Praise for

THESE BURNING STARS

"A richly imagined space opera packed with intricate worldbuilding, compelling prose, and twisty politics, artfully woven together and delivered through a cast of fallible, endearing characters. An incredible debut perfect for fans of Ann Leckie, Kate Elliott, and Scalzi's Interdependency series." —J. S. Dewes, author of *The Last Watch*

"I love a book that makes me pay attention and rewards me for it. I love even more a book with complicated, messy politics. But really, I'm here for the characters, and Jacobs's are compelling, flawed, tragic, and hopeful at the same time. What's that? There's a sequel? I can't wait." —K. Eason, author of *How Rory Thorne Destroyed the Multiverse*

"One of the best SF books I've read, period. It has it all: jump off the page action, wild twists, superb worldbuilding. Go ahead and pen Jacobs in for your Astounding Award ballot for best new author." —Michael Mammay, author of *Planetside*

"Destined to be the space opera of the decade. The vivid characters and ratcheting plot tension kept me racing through the book, and as soon as I hit the last page, I immediately wanted to read it all over again just to savor the elegance with which it builds to its explosive conclusion." —Rebecca Fraimow, author of *The Iron Children*

"With a cast of deliciously dangerous characters and a gloriously executed plot that twists like a knife, this propulsive debut heralds the start of a sweeping space opera saga in the vein of Ann Leckie and Alastair Reynolds. Bethany Jacobs is an ingenious worldbuilder and a stunning new voice to look out for in sci-fi." —Ren Hutchings, author of *Under Fortunate Stars*

THESE BURNING STARS

BOOK ONE OF THE KINDOM TRILOGY

BETHANY JACOBS

orbitbooks.net

Copyright © 2023 by Bethany Jacobs
Excerpt from *Book Two of the Kindom Trilogy* copyright © 2023 by Bethany Jacobs
Excerpt from *The Blighted Stars* copyright © 2023 by Megan E. O'Keefe

Cover design by Lauren Panepinto
Cover landscape by Thom Tenery
Cover copyright © 2023 by Hachette Book Group, Inc.
Charts by Tim Paul
Author photograph by Mary Ganster

Orbit
Hachette Book Group
1290 Avenue of the Americas
New York, NY 10104
orbitbooks.net

First Edition: October 2023
Simultaneously published in Great Britain by Orbit

Orbit is an imprint of Hachette Book Group.
The Orbit name and logo are trademarks of Little, Brown Book Group Limited.

The publisher is not responsible for websites (or their content) that are not owned by the publisher.

The Hachette Speakers Bureau provides a wide range of authors for speaking events. To find out more, go to hachettespeakersbureau.com or email HachetteSpeakers@hbgusa.com.

Orbit books may be purchased in bulk for business, educational, or promotional use. For information, please contact your local bookseller or the Hachette Book Group Special Markets Department at special.markets@hbgusa.com.

Library of Congress Cataloging-in-Publication Data
Names: Jacobs, Bethany (Novelist), author.
Title: These burning stars / Bethany Jacobs.
Description: First edition. | New York, NY : Orbit, 2023. | Series: The Kindom trilogy ; book one
Identifiers: LCCN 2023009884 | ISBN 9780316463324 (trade paperback) |
    ISBN 9780316463423 (ebook)
Subjects: LCGFT: Space operas (Fiction) | Science fiction. | Fantasy fiction. | Novels.
Classification: LCC PS3610.A356417 T47 2023 | DDC 813/.6—dc23/eng/20230331
LC record available at https://lccn.loc.gov/2023009884

ISBNs: 9780316463324 (trade paperback), 9780316463423 (ebook)

Printed in the United States of America

LSC-C

Printing 1, 2023

For Kelly, my first reader,
and for Mary, who held the hope

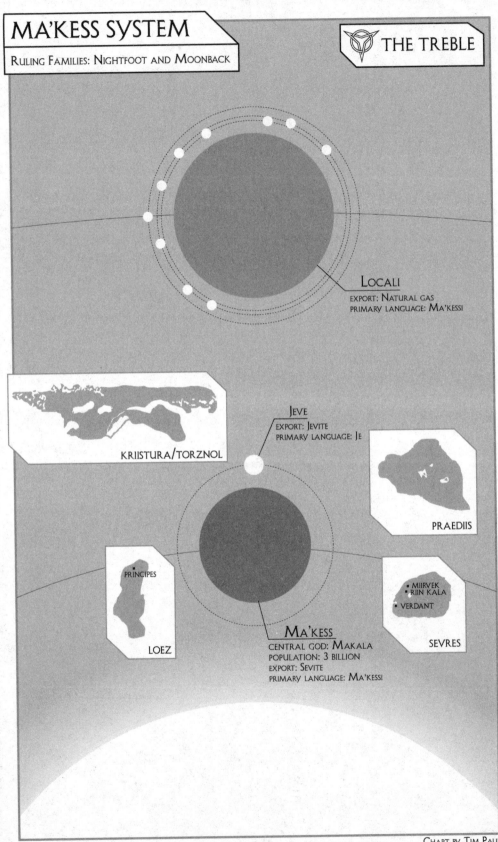

MA'KESS SYSTEM

RULING FAMILIES: NIGHTFOOT AND MOONBACK

THE TREBLE

LOCALI
EXPORT: NATURAL GAS
PRIMARY LANGUAGE: MA'KESSI

KRIISTURA/TORZNOL

JEVE
EXPORT: JEVITE
PRIMARY LANGUAGE: JE

PRAEDIIS

PRINCIPES

LOEZ

MIIRVEK
RIIN KALA

VERDANT

MA'KESS
CENTRAL GOD: MAKALA
POPULATION: 3 BILLION
EXPORT: SEVITE
PRIMARY LANGUAGE: MA'KESSI

SEVRES

CHART BY TIM PAUL

KATOR SYSTEM

RULING FAMILY: PAIYE

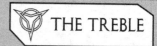 THE TREBLE

UOSTI SA
• BARCETIMA

UOSTI

TRE'M

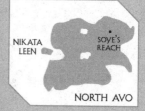

NIKATA
LEEN

SOYE'S
REACH

NORTH AVO

K-5 STATION

DUNTA

SIKATA
LEEN

SOUTH AVO

KATOR

CENTRAL GOD: KATA
POPULATION: 2 BILLION
EXPORT: AGRICULTURE, WEAPONS
PRIMARY LANGUAGE: KATISH

KRAY WEST/EAST

QUIETUS

CENTRAL GOD: CAPAMAME
POPULATION: 600,000
EXPORT: FISHING
PRIMARY LANGUAGE: QI

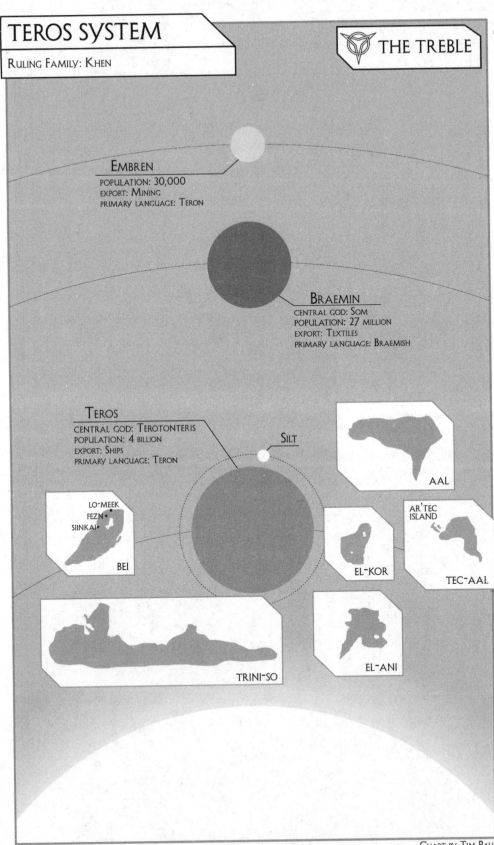

TEROS SYSTEM

RULING FAMILY: KHEN

THE TREBLE

EMBREN
POPULATION: 30,000
EXPORT: MINING
PRIMARY LANGUAGE: TERON

BRAEMIN
CENTRAL GOD: SOM
POPULATION: 27 MILLION
EXPORT: TEXTILES
PRIMARY LANGUAGE: BRAEMISH

TEROS
CENTRAL GOD: TEROTONTERIS
POPULATION: 4 BILLION
EXPORT: SHIPS
PRIMARY LANGUAGE: TERON

SILT

AAL

LO-MEEK
FEZN
SIINKAI

BEI

EL-KOR

AR'TEC
ISLAND

TEC-AAL

TRINI-SO

EL-ANI

CHART BY TIM PAUL

CAST OF CHARACTERS

The Hands of the Kindom

Esek Nightfoot, a cleric
Chono, a cleric
Aver Paiye, the First Cleric
Seti Moonback, the First Cloak
Vas Sivas Medisogo, a cloaksaan
Ilius Redquill, a secretary
Rekiav, a novitiate
Khen Caskhen Paan, a cleric, murdered
Yorus Inye, a cloaksaan

The Nightfoot Family

Alisiana Nightfoot, the Nightfoot matriarch
Caskori Nightfoot, Alisiana's uncle

The Ironway Family

Jun Ironway, a caster
Liis Konye, a former cloaksaan, and Jun's lover
Ricari Ironway, a revolutionary, and Jun's Great Gra
Hosek Ironway, Jun's grandmi
Bene Ironway, Jun's cousin

Also

Lucos Alanye, a genocider
Masar Hawks, a pirate
Saxis Foxer, a pirate captain
Phinea Runback, an archivist
Nikkelo sen Rieve, a collector

and Six

CHAPTER ONE

1643

YEAR OF THE LETTING

Kinschool of Principes
Loez Continent
The Planet Ma'kess

Her ship alighted on the tarmac with engines snarling, hot air billowing out from beneath the thrusters. The hatch opened with a hiss and she disembarked to the stench of the jump gate that had so recently spit her into Ma'kess's orbit—a smell like piss and ozone.

Underfoot, blast burns scorched the ground, signatures from ships that had been coming and going for three hundred years. The township of Principes would have no cause for so much activity, if it weren't for the kinschool that loomed ahead.

She was hungry. A little annoyed. There was a marble of nausea lodged in the base of her throat, a leftover effect of being flung from one star system to another in the space of two minutes. This part of Ma'kess was cold and wet, and she disliked the monotonous sable plains flowing away from the tarmac. She disliked the filmy dampness in the air. If the kinschool master had brought her here for nothing, she would make him regret it.

The school itself was all stone and mortar and austerity. Somber-looking effigies stared down at her from the parapet of the second-story roof: the Six Gods, assembled like jurors. She looked over her shoulder at her trio of novitiates, huddled close to one another, watchful. Birds of prey in common brown. By contrast, she was quite resplendent in her red-gold coat, the ends swishing around her ankles as she started toward the open gates. She was a cleric of the Kindom, a holy woman, a member of the Righteous Hand. In this school were many students who longed to be clerics and saw her as the pinnacle of their own aspirations. But she doubted any had the potential to match her.

Already the kinschool master had appeared. They met in the small courtyard under the awning of the entryway, his excitement and eagerness instantly apparent. He bowed over his hands a degree lower than necessary, a simpering flattery. In these star systems, power resided in the Hands of the Kindom, and it resided in the First Families. She was both.

"Thank you for the honor of your presence, Burning One."

She made a quick blessing over him, rote, and they walked together into the school. The novitiates trailed behind, silent as the statues that guarded the walls of the receiving hall. It had all looked bigger when she graduated seven years ago.

As if reading her mind, the kinschool master said, "It seems a lifetime since you were my student."

She chuckled, which he was welcome to take as friendly, or mocking. They walked down a hallway lined with portraiture of the most famous students and masters in the school's history: Aver Paiye, Khen Sikhen Khen, Luto Moonback. All painted. No holograms. Indeed, outside the tech aptitude classrooms, casting technology was little-to-be-seen in this school. Not fifty miles away, her family's factories produced the very sevite fuel that made jump travel and casting possible, yet here the masters lit their halls with torches and sent messages to each other via couriers. As if training the future Hands was too holy a mission to tolerate basic conveniences.

The master said, "I hope your return pleases you?"

She wondered what they'd done with her own watercolor portrait. She recalled looking very smug in it, which, to be fair, was not an uncommon condition for her.

"I was on Teros when I got your message. Anywhere is better than that garbage rock."

The master smiled timidly. "Of course. Teros is an unpleasant planet. Ma'kess is the planet of your heart. And the most beautiful of all!" He sounded like a tourist pamphlet, extolling the virtues of the many planets that populated the Treble star systems. She grunted. He asked, "Was your trip pleasant?"

"Hardly any reentry disturbance. Didn't even vomit during the jump."

They both laughed, him a little nervously. They walked down a narrow flight of steps and turned onto the landing of a wider staircase of deep blue marble. She paused and went to the banister, gazing down at the room below.

Six children stood in a line, each as rigid as the staves they held at their sides. They couldn't have been older than ten or eleven. They were dressed identically, in tunics and leggings, and their heads were shaved. They knew she was there, but they did not look up at her. Staring straight ahead, they put all their discipline on display, and she observed them like a butcher at a meat market.

"Fourth-years," she remarked, noticing the appliqués on their chests. They were slender and elfin looking, even the bigger ones. No giants in this cohort. A pity.

"I promise you, Sa, you won't be disappointed."

She started down the staircase, brisk and cheerful, ignoring the students. They had no names, no gendermarks—and no humanity as far as their teachers were concerned. They were called by numbers, given "it" for a pronoun. She herself was called Three, once. Just another object, honed for a purpose. Legally, Treble children had the right to gender themselves as soon as they discovered what fit. But *these* children would have to wait until they graduated. Only then could they take genders and names. Only then would they have their own identities.

At the foot of the staircase, she made a sound at her novitiates. They didn't follow her farther, taking sentry on the last step. On the combat floor, she gloried in the familiar smells of wood and stone and sweat. Her hard-soled boots *clacked* pleasingly as she took a slow circle about the room, gazing up at the magnificent mural on the ceiling, of the Six Gods at war. A brilliant golden light fell upon them, emanating from the sunlike symbol of the Godfire—their parent god, their essence, and the core of the Treble's faith.

She wandered around the room, brushing past the students as if they were scenery. The anticipation in the room ratcheted, the six students trying hard not to move. When she did finally look at them, it was with a quick twist of her neck, eyes locking on with predatory precision. All but one flinched, and she smiled. She brought her hand out from where it had been resting on the hilt of her bloodletter dagger, and saw several of them glance at the weapon. A weapon ordinarily reserved for cloaksaan.

This was just one of the things that must make her extraordinary to the students. Her family name being another. Her youth, of course. And she was very beautiful. Clerics deeply valued beauty, which pleased gods and people alike. *Her* beauty was like the Godfire itself, consuming and hypnotic and deadly.

Add to this the thing she represented: not just the Clerisy itself, in all its holy power, but the future the students might have. When they finished their schooling (*if* they finished their schooling), they would be one step closer to a position like hers. They would have power and prestige and choice—to adopt gendermarks, to take their family names again or create new ones. But *so much* lay between them and that future. Six more years of school and then five years as a novitiate. (Not everyone could do it in three, like her.) If all that went right, they'd receive an appointment to one of the three Hands of the Kindom. But only if they worked hard. Only if they survived.

Only if they were extraordinary.

"Tell me," she said to them all. "What is the mission of the Kindom?"

They answered in chorus: "Peace, under the Kindom. Unity, in the Treble."

"Good." She looked each one over carefully, observed their proudly clasped staves. Though "staves" was a stretch. The long poles in their hands were made from a heavy-duty foam composite. Strong enough to bruise, even to break skin—but not bones. The schools, after all, were responsible for a precious commodity. This cheapened the drama of the upcoming performance, but she was determined to enjoy herself anyway.

"And what are the three pillars of the Kindom?" she asked.

"Righteousness! Cleverness! Brutality!"

She hummed approval. Righteousness for the Clerisy. Cleverness for the Secretaries. Brutality for the Cloaksaan. The three Hands. In other parts of the school, students were studying the righteous God-texts of their history and faith, or they were perfecting the clever arts of economy and law. But these students, these little fourth-years, were here to be brutal.

She gave the kinschool master a curt nod. His eyes lit up and he turned to the students like a conductor to his orchestra. With theatrical aplomb, he clapped once.

It seemed impossible that the six students could look any smarter, but they managed it, brandishing their staves with stolid expressions. She searched for cracks in the facades, for shadows and tremors. She saw several. They were so young, and it was to be expected in front of someone like her. Only one of them was a perfect statue. Her eyes flicked over this one for a moment longer than the others.

The master barked, "One!"

Immediately, five of the children turned on the sixth, staves sweeping into offense like dancers taking position, and then—oh, what a dance it was! The first blow was like a *clap* against One's shoulder; the second, a heavy *thwack* on its thigh. It fought back hard—it had to, swinging its stave in furious arcs and trying like hell not to be pushed too far off-balance. She watched its face, how the sweat broke out, how the eyes narrowed, and its upper teeth came down on its lip to keep from crying out when one of the children struck it again, hard, on the hip. That sound was particularly good, a *crack* that made it stumble and lose position. The five children gave no quarter, and then there was a fifth blow, and a sixth, and—

"Done!" boomed the master.

Instantly, all six children dropped back into line, staves at rest beside them. The first child was breathing heavily. Someone had got it in the mouth, and there was blood, but it didn't cry.

The master waited a few seconds, pure showmanship, and said, "Two!"

The dance began again, five students turning against the other. This was an old game, with simple rules. Esek had played it many times herself, when she was Three. The attack went on until either offense or defense landed six blows. It was impressive if the attacked child scored a hit at all, and yet as she watched the progressing bouts, the second and fourth students both made their marks before losing the round. The children were merciless with one another, crowding their victim in, jabbing and kicking and swinging without reprieve. Her lip curled back in raw delight. These students were as vicious as desert foxes.

But by the time the fifth student lost its round, they were getting sloppy. They were bruised, bleeding, tired. Only the sixth remained to defend itself, and everything would be slower and less controlled now. No more soldierly discipline, no more pristine choreography. Just tired children brawling. Yet she was no less interested, because the sixth student was the one with no fissures in its mask of calm. Even more interestingly, this one had been the least aggressive in the preceding fights. It joined in, yes, but she wasn't sure it ever landed a body blow. It was not timid so much as... restrained. Like a leashed dog.

When the master said, "Six," something changed in the room.

She couldn't miss the strange note in the master's voice—of pleasure and expectation. The children, despite their obvious fatigue, snapped to attention like rabbits scenting a predator. They didn't rush at Six as they had rushed at one another. No, suddenly, they moved into a half-circle formation, approaching this last target with an unmistakable caution. Their gazes sharpened and they gripped their staves tighter than before, as if expecting to be disarmed. The sweat and blood stood out on their faces, and one of them quickly wiped a streak away, as if this would be its only chance to clear its eyes.

And Six? The one who commanded this sudden tension, this careful advance? It stood a moment, taking them all in at once, stare like a razor's edge. And then, it flew.

She could think of no other word for it. It was like a whirling storm, and its stave was a lightning strike. No defensive stance for this one—it went after the nearest student with a brutal spinning kick that knocked it on its ass, then it whipped its body to the left and cracked its stave against a different student's shoulder, and finished with a jab to yet another's carelessly exposed shin. All of this happened before the five attackers even had their wits about them, and for a moment she thought they would throw their weapons down, cower, and retreat before this superior fighter.

Instead, they charged.

It was like watching a wave that had gone out to sea suddenly surge upon the shore. They didn't fight as individuals, but as one corralling force, spreading out and pressing in. They drove Six back and back and back—against the wall. For the first time, they struck it, hard, in the ribs, and a moment later they got it again, across the jaw. The sound sent a thrill down her spine, made her fingers clench in hungry eagerness for a stave of her own. She watched the sixth fighter's jaw flush with blood and the promise of bruising, but it didn't falter. It swept its stave in an arc, creating an opening. It struck one of them in the chest, then another in the side, and a third in the thigh—six blows altogether. The students staggered, their offense broken, their wave disintegrating on the sixth student's immovable shore.

She glanced at their master, waiting for him to announce the conclusion of the match, and its decisive victor. To her great interest, he did no such thing, nor did the children seem to expect he would. They recovered, and charged.

Was the sixth fighter surprised? Did it feel the sting of its master's betrayal? Not that she could tell. That face was a stony glower of intent, and those eyes were smart and ruthless.

The other fights had been quick, dirty, over in less than a minute. This last fight went on and on, and each second made her pulse race. The exhaustion she'd seen in the students before gave way to an almost frenzied energy. How else could they hold their ground against Six? They parried and dodged and swung in increasingly desperate bursts, but through it all the sixth kept *hitting* them. Gods! It was relentless. Even when the other students started to catch up (strikes to the hip, to the wrist, to the thigh) it *kept going*. The room was full of ragged gasping, but when she listened for Six's breath, it was controlled. Loud, but steady, and its eyes never lost their militant focus.

In the feverish minutes of the fight, it landed eighteen strikes (she counted; she couldn't help counting) before finally one of the others got in a sixth blow, a lucky cuff across its already bruised mouth.

The master called, "Done!"

The children practically dropped where they stood, their stave arms falling limply at their sides, their relief as palpable as the sweat in the air. They got obediently back in line, and as they did, she noticed that one of them met Six's eye. A tiny grin passed between them, conspiratorial, childlike, before they were stoic again.

She could see the master's satisfied smile. She had of course not known *why* he asked her to come to Principes. A new statue in her honor, perhaps? Or a business opportunity that would benefit her family's sevite industry? Maybe one of the eighth-years, close to graduating, had particular promise? No, in the end, it was none of that. He'd brought her here for a fourth-year. He'd brought her here so he could show off his shining star. She herself left school years earlier than any student in Principes's history, a mere fifteen when she became a novitiate. Clearly the master wanted to break her record. To have this student noticed by her, recruited by her as an eleven-year-old—what a feather that would be, in the master's cap.

She looked at him directly, absorbing his smug expression.

"Did its parents put you up to that?" she asked, voice like a razor blade.

The smugness bled from his face. He grew pale and cleared his throat. "It has no parents."

Interesting. The Kindom was generally very good about making sure orphans were rehomed. Who had sponsored the child's admission to a kinschool? Such things weren't cheap.

The master said, clearly hoping to absolve himself, "After you, it's the most promising student I have ever seen. Its intelligence, its casting skills, its—"

She chuckled, cutting him off.

"Many students are impressive in the beginning. In my fourth year, I wasn't the star. And the one who was the star, that year? What happened to it? Why, I don't even think it graduated. Fourth year is far too early to know anything about a student."

She said these things as if the sixth student hadn't filled her with visceral excitement. As if she didn't see, vast as the Black Ocean itself, what it might become. Then she noticed that the master had said nothing. No acquiescence. No apology, either, which surprised her.

"What aren't you telling me?" she asked.

He cleared his throat again, and said, very lowly, "Its family name was Alanye."

Her brows shot up. She glanced back at the child, who was not making eye contact. At this distance, it couldn't have heard the master's words.

"Really?" she asked.

"Yes. A secretary adopted it after its father died. The secretary sent it here."

She continued staring at the child. Watching it fight was exhilarating, but knowing its origins made her giddy. This was delicious.

"Does it know?"

The master barely shook his head no. She *hmmed* a bright sound of pleasure.

Turning from him, she strode toward the child, shaking open her knee-length coat. When she was still several feet away from it, she crooked a finger.

"Come here, little fish. Let me have a look at you."

The fourth-year moved forward until it was a foot away, gazing up, up, into her face. She looked it over more carefully than before. Aside from their own natural appearance, students weren't allowed any distinguishing characteristics, and sometimes it was hard to tell them apart. She took in the details, looked for signs of the child's famous ancestor, Lucos Alanye: a man who started with nothing, acquired a mining fleet, and blew up a moon to stop anyone else from taking its riches. The sheer pettiness of it! He was the most notorious mass murderer in Treble history. She hadn't known he *had* descendants. With a flick of her wrist, she cast an image of Alanye to her ocular screen, comparing the ancestor to the descendant. Inconclusive.

The child remained utterly calm. Her own novitiates weren't always so calm.

"So, you are Six. That is a very holy designation, you know." It said nothing, and she asked it cheerfully, "Tell me: Who is the Sixth God?"

This was an old riddle from the Godtexts, one with no answer. A person from Ma'kess would claim the god Makala. A person from Quietus would say Capamame. Katishsaan favored Kata, and so on, each planet giving primacy to its own god. Asking the question was just a way to figure out where a person's loyalty or origins lay. This student looked Katish to her, but maybe it would claim a different loyalty?

Then it said, "There is no Sixth God, Sa. Only the Godfire."

She tilted her head curiously. So, it claimed no loyalty, no planet of origin. Only a devotion to the Kindom, for whom the Godfire held primacy. How...strategic.

She ignored its answer, asking, "Do you know who I am?"

The silence in the room seemed to deepen, as if some great invisible creature had sucked in its breath.

"Yes, Burning One. You are Esek Nightfoot."

She saw the other children from the corner of her eye, looking tense and excited.

She nodded. "Yes." And bent closer to it. "I come from a very important family," she said, as if it didn't know. "That's a big responsibility. Perhaps you know what it's like?"

For the first time, it showed emotion—a slight widening of the eyes. Almost instantly, its expression resolved back into blankness.

"The master says you don't know who you are...Is that true, little fish?"

"We don't have names, Sa."

She grinned. "You are very disciplined. From all accounts, so was Lucos Alanye."

Its throat moved, a tiny swallow. It knew *exactly* what family it came from. The kinschool master was a fool.

"Do you know," Esek said, "all the First Families of the Treble are required to give of their children to the Kindom? One from each generation must become a Hand. My matriarch selected me from my generation. It seems fate has selected you from yours."

There was a fierceness in its eyes that said it liked this idea very much—though, of course, the Alanyes were not a First Family. Lucos himself was nothing more than an upstart and opportunist, a resource-raping traitor, a genocider. Esek half admired him.

"Your family did mine a great service," she said.

It looked wary now, a little confused. She nodded. "Yes, my family controls the sevite factories. And do you know who are the laborers that keep our factories going?"

This time it ventured an answer, so quiet its voice barely registered, "The Jeveni, Sa."

"Yes! The Jeveni." Esek smiled, as if the Jeveni were kings and not refugees. "And if Lucos Alanye had never destroyed their moon world, the Jeveni would not need my family to employ them, would they? And then, who would run the factories? So you see it is all very well, coming from the bloodline of a butcher. All our evils give something back."

The student looked at her with that same wariness. She changed the subject.

"What do you think of your performance today?"

Its face hardened. "The fight had no honor, Sa."

Esek's brows lifted. They were conversing in Ma'kessi, the language of the planet Ma'kess. But just then, the student had used a Teron word for "honor." One that more accurately translated to "bragging rights." Perhaps the student was from the planet Teros? Or perhaps it had a precise attitude toward language—always the best word for the best circumstance.

"You struck your attackers eighteen times. Is there no honor in that?"

"I lost. Honor is for winning."

"But the master cheated you."

The invisible creature in the room drew in its breath again. Behind her she could *feel* the master's quickening pulse. Esek's smile brightened, but Six looked apprehensive. Its compatriots were glancing uneasily at one another, discipline fractured.

She said, "Beyond these walls, out in the world, people don't have to tell you if you've won. You know it for yourself, and you make other people know it. If I were you, and the master tried to cheat me out of my win, I'd kill him for it."

The tension ratcheted so high that she could taste it, thick and cloying. Six's eyes widened. Before anything could get out of hand, Esek laughed.

"Of course, if *you* tried to kill the master, he would decapitate you before you'd even lifted your little stave off the ground, wouldn't he?"

It was like lacerating a boil. The hot tightness under the skin released, and if there was a foul smell left over, well . . . that was worth it.

"Tell me, Six," she carried on, "what do you want most of all?"

It answered immediately, confidence surging with the return to script, "To go unnoticed, Sa."

She'd thought so. These were the words of the Cloaksaan. The master wouldn't be parading its best student under her nose like a bitch in heat if the bitch didn't want to be a cloaksaan—those deadly officers of the Kindom's Brutal Hand, those military masterminds and shadow-like assassins, who made peace possible in the Treble through their ruthlessness. Esek had only ever taken cloaksaan novitiates. It was an idiosyncrasy of hers. Most clerics trained clerics and most secretaries trained secretaries, but Cleric Nightfoot trained cloaksaan.

"You held back in the first five fights," she remarked.

The child offered no excuses. Did she imagine defiance in its eyes?

"That's all right. That was smart. You conserved your strength for the fight that mattered. Your teachers might tell you it was cowardly, but cloaksaan don't have to be brave. They have to be smart. They have to win. Right?"

Six nodded.

"Would you like to be my novitiate someday, little fish?" asked Esek gently.

It showed no overt excitement. But its voice was vehement. "Yes, Burning One."

She considered it for long moments, looking over its body, its muscles and form, like it was a racehorse she might like to sponsor. It knew what she would see, and she felt its hope. Her smile spread like taffy, and she said simply, "No."

She might as well have struck it. Its shock broke over her like a wave. Seeing that it could feel was important; unlike some Hands, she didn't relish an emotionless novitiate.

"I won't take you. More than that, I'm going to tell the other Hands not to take you."

The child's stunned expression nearly made her laugh, but she chose for once to be serious, watching it for the next move. Its mouth opened and closed. Clearly it wanted to speak but knew it had no right. She gave it a little nod of permission, eager to hear what it would say. It glanced toward its master, then spoke in a voice so soft, no one would hear.

"Burning One...I am not my ancestor. I am—loyal. I am Kindom in my heart."

She hummed and nodded. "Yes, I can see that. But haven't we established? My family owes your ancestor a debt, for the Jeveni, and I don't care if you're like him or not. The fact is, I find you very impressive. Just as your master does, and your schoolkin do. I imagine everyone finds you impressive, little fish. But that's of no use to me. I require something different."

Esek watched with interest as it struggled to maintain its composure. She wondered if it would cry, or lose its temper, or drop into traumatized blankness. When none of these things happened, but it only stood there with its throat bobbing, she dropped a lifeline.

"When you are ready, you must come directly to me."

Its throat stilled. She'd startled it again.

"You must come and tell me that you want to be my novitiate. Don't go to my people, or the other Hands. Don't announce yourself. Come to me unawares, without invitation."

It looked at her in despairing confusion. "Burning One, you're surrounded by novitiates. If I come to you without permission, your people will kill me."

She nodded. "That's right. They'll never let you through without my leave. What's worse, I probably won't even remember you exist. Don't feel bad. I never remember any of the little fish I visit in the schools. Why should I, with so many things to occupy me? No, in a couple of days, you'll slip my mind. And if, in a few years, some strange young person newly gendered and named tries to come before me and ask to be my novitiate, well! Even if you get through my people, I may kill you myself." A long pause stretched between them, before she added, "Unless..."

It was exhilarating, to whip the child from one end to the other with the power of a single word. Its eyes lit up. It didn't even breathe, waiting for her to name her condition. She leaned closer still, until their faces were only inches apart, and she whispered in a voice only it could hear, "You must do something *extraordinary*." She breathed the word into its soul, and it flowed there hot and powerful as the Godfire. "You must do something I have never seen before. Something memorable, and shocking, and *brutal*. Something that will make me pause before I kill you. I have no idea what it is. I have no idea what I'll *want* when that day comes. But if you do it, then I will make you my novitiate. Your ancestry won't matter. Your past won't matter. This moment won't matter. You will have everything you deserve: all the honor a life can bring. And you will earn it at my side."

The child stared at her, caught in the terrible power of the silence she let hang between them. And then, like a fishersaan cutting a line, she drew back. Her voice was a normal volume again, and she shrugged.

"It's not a great offer, I'll grant you. Probably you'll die. If you choose not to come to me, I won't hold it against you. I won't remember you, after all. There are other, excellent careers in the Kindom. You don't have to be a Hand to do good work. Someone as talented as you could be a marshal or guardsaan. The master says you're good at casting. You could be an archivist! But whatever you decide, I wish you luck, little fish." She pinned it with her mocking stare. "Now swim away."

It blinked, released from the spell. After a moment of wretched bewilderment, it dropped back into place beside its schoolkin, who looked most shocked of all; one was crying silently. She whirled around, each click of her boots on the stone floor like a gunshot. The gold threads in her coat caught the light until she shimmered like a flame.

She locked eyes with the master, whose friendliness had evaporated in these tense minutes. He was now marshaling forty years of training into a blank expression, but Esek sensed the cold terror in him. No one in his life had seen him this frightened before, and the shame of it, of all these little fourth-years witnessing it, would torture him.

Esek moved as if she would go right past him, but paused at the last moment. They were parallel, arms brushing, and she heard his minuscule gasp. Perhaps he expected the plunge of the bloodletter? As a Hand of the Kindom, she had every right to kill him if she judged his actions unrighteous. Still, knowing he was afraid of it happening was its own reward—and she didn't feel like dealing with the aftermath today. Instead, she studied the master's face. He was staring straight forward, as well trained as the students, and just as vulnerable.

"Graduate it to the eighth-years."

The master's temple ticked. "You've already determined that no Hand will make it their novitiate. It has no future here."

Esek chuckled, amazed at the brazenness of this master. "Let it decide on its own. Personally, I think this one will find its way. Or has your confidence in it proved so fickle?" The master was silent, and this time Esek's voice was a threatening purr. "What about your confidence in *me*, Master? I am your window to the glory and wisdom of the Godfire. Don't you believe in the power of the Clerisy?" She drew out the final word, clicking the *C* with malevolent humor.

The master nodded shortly. "Of course, Sa. I will do as you say."

Esek smiled at him. She patted his shoulder, enjoying the flinch he couldn't control. She was preparing to murmur some new ridicule into his ear, when a voice interrupted them.

"Burning One."

She looked toward the marble staircase, where her novitiates still stood. They had been there all this time, invisible until she had need.

"Yes?" Esek asked. "What is it?"

"You have a message from Alisiana Nightfoot. The matriarch requests your presence at Verdant."

Esek clucked her tongue. "No rest for a Nightfoot." She swept past the master without farewells. She heard his barely discernible exhale of relief, and then the trio of novitiates were behind her, following her up the stairs. They retraced their steps to the school gates and the tarmac, where her docked warcrow awaited them. As they went, she called over her shoulder, "Send word to the Cloaksaan that they should visit the master. I think his tenure has run its course."

Who is the Sixth God, to your mind?
Fecund Makala or Kata wise?
Is it wily Terotonteris?
Or else Sajeven, warm and barren?
Is it the devouring Som?
Or Capamame, of gentle songs?
Beware you love them more than me,
For my eye perceives everything.

A Record of the Gods, 1:1–8. Godtexts, pre-Treble

CHAPTER TWO

1664

YEAR OF THE CRUX

Riin Cosas
Sevres Continent
The Planet Ma'kess

Cleric Chono arrives on Ma'kess by spacecraft, a forty-hour trip from the water world of Quietus. She comes alone and walks the length of the tarmac with only a bag slung over one shoulder. Black Ocean sailors mill about in knots of bitter talk and cool glances flung her way. In the east, the planet's capital city of Riin Kala is a profile of spires built beneath a mountain range, purple cliffs a jagged backdrop. The city itself is a paragon of beauty and industry and art, and at the moment it seems like half its population has crowded to the docks, standing behind the metal fences. They clamor with protest, with curses and shouts. It's two days since the Secretaries officially shut down jump gate travel for all but the most essential services. Chono's own Hand, the Clerisy, has no authority to control the jump gates (such lines of authority are carefully delineated, amid the Hands), but one wouldn't know that from how the people glare and mutter at her passing.

Chono can't exactly blame them. As far as she can read the situation, there was no need to shut the gates down. Not yet, anyway. But these are tense times. The matriarch of the Nightfoot family, Alisiana Nightfoot, is dead, and she took with her all the stability of the sevite trade. Without sevite, the gates can't operate, and the Jeveni factory workers are in the midst of labor strikes.

Chono knows for a fact that the Kindom has enough sevite in storage to outlast these strikes. But still, the Secretaries have chosen a radical course, sure to debilitate trade and travel. If the people of the Treble resent them for this decision, they resent the Jeveni even more. Out in the crowd, Chono sees a hand-drawn sign: MAKE THE J BASTARDS WORK! She fears there will be attacks, killings. Already the casting net thrums with anti-Jeveni sentiment, with accusations and threats. Always such an easy target, the Jeveni.

A chant starts up in the distance: "Free our ships! Free our ships! Free our ships!"

Chono looks up into a blue sky, squinting at the pinprick shapes of idling ships that hover like dust motes on the very edge of the Ma'kessn atmosphere. It's so clear today that she easily sees the half-sickle form of the moon, Jeve. A black fingernail stamping the sky.

"Free our ships! Free our ships! Free our ships!"

A large contingent of guardsaan holds the crowds back from the main road out of the docks. There's a transport waiting for Chono, a warcat shuttle, odd to see after so many months on Quietus. The shuttle's driver, no doubt one of First Cleric Aver Paiye's novitiates, intends to ferry her the five miles to the temple, but Chono elects to walk. The driver is flustered, nearly hostile as he babbles about the First Cleric's schedule. But when Chono's stare doesn't waver, he bows under the weight of it and climbs back into the warcat. He asks petulantly if he can at least take her bag. She says no, and leaves him.

It's an hour walk to the temple Riin Cosas, and Chono needs the quiet. The Black Ocean may be silent, but warships are not. Two days ago, she was making Hasha tea for a gaggle of parishioners come to morning prayer, peaceful in her appointment to the floating township of Pippashap. Far removed from the temple dramas that so often include Esek Nightfoot. Now she's standing eight light-years away, on the borders of the largest metropolis on Ma'kess.

Quietus was a flatland of ocean, its god the gentle Capamame, the dear friend. Ma'kess is all mountains and forests and valleys, presided over by fecund and lovely Makala. Fierce and vain Makala. The change is stark, for Chono.

She adjusts her pack. Feels the crinkle of the letter in her breast pocket: Aver Paiye's summons, on real laminate. Elegantly written. Full of praise. Cryptic.

She begins the walk with shoulders back and head high, determined not to look unsteady. Adapting to solid ground and lighter gravity is giving her a slight headache, but she leaves the docks behind at a steady clip, winding her way up the hillock that ridges the temple valley. At its crest, she pauses to absorb what anyone would assume to be her consolation prize for the tiring climb. It is, after all, a gorgeous sight. Against miles and miles of emerald grass and sapphire skies, Riin Cosas is a hexagonal jewel, its walls and domed roof glinting magnificently under an early afternoon sun, as reflective as glass, as impenetrable as steel.

By any measure of beauty in the Treble, Riin Cosas is the most exquisite temple in all of the three systems. The most ethereal. Chono has studied it since childhood: the seat of the First Cleric and the birthplace of Treble civilization. She wonders at the awe their colonizing ancestors must have felt, when they stepped from the decks of their generation ships into paradise. No wonder they built the temple here, intending a beacon of joy and hope that would survive through the centuries.

Yet to Chono, it has always been a source of deep ambivalence. Today, that feeling grows and ghosts inside her, as if her soul were two pieces engaged in a battle, all feints and hiding places.

By the time she reaches the temple, her trousers are hemmed with a foot of dust. Her hairline is damp, and she can feel the sweat under her arms and at the small of her back. When she arrives at the massive double doors at the top of the temple steps, she stands a moment staring at her own face in the reflective surface, obfuscated by inlaid carvings of Makala. All of Ma'kess is united in its worship of her, but beauty has always perturbed Chono. She prefers the five-eyed Sajeven, known for her barrenness and warmth, or the humble water god, Capamame. Quiet gods. Most of all she prefers the Godfire, for the Godfire is not a personality, has no ego or character, has only the steadiness of purpose: To keep the systems alive with its fire. To be a force of justice and mercy in the worlds.

Inside the door's massive frame, there's a creak of gears and pulleys. Chono's reflection bifurcates as the doors open, and she steps through.

Is it any wonder the temple interior is just as lush and beautiful as the surrounding valley? A garden square spills before her, overflowing with flowers and fruiting trees, the bounty of the southern Ma'kessn continents displayed in all its corals and crimsons and mauves. Statues of polished serpentine hold sentry in the lively garden, the Six Gods arrayed for worship. Flittering among them, birds call, insects whistle, and some small animal darts under a rosebush. The temple's translucent roof decorates it all in fractals of light, because the Godfire is light. The Godfire is everywhere. It suffuses the temple grounds, inimitable.

Chono sees the temple novitiate scurrying toward her from one of the walkways bordering the garden. She stymies him again, carefully lowering to her knees before he can reach her. She holds out her open palms, bowing over them to recite the beatitudes. Though they are a holy order, clerics often play fast and loose with ceremony, and this is not the first time Chono has baffled a novitiate with her adherence to tradition. But she likes the beatitudes. She likes their poetry and familiarity. She likes the righteous worlds they imagine.

When she finally stands, dustier than ever, the novitiate swoops in. "Burning One. I hope your walk was...peaceful."

Clearly, he hasn't gotten over her refusing to take the warcat.

"It offered plenty of time for contemplation."

The novitiate nods, barely listening, and ushers her toward the walkway. They go through a door into the atrium of the temple's eastern corner. He says, "The First Cleric is currently in conference with the First Cloak, but he intends to see you directly afterward."

This is surprising. The First Cloak of the Cloaksaan is Seti Moonback, and he's not generally found in temples. Cloaksaan keep their own company and prefer to conduct meetings via comm or other casting technologies. If they show up somewhere, it's usually to exercise some bloody errand. His business must have something to do with the protests over gate travel, though why he would come to the Clerisy instead of the Secretaries, Chono can't say.

The novitiate leads her farther into the atrium, passing the short hallway to Aver Paiye's office. Chono catches a glimpse of a large cloaksaan outside the door. A blink and he's out of sight; Chono faces forward again. Only then does she realize the novitiate is leading her toward the clerics' private gathering room. *To burn like stars*—the words of the Righteous Hand—is blazoned above the doors in holy lettering. What flashes through her then is not some image of majesty and power, but memories of destruction, and the reluctance she's felt ever since receiving Paiye's letter pulls heavy in her gut.

The novitiate says, "I'll come for you when the meeting is over. You may wait with your kin if you like."

Apparently, it is not truly "if she likes" because he has already reached the gathering room door and pulled it open with a flourish, as if he thinks he's delivering her to a banquet. He glances to the bag over her shoulder.

"Can I take that for you, Sa?"

Chono knows she'll look like a vagabond if she carries the pack into the gathering room; nevertheless she hesitates. Her grip on the strap tightens, before at last she hands it over to him.

"I want it somewhere secure."

"Of course, Sa."

Chono holds his stare for a long moment, and if a part of him thought her order was silly, now he shifts uncomfortably, realizing how foolish it would be to disregard her. Remembering, perhaps, who she is, and that unlike most clerics, Chono has a bloody history. Relatively satisfied, she looks away from him. She steels herself, and steps through the gathering room door. It closes behind her with a *snick*.

Inside, a glass column centers the room, burning with sevite fuel stones in homage to the Godfire. They are a glittering black blanket on the hearth, treated with oils that emit something woodsy and pepper-sharp—much more pleasant than the natural stench of the burning coals. It's expensive, of course, constantly burning treated sevite, but the clerics *will* have their symbolisms.

It's warm inside the room, another disorientation. Quietus is a chilly place, all mist and rain, with occasional warm floods of sunlight across the water. But here on Ma'kess, it is the height of summer, and the Year of the Crux is turning out to be a hot one.

A dozen clerics mill about, shiny-faced in their heavy gold-threaded coats, refreshing themselves with glasses of lemon water on ice. Some recline on couches as far from the fire as possible, chatting to each other. Others walk the circumference of the room in pairs and trios. No one acknowledges Chono. But they know who she is. Do they whisper? Do they say, *There is the cleric who killed another cleric in cold blood*?

Not to her face, perhaps.

Aver Paiye's letter said nothing about it. He said, *Come to Riin Cosas, where you are always welcome*. But welcome by whom? Certainly not her kin, who must regard her as a danger now. Do they even care why she killed Cleric Khen Caskhen Paan, that scion of a powerful First Family? Probably not. Meting out death sentences is the purview of the Cloaksaan. For a cleric to kill... Well, it's the sort of thing Esek would do. Perhaps the other clerics think Esek rubbed off on Chono. Infected her with her reckless, violent ways. So unbecoming.

It's a point of some reassurance to Chono that whatever discomfort she feels, the other clerics in the room can't see it. Chono has a very old impulse to go unnoticed. Not as cloaksaan go unnoticed, but as small animals do, safe in their burrows. This impulse always manifests on her face as stoicism—a rare characteristic for a cleric. Most of them are beautiful and alluring and charismatic. Chono is none of those things, but she *is* righteous and unflappable. And she has important benefactors.

It's the sight of one of these that nearly breaks her composure. There, standing on the opposite side of the gathering room, is Esek.

Chono is very careful not to stare. It's a near thing. Something happens in her chest, a thunder of equal parts shock and childlike thrill, but she stamps both feelings down lest they somehow show up on her face. Why didn't she expect Esek to be here? The First Cleric's message summoning Chono to Riin Cosas—it's all about Esek. And yet, the older cleric's presence in the temple feels totally incongruous. Esek *hates* Riin Cosas. She avoids it religiously. Yet here she is, surrounded by her kin while very distinctly apart from them, and the sight of her after so many years is just as elating and just as terrible as it ever was. That their last meeting ended so badly makes the thought of a reunion now twist in Chono's stomach like a parasite.

Of course, Esek hasn't noticed Chono at all. Esek has always had a remarkable talent for ignoring others until their presence becomes of use or interest to her. Right now, she clearly has no use for anyone. She's standing with legs apart and hands clasped, staring up at a massive statue. Her look is clever. Serene.

Chono dithers for long moments, sweat on her palms, but this is absurd. She's not a novitiate anymore, scraping for Esek's attention. She steels herself, then walks toward her one-time mentor. The farther she goes into the room, the more aware she is of her kin. Their glances and murmuring follow her all the way to Esek's side.

"Burning One," she says.

Esek doesn't look away from the statue, but her mouth curves up in a shape like a cutlass. When Chono saw her for the first time, Esek was only twenty-two. She was the youngest cleric in a hundred years, the most beautiful, and had come to Chono's school to watch her and her fellow fourth-years fight. Well, more accurately, to watch *Six* fight, back when Chono was called Four and Six was her friend, rather than a ghost at her periphery. The memory alone makes her uneasy, just as Esek made her uneasy, that day at Principes. Esek swept into their lives like a great, gorgeous bird of prey. Now, twenty years later, time has matured what was already exquisite: sharp jawline and nose, full mouth and large eyes the color of umber. Her thick black braids are tied and wound atop her head, displaying a slender neck.

"Dear Chono," Esek Nightfoot finally answers. "How long since you were my novitiate?"

"Eleven years, Sa."

"Yet you still talk to me like a novitiate. We're kin now, don't you remember?"

Chono pauses, considering. "You've always preferred your novitiates to your kin, Sa."

Esek chuckles, glancing Chono's way. Her golden-brown eyes are far more striking than any of the blue or green or purple eye mods other Ma'kessn favor. But this time, it's not her eyes that command Chono's attention. In turning toward her, Esek has exposed the opposite side of her head. Chono doesn't react, doesn't give any indication she sees it—but how could she not? So, it wasn't just a macabre rumor. Esek's left ear is half gone. It's a rough, ill-healed injury, its origin unclear: A blade? A gunshot? Teeth? A simple mod could have repaired it, but instead she wears her hair back, displaying it like a trophy.

Far from disgusting Chono, it fills her with guilt. She was on Quietus when she heard about the pirate attack on the Nightfoots' ancestral home, an estate called Verdant some two hundred miles south of Riin Cosas. Pirates, a particular subset of Braemish sailors, have always been an unavoidable nuisance in the vast reaches of the Black Ocean—they smuggle and kidnap and murder, all while finding ways to avoid Kindom justice. But they have a certain code of honor. And a gift for staying under the radar. This attack on Verdant—it was unlike anything the Treble had ever seen before. Unlike anything that any pirate had ever tried. Dozens of the Nightfoots' private guardsaan died; four of the lesser Nightfoots, too. From reports, Esek Nightfoot fought like a godling, surviving against all odds, but the pirates still carried off heaps of wealth, of artifacts, of records, and burned half the estate to the ground. A year ago, the Kindom itself would not have dared attack the Nightfoots so, let alone *pirates*.

Of course, a year ago, the matriarch Alisiana Nightfoot was alive, her very presence a bulwark against attack.

There have been other signs that the Nightfoots are losing their primacy. This trouble at the factories, for example. The Jeveni have always been a hardworking and mild-mannered labor force, but now their union leaders are thundering for change, and with no new matriarch in place, the Nightfoots have yet to quell the storm.

Then, of course, there is the statue that Esek is staring at again. It depicts Reveño Moonback, the once First Cleric of the Righteous Hand. Reveño is a favored figure in the Moonback family, those Nightfoot rivals who control the northern continents of Ma'kess. But Riin Cosas is in the south, Nightfoot territory. The Moonbacks must have paid a fortune to have such a statue placed in this room. Its presence is a blatant shot at the Nightfoots. Anyone who didn't know Esek would think she was admiring the craftsmanship. Chono thinks what she really admires is the Moonbacks' audacity. And in time she'll travel north and make them regret it.

"It's been so long, Chono," sighs Esek, wistful.

If she remembers their falling-out on Xa Cosas in '58, her tone doesn't suggest it. Strange. "Too long," Chono agrees, half expecting some kind of trap.

"I heard about the old pervert cleric on Pippashap," Esek says. Chono shows nothing, says nothing, thinks *nothing nothing nothing*. "I hope you cut his cock off."

A flash of the old man's face when she struck—stunned rage quickly turning to terror.

Chono flinches from the memory. "I didn't know you would be here."

Esek shrugs. "You know the First Cleric. He loves meetings. Loves to get his little birds together and hear us chirp. I took a warcat up this morning. Beautiful country, this time of year. One forgets when everything around them is ashes."

"I am very sorry about—"

"Oh, stop." Esek waves a hand at her and turns fully to look into her face. For several moments they are both perfectly still, Esek's eyes traveling all over her, as if reminding herself what Chono looks like. And Chono knows she looks different, older. The year on Pippashap alone has weathered her, but she's also put on muscle. She wonders what Esek sees. But Esek only gestures at her clothes, eyes lit with amusement. "Did you miss land so much that you decided to take a roll in the dirt?"

Chono remembers very well how this minor jab might have devastated her when she was Esek's novitiate. The desire to please, the desire to be praised, were a constant ache in her belly. She feels that echo now. But other feelings take priority as she completes her truncated condolences. "I am very sorry about Alisiana."

Esek's eyes narrow. Chono adds, "I know your first loyalty is to the Kindom"—a wry look from Esek—"but I also know what your family means to you. I believe the Nightfoots will thrive in spite of this. Riiniana may be young, but she can learn."

This time, Esek's look turns flat and disbelieving. She stares for so long that Chono feels unsettled. What has she said? Esek never had anything particularly poisonous to say about Riiniana, Alisiana's great-granddaughter and fourteen-year-old heir. But maybe things have—

"So, you don't know?"

Chono hesitates, opens her mouth to respond—but Esek's bark of laughter cuts her off. Nearby, unsubtly eavesdropping clerics startle at the gunshot sound. Esek puts a hand on Chono's shoulder, stepping aggressively closer. Chono can see every detail of her mutilated ear.

"Chono," Esek says. "You've been too long on that water world. The

Secretaries read Alisiana's will weeks ago. She didn't pass the matriarchy to Riiniana, or any of her direct descendants." Esek's teeth glint. "She passed it to *me*."

Chono waits for her to say something more, something that would negate the incomprehensible words. But Esek is alight with glee, and with something else—something maniacal. A shiver runs down Chono's spine, but before she can think how to respond—

"Excuse me, Saan."

It is the temple novitiate, addressing them both. "The First Cleric is ready for you, now."

Esek starts off immediately, her commanding pace and posture attracting every stare in the room. After a beat, Chono follows, similarly erect, but with none of Esek's swagger. Chono is half convinced this is a prank. The whole thing makes no sense. To join one of the Hands of the Kindom, to be a cleric or cloaksaan or secretary, is to abandon all familial rights. Hands *can't* take leadership of their families because they are instruments of the Godfire, first. And all this to say nothing of the fact that on the complex structure of the Nightfoot family tree, Esek's branch is nowhere near the line of succession.

Focus, Chono tells herself. *Paiye said there were things you didn't know.*

They leave the gathering room with many eyes watching.

In the atrium Chono sees two figures all in black have emerged from the hallway leading to Aver Paiye's office. One of them is the large cloaksaan Chono glimpsed on her way in. Larger even than she realized. He's a great block of a man, his hands and feet like clubs, his limbs like tree trunks.

"Look at that specimen," says Esek with interest.

The other figure is the First Cloak, Seti Moonback. He is very different from his companion—shorter by a foot but sleek as a cat, and eyes a modded electric blue. He smiles coldly at their approach, a smile made grotesque by the scar wending from nostril to chin, white against golden skin. He tilts his head and rests his hand on the hilt of his bloodletter.

"Cleric Nightfoot."

"Cloak Moonback," Esek returns, and her failure to use his full honorific can't be accidental. "I didn't think you liked our sunny climes."

Again, the cold smile. "Cloaksaan are far less sensitive to the elements than clerics."

"Tell that to this one." Esek jerks a thumb at Chono. "She's been languishing on Pippashap, of all places."

Seti Moonback looks at Chono, a long, assessing look, full of banked hostility.

"Ah, yes. The cleric who tried to be a cloaksaan."

Clearly he thinks very little of her for that. Cloaksaan are...possessive, when it comes to the work of assassination. Chono supposes that if she had tried to run the economy on Pippashap, her secretary kin would take that badly, as well. And yet no one has punished Chono for murdering Cleric Paan without trial. For months she thought the Cloaksaan would darken her door. Not yet, though.

Esek clucks. "Don't be petty. It's on you that a corrupt cleric lived as long as he did. She made a good job of it. Saved everyone the trouble of a trial." This meets with a tense silence. If there was a secretary here, they'd probably throw a fit over this blatant disrespect for the legal system. Esek smiles, gesturing theatrically. "And who's this big fellow you've got with you?"

The second cloaksaan is as stoic as Chono, but Chono doubts her own eyes ever project such an unsettlingly murderous gleam.

"This is my second, Cloak Vas Sivas Medisogo," says the First Cloak, still looking at Chono. "I suppose he's your counterpart, Cleric Chono. Though I didn't realize you were Esek's shadow again."

"She can't keep away," agrees Esek. "As for your boy..." A slow perusal. Medisogo's head resembles the end of a battering ram, with a nose equally as blunted. He looks at them with the contempt of a man being forced to watch his dinner roam free in a slaughterhouse. Esek looks from him to Moonback and drawls, "Bit of a stereotype, isn't he?"

At that moment, Paiye's novitiate reappears, burdened under two black cloaks. Seti Moonback takes his, sweeping it over his shoulders with a practiced flourish. The pauldron on his left shoulder gleams with polish, the Kindom's symbol embossed on the leather: a three-pointed star against a fiery sun.

"Back to the Silver Keep?" asks Esek cheerily.

Moonback sniffs. Most cloaksaan get testy when someone references the headquarters of the Brutal Hand, whose location is a secret even from most cloaks. Chono has heard they won't even say the name of the keep to each other, bound by a strange superstition.

Moonback says, "The labor strikes on Loez are getting dramatic. You'd think the Jeveni never want us to turn the gates back on. Fucking parasites."

Chono's stomach churns.

"Punish them," Esek suggests. "Deny them access to *The Risen Wave*. Cancel their Remembrance Day celebrations."

Moonback sneers. "Thank you for the suggestion, but it's all going ahead as usual."

Chono frowns at that. Every twenty-five years, the Jeveni come together as a people to orbit their destroyed moon colony and perform ceremonies of remembrance for the Jeveni Genocide. They converge in one of the original generation ships, *The Risen Wave*, and worship their god and grieve their ancestors. It is an important holiday for them—but also a tremendous strain on the jump system. It will be even more so now, with the gates closed to everyone else.

"Wouldn't it be better to ask them to delay?" she asks. "At least until the gates reopen?"

Moonback looks at her with cool displeasure. "It's up to the Secretaries and they don't want to exacerbate the union leaders. The last thing we need is for Jeveni malcontents to get violent."

Chono balks at this. "I was under the impression the only threats of violence were *against* the Jeveni. And those threats will hardly end if you give them gate access while denying it to—"

"Ah, so you take the Jeveni for harmless pacifists, do you? That's quaint. I for one don't trust anyone who worships a barren goddess."

His words breathe with contempt, a contempt that's common in the Treble. All the gods have children, even the death god, Som—but not Sajeven. Moonback snorts at Chono's expression, adds, "But I suppose they were perfectly peaceable when Alisiana controlled the sevite industry."

This is flung at Esek like an acid attack. But Esek smiles, unimpacted. One of Alisiana's greatest accomplishments was to recruit the Jeveni as factory workers for the sevite industry. It was a natural fit. From the early centuries of the Treble's colonization, the Jeveni were religious outcasts, derided for worshipping Sajeven, and distrusted for refusing to worship the Godfire. When the Ma'kessn moon, Jeve, turned out to be a spinning rock of fuel, the Kindom saw divine providence. Jeve was named after Sajeven, and the Jeveni were her worshippers. Relocate them to the moon, out of sight, and make them mine it for the jevite rock that so masterfully fueled the jump gates. And so it went, until the beginning of the thirteenth century, when the mining contracts had stripped Jeve of its one resource. Kindom overseers pulled out, but left the Jeveni behind, to fend for themselves in crumbling biodomes. Within a century Ri'in Nightfoot had found the formula for synthetic jevite (sevite, of course), and raised the Nightfoots from a declining First Family to one of the Treble's most powerful.

The Jeveni were all but forgotten. That is, until Lucos Alanye found evidence of more jevite seams on the moon. But he was greedy, and monstrous. As soon as he realized he couldn't hoard the seam, he turned all the firepower of his three mining ships on blowing the seam up—and the last of the Jeveni with it.

There were survivors, of course—nearly a hundred thousand refugees scattered to the systems. Alisiana gave succor to those who wanted it, gave them work and protection in her sevite factories, and while many Jeveni choose to live in separatist communities, most have acquiesced to their modern conditions.

That Alisiana chose to aid the Jeveni survivors was not, Chono knows, a sign of charity, but a ruthless cleverness that makes Chono's insides crawl. She created for herself a deeply loyal workforce. A stable sevite trade. It remains to be seen whether that stability will survive her death after almost a year.

Chono tells Moonback, "I take the Jeveni for reasonable people who will understand if we ask them to delay, for their own protection."

"I'm not interested in protecting the Jeveni right now. They can save themselves if they want to."

Moonback says it with such disregard, such an utter lack of humor or self-consciousness, that Chono is stunned. She knows very well that there are people in the Treble who view the Jeveni as less than citizens, but to have it put so bluntly—

The First Cloak adds, "Perhaps Sa Nightfoot will take their protection on, hmm? Gods know you have the opportunity to do it, haven't you?"

The words hang for a beat, inviting a reaction that never comes, and at last Seti Moonback snorts. He turns from them, striding off. Medisogo gives Chono a hateful look, disorienting for its intensity, and then he is sweeping away as well.

"Ass," mutters Esek, though she looks more amused than offended.

"This way, Saan," says the novitiate.

They follow him down the hall and through the open door to First Cleric Paiye's small but beautifully lit office. The First Cleric is already on his feet, and he comes around his desk with a broad smile for Chono, arms outstretched.

"My beloved kin," he says warmly, clasping her hand with both of his. She can feel the fat Godfire stone of his official ring, round cut and warm like a sun. "In all this trouble, I am so grateful for the joy of seeing you again."

Chono is not much of a smiler but she grips his hand and allows her lips to quirk at the corners. Some years ago, Paiye made her his assistant on a two-year tour of the Treble systems. She has fond memories of it, of him. And ambivalent as she is toward so many of her kin, she has always trusted the noble intentions of the First Cleric, who chuckles at her meager smile. There is something fatherly in his regard.

"Ah, Esek." He turns with only a slight dip in warmth. "It seems crass to ask if you have enjoyed your leave from duty."

"Not at all, First Cleric," returns Esek. "The work at Verdant is very refreshing. No one expects you to pray when you're shoveling through rubble."

Chono looks away, embarrassed. Paiye *hmms*, though it's not without humor. He gestures them to the two chairs across from his desk, and then sits down himself. The light from the ceiling pours over them in buttery sheets, and there's a rich smell emanating from the flowers standing in vases throughout the room. The First Cleric folds dark, weathered hands on the desktop, regarding them both before he lets out a heavy sigh.

"Well. I won't draw things out. I've asked you both here because we may have found a link to whoever plotted the attack on Verdant."

Chono shifts subtly in her chair so she has a better view of Esek, and waits for her to respond. Paiye, too, watches Esek for a reaction, but remarkably, she gives nothing away.

Chono has read enough about the aftermath of the Verdant sacking to know the Nightfoots put a bounty on every pirate who participated in the attack. Hundreds have scrambled to claim the reward—accusing business rivals and neighbors and inconvenient relatives of colluding in the attack. But while everything from Nightfoot portraits to Nightfoot jewelry to Nightfoot underwear has resurfaced in various markets, none of it has been reliably tied to any of the accused. In the history of criminal undertakings, none has so absolutely managed to hide its operatives from the investigations of the Cloaksaan—or the retribution of the Nightfoots. Esek ought to be vibrating with the chance of some revenge, but her expression is calm.

Paiye clears his throat and spreads his hands. The light catches on his Godfire ring.

"As you know, among the possessions marked as stolen from Verdant were a great many archival records: antique documents, memory coins, that sort of thing. The Cloaksaan believe they may have tracked down one of those coins. A pirate ship called *The Swimming Fox* has been communicating with a caster who goes by the handle Sunstep. It's unclear from communications which party is actually selling the coin, but the sale *is* scheduled to occur tomorrow, on Teros."

Again, Esek is silent.

Chono asks, "Do you believe *The Swimming Fox* was at Verdant?"

Still looking thoughtfully at Esek, Paiye says, "No. In fact, they have a tight alibi. And Sunstep's admittedly incomplete records don't paint them as the type to raid a stronghold."

Finally, Esek joins in. "How auspicious, to be the only coin we've found." Her lips spread in a lupine grin. "Are you hoping to use it to track down the original attackers?"

"We could try. But the coin itself is what interests us."

Esek's brows lift. "Really. And what is on this little coin?"

"Something with the capacity to erode public trust in the Nightfoot family."

For a moment no one speaks, and Chono is suddenly hyperaware of the powerful families in her orbit—the Paiyes themselves, and the Moonbacks up north, and the Khens out on Teros. These First Families of the Treble have long-standing rivalries with one another, and with the Nightfoots, and any of them would have a stake in seeing the public turn on the Nightfoots. But Aver Paiye is not an agent of his family, not since he took his vows. He is an agent of the Kindom. And the Kindom wants order, above all.

Esek says at last, "That's very vague and mysterious."

"We are limiting further details to the most essential people."

Esek's eyes narrow, the first hostile sign. "Am I not *essential*, where the Nightfoots are concerned?"

"You are a cleric of the Righteous Hand." He meets her tone with a coolness few would dare direct at Esek. "You are a servant of the Kindom. It is in that capacity that I have invited you here. Not as the possible matriarch of your family."

Esek smiles coldly. "Of course. That is not a position I have accepted."

The "yet" hangs unspoken.

Aver Paiye clasps his hands again. "Very good. Then let me make your responsibilities plain. The sale will take place in the city of Lo-Meek on

Bei continent. We would like you to go to Teros and intercept both the pirates and the caster. If possible, all parties should be placed under arrest with the local marshals. If it is a choice between killing them and their escape, you have permission to kill them."

Chono's skin prickles. Esek raises her eyebrows. "Really? And there was Seti Moonback not ten minutes ago, giving us shit because Chono killed a pedophile."

"Pirates are not always redeemable," says Paiye, unrattled by Esek's mocking tone. "And the caster Sunstep is a known criminal, with ties to illegal cloaking technologies, not to mention some of the worst offenders in the Treble. They've managed to scramble their communications with *The Swimming Fox* so expertly that even our best couldn't recover everything. We don't know what they look like, where they're from, who their allies are. The most personal thing we know about them is that they seem to do a lot of sniffing after the Nightfoots."

Chono's fingers bite a little deeper into the arm of the chair; her thoughts roil with possibilities. She knows Esek's must be as well, a single name ticking in both their heads, like a countdown to disaster.

"Nuisance though they are, the Cloaksaan don't seem to think Sunstep is particularly valuable. Nor are the pirates, for that matter. If they can't be taken alive, they must be put down. Honestly, Esek, I didn't expect any pushback from you on the matter."

A beat of silence. An *invitation* to argue.

Esek merely says, "I see."

Chono is surprised. She, for one, does not "see" at all. Lines of authority are firmly delineated between the three Hands of the Kindom. Clerics don't practice the law; secretaries don't administer death rites. And a task like this should rightly fall to the cloaks, who are the Kindom's ruthless constabularies. It's true Esek has all the skills of a cloaksaan (except, perhaps, the ability to go unnoticed), but Chono has never known the Righteous Hand to officially send one of its clerics on a mission of this type. It's...bizarre.

Esek gestures at Chono. "And what's her involvement?"

Aver Paiye smiles. "You and I both know from experience that Chono is a valuable companion."

It's a compliment, but the phrasing stabs her with memories she would like to forget.

Esek chuckles. "Ah. Of course. You want me to have a chaperone." She tells Chono with mock seriousness, "You see, while you were on Quietus praying to Capamame for absolution, I was fighting a battle to the death for the Nightfoot estate. It all got very bloody and chaotic. Apparently, I attacked a guardsaan for trying to evacuate me. Nearly killed him. And now, they send me off to Teros to capture the very mongrels who are trading in my family's stolen goods. Best to have someone keep an eye on me."

Chono doesn't know how to respond, so she looks at the First Cleric. His generally easy demeanor has started to frost at the edges. He stares at Esek with disapproval, bushy brows gnarled above his dark eyes.

"Everyone needs friends sometimes, Cleric Nightfoot. I approved your leave request so you could be with your family as it works to rebuild Verdant. But just because you've been away doesn't mean I haven't had my eye on you. Alisiana only died a year ago. I know it hit you hard. I want to make sure this secondary blow hasn't pushed you too far. Chono is uniquely qualified to protect your best interests, even when you act against them. Never forget my duty as First Cleric is to see that you are safe and well."

Chono thinks if this is indeed his duty, sending Esek to Teros is a peculiar way to perform it.

Esek smirks at the First Cleric with such insulting condescension that Chono wonders how Paiye can bear it as peacefully as he does.

Apparently, he doesn't mean to bear it any longer.

"So," he says, with finality. He stands up, Chono rising with him. Esek takes her time following. "You will have a warkite for the duration, *The Makala Aet*. It has a capable crew and will accommodate your novitiates, since I know you'll insist on bringing them. They are completing their preflight checks and will depart late this afternoon."

Esek says, "I have business in Riin Kala, first."

Paiye's expression goes flat. He is reaching the end of his patience. Esek smiles placidly and shrugs. "It shouldn't take more than a couple of hours."

After a tense moment, the First Cleric nods once. "Fine. You will depart after your errand is complete. The trip to Lo-Meek will not take more than ten hours, and you'll find a garrison of marshals available for your use. The meeting is at 8:00 a.m., local Teron time. We'd like as little mess as possible, so I trust Chono to be your conscience in these matters. Bring the coin directly back to Riin Cosas once you have it. Understood?"

Esek bows over her palms, low enough to evacuate the holy gesture of all sincerity. "Of course, Sa. Gods keep you well."

Chono gives her own, genuine bow, and turns with Esek to go, but Aver Paiye says, "Stay a moment, Chono."

Esek pauses only to shake her head as if at two silly children, and then she flounces off, shutting the door after her with exaggerated consideration. Chono, still standing, looks to the First Cleric with an uncertainty she's not used to feeling in his presence. They had such warmth between them, when they toured the Treble together. He had taken her under his wing, trained her, equipped her with patience and care for the true work of being a cleric—things Esek never taught her. And yet now, he is doing such strange things...

He sighs and goes to a tea tray on a nearby table to pour himself a cup. He offers her one, but she shakes her head no, watching him. He carries the cup and saucer with him back to her, sips contemplatively. Then gives her a rueful look.

"You must have questions."

She hesitates. "I assume you'll tell me whatever I need to know."

His smile is affectionate. He takes another drink of tea, and then places saucer and cup on his desk. "I also trust you to ask what you need to know."

Chono shifts her stance and folds her hands in front of her. She has never had the luxury of complete honesty, with anyone. But whatever honesty she has given Aver Paiye over the years, he's accepted without reproach.

"The business with the factory unrest, and with the jump gate rationing. Is it connected to this mission on Teros?"

Paiye regards her shrewdly. "What connection do you imagine?"

"I'm not a secretary, but I have access to the same ledgers as any cleric, and it's clear that the Clever Hand has reserved enough sevite fuel to make these recent rations unnecessary. Yet here we are, with protests ratcheting up, and the factory unions growing even more recalcitrant, and now I find that Esek has been named the matriarch of her family. I don't think you're rationing because of what's happening now. I think you're rationing because of what you think *may* happen."

He nods approvingly. He twists the ring on his finger, as if it were a key in a lock.

"Alisiana was always supportive of the factory unions," he says musingly. "She treated them well, protected their autonomy. She did this so they would be loyal to her, and it worked. You know as well as I that the factory workers view themselves as ancillaries to the Nightfoots. The unions don't care that the Kindom itself controls the gates. They care that their work remains the purview of the Nightfoots, whom they trust to grant them at least some freedoms. Since Alisiana's death, union leaders have openly demanded that Esek take her place."

Chono considers this, surprised. Alisiana was always personally involved in monitoring sevite production, an empire she inherited and made thrive. Esek has never been anywhere near the family business (at least, not in any official capacity). Why would the Jeveni want *her* for their matriarch?

She asks as much. Paiye says, "It's something we've anticipated for some time. Alisiana was a force of nature. So is Esek. If the matriarchy passes to a child, like Riiniana, the unions fear an erosion of Nightfoot authority, and that Kindom oversight will take its place."

"Are they right?" Chono asks.

Paiye chuckles. "I sympathize with the Jeveni not wanting their way of life to change. After all they have endured, it's natural. But the Kindom chose its words for a reason: Peace, under the Kindom. Unity, in the Treble. Without our mediation of the sevite trade, the individual families would turn on one another. There would be monopoly and war. Alisiana understood that, but she still fought for every crumb she could take. She was a strategist. She took care of the unions and workers so they would protect her independence from us. She offered employment to tens of thousands of Jeveni survivors so they would see *her* as their ally, not the Kindom that rescued them. But her methods never went so far as to force a Kindom response. She kept a delicate balance. If Esek becomes the matriarch of the Nightfoots, do you think she will be able to keep that balance?"

"Esek is a strategist, too."

Paiye nods, a conciliatory gesture. "I know she is. Which is precisely why I prefer her to remain a Hand of the Kindom. I do not seek the day when she is at odds with our interests."

Chono reflects, the pieces coming together. "If Esek becomes matriarch, it will pacify the unions and restore order to the trade. But the Kindom does not trust her with that sort of power. So we are rationing access to the jump gates in order to further stockpile the sevite—as an insurance policy against her intransigence." Paiye looks at her quietly, an invitation for her to continue. "If, on the other hand, she remains a cleric, there will be more uproar in the factories. We will have to break up the unions—install new leadership and loyal workers, which would displease the Jeveni. Rationing sevite now is a security against the time it will take to rebuild."

The move is typical of Kindom leadership, and especially of the Secretaries—farseeing and practical. And it explains, in a roundabout way, why Paiye is sending Esek after this memory coin. It's a test. Will she obey the Kindom? Or act according to her own desires? Will she be a Hand . . . or a matriarch?

Of course, in the meantime, it's the people of the Treble who will suffer the consequences. And the Jeveni who will bear the brunt of the blame.

Chono asks, "Don't you think it would help our mission, Sa, to know the contents of this coin?"

He gives her a sympathetic smile, but there is steel behind it, and Chono knows that she has touched too close to the quick. He shakes his head. "On the contrary, I think it would prove a distraction. You must trust me on this, Chono. The contents of the coin are not your concern. Only bringing it back to me."

Chono knows better than to argue, yet through her curls a premonition of that coin's import. She more than any non-Nightfoot in the worlds (and more than many Nightfoots themselves) knows the kinds of secrets that family carries. And if she's right about the contents of the coin, then it can only mean one thing: Six is involved.

Suddenly Paiye is looking at her with a deep warmth and gentleness, as if to soften his refusal. "You are the most righteous Hand among us, Chono. And you are also devoted to Esek. You will protect her, counsel her. Remind her of the loyalty she owes our kin. At the end of it all, you will keep your vows to the Godfire. You will be my ears."

At those words (expected, dreaded), Chono hazards to remind him, "Esek won't appreciate being spied on, Burning One."

"I don't ask you to spy on her. I ask you to report to me on the progress with this mission, since I know Esek will not. Whatever else is at play, I want that memory coin. If someone like Sunstep has it, or gets it, I fear the repercussions."

Chono clears her throat, banishing thoughts of whoever Sunstep might or might not be. There is only one answer she can give to the First Cleric.

"Of course, Sa. I am your servant."

"Good." He smiles again. "Good. Do you know anything about this business she has in Riin Kala?"

It's a loaded question.

"I don't, Sa."

"Go with her."

Chono hesitates, about to point out that Esek may not allow it, but then he is moving toward the door. "And if there is anything you need, contact me directly."

"Thank you, Sa."

"Gods keep you well, Cleric Chono."

"Gods keep you well, First Cleric."

But just before she is about to go through the door, she stops, and looks at him again. He frowns curiously, an invitation, and though something in Chono tells her to keep quiet, she can't help herself.

"Seti Moonback says that Remembrance Day will go ahead as planned." Paiye looks at her without answering. A confirmation. "Isn't that dangerous, for the Jeveni? People already blame them for the gate closures. Now they'll think they're getting special treatment."

"It is not special treatment. Remembrance Day is built into the Anti-Patriation Act; it is crucial to Jeveni autonomy. We cannot break our own laws."

The irony of this, of course, is that the Anti-Patriation Act never had anything to do with protecting Jeveni autonomy, but rather curtailing it.

Chono says, "Surely a delay while we resolve—"

"The Jeveni are intransigent. They would not accept a delay, even to save their own lives. They refuse to see us as anything but their persecutors."

His tone creeps close to the one that Seti Moonback used. It unnerves Chono, wondering at this attitude from a man who has always regarded the Treblens as his own children. She says quietly, "They have reason, you know... to distrust us."

Centuries' worth of reason, in fact. They were treated as little better than slaves on Jeve. After the Kindom abandoned them there, they at least had the benefit of worshipping their goddess in peace, creating their own government, and avoiding the attention of the larger Treble. The genocide stripped them of those freedoms. Now they are tightly controlled, their separatist communities forbidden by the Anti-Patriation Act to exceed a hundred people, their one-time government disbanded, their very existence occupying a liminal space: rejected as Treblens, but beholden to the laws of the Treble.

Paiye says, "Your concern for their well-being is admirable, Chono. Rest assured, I will take your thoughts to heart."

It is a definitive close to their conversation. Chono hesitates, and Paiye looks at her in a way that says, *Enough*.

She nods curtly, and leaves. The door snicks shut behind her. In the empty hallway, she's momentarily disoriented. She needs to find Esek. She needs to speak to the novitiate who took her bag. She needs to decide what to do with that bag, and with the thing inside it, her dearest possession of all. Should she bring it with her? No, not with Esek here. Esek, who makes chaos out of peace.

Breathing out, Chono marshals a career of meditative practice, trying to quiet her mind. Trying to remember what the air tastes like on Pippashap, how the breeze swoops in through the shanty curtains, and how the floor always moves gently, rocked by a world-covering ocean...

Instead, her nostrils are full of the Riin Cosas gardens, and the shifting ground underfoot is of an entirely different type.

CHAPTER THREE

1664

YEAR OF THE CRUX

Lo-Meek
Bei Continent
The Planet Teros

*T*he *Swimming Fox* makes port in a prepaid station on Ton Street, directly across the way from Jun's window seat in a snack shop. The ship's oblong bulk hangs in midair over the Lo-Meek Canyon. Hacking their firewall is child's play, and now she's got a direct view into what they're packing behind that grim metal prow: twenty-person crew, all Braems with rap sheets the length of the ship itself; quad engine pieced together from stolen Kindom ships; state-of-the-art casting array; and, of course, military-grade armaments. It looks like a torpedo fit to blow the nearest threat to pieces, and Jun is planning to walk right into it. Most of her gambits happen at a remove, clever cons that hit before anyone knows what's happened to them. *This*... Well, this may be the most reckless thing she's ever done.

Jun takes a grimacing drink of her coffee, cold and sickly sweet with condensed milk. Her appointment with the captain of *The Swimming Fox* is half an hour away, but she's been nursing the same cup for two hours, and this is hardly a pleasant place to spend the afternoon. The Grum Bowl's half-stocked shelves boast evaporated soups, snack packs, and candy bars, none of which are less than a standard year old. The floors are grimy, and the lights are eye-stabbingly fluorescent. Patrons glare at her when they see her gun, flashing their own sidearms like a dare she ignores. On one wall there's a crude mural of Terotonteris, god of revelry and risks, his round body jutting with arms and legs, his mouth open to swallow from a pitcher while some of his hands play a game of tiles and others clasp at shiny things.

The only thing to recommend this shop is its floor-to-ceiling windows with a perfect view of the street. Hundreds of ships are docked in the canyon, many still radiating heat after the blazing reentry. Heat is a staple of Teros, thick and unctuous. Red dust covers everything, including the people: vagrants, hawkers, drunks, Black Ocean sailors. The skies over the canyon are as muddy red as the Teron soil, radiation shields in the atmosphere reflecting back the surface. It's a mucky, rough-hewn disaster of a planet, and Jun can't wait to get off it.

In the corner of the shop, a staticky casting view blares with advertisements and news snippets from a local info hawker with an affected grandiosity:

"The Ar'tec work colony secures three new contracts with the Moonback family. Looks like anyone can be redeemed by hard work!"

"Union talks break down! Jeveni dissidents refusing to work until their demands are met. The Secretaries won't estimate when gate travel embargos will lift."

"The seventy-fifth anniversary of the Jeveni Genocide is four days away, and preparations for Remembrance Day are in full swing! Will union troubles interrupt the celebrations? If not, visit Sa Saboshi's Sips and Surprises Shop on Ton Street for all your holiday needs!"

Then, suddenly, a louder bulletin streams through, flashing lights and a newscaster's face appearing by hologram.

"Breaking news! We're receiving reports of a pirate attack on the transport vessel *The Wild Run*. What looks like a standard act of piracy has escalated to full-blown annihilation!"

Jun's eyes shift from the street to the cast.

"*The Wild Run* is destroyed. I repeat, the transport vessel *The Wild Run* has been completely destroyed. Reports indicate that the ship was contracted to transport a casting corps to South Avo on Kator."

Jun's heart thumps.

"In the most stunning detail to come out of the destruction site, officials confirm that the casters were composed entirely of Jeveni citizens. Over three hundred Jeveni and ship's crew are presumed dead."

Her lips part in disbelief. Three *hundred*?

"This is a developing story, but I can confirm that no single event has killed this many casters, or this many Jeveni, since the Jeveni Genocide of 1589."

Jun dives into the casting net, seeking out the virtual forums where legal and illegal casters gather. Already hundreds are discussing and drawing on the reports, an entire community of tech heads brought to their feet. Jun has never met a Jeveni caster, but it makes no difference. If she belongs to any people, it's not the Ma'kessn who share her genetics—it's the casters who share her calling. A deep ache and horror pool in her gut. Three hundred. Three *hundred*!

A sound from outside grabs her attention. *The Swimming Fox* has let down its gangplank, the huge metal shaft groaning into place with a final *bang* that connects it to the street. No one disembarks. No one approaches. She checks the time. Twenty-four minutes to go.

In the forum, casters debate what so many Jeveni were doing in one place. Some are cruel, dismissive—others smell foul play. Jun has half a mind to jump into the debate herself (even if she's running out of time), but a messenger bot starts beeping at her.

Jun mutters a curse at the signature. She considers ignoring it, but this is the third time in as many hours, and she knows Liis will keep pinging her until she reacts. With a practiced flick and bump of her wrist, she casts the message to her ocular, and Liis's glowering face appears.

"When you get back, I'm going to smack the shit out of you."

The hostile words in Liis's hypnotically low voice make Jun grin, thoughts about *The Wild Run* taking a back seat.

"Domestic abuse is no laughing matter, dear," she says.

"Where are you?"

Jun sighs, clears her throat. She glances around, pleased the shop is empty at the moment. Only the sullen-looking teenage cashier remains, and he's ten feet away and clearly watching something on his ocular screen. She doubts he can hear anything over whatever program is blowing out his eardrums. He's stocky and shaggy-haired and reminds her in a vague way of her sweet younger cousin Bene—but no, she can't think of him right now, any more than she can afford to think about three hundred dead casters. She pushes those thoughts away and focuses on Liis again.

"I'm in Lo-Meek. *The Fox* just docked. Our appointment is in twenty minutes and don't worry, I left *The Gunner* with a first-rate docking agency two miles away. Our baby will be fine."

"You've got to call this off."

Jun blows out an exasperated breath. "Liis, I've had my eye on this coin for months, and for most of that it was about as attainable as Kata's tit, okay? I can't call this off."

"They pushed the meeting up by fifteen hours." Liis speaks evenly but her eyes add, *That is* not *good.*

"They pushed it up because the gates are closed and they had nothing better to do," Jun argues. "I mean, shit, you should see this place. I've never seen so many angry merchantsaan."

Somewhere, someone whistles. A troop of Lo-Meek marshals appears at the end of the street. Jun goes still, watching them march. In their cream-colored, dust-resistant uniforms, they're a sharp contrast to the red everywhere else, and the people on the street stand aside for them, leery. Lo-Meek marshals are more thugs than law-keepers, and they've been pretty active lately, as far as Jun can tell. All the unrest about the jump gates. All the trouble in the factories. As the marshals approach *The Swimming Fox*, Jun's heart thuds steadily harder. But then they reach it—and carry on without a glance. She lets out her breath.

"What is it?" asks Liis.

"Nothing. Just some marshals walking by."

There's a tense pause. "Any cloaksaan?"

Jun stops eyeballing the street in order to focus on Liis again. She knows what people see when they look at Liis. A gouge in her cheekbone; the three-inch, mottled patch on her jaw where a burn repair went shoddy; the coldness of her dark eyes and the definition of muscle visible through her clothes. She looks terrifying. And she is terrifying—an exquisite combination of wreckage and beauty and danger. But Jun will never forget her soft voice the night they met, how she murmured, *I won't hurt you.*

And now that one word—"cloaksaan"—reminds Jun of all Liis has lost and stands to lose. As she watches, Liis tugs her cap farther down, tucking away a few twists of black hair.

Jun says, "No. I haven't seen a single cloak since I got here. You know how it is in these marshal-run towns. They like to keep the Kindom out of their business if they can."

"And they're the smarter for it."

"I'm not inviting the Kindom into my business," mutters Jun.

"You're buying an artifact that was stolen from the Nightfoots," Liis answers coolly.

"People have been selling Verdant stash all over the place. The Nightfoots care a lot more about finding who took it than finding who has it now. And all I'm buying is a cache of memory coins on behalf of an archivist consortium I made up. It's nothing to attract anyone's attention."

"Then why didn't you bring me with you?"

Jun scowls. In the corner of the shop, the info hawker is now jabbering about the strikes on Loez. A skinny Jeveni worker appears, face hidden behind a bandana, speaking in rapid Ma'kessi about the draconian conditions since Alisiana Nightfoot died. The Treble is a powder keg, and Jun can't answer Liis truthfully. Not unless she wants to admit how dangerous this is. But she can't back down now. *Months* of work. *Years* of planning…

"I know what you're doing," Liis says.

"What am I doing?"

"You're trying to protect me. I don't need you to protect me."

Tough shit, Jun thinks. "Look." She draws out the word, stalling. The fact is that counterfeiting jump gate clearance was easy, but it may be harder getting back. More crackdowns. Harder to stay under the radar. In this moment, Jun grasps the full weight of what separates her from Liis, and her stomach drops.

"I have to go, all right? I'll call you as soon as it's done."

Liis only nods. She's not one to blubber or beg. That she called at all is…sort of romantic. There are muttered words of love, and the comm goes dark.

Jun breathes in and breathes out, checking the time. She looks across the crowded street at *The Swimming Fox*'s smooth nose. Reaches for a comprehensive view of her six bank accounts, scattered across the planets and attached to various pseudonyms. She may not be rich by First Family standards, but the numbers gazing back at her are good. Good, and *close* to what she needs. To what this job will give her. If she can just pull it off.

The pirates of *The Swimming Fox* are restless from the moment she introduces herself ("Junian Graylore," she says, because it sounds like an archivist's name). They barely let her onto their ship, opting to conduct business in the docking chamber. The captain watches her closely, eyes pale blue and cold. He sits across from her, leaning back in his chair with the indolence of a resting tiger. His three comrades are rangy, well-armed men with perpetually glowering faces. One of them has fresh bruising on his face. The situation is...fraught.

On the other hand, they've turned over the case of memory coins without incident. Now Jun pieces through the stacks, slow and methodical, examining ID numbers through her magnifier as if she doesn't know exactly which one she's looking for. It's stifling in the chamber, that deep swamp humidity leaving a film on her skin and dampness in all the most uncomfortable spots. No doubt the captain is eager to get his merchandise back into cooling before the air does any damage. If you can call this air. More like breathing steam, acrid with the stench of the docks, and of the planet itself. Jun blocks it out, melting into concentration...

But after a few minutes, it's clear the coin isn't here.

Don't react, she tells herself. *Stay calm.*

"This is a very impressive collection, Captain Foxer," she says, still surveying the utterly useless coins with the mask of academic curiosity. "My cohort will be very pleased. There is a discrepancy, however. In our correspondence you listed seven hundred and twelve coins." She stops, looking up to meet the captain's stare. "My scan shows seven hundred and *eleven*."

One of the pirates, the one with the bashed-in face, chuckles darkly. Foxer throws him a quelling glance, then looks at Jun.

"You sure you haven't counted wrong?"

Jun smiles, and makes a show of rescanning the stack and projecting the reports, as if she doesn't have the identifier memorized.

"Yes, according to this, coin MSNV-1575-12-14 is missing. It appears on your manifest, but not in this stack."

"We can deduct it from the price."

Jun stays friendly, stays smiling. "Does that mean you don't have it?"

The bruised pirate chuckles again. More like a snort, and Jun isn't sure who he's snorting at. He's younger than the others, slimmer, but brutally built, his long straw-colored hair woven into a few dozen tight braids. Signs, each of them, of combat kills.

Foxer ignores him this time, focusing on Jun for a long stretch before he suddenly reaches for the case of memory coins and snaps it closed, handing it off to one of his crew. For a terrified moment she thinks it's over, then he reaches into his shirt pocket. He withdraws something square and metal and about an inch across, placing it on the table with a carefulness that belies his gruff performance so far.

"Let's stop pretending you care about any coin but this one."

Jun holds perfectly still, though the desire to reach out and snatch up the coin is a physical ache. She flicks her eyes from it to the pirate captain, and her smile is less friendly this time.

"I was never dishonest with you. I asked to purchase this cache with all its listed coins. Why the games, Captain?"

"Because I wanted to see if it was really this coin you wanted."

"Why?"

He doesn't answer. Jun clears her throat, finally moving—but only to lean back a little in her chair. Her hand strays casually toward the butt of her handgun. They're all armed, but she's a cracking shot, and she might—*might*—be able to get out alive.

To her surprise, it's the young pirate who speaks next. "You probably didn't expect us to actually look at the coins, did you?"

"At over seven hundred memory coins? No, I didn't."

"So, you planned to pull one over on us?"

"That's enough, Masar," says Foxer. Then, to Jun, "Although, he has a point. You seem to have banked on us not realizing what this coin is."

"And what is it?" Jun retorts, the tension making her brash. "I haven't even seen it yet."

"Then you don't know who's in it?"

"I know who... *might* be in it," she admits.

"Lucos Alanye," blurts the pirate Masar, like he's been desperate to say it, to speak the name they've all been thinking.

Foxer makes a growling sound, and the look he turns on Jun is deadly, volcanic. Jun shivers. People romanticize the Braems. Say they're wild and dangerous and sexy, all big muscles and tight braids. But in the captain's pale blue eyes, Jun sees nothing romantic. All she sees is the life he's lived Out There, in the dark, icy chasms between the planets, the black reaches of that inimitable ocean. It's the same place where Jun has spent most of her life, and she knows who the apex predators are.

Suddenly, he folds his arms and jerks his head at his three comrades. It's an unmistakable *Get out*. Masar looks mutinous, while the others are already turning to leave the chamber. The airlock door leading deeper into *The Swimming Fox* whooshes open for them. After a tense staring match between Foxer and Masar, the latter goes, though not without a last look at Jun. When the door irises shut, the vacuum seal shuddering the antechamber, she isn't sure if this is a good development or not.

Foxer unfolds his arms and stretches out one of his legs. An unsheathed dagger is strapped to his thigh, the angled blade gleaming. Jun doesn't move, watching him. She lets the silence stretch for as long as she can bear it.

Which isn't long.

"May I view the coin before we talk price?"

Foxer continues staring at her. She's struck by the paleness of him, the geometrically patterned dots tattooed down the side of his face, the thinness of his braids (necessary, to accommodate his kill count). He asks, "What if the coin isn't what you want? Will you call it all off? Will I have come here for nothing?"

Jun hesitates. "I'm entitled to view the product before I agree to the sale."

Foxer smiles thinly. He reaches across the table, picking up the square case with its valuable occupant. Jun is irrationally afraid he's going to crush it in his palm. So, when he suddenly tosses it across the table at her, she barely has the wherewithal to catch it.

"I'll tell you what, *Junian Graylore*"—clearly he never bought the name—"why don't you take it? No charge."

His words hang in the air, thicker than the humidity. At first, she thinks it's a joke, but his stare is level. She glances down at the case in her hand, then looks at him again. She feels suddenly as if she's surrounded by a field of explosives. The wrong word will set off everything.

"Why?"

Foxer shrugs. "I can't sell it," he says, as if they're discussing expired snack packs.

She blinks. Reminds him, "I'm...offering to buy it. I can transfer the credit to you in any currency you want."

His stare frosts over. "I don't want your credit. I don't want that coin, either. Lucos Alanye destroyed every biodome on Jeve just so no one else could get at the jevite. You think pirates are bad? Bah! We've never destroyed a moon. I may murder as I need, but *genocide?*" His lip curls. "Som themself isn't that bloody, and I'll take the advice of my god. If Lucos Alanye is what you're after, I want no part in it. Either you take the thing, or I drop it in the canyon."

Jun stares, amazed. She would never have expected a pirate to reject a deal on *religious* grounds. Pirates are businessaan first. This can't be the whole story, and yet—

"Well?" Foxer demands. "Do we have an accord...archivist?"

He uses the term like a slap, which has a clarifying effect. His threat to drop the coin in Lo-Meek Canyon clearly extends to her, and while she may not understand, she'll be damned if she's going to get herself murdered because some pirate is superstitious. Jun carefully tucks the memory coin case into her pocket, absently aware that if it ends up being empty, she'll feel a damn fool. Foxer continues to watch her, placid, dangerous, and she very carefully stands up.

"I see that our business is over, Captain."

He smiles thinly. "Yes, it is. Let me show you out."

A fresh wave of that Lo-Meek smell and heat flows over her as he leads her back onto the gangplank—ferric oxide and garbage. The docks are thick with people; nobody blinks an eye at a frigate ante-chamber disgorging her. Jun pauses at the end of the plank, Foxer right on her tail, as if he thinks she's going to try to double back. Now, looking up at him, she's struck by his formidable height.

"All the best to you, Sa." His eyes are cold.

It's a dismissal, and with the coin sitting heavy in her pocket, Jun offers him a weak smile and hurries down the road. Muscling past dockworkers and merchants and travelers, she's insensate to the clamor and movement, lost in thought, until the whistle.

That universal signal: The marshals are coming.

Everyone knows when you hear that sound, you should keep your head down and move on. But something prickles the nape of her neck. Something shocks the common sense out of her. She looks back over her shoulder, toward *The Swimming Fox*'s metal bulk, suspended over the port chasm. Six marshals, their cream uniforms unmistakable under the streetlights, stand at the foot of the gangplank, where she was moments ago. Captain Saxis Foxer has not retreated into his ship. Instead, he stands with arms raised away from his body, away from his weapons. The marshals aim rifles at him, and though Jun can't hear it, there's clearly a rapid back-and-forth happening. The surrounding passersby make a wide berth. Jun has no idea what compels her to stop walking, to keep looking. A moment later, all seven heads swivel toward her. She meets Foxer's stare for a split second, sees it in his mouth and eyes, and then he points. Right at her.

"Shit," she whispers, the marshals zeroing in on her with sniper precision.

"You!" the leader shouts. They're already on the move. "Stop there!"

"Shit," she growls, louder. And turns. And runs.

The streets are full. That's her only advantage. People weave incongruous paths around her. Trolleys and wares are stacked against the walls of the surrounding city. Everywhere is mud and potholes and convenient alleys tucked between buildings. And Jun is unencumbered by the marshals' body armor, which she hears clanking furiously behind her as they pursue.

"Stop *now*!" the same voice thunders.

Some fool playing at good citizen grabs her arm, trying to stop her. She throws the whole weight of her body behind a single fist, cracking against his cheekbone, then hurls herself down one of the alleys. Gunfire ricochets off the wall; something sharp strikes her cheek. She stumbles for an instant and keeps running. She knows this neighborhood. She knows if she can get ten blocks over and cut across onto the Westside docks, her ship is waiting. It's fifteen minutes tops, at a run.

Another gunshot. She darts left. These marshals are terrible shots, but *godsdamnit this alley is a dead end shit shit shit!* She doubles back. Goes right instead and they're practically on top of her. She stumbles down a flight of stairs.

"Stop or we'll shoot!"

And they won't miss this time. But the stairs are steep, she's got too much momentum, she can't stop even if she wants to—

A door flings open. Someone grabs her, hauling her inside as gunfire explodes in the alley. The door slams shut, pitching her into blackness. She can't see a thing, but she hears it when the marshals reach the door. Hears them pounding against the solid metal of it.

"Come on," someone grunts, pulling her forward. She stumbles in the dark. There's wetness on her face, thick and stinging, but she manages not to trip as she's hustled down a hallway. Behind them, there's a cracking sound as the marshals hammer at the door, but Jun doesn't look back. Heart throbbing, she follows the figure ahead of her, nearly barreling into them when they grind to a sudden halt. They're bigger than she is, a blocky shape in the darkness. There's the sound of jangling keys, and a new door opens, spilling her into piercing light and the smell of booze and urine. It's one of the service alleys that run behind the bars and shops, easy access for vomiting drunks and trade deliveries. She's standing under a streetlamp, bright enough to stagger her. The door slams shut after them and she spins to face her savior.

It's the pirate Masar.

Jun draws on reflex, pistol lining up with his head in an instant. He doesn't even flinch. Great Gra's voice fills her ears: *Steady your grip. Stand outside their range. Breathe.*

They stand like that for ten seconds. She counts, not only the seconds but the incongruities: How did he get off *The Swimming Fox?* How did he catch up to her in the alley? Where did he get *keys* to one of the shop doors? Masar watches her with the bored contempt of a teenager, his unbruised eye trained as steady as her pistol. If there's one bright spot in all this, it's that she hears the crew of marshals through the closed door, trooping past and none the wiser—though they may double back when they find they've lost the scent. There's no time to waste.

"I'm not giving it to you," she tells him, reckless.

He glances at the door behind them, closed and hopefully locked. He looks back at her. It's in this moment she realizes he has a double-barrel shotgun strapped to his back. It's almost as big as him. He doesn't draw.

"What are you going to do with it?" he asks.

She blinks, genuinely startled. *Don't let your guard down.* She tightens her grip on the pistol.

"What am I going to *do* with it? Sell it, make a fortune, get out of this system, start over, blah, blah, blah! What would *you* do with it?"

He doesn't answer. Somewhere in the distance, a siren begins to wail. Jun's blood runs cold.

"You'll never get out of the city now," says Masar.

"Let me worry about that, asshole."

"I have a warhorse."

For a second, Jun's legs turn to water. She nearly shoots him, she nearly runs, her body flooding with terror and—

He reads her thoughts, rolls his eyes. "I'm not a *cloak.* Fuck's sake, the warhorse is stolen."

Jun still hesitates. After all, an undercover cloaksaan would not admit to being an undercover cloaksaan. Yet there's something about him, a kind of youthful impertinence, that even the best cloaks wouldn't want to emulate. Obsessed as they are with their own gravitas.

Finally, she says, "I don't need a warhorse. I have a battle shuttle."

He lifts his eyebrows mockingly. "Nearby?"

Jun hesitates. Their route has taken them farther away from the Westside docks. And with how many checkpoints will be on guard, now the siren's gone up, her ship may as well be a hundred klicks away. A warhorse is an official transport of the Cloaksaan. It won't be subject to the checkpoints...

When she doesn't answer him, Masar jerks his head down the service alley. "Mine is two blocks east. All backstreets."

"What about your captain?" she snaps. "Won't he be—"

"My time on that bucket is over. It was the second I found that memory coin."

Jun's brows shoot up. *He* found it?

"Why should I trust you?"

"Do you have a choice? If you want, I can leave you for the marshals."

He looks earnest, but she has a feeling he's bluffing. He wants the coin. And the fact he didn't simply attack her in the alley and take it means something. She's not sure what, but something. And he's right. There are lots of places to hide in Lo-Meek, but nothing as secure as the interior of a warhorse.

Slowly, cautiously, waiting for him to spring, she holsters her gun.

"Your scarf is bloody," he says.

She glances down at the gauzy piece of blue muslin wound around her neck. Something she stole from Liis. And he's right, there is blood on it. She carefully unwinds it from her neck, using it to wipe at the cut on her forehead (at least the bleeding is sluggish). When she's done, she stuffs it behind a garbage bin near the alley door. Underneath the scarf, she's wearing a hooded jacket, and she pulls the hood up over her head. The jacket belongs to Liis, too. She better not lose any more of her stuff...

Without another word, Masar is on the move. His legs go to her waist; she practically has to jog to keep up. They skirt between narrow buildings and stacks of crates and garbage.

There's a reason people call Lo-Meek the most claustrophobic port city in the Treble. Yet already the sirens have driven most people indoors, so they pass hardly anyone. After two blocks the alley opens into a pavilion. There, as promised, stands a warhorse, gleaming under streetlights, with engines for haunches and a double saddle of burnished leather. Its spherical shields are down, its base resting on the ground rather than hovering above it. Three kids are crowded around it, oohing and aahing, while a fourth, old enough to have a gendermark, whacks them with a stick to keep them back. When he sees Masar coming, he jumps to attention.

"Here you are, Sa. Just like you said!"

"Good boy." Masar gives him four Teron marks. He looks at the three other children. "And what do you all say when the marshals and the cloaks come asking?"

"Never saw you!" they vow in unison.

Jun nearly scoffs. These are Teron street brats; opportunists, the lot of them. They'll sing the truth to the first person who offers them cash. Yet Masar gives each of them a mark, and off they race, gleeful. Masar runs his hand over the steering grips of the warhorse, and the engine recognizes him, purring to life. It levitates three or four inches off the ground, the thrusters rumbling. He climbs into the front saddle and gives Jun an expectant look.

She could always run. Take shelter somewhere and wait it out. No need to throw herself in with a stranger. She's got the memory coin. That's what matters.

Masar looks at her knowingly. "I have a buyer."

This time, she does scoff. "What makes you think I don't?"

"Do you?" he tosses back.

Jun refuses to dignify the remark, but in that moment the fresh wails of sirens split the air and all her bravado disappears. With a growling sound she climbs onto the machine behind him, his great shotgun like a bar dividing them from each other as she grabs the horn of the second saddle. As soon as she's in, the armored shields engage, tinted plates shooting up from the horse's foundation to form an impenetrable shell all around them. Masar hunches forward over the grips, guns the throttle, and they sprint out of the pavilion.

CHAPTER FOUR

1648

YEAR OF THE GAME

Barcetima
Uosti Sa Continent
The Planet Kator

Esek was bored. These kinds of parties always bored her, rife with sycophants and self-congratulatory elites, somebody always talking too loudly. Her host, Ashir Doanye, was seated on the couch across from hers and droning on about weapons contracts, and that was the most boring thing of all.

She had come to Kator, nominally, to bless just such a contract: one between the Kindom and the Katish arms syndicate, of which Doanye was a member. Now that task was done, and she would have liked to relax and drink and maybe fuck someone.

But her real reason for being here was not the Kindom contract. It was her family: The Nightfoots required fresh weapons inventory, as well. They couldn't go to the markets on Ma'kess—all those belonged to the Moonbacks, whom they had been fighting for complete control of the home planet for centuries. A bitter rivalry that went all the way back to...someone insulting someone's husband, Esek didn't really know. At the moment, Moonbacks held the northern continents and Nightfoots held the south, and Esek was hardly going to go north for a few extra guns. So here she sat on Kator, glad-handing local merchantsaan over the Kindom's four-trillion-plae weapons contract, while simultaneously cementing a quieter deal on behalf of her family. Dull, dull stuff.

A server walked by, and Esek snapped her fingers at them; they brought her a flute of bright and bubbling keel, a local vintage. She was normally a praevi drinker, partial to distilled liquors, but the keel felt good in her mouth, a moment of pleasure in the midst of so much mediocrity. Say this for Katishsaan—they made good jump gates, good guns, and good alcohol.

Speaking of guns, Ashir Doanye was still rambling: "—designed some excellent new rifles, better even than the latest Katish design, but fucking *fires* do those Braems charge through the roof. And of course, the engineers are annoyed with me for going elsewhere. I had to invite three of them here tonight to smooth things over; they drink like fish. Look at them."

Esek did look. The room was full of rich Katishsaan and visiting Ma'kessn dignitaries. As usually happened when persons of those separate worlds came together, there was a stench of competition in the air.

Another server went by. Esek grabbed a bunch of grapes from his platter and began to lazily bite the fruits from the stems. She got a bit of stem in her mouth and spit it at a passing Katishsaan who, sadly, didn't notice.

Doanye said, "After your success on behalf of the Kindom today, I'm sure you're eager to settle this other business for your family. And I'm eager to settle, too, Esek, if we can agree on price."

Esek sighed. Tuned him out again. She watched the wealthy party-goers show off their new body mods to one another: new breasts, new eyes, new digital tattoos that swam and flexed on their bodies. One Katish engineer with hair arrayed like a sculpture on his head was showing off the sixth and seventh fingers of his hands by playing a drum harp; his finger bracelets tinkled as he played. Ma'kessns stood around him, admiring with ice in their eyes.

Esek spit another grape stem, hitting a passing Katishsaan right on the neck. The woman turned, indignant—but when she saw it was Esek, she quailed and went on. Esek huffed through her nostrils. How she *scorned* the socialites and politicians and entrepreneurs around her, the complete absence of any worthy competitor.

To her annoyance, Doanye kept talking of inflation and price goug-ing, kept throwing in barbs about the rudeness of Ma'kessn traders. He had been remarkably free with her all night. Honestly, a few throw-away fucks and people became *insufferably* presumptuous.

"—and you add to that the factory explosions in Dunta! Suddenly production is down thirty percent. Thirty *percent*! Do you know what that does to my margins?"

"Very inconvenient, that explosion," drawled Esek.

Ashir Doanye gave her an unimpressed look. "Two hundred work-ers died. The Katish Council required all the barons to pay damages. I had to shell out over five million plae. The Secretaries didn't raise a finger to help."

"As I recall, the Secretaries issued fifty million plae in relief funds," Esek replied.

Doanye blew out an annoyed breath. He snapped at the nearest ser-vant, who brought him a cigarette. Esek ran her fingers through the minkat fur couch she was sitting on, luxuriating in the fine fibers. At least Doanye's home was comfortable. She sipped the keel. *Delicious.* Doanye lit his cigarette with a silver lighter engraved with the image of Kata, Kator's god. A slim, scarred creature with no eyes and one volup-tuous breast. A god of spies and cleverness and stark honesty. How crass, to stamp their image on a trinket.

Doanye waved the lit cigarette. "That money went to the workers, not *me*. I'm shit out of luck. And, of course, I could go to a different factory, a cheaper factory, but I'm *principled*. Only the finest metals for my guns. No offense, but some synthetics don't do the trick."

"Why would I be offended?" said Esek coolly. "Sevite fuel is *better* than jevite, wouldn't you say?"

He gave her a look, and if Esek weren't so amused by his careless-ness, she might have had to hit him for the sheer insolence of it. Night-foots were very bad-tempered when it came to anyone insulting the quality of their product. Acknowledging that the synthetic jevite they manufactured was inferior to the organic jevite once mined on Jeve was an insult. Esek had never actually held a position in the business, but still. Family loyalty and all that.

Doanye was talking again. "If I gave you ammunition made with synthetic copper, you'd cancel my contracts."

She shrugged. "Our contracts *stipulate* natural copper. You would be in breach."

"And so that's what I use! But I'm not immune to market forces! If my costs go up twenty-five percent, I have to pass some of that off to my buyer. It's basic business. And gods know you people can afford it!"

" 'You people'?" she repeated dryly. The phrase, uttered in Katish, included a religious signifier that indicated he was not, in this moment, speaking about the Nightfoots, but about the Kindom. He had switched the script. Esek held up her half-finished glass. In moments, a servant refilled it from a diamond-stippled decanter. Doanye's whole lifestyle could be funded with half of what the Nightfoots paid him. And yet, now it was apparent he had a bigger fish in mind. "If you're referring to the Kindom, surely you don't mean to suggest you are not equally a part of our own cherished Body?"

"I am not a *Hand* of the Kindom," Doanye shot back. He was being very peevish. He dragged on his cigarette but didn't even take the time to inhale properly. Wasteful. "I am not a secretary or a cleric or a cloaksaan. Yet I've been making weapons for the Hands for ten years. A six percent renewal markup is more than generous, given the state of things." He paused and drank some keel, looking at her sidelong. "And it would make it *much* easier to keep costs down for my other clients."

Ah, *now* it all made sense. He wanted her to reopen the Kindom contracts in his favor, and in exchange, he'd cut a better price for her family. Such brazenness. Such *industry*! Such—an *invitation* to the Cloaksaan: *I am corrupt. Come darken my doorway.*

The insipid Katish engineer missed a note on the drum harp, laughing drunkenly, and Esek flinched in irritation. Time to put Doanye in his place.

"The barons and the Secretaries have already signed the Kindom contracts with a four percent markup. And *you* have already agreed to give my family the weapons upgrades for fourteen million plae. Trying to change the terms isn't simply impolite, Doanye, it's an insult to the Clever Hand. It's also an insult to my family. You know, some of my kin thought I should offer you twelve million."

"Twelve million?!" he bellowed, and threw his cigarette on the ground. A servant darted forward to stomp it out. More than one pair of eyes shifted toward their corner. "Are you completely—"

"Have a care, Doanye. You are speaking to a cleric."

He spluttered. "Don't you throw that in my face now, Esek, you—"

"Cleric," she corrected him, clicking the hard consonants in such a way that finally penetrated his bluster. He paused. "Burning One. Sa. These are all appropriate ways to address me." His mouth opened; his brow furrowed. He was clearly unsure of her seriousness. Esek smiled at him, and on another person's face this might have been the signal he could relax. Her smile, however, had the opposite effect. "You seem to think I'm here as a friend," she murmured. "I am not, and have never been, your friend. I am here representing the Kindom. When I went to bed with you the first time, I was representing the Kindom. The second time, too. I go to bed with a lot of people. And sometimes I kill them afterward." She tilted her head to one side and asked sweetly, "Do you think you're special? Do you think, just because you please me in bed, I don't care that you're trying to steal from my kin?"

Doanye had been a ball of energy before. Now, he went remarkably still. How badly had he miscalculated? Would she share this conversation with the Kindom?

"Burning One," he said, the words awkward in his mouth, "Sa Nightfoot, please understand, I'm only trying to honor my very long relationship with your matriarch, Alisiana—"

"It's not often a cleric is treated this way," interrupted Esek musingly. "So informal. So...without reverence. Why, where are the beatitudes? Where are the offerings to the Godfire? Why have your family members not come to ask for my blessing? Aren't I holy enough for you?"

He blinked at her. She gazed back, steady and without humor. She had wrong-footed him.

A few more seconds passed, and then he cleared his throat. He barked at the nearest servant, "You. Go to the cellars. Have them take six cases of keel to Cleric Nightfoot's warcrow, as a gift. And you"— pointing at another—"tell my partners to get the children down here for their blessing. Wake them up if you have to. It's not even ten."

The two servants scuttled off, and Doanye looked at Esek again, clearly hoping this was sufficient. But she raised her eyebrows, expectant. He muttered something under his breath, then addressed the room, "I haven't been to temple in five years. Who here knows the beatitudes?"

The two remaining servants glanced at each other. The other partygoers flicked them wary glances and pretended not to hear. Ashir Doanye raised his voice to a snarl. "Who here knows the *fucking* beatitudes?!"

Everyone within hearing stopped, startled. Even the fool engineer stopped playing. Esek looked around at all of them, delighted, waiting. Not only had she made a Katish baron admit his lapses, but now the Katish and Ma'kessn elite had been found out, too. They might stamp their gods on their lighters and deliver offerings to the temples, but not one was truly devout.

Then, a quiet voice arose from the group. "I know them."

Everyone shifted to reveal the speaker, and Esek's delight sky-rocketed. It was a *kinschool* student! She blurted a laugh, which no one dared copy. There was a man standing by the child, a kinschool teacher, posture erect and smile lit with pride. When Esek looked at the child again, she saw a shadow of anxiety in its eyes, and sensed that its teacher had made it speak up. Even now, he hurried forward, the child following reluctantly behind.

"Burning One." He bowed over his open palms. He was flushed from alcohol, his violet hair hanging limp and damp across his green eyes, which were probably mods. Had he gotten them for the party? He must have been unused to drinking. There was a clumsiness to him. "Forgive me for not greeting you. I didn't want to presume."

"It is always presumptuous, to seek the attention of the Godfire. A wonder we aren't burned up, every time."

"Oh yes," the teacher agreed vapidly. "Quite so."

Bored of him, Esek focused on the student, who was taller than she originally realized, and older. Fifteen, sixteen? Head freshly shaved. Its trousers and tunic were clearly new, tailored, unlike the hand-me-downs it must wear at school. The teacher wanted it to look good. Esek's perusal ended when she looked into its face. It met her stare with large gray eyes, which surprised her. It looked to be a Teron, and gray eyes were not common among Terons. But this was its only interesting feature. It was actually quite ugly, otherwise, and not in the adolescent way that some outgrow. It wore a shadowy bruise on its jawline, which intrigued her.

"Who is your little hanger-on?" she asked the teacher.

"Sa, this is a student from the kinschool where I teach. Enrollments are down in this part of Kator, and the masters have sent me with this one, to recruit from the best families."

"I see you've dressed the part." She gestured dismissively at the teacher's uniform, also clearly new. He flushed. "However did you get into Sa Doanye's party?"

There was a moment of awkward silence. Esek, who was still watching the child, noticed color tint its cheeks; its eyes dropped.

"Sa Doanye was kind enough to extend us an invitation," said the teacher.

Esek barked a laugh. "Kindness, Som's ass! Doanye isn't *kind*, are you, Doanye?"

Doanye looked sulky but still cautious. "I don't know all my guests. Someone else must have invited them."

"And whoever it was, you paid them for it," Esek said to the teacher. "*That* I'm sure of. I'm just wondering what you had to offer." She paused, pondering. She dragged her eyes up and down the child again, and guessed, "A night with the student, maybe? It's old enough, I see. Though not very good-looking. The clerics will never take it."

The student flushed harder; the teacher paled. Esek nearly crowed at being right. Even an ugly student was still a novelty to the rich, who often paid for the chance to bed a future Hand.

Beside her, Doanye made a squawking sound. "No one in my house will take a kinschool student to bed! Not even with consent."

Esek gave him a droll look. "Of course not. That would be illegal."

She held his stare, and he shifted nervously. Then, clearly wanting to change the subject, he said, "If it knows the beatitudes, let it say them."

"Is it true, little fish?" Esek asked. "Do you know the beatitudes?"

The student had gotten control of its blush and was looking at her again. Esek wondered if there were other bruises under its clothes. She wondered how many other party invitations were bought with the child's body.

It spoke in a quiet voice, "I do, Burning One."

"Go on, then."

It began. The whole room watched it. Its skin was unhealthily pale. Its body was like a block—shoulders, hips, waist all in-line. Its face had a muddy, indistinct quality.

But its voice. Gods and fire, its *voice*...was low and strong and rumbled with feeling. It spoke in Ma'kessi, not Katish, and that beloved language filled the words with an especial gravity. It spoke the beatitudes, not as the rote recitation of a prayer everyone memorized in childhood—but as the performance of a beautiful, beloved poem. It seemed to disappear into its own words, to forget everything around it. Its eyes grew distant, its body peaceful, its confidence surging with the love it found in what it said.

All around, the partygoers were still. Amazed that such old words could feel so new. So *true*. Had any of them ever even heard a *cleric* recite this way? As they described the liveliness and joy of Makala, the keen intelligence of Kata, the warmth of Sajeven, and the revelry of Terotonteris—had any cleric captured it all like a spell to be woven over the Treble? Where had the student learned such love for its gods? For devouring Som and mild-mannered Capamame? And when it described the virtues—did it actually believe what it was saying? About justice and unity? Did *anyone* really believe any of that? Remarkable!

When it finished, the silence was absolute, the whole room hypnotized. The kinschool teacher was the only one who appeared unmoved. His eyes flicked back and forth between his charge and Esek. He looked hopeful. And nervous.

"Gods keep you well, child," said Esek finally.

The whole room seemed to breathe out, relieved. A few patrons echoed the blessing. This was the thing that brought the child back to the room. It blinked, looking disoriented, and then sad. It blushed again and bowed its head.

Ashir Doanye, still antsy, couldn't stop himself from asserting some authority over his own home. "You honor us with your piety." He looked at the teacher. "What school are you from?"

"Principes, Sa," the teacher replied.

Esek's heart leapt. She looked at the student anew. For a split second she hoped, ridiculously—but no. Despite her promise five years ago, she had not forgotten the face of Lucos Alanye's descendant. It was a face that came to her often, in errant thoughts, and in dreams. Like most clerics, Esek was not particularly spiritual, but the constant recurrence of that child in her thoughts had tested her unbelief. This was not that child's face.

A line from the beatitudes came to her again, now forever in the kinschool student's voice: *Praise the goddess Makala, fecund and lovely, who births all destinies. When your destiny arrives, it will consume your soul as the newborn consumes its mother.*

Hadn't Esek been consumed by thoughts of the Alanye child since she met it?

She looked at the gaping crowd, and then at Doanye, who took her meaning.

"Back to your revelries," he snapped. "Tem, keep playing that song."

After a beat of hesitation, the engineer started playing the harp again, his fingers fumbling slightly before finding the tune. The other guests, at first nervous, then desperately relieved, moved away from them, everybody snatching up the nearest glass of keel. Esek spoke to the student, who had not moved.

"What year are you?"

The student's pause confirmed what Esek was already suspecting. "I'm a ninth-year, Sa."

Esek smiled. "Hmm. Then you have performed for me before."

"Yes, Burning One."

"Do you remember me well?"

The child was looking at her steadily now. Perhaps speaking the beatitudes had given it strength. "All the ninth-years remember, Sa."

"And what about your master's favorite? Six, wasn't it called? Does it remember me?"

The child hesitated. Beside it, its teacher muttered a command in Teron. Annoyed, Esek hissed at him, startling him so much he jumped.

"You are not a part of this conversation," she said, also in Teron. "You were not there. This student and I are old friends. You are a stranger and will be quiet." Esek turned to the student again and switched to Ma'kessi. "You were saying?"

The student's throat bobbed; its bruised jaw flexed. One nervous glance at its stunned teacher, and then it said, "They left the school, four years ago."

Excitement sparked within her. Most likely the child gave up in the face of her offer. But Esek couldn't silence the hope that perhaps this meant something different—that perhaps the child was already on its way to meeting her demands.

Then she realized—

"*They?*"

She expected the student to pale as it realized its mistake. It had called Six "they," and not the neutral Ma'kessi "they" that was given to children before they gendered themselves. No, it used the Katish "they." A proper pronoun.

To call a student by this pronoun was to imbue it with humanity. But the student did not look apologetic. It said, "When they left the school, they ceased to be a student. They...must have gendered themself, since then, Burning One. And their family was Katish born."

Esek couldn't argue with that logic, daring though it was. It suggested a precision to the child's mind, a taste for accuracy. Or...it suggested Six was never "it" to its fellows. That they had afforded it an identity no student deserved. Could it have been so beloved, so powerful among its peers, that they risked flogging or expulsion to show it their respect?

"Where did it go?" asked Esek, finding the only way to conceal her excitement was to be so quiet the student must strain to hear her. Unnerved, it looked at its teacher. Esek blew out her breath, demanding, "Do *you* know?"

The teacher, unsure if he had permission to speak again, stuttered. "I—we—it slipped away in the night. We learned later it stowed away on a Braemish ship. We didn't pursue it. We...never pursue the runaways, Som devour them."

"*I* devoured that student," Esek returned coolly. "I gobbled up its dreams and spit out the bones. I cursed it, by the Godfire and all the Six Gods. Can you blame it for running?"

The teacher had no response. Esek dismissed him with a look, turning to the student.

"Which number are you?"

"Four, Sa."

"I was called Three. Are you a very good student? You must be, for the master to send you on a recruitment mission."

The student hesitated. The teacher said, "It's the best in our school, Sa."

Not in its year. In the school. But if Six had remained, mused Esek, then Six would be the best. She was certain. Still, she liked this little fish, with its ugly face and box body, and its voice like a dipper that poured out dark, rich music. But the bruise on its jaw displeased her.

"When I was your age, I went to bed with several people who were not students. And I enjoyed it. I don't think I would have enjoyed being sold, though. But some people like that sort of thing. Do you like it?"

The child grew pale. Its teacher actually squeaked. Esek ignored him, willing the student to answer her, but it could not. No doubt it was remembering her cruelty five years ago and thinking how much crueler this was. Now it must either betray its teacher, and no doubt be punished for it—or lie to a cleric of the Godfire. A Nightfoot, no less. Esek decided to be merciful. She looked over her shoulder, toward the wall behind her. There, in silence, her chief novitiate had stood all this time.

"Inye," she said. "Take this one back to the ship. It will be one of us, now."

The student blinked owlishly. The teacher made a garbled sound.

"Burning One. You—you honor our school. You—you *rain* glory on us. But the child has only ever expressed an interest in being a cleric, and you—great cleric that you are—only train cloaksaan novi—"

"Has it ever expressed an interest in getting as far away from you and your lecherous friends as possible?" interrupted Esek. At his horrified expression, she nodded. "Of course not. That shows it has survival instincts. And survival instincts are essential in the Cloaksaan. I wonder, do *you* have survival instincts, Sa? Will you be able to survive the Cloaksaan when I send them to discuss your 'recruitment' methods?"

He looked sick. Gods, what was it about Principes, to produce so many troublesome teachers? Then again, Esek had already gotten one Principen master killed this decade. Her family might not like her setting the Cloaksaan on another. Principes was Nightfoot territory, after all.

"Perhaps you should run home," she said to the teacher. "Run home, and tell your master if any Principes teacher ever sends another student into the bed of the highest bidder, I will cut out all your genitals, and string your intestines in the street for Som to devour."

Stricken, he raised his open palms, bowing over them repeatedly as he retreated. Esek gestured at her novitiate Inye, who came and leaned close. "Find out who bid for the child. I'll handle it personally. And take the child away. Make sure it's clothed, and let it have whatever gender and name it wants."

"Yes, Sa."

Inye took the stunned student by the shoulder and drew it away from the room. A few partygoers who dared to eavesdrop were now making themselves scarce. Esek's corner of the room had become very quiet, very quickly. Across from her Doanye seemed most quiet of all. His party had gotten away from him. Esek stood up and went over to his chaise. She sat down, right next to him, thigh pressing to his thigh. He seemed to fight not to shift away. She wondered if *he* was the bidder. Regardless, his house was implicated in a crime. Students belonged to the Hands. A threat against them was a threat against the future power of the Kindom. Doanye's throat bobbed as she ran her eyes over him.

"My children are here," he said. "Will you...will you bless them?"

Esek crooned. "Of *course*. And you will be content with *ten* million, yes?"

His whole body tightened; his skin flushed. He looked on the verge of some outburst, but the words choked in his throat. At least he had the intelligence to know he had lost. When he finally gave a curt nod, her smile brightened. "Good. And you will retire to your room for the night. I'll come to you shortly. Then you can prove your devotion to me another way."

He blinked rapidly, wetly, but nodded again. Esek leaned even closer. She breathed him in, running her nose down his ear and jaw-line. She put her mouth against his throat—let her teeth prick against the hammer of his jugular, and smelled the sweat rolling off him. Then, abruptly, she stood. Behind him, his partners stood frozen, their children looking sleepy and confused.

"Beloved children." She stretched out her arms in greeting. "Come and be blessed."

For Kata's mind is a sharp blade, wise. And Kata is the keeper of many spies. Gods preserve you, if ever they should come to haunt, for they will ride you like a ghost. Most persistent. Kata is not cruel and they are not tender, remember this. They are honest like the wind and the wave and the rock. Be the rock. Be the rampart in the storm and they will warn your enemies off. Beware—

The Many Blessings, 14:27–30. Godtexts, pre-Treble

CHAPTER FIVE

1664

YEAR OF THE CRUX

Riin Kala
Sevres Continent
The Planet Ma'kess

Her first impression is that the room is more like a museum than the office of a Hand. The sheer number of books makes her pause in the entryway, staring. Printed books, while common enough in the Treble, are an impractical medium compared with cast technology, and these floor-to-ceiling bookshelves are crammed full. It's... eccentric, and despite her nerves, Chono feels a flicker of amusement. She lets the door slip shut behind her.

The room is empty, which she wasn't expecting. Overhead, a holographic model of the Treble star systems lazily rotates, full color orbs glittering like glass baubles. The model is oriented not around the planet Ma'kess, but the planet Kator—in a system several dozen light-years away. There's also a small shrine to Kata in the corner of the room, their single large breast cradled in their hands, their belly flat and cut with scars.

Only someone proudly Katish would so openly display a shrine to Kata in the heart of Ma'kess. Ma'kess, with its rolling hills and verdant forests and rivers running into crystalline seas, is the planet of Makala, fecund and lovely. Kata is for cool purple plains and southern wetlands, for snowy mountains in the north. The wisdom god. The god with many spies.

Chono, fighting her anxious stomach, goes to the shrine. She observes the little stack of Katish plae that constitute an offering. A Teron herself, Chono grew up offering marks to Terotonteris, for whom she felt no more special affection than she feels for Kata now. Nevertheless, she takes out her purse and finds a plae buried under the ingots, and puts it on the stack. She recites the Many Blessings of Kata. The god, eyeless, still seems to stare back at her, impassive and clever. Chono turns away.

She wanders. Apart from its opulent bookshelves, the office is all ornaments and centuries-old furniture, floating light fixtures that burn gold, and windows draped with tapestries that depict the colonization of Ma'kess. There's a pedestal bookstand in one corner, with a giant tome protected under a holo shield. The leather cover, old and worn, boasts a single image: the bright eye of the Godfire.

A door opens behind her. The sound of feet juddering to a halt. A startled voice says, "Chono?"

Swallowing once, she turns. A man has come into the office through an adjoining door, and he looks at her in naked surprise. He is the very image of a Clever Hand in his blue suit with its wide white tippet, silver buttons down the jacket, and collar high on his throat. And yet an errant curl falls over his forehead, just as recalcitrant as Chono remembers. She swallows again. She doesn't know why she expected him to look different. It's only been a year.

Chono hides her reaction with a bow. "Good afternoon, Prudent One."

His eyebrows shoot up, his expression baffled. He stares at her for a moment and then asks, half amused, half incredulous, "Are we not on a first-name basis anymore?"

Chono winces. Yes, maybe that was too formal. She's never been particularly good with social interactions. She amends her greeting. "Hello, Ilius."

Secretary Ilius Redquill huffs, steps farther into the room, and gives her a long, frank appraisal. She returns it. For all his obvious devotion to Kata, Ilius is not Katish born. His skin is fair, his hair nearly blond, like a Braem. Very un-Katish hair. And Redquill is a Ma'kessn name. Nevertheless, he wears the delicate three-chained finger bracelet of a Katishsaan, its hundred pin-sized beads of gold glittering in the light of the office.

"You—I—you didn't say you were coming?"

Chono clears her throat. "I was summoned to Riin Cosas. I didn't know how long I would be here."

"Oh."

He smiles, though it's awkward. They haven't seen each other since before she went to Pippashap. She hurt him, when she left, and hurt herself in a way, but it couldn't be helped. Still, when he takes off his glasses and wipes the lenses with his tippet, the familiar gesture makes something odd happen in her chest.

He puts the glasses back on. "Well, uh—you look well!"

Chono very nearly laughs. When they first met some ten years ago, it was via correspondence. She was looking for information about recent events in the northern wilderness of Kator, and her investigation led her to stories about a secretary with a penchant for investigation, a man with many informants and, most importantly, discretion. All these years, they've *never* resorted to small talk or pleasantries. This was something that always endeared him to her. He is a reliably honest and straightforward person. Though, at the moment, he looks a little lost.

"I—" Chono blunders. "So do you. Look well."

Or, as well as Ilius ever looked. He has a rangy, underfed build, all joints and angles. With his sharp jaw and round spectacles, and his eyes like pale brown searchlights, he's not handsome—but he is striking. He strides over to his desk, all nervous energy. The desk is covered in books and stacks of laminate records. He straightens them, and puts one stack away in a drawer, like he's embarrassed of the mess.

Most secretaries are stationed in Nikapraev on Kator, but Ilius Redquill has the dubious honor of a foreign appointment. Though his field is nominally contract law, they put him in Riin Kala because he's an exodus scholar, as well educated as anyone about how their ancestors settled the Treble seventeen centuries ago. He is often called to give lectures at the Riin Kala Academy of Archivists. *It's a vanity position*, he told her once. *So the Kindom can keep its fingers in academic conversations.*

Chono had liked him for the self-deprecating honesty of that assessment. She had liked him for his well-researched and thoughtful responses to her casts. She thought he liked her, too—and that was strange. Fresh out of her novitiancy, she'd had no friends. Nor had since Six.

"What brings you into the city?" Ilius asks.

Chono hesitates. By the time she finished her conversation with Aver Paiye, Esek had already secured a ride into Riin Kala—she'd simply left Chono behind and gone about her business. Irritating though it was, Chono wasn't surprised. She had never thought that Esek would allow Chono to accompany her. Esek might surround herself with novitiates, but she was always one for secretive, solitary errands.

This was no loss for Chono. She had her own errands to complete. Though now that she's facing Ilius she wonders if this was a mistake. She doesn't want to mention Esek to him. Ilius can be a little prim when it comes to Esek. Like Chono, he's a devout Hand, rigorous in his duties and committed to the Kindom. Never having had to work with Esek before, he can afford to be disapproving.

"I—have a friend in the city," she says, then quickly asks, "That book. Is it new?"

She gestures to the book on the pedestal. She isn't particularly interested in its contents, but her deflection works. Ilius's eyes light up. He hurries over to her, casting a lock release that makes the holo shield drop like a curtain. He flips the cover open, showing her pages dark with real ink. Chono hasn't read a real, physical book since her kinschool days.

"Isn't it beautiful?" he asks. "It's third century. Look." He shows her an image in the front matter, a re-creation of *The First Portrait of the Six Gods*, artist unknown. "Look at the color!" he says admiringly. "The original has faded, you know—you can't expect something painted on a generation ship hallway to last forever. Hold on. See this? This is what it looked like in the beginning. Look at how they drew Terotonteris. Incredible—"

He starts eagerly describing the virtues of the re-creation, which Chono has seen a thousand times in holograms. But his excitement is just as infectious as she remembers, his hungry fascination with the origins of their people sparking a response in her. Chono has dozens of memories of Ilius like this, prattling away like an enthusiastic child, and against her will something deep and fond and lonely rises in her throat.

He looks at her again. Maybe he sees her loneliness, because he trails off. That fair skin of his gives everything away, the tips of his ears pinking as he puts the book back down. She clears her throat, stepping back from him. Ilius, looking more awkward than ever, tries to move another stack of books next to the pedestal, knocks them over, curses, and fumbles them back into place, saying, "My novitiate didn't announce you."

"I let myself in. They weren't at their desk." He frowns, and for the first time, she smiles. "Don't punish them," she chides, knowing how exacting he can be with his novitiates. "It wasn't some terrible dereliction of duty. I waited until they were in the back room, then slipped inside."

"Always so mysterious," he says dryly.

The old joke makes her feel both uncomfortable and oddly pleased.

When they began corresponding, Chono used Ilius like her own personal database. She was desperate for answers that she couldn't find on her own—answers she couldn't seek with Esek. A rabid intellectual, he was always so delighted to be asked, and to share what he knew. His excitement bled through his casts. But when he asked her questions in return, tried to find the cause behind her far-ranging interests, she was vague. Ilius has an unshakable moral framework, a sense of what is right in the worlds, and what is impermissible. If he knew the truth of all she had done with Esek, he could never forgive her. He would probably turn her over to the Kindom. So she withheld from him, for his sake and her own. Mysterious Chono, he called her, and it stuck between them.

"I'm not being mysterious," she says. "I just...want to avoid rumors."

Ilius frowns, eyes cutting away. This time he sounds exasperated. "I forget how paranoid Esek made you."

So of course, Esek comes up anyway. No avoiding it. Chono says flatly, "I'm cautious. Surely a secretary can appreciate caution."

Sighing, he goes back to his desk and shuffles some things, and while he's fussing Chono considers him. She has taken so few lovers in her life that she can count them on one hand, and toward each of them she feels a kind of uncomfortable curiosity, as if once the affair is over, she can't understand what compelled her to be with them in the first place. Ilius...was different. Their relationship had been strictly correspondence until just over a year ago. When she met him in person for the first time, the *way* she liked him had shifted.

It had been brief, like the others, but not an affair of opportunity. And not something she regrets, even if it had to end. She never loved him, exactly, but with him she had the unprecedented experience of *trusting* her lover. That, in the end, was the problem. Liking him too much, trusting him too much—and having too many secrets of her own. The closer she grew to him, the more untenable that burden became. She ended things shortly before her appointment to Pippashap.

But the trust never died.

"I've come to ask a favor."

Ilius pauses. He still has a way of looking at her like he can see directly into her brain.

"Has this got anything to do with what happened on Pippashap?"

Shivers waterfall down her arms. She gazes up at the holo model of the star systems, seeking an excuse not to look at him. She wasn't aware that what she did on Pippashap had reached the ears of rank-and-file secretaries, though she should have guessed. Ilius has informants everywhere.

She says, "No."

"Because if you need help, Chono, I—"

"It's not about Pippashap."

Her voice is sharper than she intends. Ilius subsides, blinking. It occurs to her that if he knows about Cleric Paan, and is still willing to help her, then his morals might be more flexible than she thought. She changes the subject.

"I have something. It's a...personal effect. It's very dear to me, but I've been sent on a mission abroad. I need to leave it somewhere safe. With someone that I trust."

His brows hike up in surprise. Some would call it suicidal to entrust a secret to a secretary. Just as the Cloaksaan words "to go unnoticed" fail to capture the brutality of that Hand, so the words of the Secretaries, "to prove prudent," elide their actual reputation. In the Treble, many say a true secretary's mission is "to prove vicious"—in mind and machinations. Ilius, with his particular penchant for accruing knowledge of all types and origins, with his vast network of informants and his access to people far more powerful than Chono, would make a formidable foe.

But not every Hand matches the reputation of their kin. Chono is a cleric who eschews arrogance and pomp. So, too, Ilius is a secretary who eschews power-grabbing. In all the years she sent him her careful questions, he never betrayed her confidence to anyone.

"All right," he says now. "What is it?"

She takes off her pack and reaches inside to withdraw the thing it carries. It's a small chest, artisan-made, crafted from thick, burnished wood, and no larger than the Godfire tome on Ilius's pedestal. It looks more ornamental than secure. But it has a cloaksaan-grade lock, and an internal self-destruct mechanism. It is a chest for keeping secrets. It is a chest that normally lives under her bed, where it can sometimes be forgotten. Like a treasure. Or a monster.

Ilius regards it curiously but doesn't ask what it is. It's this, his very ability to not pry, that gives her the confidence to leave the chest with him.

"I'd like you to keep it in your vault," she says.

He gets up from his desk and comes around it to pick up the chest. She watches him carry it, all her energy focused on concealing what it does to her, to see someone else touch it. He goes to one of the walls and pulls open a piece of the bookshelf to reveal the vault behind it. After a succession of biometric readings, the vault opens, and he puts the chest inside. Chono knows what its bedfellows are: ancient records, rare artifacts, and a piece of petrified driftwood that supposedly comes from one of the forgotten worlds of their ancestors—a place from which they rose, and set out through the stars, and colonized these three adjoining systems. Most of the records are lost. Those prior worlds are as untouchable as the gods. Maybe this is the best possible place for the chest. Somewhere untouchable.

Ilius shuts the vault with a thick, suctioning sound that Chono feels in her chest, and then he turns to her again. He must see something on her face, some hint of what it costs her to be divided from it, because his brow furrows.

"Why not take it with you? I mean...I *assume* you'll have locks on your door, wherever you're going?"

Yes, no doubt. But no lock could quell her fear of Esek's scrutiny. Esek, unlike Ilius, has no respect for other people's privacy. It would be like walking around with a bomb held behind her back, just hoping that her old mentor didn't notice.

At her silence, Ilius's face resolves with understanding. "This mission...It's to do with Esek, isn't it?"

Annoyed at his perceptiveness, Chono says shortly, "Esek is... involved."

Now, he looks shrewd. A true secretary. "So it's about the sevite trade?"

"What makes you say that?"

"Isn't everything about the sevite trade right now? I've seen Alisiana's will. I know that she named Esek her successor to the trade."

Chono wonders how everyone in the worlds knew about this will besides her. Pippashap isn't *that* isolated. "It's not about the trade." At his doubtful scowl, she smiles a little. "It's not *only* about that. It's about the Nightfoots. I really can't say any more."

Still doubtful, he asks, "Then why did you come here?"

She gestures toward the vault. "I told you, I—"

"This is Riin Kala," he interrupts. "There are dozens of secure vaults where you could leave your possessions. Not to mention the temple itself. You don't come to me when you need storage space, Chono; you come to me when you need questions answered."

The words clip her pride, make her feel stiff and inhuman. Or like he sees her as inhuman. Apparently, it hasn't occurred to him that she brought the chest because she trusts him. Cares about him, even, in a way she can't interrogate. No, he's blown right past that possibility and focused on the other thing. The thing that first brought them together. Information.

She could prevaricate, make excuses. But that was never their way.

"Do you know anything about a caster called Sunstep?"

The secretary's eyes light up, but he tries to be cool. "Aren't they some kind of...con artist?"

"You tell me."

At that permission, he gives up any pretense. He's a lecturer set loose on his subject, words tumbling out, the beads of his finger bracelets jangling as he gestures. "Well, their name is all over the casting net, that's for certain. Bit of a celebrity in the dark forums. Over the years they've used a number of aliases, but nothing has ever turned up a real identity. Whoever they are, they're tied to first-rate tech—the kind that even our Kindom casters don't understand. Incredible stuff. Hood programs. Communication scramblers. Oh! I saw a translation program once that floored me. People say Sunstep created it."

"Floored you how?"

"It could accurately translate Je!"

Je is the Jeveni's native dialect, a dialect that combines Ma'kessi and Katish. Chono shrugs. "My own translator can do that."

His eyes sparkle. "Not *accurately*. Je is practically a code language. It evolved out of the Jeveni desire to communicate without the Kindom understanding them. It relies heavily on inflection and idiom. The same sentence can have as many as six translations, depending on the tone of the speaker. Nearly impossible for translator tech to re-create that. But Sunstep did it."

"So, they're a genius."

"I'm sure they'd be delighted to hear themself described that way."

"And is it true they've shown a particular interest in the Nightfoots? Specifically, in a memory coin that was taken from Verdant?"

Ilius pushes back his hair, looking surprised. "Is Sunstep after that coin?"

"You've heard of it."

He nods. "Yes. There was chatter about it a few months before the pirate attack."

Chono frowns. "*Before?*"

"Yes, from what I can tell. I wasn't aware Sunstep took an interest."

"Then—were the pirates trying to get the coin? Is that what motivated the attack on Verdant?"

Ilius scoffs. "I doubt it. All those ships seem like overkill for a single memory coin. Braems tend to fix their eyes on bigger loot." Yet, though he dismisses the idea, Chono can't imagine who would have advertised a coin that was locked inside Verdant, nor how the Nightfoots could have been unaware of such an advertisement, or could have failed to secure the coin themselves. Ilius carries on. "As for Sunstep caring about the Nightfoots—it seems to me what they care about is making money." Then, with a sharp crest of his eyebrows, "Is this your mission? To find that coin?"

Though the First Cleric never explicitly said, *Discuss your mission with no one*, it was, of course, implied. And the Hands, for all their dependence on each other, can be rather insular. It wouldn't please Paiye to know that she sought answers he wouldn't give from a secretary he didn't know.

"According to Aver Paiye, yes," she says.

At that, Ilius frowns. "Didn't *he* tell you everything you wanted to know?"

Chono says flatly, "It's not his obligation to tell me everything I want to know."

"I thought you trusted Paiye." Ilius looks at her in distress.

She tenses. "Of course I do."

"And I thought he trusted you. After that tour, people said you were his favorite. People kept saying it, until the thing in Pippashap happened."

Stung, Chono doesn't answer. Here before her is the lawyerly Ilius, the investigator Ilius, the one who unravels mysteries and yet tactfully reduces the murder of Cleric Paan to "the thing that happened." Is Ilius right? Is Aver keeping secrets from her because he no longer trusts her? During their two-year tour of the Treble, the First Cleric was a warm and generous mentor, so different from Esek. In his service, she devoted herself to the cause of the Godfire, to the uniting faith of her people, to the principles of justice and self-sacrifice that first drew her to the Clerisy. Aver supported her, encouraged her. She took relief in his approval. But maybe something has changed?

"I was never looking for Paiye's favoritism," she says woodenly.

Ilius shrugs. He's looking at her, not unkindly, but not gently, either. "That's probably why you had it."

Neither of them says anything for several moments, and at last the secretary appears to accept that he won't get more from her on this topic. He lets out a breath, thoughtful. "Well, as far as this coin goes . . . I don't know what's on it. The original chatter said it endangered the reputation of the Nightfoots. But I've seen certain forums that insist it threatens the Kindom, too."

All the anxiety about Paiye's trust in her vanishes at those words. Paiye never said anything about the coin threatening the Kindom.

"Threatens it how?"

"To be honest, Chono, it's all conjecture. One forum suggested it had to do with the Jeveni casting corps."

Taken aback, Chono wonders if she misheard him. "The Jeveni have a casting corps?"

"I suppose calling them that may be an overstatement. The Jeveni have about three hundred formally trained casters spread across the Treble. Had, I should say. Didn't you see the newscasts? Every so often those casters attended conferences together. It got them around the Anti-Patriation laws. They had chartered a ship bound for a conference on Kator. Pirates attacked. They were all killed."

For a moment Chono is too stunned to react, wondering how, yet again, vital news hasn't reached her. Why isn't the story everywhere? Why didn't Paiye mention it? At the very least, no pirate attack has taken that many lives in a century—not even the attack on Verdant was that deadly.

"What—what does it have to do with the coin?" she asks.

"Probably nothing. But the casters have been accused of trying to undermine the Kindom. And maybe the coin would have helped them to do so."

Chono grimaces. "That seems pretty thin."

He shrugs. "Rumors often are."

"What if I wanted more than rumors? What if I wanted facts? Are there facts to be had?"

He ponders. "I can certainly do more research."

"Can you do it without telling anyone that I'm asking?"

"I never tell anyone that you're asking."

This, said so casually, so easily, makes Chono feel a surge of guilt. When she ended things with him, she offered almost no explanation. And yet here, again, he's willing to help her.

"I'd appreciate it," she says.

They stare at each other without speaking. Conversational denouements were never Chono's strength. Luckily, he goes for a transition. "Where are you headed?"

Chono looks to the cluster of spheres above them that represents the Teros System. Tall as she is, she can just brush her fingers through the holographic curve of Teros.

"Lo-Meek," she tells him. "Out on Bei continent."

"There are isolationist Jeveni on Bei continent," Ilius muses. "South of Lo-Meek."

Chono frowns, wondering why this matters. "All right."

"There are bad protests, too."

She snorts humorlessly. "Whose fault is that?"

He bristles. "It was hardly *my* decision."

"You secretaries vote on everything."

She's got him there, and wonders if he voted for or against the gate closures. Gets her answer when he says defensively, "We're being far-sighted. What do you think 'prudence' means? And would you prefer we turned our backs on what's happening in the Treble right now? When the Secretaries turn their backs, all law is lost."

It has the flavor of an axiom. Chono looks at him drolly. "You are an institutionalist, Prudent One."

He sniffs at her teasing. "Well, aren't you?"

Is she? She always *was*. It was a point of connection between them. That they both believed, fundamentally, in the institutions of the Kindom, in the ability of those institutions to maintain order and, thus, peace.

Not waiting for her response, Ilius says, "Even if the Nightfoot matriarchy was secure, I wouldn't trust the trade to stay stable. Not now, with the Jeveni on the verge of open rebellion."

"The Jeveni seeking better working conditions isn't *rebellion*," Chono reproves him. "We took their government away. The least we can do is let them have their unions."

Ilius looks as though he doesn't quite agree with that, and Chono remembers that the Jeveni government itself has always been one of his scholarly pursuits. More than once he has lectured her on the peculiarity of the pre-genocide ruling body, a court of five leaders called the Wheel. Unlike other governments on other planets, the Wheel never received Kindom sanction, and after Alanye's ships irradiated Jeve, the Kindom used it as an opportunity to dissolve the Wheel. Ilius approves that dissolution. Chono always thought it was cruel. But what good are those regrets now?

She checks the time. *The Makala Aet* departs in less than two hours.

"I have to go. I appreciate everything you've told me. And—" She makes a short gesture toward the vault, her very blood seeming to surge toward it. "Thank you, for that. I'll be in touch."

She's halfway to the door when his words stop her.

"Aren't you afraid to work with Esek again? After last time?"

She turns slowly toward him, unnerved. "Last time?" she repeats.

Whatever vague accounts she's given him over the years, she never told him the details of what happened the last time she saw Esek. How could she, when it was all wrapped up in Six?

"I know she hurt you," says Ilius.

Chono almost laughs.

"It is Esek's prerogative to hurt me."

He looks baffled, and then urgent. "You must realize the Hands distrust her. You must realize she's dangerous."

"It is what it is, Ilius," she murmurs, and turns again.

"Wait. Chono. Lo-Meek is teeming with Khen family loyalists. You murdered one of their own. You have to be careful."

With a hint of anger, Chono says, "Murder implies injustice."

He raises his eyebrows. "Then it was just? What you did?"

It's clear he needs to believe it. Needs to believe that the Chono he cares about is righteous, still.

"It was necessary," she murmurs.

"The Khens don't agree."

Suddenly Chono recalls the first time Esek took her to Teros. She had not been to her home world since leaving for school. She was terrified to be among her own people again, and terrified most of all that she would somehow encounter a member of the Khen family, with whom she had her own history, even then. Esek found her almost shivering as they prepared to disembark the shuttle onto that red, hot world, had grabbed her shoulder hard and leaned into her. Chono can still feel her breath on her ear, the vibration of her rumbling voice.

"Don't you know, Chono?" she had crooned. "The Khens are all spendthrifts and degenerates. I have honed you into a knife with a hook on its end. You could flick your wrist once and disembowel every one of them."

Then Esek had looked her in the eye, and Chono had felt the blood transfusion of her mentor's confidence, and all her fear melted away.

"Yes, Burning One," she whispered, and believed it.

Now, she looks at Ilius Redquill, and fears that she has deceived him all these years. Made him think that she was only ever a reluctant servant to Esek Nightfoot. He believes she feels guilty because she has been the tool of a monster. But Chono feels guilty because she has loved the monster, and loved the strength she drew from her. So how can she ever know if killing Cleric Paan was righteous, when in the moment it had simply felt good?

"Thank you, Ilius," she tells him. "I will be careful. I promise."

He doesn't answer, and Chono bows over her hands.

"May Kata's Many protect you," she says, and leaves him in his office.

CHAPTER SIX

1664

YEAR OF THE CRUX

Fezn
Bei Continent
The Planet Teros

They stop once on a back road to pee in the knee-high scrub grass. He tells her his name is Masar Hawks. She tells him to call her Jun. They agree to bypass the cities and spend the night in a village called Fezn, three hundred miles south through rocky foothills. It's a gamble. In a city, there are more places to hide. In a village, there are no marshals. The drive takes four hours, and by the time they reach the village the murky orange sun has set, and the giant yellow moon, called Silt, fills the sky like a searchlight. Fezn is several miles off any highways, and Jun feels good about the choice. Until they pull into an inn with a five-spoked wheel hanging over the door.

Hopping off the back seat, Jun glowers at Masar, who is focused on powering down the warhorse. He pulls a tarp from the compartment under his seat, covering the vehicle. They don't want anybody thinking there are cloaksaan around.

"Is this a Jeveni village?"

He shrugs, still not looking at her. "It's a village. Clearly Jeveni live here."

Before she can tell him all the reasons they might not be welcome in a Jeveni village, he starts toward the inn's back door, throwing over his shoulder, "Wait here while I get us a room."

Get them a room. They'll be lucky if the owner doesn't run them off. Most Jeveni live in the factory towns on Ma'kess, working for the Nightfoots and worshipping Makala and enduring their assimilation. Small Jeveni communities like this one, isolated and poor, generally spell very little in the way of welcome. Jun can respect a little anti-socialism, same as the next criminal caster, but if these Jeveni run them off, they'll have to sleep on a rock somewhere, and she does not relish the thought.

Kicking the dirt, she mutters curses to herself and checks her comms. Nothing from Liis, which is itself a damning report. When they stopped outside Lo-Meek, she took a minute to send Liis a quick message:

Complications. I'm fine. Had to leave The Gunner *behind. Will call you when I can.*

She got no answer. That was a bad sign. Not that she can blame Liis. Her message was...laughably inadequate. She'll probably never get their ship back, and it's worth three million marks, easy. Liis is going to eviscerate her. Probably hide her body. She knows how to do that.

Jun glances toward the inn, but there's no sign of Masar. Under the Silt moon's brassy light, she can see notices posted on the wall. It's clearly some kind of public message board, but in addition to the notices about jobs and donations, there are hints at the community's artistic members: a clay mask of Sajeven, her five eyes crinkled with laughter; a low-tech hologram of *The Risen Wave*, the ancient generation ship that will ferry them through Remembrance Day in a couple of days. There's a poster of the Jeveni wheel, with the words WE HAVE OUR OWN WAY underneath, and near these hangs a placard with dozens and dozens of mini-wheels, labeled OUR LOST CASTERS. MAY THE BARREN FLOURISH.

The casters. Murdered in a pirate attack. Jun isn't religious, but she sends up her own awkward prayer for the dead.

Then one of the largest images on the board draws her attention. It shows the three-pointed star of the Kindom, with a red slash across it.

REMEMBRANCE DAY IS OURS!

the block letters shout.

RESIST KINDOM APPROPRIATION!
BOYCOTT ALL KINDOM BUSINESSES!

Fan-fucking-tastic.

Jun takes out her sidearm and checks the chamber. The gun is a Som's Edge, a gift from her Great Gra, a relic. But Jun's obsessive maintenance has kept it in pristine condition. She cleaned it this morning, but she gives it a look anyway, because the routine of its various parts is soothing.

She stares at the message board again. The bulletins speak to a community of close ties but few resources—short-term jobs, requests for childcare, reminders of local goods shortages and rationing. Jeveni are no strangers to poverty. Their moon colonies were impoverished, too—overtaxed and exploited by the mining operations. Lots of disease and hunger. These days, the ones who work for the Night-foots live marginally better. But they have to stomach working for the Nightfoots. A bad deal, either way. Jun, for her part, believes in third choices, in making your own way.

She holsters her gun again and takes out the memory coin case that's been tucked in her pocket since Lo-Meek. The temptation to slot it into her neural port and cast the contents to her ocular is intense. It's been over a year since rumors of this coin started licking at the darkest corners of the casting net, whispers of Nightfoot secrets, Nightfoot failures, Nightfoot destruction. Nothing in the systems could stop her going after *that*.

The back door of the inn opens abruptly. Masar comes out, carrying a paper sack in one hand and using the other to signal something on his ocular—probably a message to his buyer. Jun is legitimately surprised his other eye hasn't been blackened.

"I got us a room," he says, holding up the paper sack. "And sandwiches."

Jun is amazed. Her stomach rumbles. "They gave you *food*?"

Masar Hawks shrugs, already walking toward the row of rooms across the parking lot.

"I speak Je," he says.

"*Why?*"

"Why not? I like languages."

Jun narrows her eyes at this, but makes the rare decision to keep her mouth shut. He takes them to the second door in the line of rooms, waving a fob in front of the sensor till it beeps. At least the room has two beds, and a bathroom with a shower. Jun can smell the ripe fear-sweat stench rising off her own body, and the prospect of bathing makes the tightness in her shoulders relax fractionally. Masar goes to the room's small table. He takes his gargantuan shotgun off his back and sets it down. Then he empties the paper bag. It holds two large sandwiches that appear to be stuffed with meat and vegetables.

Jun's mouth waters, but no shower, no food, no bed (gods and fire, she's exhausted) can distract her from her purpose. She's still holding the memory coin case in her hand, and it's the work of a moment to flick it open. She pushes back her hair and feels for the subdermal port under her ear, slotting the coin into place. There's a low vibration, then she casts a large view against the nearest wall of the room, visible to both of them.

Masar pauses with the sandwich halfway to his mouth.

"You don't want to eat first?"

"No," Jun mutters.

She images the coin's internal organization interface as a library of bookshelves—it's one of the first mental tricks they teach archivists: turn the code into a narrative. She finds the principal file in the library center. Her fingers, normally steady as she weaves her way through the holograms her castings create, tremble now. She's stopped blinking. She rotates her wrist and makes a flicking motion with her finger, and the view comes to life with the memory coin's bounty.

She's not expecting the initial distortions, flinching as sparks spit across the view and warped images stutter, then resolve. After that, the picture is notably grainy, but that doesn't stop Jun recognizing the figure who has appeared in frame: Alisiana Nightfoot, just a child, sits in a throne-like chair some ten feet away from the person watching her—the memory's source. Jun's breaths become shallow.

"Why isn't there sound?" she demands.

"Keep watching," Masar replies, mouth full of food.

Jun blows out an irritated breath, but obeys.

The large room is festooned with decorations, and Jun knows from the coin's ID markers that this is Alisiana's eleventh nameday party, and the memory itself belongs to a Nightfoot guard identified as A-12-6. Even without sound, everything in the guard's line of sight is chaotic. Dozens of kids run around, trailed by nannies. The wealthy adults stand in gossiping knots, while servants move through the throng with platters of food and drink. There's also some kind of performer, an acrobat, Jun thinks, doing complicated flips and contortions. All this cacophony is only exacerbated by intermittent flickering—proof the coin has been damaged at some point.

Against all the commotion, Alisiana Nightfoot is a single point of stillness.

The guard's eyes are never far from her. She is, after all, the most important person there. Alisiana, future matriarch of the Nightfoot dynasty, sits in her chair with wide, watchful eyes, observing the revelry around her but not participating, her hands planted on the armrests and her feet barely touching the ground. She's still a child, but already so refined.

This goes on for nearly a minute, the guard never shifting. Jun can hear Masar chewing, and she starts to grow impatient. Why isn't there any sound? Why is the coin damaged? Where is Alisiana's mother, the at-that-time matriarch, Ti Nightfoot? What can be remarkable about a child's party?

Then it happens.

A new figure steps into the frame, a young man who crouches beside Alisiana's chair. For the first time, the girl smiles, bright and genuine. Alisiana's fondness for her uncle Caskori is well-known, shamelessly romanticized by the historians. Caskori, a mere nineteen years old, beams at his niece. With a flourish, he pulls a package from behind his back, setting it in her lap. Delighted, she loosens the ribbons and lifts the lid. Her eyes instantly widen. She says something to Caskori, and he nods, urging her on. Damn, what Jun would give to hear them. Alisiana reaches into the box, withdrawing a stone of purest black—

And threaded with the unmistakable red veins of organic jevite.

Jun sucks in her breath. Within that single dark stone, no bigger than Jun's fist, there is enough power to run a jump gate for a month.

Alisiana gazes at it with wide-eyed amazement, though she probably doesn't know what it is. Even when this party occurred a hundred years ago, the moon of Jeve had long since been stripped of its only valuable resource. The jump gates had been running on Ri'in Nightfoot's sevite for decades. It wasn't as potent as jevite, but it was renewable. For people like Alisiana and Caskori, *sevite* was the miracle fuel that made communion between the Treble star systems possible. Jevite was just a history lesson.

In that moment, the memory projection shifts. The guard is moving forward.

Come on, Jun thinks. *Come on.*

Within moments he stands before the two Nightfoots. Alisiana looks up at him with a grumpy pout, and it's so strange, to see that woman as a child. All baby fat and jet-black curls, eyes like sapphires in her golden face. Beside her, Caskori scowls, but now the guard has extended his hand for the present. Finally, petulant, Alisiana hands over the jevite, and when the guard holds it up close to his face, Jun's whole body tightens in disbelief, too sharp to register as joy or relief or *success*. The jevite has been polished into a perfect dark sphere, smooth and bright. Its round curve reflects the guard's face like a dark mirror, distorted but recognizable: Lucos Alanye, mining contractor, who led his operation into the heart of Jeve.

And then murdered millions.

On the memory projection, Alanye examines the jevite for several seconds, his reflection shifting into peculiar bulbs and angles. Though his expression is flat, the distortion enlarges his eyes—bright with revelation. He was the descendant of Katish engineers. He would recognize organic jevite if he saw it. He would realize what Caskori and Alisiana clearly do not: jevite very slowly turns gray once it's exposed to oxygen, its red striations paling to pink. The transformation takes less than a hundred years. Which means what Caskori gifted to Alisiana was not only that rarest of minerals, it was *freshly mined*. And Lucos Alanye knew it.

When he finally returns the sphere to its owner, Jun imagines she can feel the reluctance in him. Alisiana snatches it back and cuddles it to her chest as if it's a doll and not a key to reopening the jevite trade. Caskori says something; he looks impatient, defensive, but Jun can't read his lips.

With a *ffftzz* of static, the image half dissolves, crooks sideways, and freezes.

Jun is so startled she takes a step back. She stares at the incomprehensible mash of colors on the wall, then throws an incredulous look at Masar. He is finishing up his sandwich.

"Where's the rest of it?" she demands.

He gives her a droll look. "What makes you think there's more?"

"It—it—" She makes an apoplectic sound. "It's damaged! What happened to it?"

He scarfs the last bite. There's no humor in him now. The unbruised side of his face is pixelated with a typical Braemish tattoo—pinpricks of ink made into geometric shapes. But for the first time Jun realizes—his skin is a little dark for a Braem. Not the bronze of a beach tan he might have achieved on furlough to the home planet, but intrinsically warmer than any pale-ass Braem Jun has met. And the Braems are notorious for only reproducing with other Braems.

The questions that assailed her in Lo-Meek come again. *How did he find her in the alley? Why did he have those keys? Why does he have a warhorse, for fuck's sake?*

"Who are you, really?"

Masar grins mirthlessly. His eyes flick over her.

"Who are *you*?" he asks.

Jun pauses, making sure there's enough distance between them for her to shoot if she needs to. This is why Liis always votes against partnerships. Too many unknown variables. Masar goes on, "When I was in the front office, I saw the inn's security cameras. One of them panned the back lot. You were invisible."

Jun's hairline and the back of her neck prickle.

"I was out of frame."

"Nah." He wipes his hands and belches enthusiastically. He sits back in his chair, a relaxed posture she knows better than to trust. "The same thing happened on *The Swimming Fox*. I think you're wearing a Hood."

Jun's jaw clenches. She considers a flat denial, or laughing at him or drawing her gun—but he doesn't wait for her to act.

"You're Sunstep, aren't you?"

This time Jun does laugh, a sharp blurt.

He's unaffected. "You're kinda famous, aren't you? You robbed the Paiye family, that one year. Nice work."

"What's a fucking pirate know about Sunstep?"

"I'm not a pirate," he replies.

"Yeah, no shit."

"I'm a collector," he says. "That is, I work for a collector. I joined up with *The Swimming Fox* six months ago, when I heard there was an imminent attack on the Verdant Estate. I thought it'd be my chance to get the coin. But Foxer bailed on the mission, and I've spent the past two months finding a way for us to acquire the coin cache from the ones who did take it. Honestly, it was a stroke of gods-damn luck someone stole it from the estate to begin with. But I found the coin, even convinced Foxer to buy the cache. Then *you* came calling."

Abruptly, he stands. Jun manages not to flinch, but she's ready. Only he doesn't come toward her. He strolls over to the bathroom, flipping on the sink to wash his hands. Jun watches him. In the Treble, "collector" means one of two things: Either you're an archivist hoping to collect valuable historical artifacts, or you're an opportunist looking to collect valuable weapons. "Weapon" being a loose term, which could absolutely encapsulate blackmail.

That Caskori Nightfoot somehow acquired fresh jevite without seeming to know it was fresh, gifted it to Alisiana, and in so doing alerted Lucos Alanye that there must still be untapped jevite seams on the moon... *Gods!*

The Jeveni Genocide may very well be traceable to the ignorance and ineptitude of a Nightfoot princeling! The very Nightfoots who have courted the goodwill of the Treble (and gained some very lucrative tax write-offs) by employing any Jeveni who wants it. The irony is... *fantastic.* Jun can *taste* it, the flavor of a priceless find. But that taste has made her greedy.

"What happened to the memory coin?" she demands again.

Masar runs wet hands through his mane of loose waves and braids. He examines his bruised face with unmistakable vanity, and sighs.

"Foxer caught me trying to break its encryption."

Jun's chest seizes. "Encryption?"

She whirls back toward the casting view, batting aside the distorted memory contents to bring up the library again.

"He beat the shit out of me," Masar muses. "I had to let him."

Jun doesn't care. She forgoes the library and delves directly into the code, sifting strings of Ma'kessi numerals through her fingers. The encryption is a net ensnaring the entire memory file. Someone tried to hack open a corner. But they hacked at the memory, too, spilling guts and blood in equal measure to the bits of the encryption they destroyed.

"Kata's *tit*. What did you do?"

Masar comes up beside her. He sounds petulant. "I've *had* casting training. But the encryption was more sophisticated than anything I'd ever seen. I tried to do a frame-by-frame recovery but—well, I decided to stop before I made it worse."

Jun huffs, shocked he had that much sense. "You're lucky you didn't shred it."

"Well, how was I supposed to—"

"Just—just shut up for a second. Let me work."

To her surprise and relief, he does. The next few minutes are swallowed up by silence. Jun goes so deep into the code she might as well be swimming through the net's tiny gaps and fissures, a lattice as delicate as snow crystals. She doesn't dare touch anything, but she works through what Masar did for clues. It's soon apparent that whenever a single thread of netting collapsed under his clumsy assault, it disintegrated the surrounding memory frames in uneven fits and starts. That's why some of the memory survived (if damaged)—and it's why it cut off so abruptly. He clearly snipped too close to the quick and almost created a domino effect that would have eaten away the entire memory, like acid on skin.

Jun does her best; she uses her comm link to pull assistance from the casting net, drawing from the cluttered databases of a hundred local casting hubs. No one sees her come or go. But even so, she can't sever the encryption. What she needs is equipment. *Sophisticated* equipment, like what she had on *The Gunner*.

Finally, she pulls out of the code, folding the entire thing up and vanishing it from the air. The memory coin, still slotted into her neural port, purrs into quiet, sending a shiver down her neck. Jun takes a moment to reorient herself to her surroundings, always a little fuzzy in the aftermath of a deep dive. Masar is staring at her hopefully. She scowls.

"You almost destroyed it."

His lip curls. "That's why I *stopped*."

"Why did your captain give it to me? Why beat you up for stealing it, then give it to me?"

"I don't know. When you contacted us about buying the cache, he was relieved. You were offering a good price, and it would get Nightfoot merchandise off our ship." Masar shakes his head. "Then, two days ago, he got weird. Jumpy. He started blaming me for bringing trouble onto the ship. We skipped two stops on Trini-so continent so he could move the Lo-Meek meeting up."

"But did he know what coin I wanted by then?" Jun asks.

Masar shrugs. "He must have. He started carrying it on him, like he was afraid I'd try to take it. Fuck if I wouldn't, given the chance. But the minute you started going through those coins, I knew it—you were after the same thing I was."

Jun realizes he's standing closer to her now—close enough to attack before she could draw on him.

"Why pick me up in Lo-Meek? Why help me? Why not try to take the coin and go?"

Masar narrows his eyes. He glances away, then back at her.

"Lots of people have been pecking at that coin since the rumors started last year. I may not be a first-rate caster, but I know who Sunstep is. And then you came to *The Swimming Fox*, and there was no sign of you on our scans. The crew didn't know what that meant—weren't even paying attention. But I knew. The Kindom doesn't let anyone but their own Hands use cloaking technology, and even they haven't figured out how to cloak individuals. But Sunstep... Well, Sunstep's famous for it. So, either they leased you their Hood program—or *you're* Sunstep. Given the way you tore through that code like you're made of code yourself, I'm inclined to think it's the latter. Either way, you'd have to be top tier to use a Hood properly. And that's what I need. A top-tier caster who can break this encryption and give me what my collector wants."

"Why not take the encrypted coin to your collector?" Jun retorts.

Now he's clearly annoyed. "Because, I don't take things to my collector unless I know they're worth something."

Well, that's believable, anyway. Jun has run jobs for collectors herself and bringing them unverified goods is a quick way to get yourself killed. Jun's curiosity gets the better of her. "Who's your buyer?"

He gives her a *yeah, right* look and Jun can't help a tiny amused smile. Yeah, that was a long shot. But when it comes to information that threatens the Nightfoots, there are only so many options. The First Families have the most to gain, so Masar's buyer is either one of them, or some middlesaan player who will buy the coin and then turn around and sell to a First Family themself. The details don't matter to Jun. What matters is that she gets paid.

"So, what are you proposing?" she asks.

"That we work together. There's more on that coin than what we've seen—loads more, and who knows how valuable it is? If you can decrypt it, my buyer will pay us well enough we won't even mind splitting the haul."

Jun considers this in silence. The question isn't whether she can make money off the coin. The question is whether he's telling her the truth. Right now, she can't see a lie in him, and she's generally a good judge of character. Or at least a good judge of when someone is trying to swindle her. Fact is, if the marshals are onto them, she could use a big brawny mountain of a guy to help keep her alive. Which reminds her...

"Why did the marshals show up?"

He shakes his head. "I have no idea."

"Whatever they said to Foxer on the gangplank, he pointed them at me. He must have meant the coin. That must have been what they were after. That's bad, all right? If we're gonna work together, you need to understand that."

Masar scoffs. "Are you trying to warn me off?"

"Call it a professional courtesy."

"Yeah, well, no need. Now tell me whether you can break the encryption."

Jun considers him for long moments. When she murmurs, "No," his eyes widen, so she adds, "Not here. I don't have the equipment. Frankly, there aren't many places that will have what we need and be sufficiently off the grid to give us cover."

"Well, where?" he demands.

Jun sucks her teeth. "Ever heard of the Silt Glow Cliffs in Siinkai?"

Masar deflates. "You mean the Caster Junkie Grand Hotel?"

"Don't be a snob," she retorts, and brushes past him to approach the room's little table, and the still-wrapped sandwich. She reaches for it, famished. "Siinkai is only about five hours south. We should ditch your warhorse and catch the first transport out in the morning."

"This is a Jeveni village," Masar reminds her. "There are no transports to Siinkai."

"Well, you speak Je," replies Jun, and takes a bite of the sandwich, flavor flooding her mouth. She groans with pleasure, and looks at him again. "Maybe you can convince someone to give us a ride?"

CHAPTER SEVEN

1664

YEAR OF THE CRUX

Lo-Meek
Bei Continent
The Planet Teros

Bei continent, and the city of Lo-Meek itself, are nothing like the southern coastal cliffs where Chono grew up. Life on Trini-so was full of wide-open spaces, torrential rains, and watching eyes. In Lo-Meek, even at eight o'clock in the morning, the air is hot and fetid, funneling between close-set, rickety buildings. And Chono is the watcher now.

When she was a novitiate, she learned to take every opportunity to study Esek, observing her, anticipating her desires and demands. Confronted by the endless cyclone of Esek's energy, that was a useful gift. Other novitiates had other gifts—they were investigative masterminds, or efficient killers, or otherwise predisposed for the Cloaksaan career Esek was training them to enter. Chono never wanted to be a cloaksaan, never viewed herself as talented in those ways. Since taking her cleric's coat, she's told herself she has no more use for the brutal lessons Esek taught her. But as she and her former mentor survey the narrow alley where they're standing now (squeezed between a bar and a warehouse in the sweltering backstreets) she realizes she retained those lessons, after all. Crouched beside a waste can, she plucks at a barely visible edge of fabric, then pulls a full-length scarf into view.

Chono stands up, taking in the unfurled piece of muslin. It's soiled, but not so much she can't see the clean blue color underneath, and that the stains aren't dirt or muck—they're blood.

She holds it up for Esek to see, and Esek clucks her tongue.

"These marshals are shit. The least of my novitiates could have found that."

Esek's novitiates are back on their ship—an unusual choice. She usually prefers them to follow her like the train of a gown.

"In defense of the marshals, they've had quite a lot to manage with Saxis Foxer's crew."

Esek chuckles darkly. "Yeah, and they botched that royally, didn't they? Wait till Seti Moonback finds out!"

Chono says nothing, still perturbed by the mess they inherited when they arrived in Lo-Meek two hours ago. The meeting between pirate and caster had come and gone the afternoon before. The marshals were now trying to make up for losing Sunstep by pummeling their captives into pulp. None of this was helped by the overall unrest in the city, by the raucousness of local crowds, hundreds of Terons gathered to the marshals' headquarters and the city docks in protest of the jump gate closure.

Then, last night, the Secretaries released a bulletin officially announcing that the Jeveni would be permitted jump gate access in order to proceed with their Remembrance Day ceremonies. In Lo-Meek, this announcement corresponded with the marshals unleashing the sirens, which confined everyone to their homes as they searched for Sunstep. The combination of perceived Jeveni fortune with non-Jeveni hardship has pushed the city to the edge.

Esek insisted that Chono carry a weapon.

And, strange and unwelcome as the handgun feels on her hip, Chono has to admit it's not Esek's worst idea. There's a dark energy in the streets, heightened by the heat and close air. It's the energy of a match flickering near a slick of oil. Teros, a mostly nonarable planet that relies on other parts of the Treble for the majority of its food supply, is especially vulnerable to these gate closures. Chono has seen that vulnerability on the faces of the people in Lo-Meek. Anger and despair and entreaty, so many of their fortunes in peril, until they can use the gates again. Somewhere in the distance, gathered crowds are chanting their anger and demands. Esek must know her own power to end or perpetuate the limbo...

For the third time since their reunion, Chono nearly broaches the issue of the Nightfoot matriarchy, but then a trio of marshals come into the alley. The first of them, by his appliqués, is the commander of the city garrison, the one responsible for the aforementioned mess with the pirates. He looks harried, which is no surprise. A smell comes off of him, possibly praevi liquor, possibly perfume. His head is shaved, which Terons only do to signal mourning.

"Burning Ones." He bows over his hands with minimum deference. "You are welcome in our beloved city. I am Chief Marshal Vine Oo-vine Norun—"

"Yes, yes, shut up. Now tell me, is this really *all* you have?"

Esek flicks her wrist, projecting an image into the air. It's a sketch, a composite from a few marshals' rough memories of chasing Sunstep through the alleys. Chono was shocked by its uselessness, by how obviously the marshals depended on their oculars to make observations for them. The hair is dark. The skin is a common brown. The accompanying details predict someone between five and six feet tall, between

130 and 180 pounds. Someone possibly carrying a gun. The only distinct characteristic of the sketch is the bright blue scarf around their neck. Marshal Norun grimaces.

"Did they see a gendermark, at least?" Esek sneers.

"My marshals only got a glimpse. Whoever they were didn't appear on ocular recordings."

"Which you should have expected, given our warning that you were dealing with a Hood. I assume the surviving crew members have been useless, too?"

"They all claim not to have seen the caster, Sa. We pressed them hard."

"Tortured them, you mean," says Chono.

Norun looks at her for the first time, a scathing look that takes her off guard.

Esek doesn't appear to notice. "Yes, we saw how effective that was. Your main prison is a travesty, by the way; it stank worse than this alley. What about Foxer? Foxer saw them, whoever they are. Where is he? I sent for him half an hour ago."

The marshal clearly wasn't expecting this reception, nor that he'd have to grovel for the Kindom. His resentful glance at Chono turns to a resentful glance at Esek. If he's not careful Chono fears what Esek will do to him.

"We placed Foxer in a different brig from the crew. Better to keep them separated from their leaders, we find. He's uptown. I must say, it's . . . unusual to question a prisoner *outside* of the prison. With all the unrest in the streets today, I worry that—"

"Does that mean he's not coming?" Esek interrupts.

Chief Marshal Norun retorts, "We're bringing him now."

"Good." Esek reaches toward Chono, snapping, and Chono hands over the muslin scarf. Esek balls it up and flings it at Norun. He barely catches it. "Test that. It's got blood on it."

He looks at it skeptically for a moment, then passes it to one of his party, who rushes off. Esek turns her back on the chief marshal, an obvious dismissal, and faces Chono.

Chono says, "The blood won't lead us to Sunstep. They can't have avoided detection all these years if their medical signature is on file somewhere."

She would like to have enough faith in Kindom casters to believe it's impossible to erase one's medical identifiers. But Six proved otherwise, long ago.

Esek says, "But the blood *will* still tell us useful things. Sex, if not gender. Birth origins. Transfusion type."

That's true. One of the only medical facts they have about Six is their universal donor status—Sunstep's blood could rule certain things out. Chono expects Esek to berate her for not thinking of it, but Esek turns from her as well, looking distant. Distracted.

She's different.

Chono didn't want to think so at first, but it's true. The first time she saw Esek Nightfoot, the young cleric roiled with energy, with humor, with poison. She was like a walking lightning strike. Later, as her novitiate, Chono saw a new side to her: caprice, but also, fortitude. She trained all her little fish to be unstoppable. She trained them as if she always hoped they would be someone else, and would torture them until they satisfied her. But they never satisfied her. Not even Chono, who may have come the closest. Yet even in their failure, all Esek's novitiates worshipped her. It was terrifying to be around Esek, but also inspiring. How could you live in that orbit and not be inspired?

But in the hours they've spent together since leaving Riin Cosas, Chono has realized that Esek's energy is deeper now. Colder. Throughout the brief trip from Ma'kess to Teros, she chattered restlessly, and yet, at the same time, seemed *quiet*. It's as if some living, breathing darkness perches on her shoulder now, whispering in her ruined ear, and she is too absorbed by the passenger to fully pay attention to anything else. What happened to her, at Verdant? Was it Six? Could anything else impact her so?

Chono turns to Chief Marshal Norun. "What about the missing pirate?"

He hesitates, lips twisting into a moue of distaste, as if it offends him to talk to her. He grits out, "We're looking for him. We found some children who watched his stuff for him. They said he went north, and someone was with him."

Esek chuckles, incisors gleaming in the dark alley. "The Teron scrap kids say their employer went north. Well then. I suppose he's practically ours, isn't he?"

Cowed, the marshal says nothing. There isn't much north of Lo-Meek besides cliffs and ocean. Certainly nowhere to run.

"They said he had a warhorse. That would explain how he got out of the city."

"A warhorse?" Esek tilts her head, raising her eyebrows at Chono. Chono gives a slight headshake; this part of the story is probably a fabrication, too. Nevertheless, Esek hums. "A pirate with a warhorse. That *is* interesting."

The marshal puffs up. "Yes, and it's possible he—"

"Never mind. Here comes the captain."

Two marshals march into the alley, each holding the arm of their shackled charge. Trussed up though he is, Saxis Foxer looks relatively unperturbed, observing his surroundings with interest. Bruises and small cuts add texture to the geometric tattoos on his face, and he's favoring one leg. He meets Chono's stare for a moment, before settling on Esek. She is the unmistakable center of gravity in this close space. Unlike most, he shows no terror in her presence, and despite a night in the brig, his braids are cleanly woven.

"Captain Foxer," Esek greets him. The marshals have not let go of him, but at one quelling look from her, they step back. Only then does Saxis Foxer lift his manacled hands, bowing shortly over them. Esek gestures at Chono. "This is my kin cleric."

He bows again, with no hint of irony. When he tries to turn back to Esek, she's staring up at a patch of orangish sky between the buildings, as if suddenly forgetting she was talking to someone.

"Tell us about the caster," Chono says.

Foxer gives her a narrow look. "I talked to the marshals for three hours last night."

"But you didn't give them a description," Chono replies.

"I gave a... rough description. I said they were a caster."

Esek, still gazing at the sky, lets out a laugh of genuine amusement. Chief Marshal Norun glowers. Chono says, "In that case, perhaps you'd like to be more specific now."

He shrugs. "A woman."

"They had a gendermark?"

"How else can I say she was a woman?"

Chono considers this. Six has taken many identities these twenty years, but never a female gendermark. And yet, Chono has developed a sense for when Six is involved in something. Everything about this mission makes those senses catch fire. Perhaps this Sunstep works for Six? Gods know they have employed plenty of criminals over the years.

"What else?" Chono asks.

"She said she worked for a consortium of archivists, though she clearly wasn't one herself. She called herself Junian Graylore, but that had to be a lie. She was no Ma'kessn. I'll bet she grew up on a station. She had that half-starved hustler look."

So, not six feet tall. Not 180 pounds.

Saxis Foxer pauses, looking between Esek and Chono, then arches his eyebrows. "I don't know what you want me to say about her. Average height. Average looking. You know. Brown eyes, brown hair, brown skin. She spoke Teron pretty well. She seemed... eager."

Back still turned, Esek repeats, "Eager?"

"Eager to sell the coin cache, yes."

So he claims that Junian Graylore was the seller.

"Of course," says Chono. "And you were eager to buy it, I'm sure?"

He smiles. He doesn't look remotely nervous.

"You know I didn't buy it. It's nowhere on my ship, is it?"

"Your ship has a back door overhanging a canyon."

"What kind of businessaan would I be? Buying something and throwing it overboard?"

"Yet you *did* agree to the sale in the first place?"

"I thought it would be trade secrets, something like that. Soon as I realized it came from Verdant?" He shakes his head. "I was done with it. That whole business went too far. I didn't even look at the cache—just sent her packing."

Some people struggle to keep their expressions neutral in the face of blatant lies, but not Chono. Her gift for complete expressionlessness has sometimes unsettled even cloaksaan. "That's very pious," she says, voice as flat as her stare.

"Not really. I'm a survivalist. If I'd gone the other way, you'd be coming after *me*, not her."

Esek faces them again. "We'd be coming after both of you."

Foxer is silent, but the comment lands like a stone on water, leaving a ripple behind.

"Archivists don't usually sell," Chono says. "They buy."

He flicks his eyes back and forth between the two of them, perhaps unsure who he should focus on: Chono, a point of stillness, or Esek, a roving flame.

He says, "I've purchased from more archivists than you'd think. Sometimes they come into a record that will make them a fortune. Forgive my bluntness, Saan, but those are the times when the elite are grateful they've got people like me to sell to."

The chief marshal growls, "You lying trash—"

"Now, now," interrupts Esek, lowly. "There's no need for that. Every actor has a place in the worlds—even pirates play their role. Captain Foxer is speaking frankly with us. Frankness is holy. Disobedience is not."

Norun scowls. Foxer watches Esek for a moment, then looks at Chono again. Chono has not taken her eyes off of him.

Esek says, "Forgive our passions, Captain. Everyone is very touchy about pirates, since Verdant. Oh, don't worry. We know you were nowhere near it."

He gives a cool nod, as if to say of course he wasn't, but there is something different in his face now. A subtle tightness around the mouth.

"The trouble is..." Esek gazes at the ground. She waves a hand, looks up, and says brightly, "Well, let's lay our cards on the table. No need to flirt around the bitch. See, while Chief Norun here was interrogating some local street brats, I was at the downtown prison. I spoke to your second-in-command an hour ago."

Foxer's very expressionlessness is the surest sign of the words' impact.

"You ought to keep disloyal people out of leadership positions. Let me guess, family deal, right? Somebody's worthless cousin? You give him a good spot on your ship, and his ma funds your next expedition? Well, I guess I can't berate you for nepotism. I mean, kettle meet pot, right? Still, you made a pretty bad call with this one. He was actually naive enough to think he'd gain the ship by telling us the truth."

Foxer doesn't respond, doesn't move, but in his eyes, a shovel digs a grave.

Chono doesn't have her mentor's appetite for playing with her food. "According to your first mate, one of your crew members convinced you to buy the cache at a Braemish bazaar last month. He says you arranged the resale with Junian Graylore. You were delighted about it. She was offering good money. Then, three days ago, your tune changed. He says you realized there was only one coin she actually wanted. That you were determined to get rid of it as quickly as possible. You erased some of your sales records so the cache couldn't be traced to you. Yet you insist you never looked at the coin she wanted?"

Foxer says nothing, clearly considering his options. In the silence, Chono becomes aware of a distant clamor, somewhere beyond the alley's closeting walls. It's the rumble of many voices, raised in shouts and chants. The protests, getting closer. Esek appears to hear it, too, for she cocks her head, putting the mangled ear on stark display. She laughs.

"Ah. So, they've decided to form a parade, have they? We saw the crowds when we arrived. It seems they're very upset about losing access to the jump gates. Something about being cut off from the rest of the Treble, reduced data floods, et cetera, et cetera. Things are bad all over."

Her smile is razor-edged, as if to say she holds Saxis Foxer personally responsible for the disruption to the sevite trade.

He asks, "If you're convinced of what my first mate told you, why the interrogation?"

Esek laughs. "Theater, of course!"

"There's information we don't have," interjects Chono. "The crewsaan who convinced you to buy the cache in the first place—Masar Hawks. He appears to be missing."

"That boy is barely crew at all. He's not even a pureblood Braem." Foxer spits on the ground. "I took him on six months ago because I needed extra labor, and he's worked on half the ships in the Black. I don't know him or trust him."

"Someone saw him leave Lo-Meek on a warhorse," Esek says. Chono, not realizing they had decided this story was reliable, keeps her expression cloistered. "They say there was a woman with him. This would have been the same time your Junian Graylore evaded our highly trained and celebrated marshals." Esek's voice bleeds disdain. "And if he was the one who found the coin cache to begin with, I have to say, I smell a collaboration."

The sound of the clamoring protesters is growing louder. Chono suspects they are marching down Ton Street, parallel to both the ship docks and this alley. Someone must have a bullhorn, for she distinctly hears a voice cry out:

"And where are the Khens? Where is Khen Ookhen Obair? We work and slave to build his ships! Does he protect us?! Does he advocate for us?! No!"

Chono feels that name, Khen, like nerve pain. Chief Marshal Norun mutters something at one of his marshals, who darts off. When he faces them again, his eyes lock with Chono's, cold and spiteful. Suddenly she remembers Ilius's warning: *Lo-Meek is teeming with Khen family loyalists. You murdered one of their own. You have to be careful.*

Chono holds Norun's stare, never buckling. The voice on the bullhorn shouts, "The Khens are Kindom puppets! The Khens are Kindom pets!"

"Ho-ho!" crows Esek. "Obair won't like that!"

Captain Foxer snorts, and for a strange moment he and Esek seem to be in accord.

Chono, on the other hand, is thinking of the Khens and their iron grip on the ship manufacturing industry—itself as badly dependent on sevite production as any other business in the Treble. She is thinking of Khen Ookhen Obair, their family head. It was his uncle she killed on Quietus. And now Marshal Norun glares at her. Is his head shaved in mourning for a family he serves? Given half a chance, would he seek revenge for his Khen masters? Probably.

Then Esek snaps her fingers, breaking the impasse. Chono looks away from Norun and back to Esek. "What *do* you know about Masar Hawks, Captain? Besides his failure to be a pureblood."

Foxer's smirk disappears. He gazes balefully at Esek, not answering. He has been betrayed by at least one of his own, and yet the Braemish tradition for loyalty to one's crew still beats in his breast.

"You are caught in a crime, Captain," Chono says. "If you have a hope for your life, you'll answer our questions."

"My life?" laughs Foxer, a new fire in his eyes. "Is it so bad if you take my life? I've plundered the Black Ocean for thirty years; I've stolen from every great family in the Treble. I've hoarded up so much treasure, Great Som themself will herald me home."

Unmoved, Chono asks, "What about your crew? What about their lives?"

He doesn't answer, but the blow lands, tightening his mouth and the lines around his eyes. By the captain's face, she knows he will make a deal. Esek knows it, too, for she's on him again. "Tell us what you know about Hawks."

Angrily he says, "There's nothing to tell! Young and brash and ambitious. He's a good fighter, trained, but not much for taking orders. Good at making friends. He was friends with everyone! The crew loved him. The ports loved him. He speaks all the languages, even Je. He—"

Esek steps suddenly forward, a javelin strike interrupting Captain Foxer's angry account.

"He speaks Je?" She looks at Chono, demanding, "Who speaks *Je* anymore?"

"Some archivists," says Chono. "And the Jeveni isolationists, of course. But he had no Jeveni markings, I assume?"

Foxer sneers. "I'd have never taken a Jeveni on my crew."

"Deplorable," hums Esek. "Are there Jeveni collectives on Bei continent?"

Chono remembers what Ilius said in his office. "South of here," she offers, and looks at Norun. "Aren't there?"

Norun grunts with distaste. "A hovel called Fezn. Nothing but paupers."

"Excellent," says Esek. "That's where we'll start."

She seems to have suddenly forgotten Foxer altogether, pacing away from him with a pleased sound. She passes two gloved fingers over the stump of her ruined ear. Chono, at a loss for her sudden excitement, won't let the Braemish captain disappear into Norun's clutches yet.

"Captain, why did you decide to change your meeting with Sunstep? You moved it up an entire day. Why?"

Foxer hesitates, clearly debating whether or not to tell them. Finally he admits, "I got a warning. Someone sent me a message, saying the Kindom knew I was involved in the sale of an important coin. Saying the only way I'd get out alive is if I found a way to convince the Kindom I never had it."

Chono glances between the captain and Esek, expecting to see some reaction from her. But she is still toying with her ear. Who would have sent such a message to Foxer? It smacks quite blatantly of Six, but if Six is aligned with Junian Graylore—

Foxer asks, "Will you spare my crew?"

Chono breathes out through her nostrils, feeling an unexpected twinge of compassion.

"We'll spare your crew, Sa," she promises.

But then, still half turned away from them, Esek says, "Well…we'll spare what's left of them. Some didn't take well to arrest and had to be put down. But that was only about half."

The look that sweeps across Captain Foxer's face is terrible. Chono barely hides her own shock. This is reckless, even for Esek, who turns toward them abruptly.

"The others will be removed to a work colony. To reform and earn their freedom. You'll share the same sentence."

Foxer is silent, gray with horror and disbelief. Esek looks at him without pity, and Chono can only glance back and forth between them in mounting tension. A moment later, the fingers of the captain's right hand start twitching. His lips barely move with soundless words. Chono recognizes the Braemish gesture. He's counting the souls of his dead, commending them to Som's tireless hunger—preparing his own soul, too.

"Captain Foxer," Chono says, with a low note of caution. "Your people will need a leader in the colony. Someone to give them hope. To help them earn their freedom."

Foxer stares unblinking at Esek, who stares back. There is something between them, now. A kind of understanding. Respect.

"No one earns their freedom in the colonies," Foxer says.

Esek's lip curls on one side. "'Better dead than a slave,' right, Captain?"

Chono's stomach clenches at the pirate adage, offered in Braemish. Foxer's fingers stop twitching. He has finished his count. Chono's body draws up in preparation.

"For what it's worth," murmurs the pirate, "I wish I'd been at Verdant. Lots of great pillage that day. I know one man who stole the underwear right off Tunistia Nightfoot's ass. He wears them as a scarf now. They slaughtered dozens, didn't they? Why, even you ran off with your tail between your legs."

Esek looks amused, even pleased. "Tunistia's ass was very small. Your friend should be careful his pillage doesn't strangle him."

Foxer nods, the conversation over. He moves with whipcrack speed, even favoring the one leg. The small knife glints in the shadowy light. Chono and Esek draw at the same moment, their shots going off in tandem. When Saxis Foxer hits the ground, it reminds Chono of the Pippashap fishersaan, felling a sea elk that leapt right onto their decks.

All that power and size and weight brought to a crush of stillness. The fishersaan sent up prayers to Capamame, singing in Qi—the Quietan language—their voices resonant with sorrow. They had killed the creature to defend themselves, but they hadn't wanted to.

Esek wanted to.

The Teron protesters have moved far enough along that their cries are distant. It's quiet in the alley now. Chief Marshal Norun looks stunned. Esek, holstering her gun, considers him pensively.

"The captain had a knife," she remarks.

He doesn't answer, his bluster and bravado disappearing as he realizes the import of letting an armed prisoner near a cleric. It's reason enough to have him stripped of titles.

Esek shrugs. "That's all right. I prefer a bit of sport. Tell your marshals to give him a Braemish burial, along with his dead. There are nine surviving crew. Transfer them to the custody of the Cloaksaan." Then she looks at Norun, and her expression is suddenly so cold and merciless that the man hardly breathes. "If I learn that fewer than nine are delivered, I'll drop you in the canyon myself."

Before the marshal can respond, she is brushing past him, striding down the alley the way they first came. Chono goes after her, feeling slightly sick. It may not be Esek's fault that the marshals over-zealously killed half of Foxer's crew last night, but it is her fault that there will be nine prisoners, instead of ten. This isn't even the worst of the vicious things Esek has done, but it's been years since Chono witnessed the carnage up close. She's no more inured to it now than she was then.

They walk briskly, Chono a half step behind. When they leave the labyrinth of the back alleys and step out onto Ton Street, the evidence of the passing parade is everywhere, in rucked-up red dust and littered flyers and graffiti sprayed on shopfronts and walkways. There is no way Esek doesn't know the factory unions are demanding her for their matriarch. There is no way her actions in the alley are less than calculated. But what is she trying to calculate?

Esek breathes in deeply, as if the noxious air is refreshing. Chono stares at her profile, at her mutilated ear. After what seems like a very long time, the other cleric looks back at her.

"Yes?" she drawls.

Chono considers her words for several breaths. "You goaded him."

There is no inflection in her voice. Esek's eyebrow twitches. "I was honest with him. I'm always honest with those I respect."

"We were ordered to deliver him to the Cloaksaan."

Esek says unconcernedly, "Our kin made it very clear what they cared about was the *memory coin*, not the survival of the parties involved."

In the past Chono might have backed down after that, but she surprises herself by pressing: "We didn't get the memory coin. The captain might have helped us track down the people who have it. Killing him was premature. Now, everything he knows is lost to us."

"Yes, of course, no one likes being left in the dark. Seti and Aver will *hate* it." Esek's musing tone is backlit with sarcasm. "Believe me, Chono, I feel for them."

She must be referring to the First Cleric's choice to hide the contents of the coin from her. Chono wants to think this is too petty for Esek, but of course it isn't. Not for the first time she considers telling Esek about her conversation with Ilius, and his research into the contents of the coin. The possibility that it threatens not just the Nightfoots, but the very Kindom. She refrains. It's not as if Ilius has sent her any conclusions yet.

But Esek must read something in her expression, for she makes a permissive gesture. "Don't worry that *you'll* be blamed, little fish. Show them your ocular. Show them what happened. The Six Gods themselves will stand you up."

The use of "little fish" touches a fragile nerve. She asks, "Is this a test, Sa?"

Esek grins. She claps Chono on the shoulder, and Chono instinctively tenses.

"Oh, Chono. You're *definitely* being tested. Now, if you want, we can fight about this some more, but let's do it on the warkite, where it doesn't smell so bad."

She strides off, and Chono is forced to follow. Their ship is docked a half mile down Ton Street, and Chono is suddenly as eager to get there as Esek. She feels haunted by this ugly place, by this planet, by its memories, and by this new Esek-driven disaster, unfolding on its soil. A wind picks up, splattering them with thick red mud, and one of the flyers gets caught in Chono's coat. She picks it free, startled by its message. The three-pointed star of the Kindom, anthropomorphized into a body with a face, is on its knees, sucking the penis of a figure with a Jeveni tattoo. Behind the Jeveni whirls a vibrant jump gate. No words adorn the flyer. They aren't exactly needed. Esek leans over her shoulder.

"Oh, that's good. Imagine how the Secretaries feel about that." She chuckles.

"There will be attacks on the Jeveni. It's not their fault we're rationing jump gate travel."

Esek *hmms*. "Not at all. It's mine."

Chono doesn't know how to respond to this first acknowledgment of how Esek's choices stand to impact the Treble. And apparently, that's all the acknowledgment she intends to give, for a moment later she's cracking her knuckles and heaving a sigh.

Chono starts to fold up the flyer. Esek demands, "What are you doing?"

"I'm going to put it in the waste—"

Esek snatches it from her, throws it on the ground, exasperated. Chono watches it slip away in a breeze. For a few moments they walk in silence, as if the flyer itself was a symbol of some greater rupture between them. Something that began years ago.

Chono, steeling herself, says, "We have neither Sunstep, nor the coin. We should ask the Cloaksaan to help us track them down."

Esek's irritation seems to evaporate. She huffs a laugh. "Aver set *us* on this task, if you'll remember. Besides, we already have a lead. A Je-speaking, warhorse-stealing, pretend Braem won't be too difficult to trace. And I'm convinced Sunstep will be with him."

Chono is *not* convinced, but whether or not this is a *good* lead, it is their only lead. They've tracked Six on less reliable information before.

A siren goes up in the city west, the same direction the protesters traveled. Chono knows what those protesters will face as punishment for deriding the Khen family: a brutal crackdown, by marshals itching to fight. Even if Chono could stop it from happening, they have reached their ship. And Esek seems antsy now. The hunt is waiting.

And if you seek hope and purpose, if you long for rebirth, lift your voice in praise. Praise the goddess Makala, fecund and lovely, who births all destinies. When your destiny arrives, it will consume your soul as the newborn consumes its mother. Then you will be like your goddess. You will breed life from dreams.

The Beatitudes, 1:4. Godtexts, pre-Treble

CHAPTER EIGHT

1649

YEAR OF THE INGOT

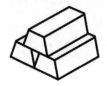

Verdant Estate
Sevres Continent
The Planet Ma'kess

The Nightfoots built Verdant at the end of the fourteenth century, when the sevite trade was blooming and Ri'in Nightfoot had money to burn. It was a massive estate of sculpted trees and manicured lawns and wildflower gardens. Its main structure took the form of a warbird in flight, with two main wings above and below the ground. It was all domes and arches, whites and blues, stone and glass. As glittering fine as Riin Cosas itself, and more expensive. Three diamond-shaped exterior buildings stood sentry behind it, a headquarters for the security systems and forces, and an opaque holo fence limned the grounds, impenetrable as steel. At the center of the estate, a focal point for the warbird's flight, rose a single black tower, fifteen stories high and swathed in flowering vines. It was once Ri'in Nightfoot's personal dwelling. Indeed, in the many generations since Verdant was built, the Nightfoot matriarch had always occupied that tower, setting herself on a perch far above the estate, from which she could review her family both figuratively and literally.

But Alisiana always did things her own way.

For appearance's sake, of course, she kept the upper rooms. She conceived her daughter there, and birthed her daughter there, and always received important guests in its sitting room, flanked by portraits of her predecessors. But when Alisiana was not performing the role, she kept a different home, in the underground levels of the tower, near the family temple.

If anyone discovered this idiosyncrasy, it was easy enough to explain: Alisiana was devout. Makala's temples were always underground. If Alisiana wanted to be able to pray at a moment's notice, she must go into the womb-like earth, where her goddess lived. And so, the underground apartment made perfect sense.

Esek, taking the stairs two at a time, could have laughed at the absurdity. Alisiana was about as devout as a businessaan doing their taxes.

There was an elevator of course, but she preferred the spiraling staircase, the walls pocked with sevite lanterns—an expensive, ethereal glow. She swept down two, three floors, until she reached the temple level with its soft soil ground and the oversized statue of Makala, in her birthing state and shiny with oil. Esek took a short hallway to the living suite, and shoved open the double doors at its terminus. Inside, six doctors and nurses stood milling in front of another door, which was firmly shut. They blanched at the sight of her.

"What the fuck are you all doing out here?" she demanded.

One doctor said, "She dismissed us, Burning One. We can't ignore her orders. She's perfectly comfortable, though. We will—"

Esek made a snarling sound, shouldering past them to reach the door to Alisiana's bedroom. One of them had the gall to try to stop her—she hurled them away and there was a hard smack as their head hit the nearest wall. Esek didn't look back. She simply shut the door behind her, turning toward the four-poster bed in the center of the room.

Alisiana was sitting up already, hands folded over her lap and brow arched. Esek stopped short, conscious suddenly of the near panic in her own expression. She schooled it away, affecting her usual mask of supercilious humor. A mask very similar, though not quite so perfect, as the one Alisiana always wore.

"Esek." Alisiana's voice was rough with exhaustion. "Tell me you haven't killed any of my doctors."

Esek paused. "Not that I'm aware of."

Alisiana sighed and made the slightest gesture with one of her fingers. Esek found a nearby chair and brought it up to Alisiana's bedside. When she had dropped into it, she leaned over, kissing her aunt on the cheek. In reality, Alisiana was a cousin many times removed, but "aunt" suited their relationship. Near to her, Esek could smell pungent medicines, and underneath them, the still healing wound: a bullet, right through the shoulder. Barely missed her heart. Esek had been performing funeral rites in an isolated village on Praediis continent. Her kin wouldn't let her leave until this morning, two days after the assassination attempt; even then it was only because Alisiana called for her, and the First Cleric probably didn't want to get in a fight with a recently shot Alisiana Nightfoot over access to her favorite niece.

"Who was it?" Esek demanded.

They caught the assassin right away, of course—but he was only a tool. Everyone claimed not to know who he worked for, but Esek trusted Alisiana's intuition.

"The Moonbacks, probably. Though I doubt it was sanctioned. Some little cousin trying to make a name for herself."

"Let me talk to him," said Esek.

Alisiana snorted. "You mean slaughter him in his cell?"

"I'll interrogate him first."

"He's been interrogated," sighed the matriarch. "The contract was anonymous. He's given everything he knows to the Cloaksaan."

"Then let me slaughter him in his cell."

She waved this off. "You must learn to curb these bloody impulses. They're unbefitting a cleric. The assassin will be relocated to a work colony. He'll suffer and die mining some gas planet like Locali. Be satisfied." Esek made to argue, but Alisiana said, "I didn't call you here to discuss this latest, paltry attempt on my life."

Esek closed her mouth. She sensed a reckoning. Alisiana was an old woman now, but not so old. A series of body mods had blunted the evidence of her eighty-five years, and she might live thirty more. True, Esek could see her age upon her. Alisiana was always small, but she seemed a slip of a woman now, wrinkled, with lank white hair, and a kind of brittleness in her wrists and collarbones, as if all of her could be snapped into pieces with the merest pressure. Yet those sapphire eyes still glittered like torchlight, and in her whole small person she radiated such power and barely banked threat that Esek wondered if any bullet could snuff it out.

"I thought you called me here because you were hurt."

"And tear you away from your work? Why would I do that?" Alisiana retorted.

"Well, because—"

"You must be careful, Esek. People will think you love me too much."

Inside, Esek recoiled from the idea. She wasn't sure she had ever felt "love" in the most basic sense of the word. There were people she enjoyed, and she took many lovers. And she felt a certain savage affection for her little clutch of novitiates. As for loving Alisiana—well, perhaps it was true. She hated anyone else Alisiana might favor. She took great satisfaction in pleasing her. Threats to the matriarch's life made Esek furious, rabid. But these feelings, if they were love, so often toed the borders of other, more familiar emotions: possessiveness, jealousy. She had even wondered, more than once, if what she really felt for Alisiana was hatred. If the thing she experienced when she heard about assassination attempts was not panic for a loved one, but rage that anyone would dare to take the right that was her own.

Sniffing, Esek said to the matriarch, "So you didn't want me for your own sake. Very well, Riin Matri. How may I serve?"

Alisiana snorted at the use of the formal family title. "Don't be petulant. We both have responsibilities, and just because you're my favorite doesn't mean I can let you come here every time there's a mishap. Honestly, you are *just like* Caskori sometimes. I worry about you."

Despite the censure (and the comparison to an ancestor Esek despised), she grinned, swallowing down Alisiana's favoritism like cool water. "Worry, Auntie? About me? No one has tried to kill *me* in a week."

"Stop being clever. Tell me about this new novitiate of yours."

This was not what she'd expected at all. Alisiana never gave two shits about Esek's work as a cleric, beyond how it influenced the family's fortunes. "Do you mean Chono?" she asked. "I've had that one for eight months already."

"Fine, tell me about her."

Esek shrugged, still perplexed, and not sure how to answer.

"I like her," she finally admitted, like she was reflecting on a recently acquired piece of furniture. "She's *ridiculously* solemn. *Comically* religious. That's great fun for me. She's more intelligent than I thought she'd be, and a better fighter than she gives herself credit for. Some of the other novitiates are scared of her."

"She's also young," said Alisiana. "You fished her out of her school early, didn't you?"

"Oh, that. I met her at a party in Barcetima. She was on a recruitment tour. Her master was clearly trading her around to fetishists."

"So?" Alisiana asked, eyes cold. "You yourself performed sexual favors as a student. Don't tell me you cared about the legality of it."

"Of course not! But when I was coming up, they only gave that sort of work to students who wanted it. This one—you could see in her sad little face she'd been coerced. She's the type that, if it went on, it would have destroyed her. Wasteful. Also, it was an opportunity to make a point with one of our business contacts on Kator."

Esek finished her story with a *that's it* gesture. Alisiana stared at her for several moments, before finally asking, "And I suppose this was the first time you've interfered in the life of a kinschool student, hmm?"

Ah... So now we are coming to the crux of the thing.

"You mean Six."

Alisiana narrowed her eyes. "I mean the Alanye spawn."

As always, Esek felt a flutter of excitement, thinking of that little creature at the kinschool on Principes. That Alisiana knew it was an Alanye only quickened her excitement, her curiosity over where all this was headed.

"They called it Six, at the school. It disappeared years ago. Who knows what it calls itself now?"

Alisiana's eyes bored into her. "Who, indeed?"

Esek frowned. "I'm surprised it matters to you, Auntie. As far as I know there are hardly any Alanyes left. Scattered to the winds. They're no threat to *us*."

"Oh, no?" Alisiana asked, with a new coldness. "You're certain of that? Expert on the family that you are? Born to the center of the tree, were you?"

Esek balked, not only at the tone, but at the bald reference to her status in the family. Nightfoots were...eccentric about gender; they tied it to sex, and only women from Ri'in Nightfoot's line could be matriarch.

Esek was a descendant of Caskori Nightfoot, and he was descended from Ri'in Nightfoot's son, Arso. In the complex genealogy of the Nightfoot tree, Esek was insignificant, just as Caskori had been insignificant. She had only Alisiana's affection to buoy her, which could be taken away in an instant. But no one in the Treble, except Alisiana herself, would dare to point this out to Esek. Esek, who took her small place on the outer branches and made it bloom with the favor of the Godfire.

"Riin Matri," she said, affecting gravity. "Tell me what I've done. I'll make it right."

Alisiana sniffed. She shifted a little, settling back against her pillows with a wince.

"You are unfathomably capricious, Esek. You rescue one student, and curse another."

"I was curious what the child could make of itself. It was a remarkable fighter."

"Your bargain was cruel," Alisiana said, though this could not be what bothered her.

"It was an opportunity. If that child shows up again, it will make my best novitiate ever."

"And become another of your rabid devotees, I'm sure. Psychological torture can do that sort of thing."

This was too much.

"You know very well why I've built a following. I never wanted to be a *cleric*! But I accepted it out of loyalty to *you*, because you wanted our family to have a fistful of the Righteous Hand. And I started training cloaksaan so that we could undermine Seti Moonback's fistful of the *Brutal* Hand. And I've succeeded. On *your* orders."

Alisiana looked unimpressed. "Yes, you're very good at what you do. You're ignoring certain histories, of course. For example, the trouble it took to get you a position at all. No one wanted you for any of the Hands. Volatile little monster that you are."

"So, how'd you do it?" Esek retorted.

"By promising to keep an eye on you," she said. Esek had no answer for this, and Alisiana wasn't done. "Sometimes in life we are presented with dangerous animals. If we train them, guide them, watch them, they can become useful instruments. This is what I have done with you. What *you* have done is set a dangerous animal loose, in the unfounded hope it will return to you anything better than feral."

"It won't be feral," Esek said, remembering the composure and discipline of the student. "If it is, I'll simply kill it."

"*Or* it will not return at all," said Alisiana. "It will become a wild thing in the woods, threatening our interests."

"How can an Alanye orphan with no family and no power and no wealth possibly threaten us?"

Alisiana stared at her for a long moment, icy calculation in her eyes. She was clearly debating what to reveal, and Esek perked up at the thought of some secret family intrigue. What she did not expect, however, was for Alisiana to reach under the covers and withdraw an envelope, scrawled with Esek's mailing stamp. Esek stared. The stamp should have ensured this package got to her, wherever she was. The date was three days old. And the envelope had clearly already been opened.

"You *stole* my *mail*?" she cried, incredulous.

"And don't I have that right?" retorted the matriarch, equal parts arrogance and warning. "You are my agent in the Treble. I am your matriarch. If I want a look at your mail, aren't I as entitled to it as every other thing you own?"

Esek scowled but managed to tamp down her recriminations.

Alisiana told her, "You know we have to be careful. My guardsaan meticulously monitor anything that comes in contact with us, including our mail, and if they see something worrisome or suspicious, they bring the matter to me for my judgment. You may be shocked to hear it, Esek, but you have made quite a lot of enemies, and this is hardly the first time I've had to make sure no one delivered a bomb to your rooms."

Esek gestured peevishly at the envelope, which Alisiana still withheld. "*That* is hardly a bomb. What about it put you in a huff?"

"Its origin."

"Which was?"

"The dome city of Dewbreak, on Jeve."

This was enough to scatter all Esek's anger. Dewbreak was as ruined as every other biodome on Jeve, just a crater in the moon. Nobody *lived* there. Alisiana nodded at her expression.

"Yes, you can imagine why that caught our attention."

"So where did it *really* come from?"

"We don't know yet. My archivists say whoever sent it is clearly a sophisticated caster, and the origin coordinates must be part of the message itself."

Esek looked greedily at the envelope. She felt like a dog at its master's dinner table, whining for a piece of the feast. Finally, magnanimously, Alisiana let her have it. Esek snatched out the contents, surprised and a little confused to find it only contained a small memory coin. There was no point trying to hide its contents (Alisiana had surely viewed them already), so she cast to its activation signal and pulled a series of images into the air. The first showed a very young Alisiana. She was seated in the matriarch's formal receiving room (some fifteen floors above Esek's head), which meant her mother, Ti Nightfoot, was already dead. Esek guessed she was...fifteen? Sixteen? A proud and solemn little thing. There was a man standing in front of her, no more than thirty, with a lean and hungry build and a broad-nosed face, eyes closely set. It took Esek a moment to recognize him: Lucos Alanye.

She looked at Alisiana in undisguised shock.

"You *knew* him?"

Before Alisiana could answer, Esek moved to the next image: Alanye, in the process of bowing over his hands, and Alisiana holding out some kind of rolled document. Esek knew a ceremonial appointment when she saw it.

The next and final image only depicted Alanye, Alisiana cropped out. He held the rolled document in his hand. The appointment given and received. But even more spectacular than this was the scrawl of lettering superimposed on the image. Esek couldn't read what it said, but she recognized the language.

"It's Je," Alisiana said. "My archivist translated it."

She projected the message in Ma'kessi into the air beside them:

Does this impress you, Esek?
Who would have thought our elders kept such company?

Esek fought very hard not to snatch the memory coin up and crush it in her hand. She was an easily delighted person, and an easily enraged person, but she had rarely felt such an immediate surge of glee and fury together. Six years of wondering whether her game would bear any fruit. And now, here, this—the first harvest. But what kind of fruit was it?

She asked Alisiana, "What did you give him? Alanye?"

The matriarch pursed her lips. But instead of answering Esek's question, she murmured, "Suffice it to say, this sort of thing would look very bad, if it became public."

Esek nearly laughed. Look bad? That was an understatement. More than half the sevite factory workers were Jeveni, people who viewed the Nightfoots as their allies because Alisiana gave them employment after the genocide. This would certainly fuck with that image!

But Esek refused to be distracted. "What, exactly, is this thing that my little fish has found?"

Alisiana clearly disliked that phrasing, for her glare grew murderous. "You think I'm going to lay all my secrets bare to you, you irresponsible child? You think I'm prepared to show you that level of trust, after all the trouble you've caused me? I wouldn't even share that much with my heirs!"

Esek looked at her flatly. Alisiana's daughter, Ev, became a debauched mods addict in her teens. She'd gone so far as to completely reengineer herself to look identical to her mother. (Or nearly identical. The eyes and shoulders were a little off. The height was wrong.) Alisiana responded by having her face disfigured. Currently, hope rested on Ev's daughter, Melicini, but this one was bucking against her female gendermark, bucking against family tradition, and if she got her way, she'd be off the list. The question was, could she give birth to a child first? Someone with Alisiana's gravity?

If Alisiana withheld family secrets from her direct bloodline, it only meant she was wise enough not to throw jewels into mud. And it meant she carried all those secrets on her own. There was a time when she had confided in Sorek Nightfoot, her cousin and second-in-command, a man who'd run the sevite factories with savvy ruthlessness. But he was decades dead, and Alisiana was old now. She couldn't survive on her own counsel alone.

Esek softened her voice. "Show me trust, Auntie," she coaxed. "How can I help you?"

Alisiana's eyes were sharp. "You can help me by finding the person who sent this message. And if it is your wretched little student, you can help me by killing it."

"Done," said Esek.

Alisiana paused in surprise, eyes narrowing. "Will you?" Her question was pointed, her tone doubtful. "Will you find it easy, to kill the 'little fish' you've been dreaming of all this time?" Esek gave nothing away, though secretly she balked. What right had anyone to know her dreams? The matriarch went on, "I know this Chono came from the same school, the same class. I have reports that she was friends with it. What if she…sympathized with it? And still does?"

This had never occurred to Esek. The prospect was actually delightful, but she didn't think Chono had the artifice for it. Nevertheless, she knew what game she was playing now, and responded accordingly.

"Chono means as little to me as her schoolkin. Say the word, and I'll kill her, too. I'll kill both of them."

Esek waited. Alisiana stared her down. It was an exciting moment. If Alisiana said the word, she would fulfill her promise. But it would make her *very* unhappy to lose Chono.

At last, the old woman let out a sigh. "You may keep your wounded bird. Use her. Use everything. I want this Alanye brat eradicated. Along with everything it might know."

"That would be easier if *I* knew what it might know."

"Then I suppose you'll have the pleasure of achieving something that isn't easy."

Annoyed, Esek stood up, withdrawing the images from the air and taking the coin. She looked about the room, this sanctuary to Alisiana's private life. Obscure art on the walls. Expensive clothes in the open wardrobe. A small watercolor of Caskori amid larger, more appropriate portraits of Alisiana's descendants, and of the original matriarch, Ri'in Nightfoot. There was also a plinth in the far corner, supporting a rather unremarkable box. Esek had always wondered what was inside it. She always wondered what was inside everything—what was inside Alisiana. Many secrets she'd uncovered through her own machinations, but now she knew there were things she had not even guessed at. And she wanted them.

"Nothing I learn will make me less loyal to you," she informed her aunt.

Alisiana chuckled, amused but grim. "Yes, I know. But I've had snakes in my garden before. Spies and traitors even in my own family. And your loyalty to me will always come second to your loyalty to yourself."

"Can I earn it?" Esek asked. She stared directly into Alisiana's brilliant, calculating eyes. "Can I *earn* your confidence?"

Alisiana shifted on the bed, wincing badly this time. She looked suddenly tired, and hurt, and the reminder of her near death sent a bolt of that not-love feeling through Esek. But it also made her greedy. Alisiana would not live forever, and then what? Fragile, deformed Ev? Recalcitrant Melicini? Or some infant created through coercion? Could Alisiana let the family fall so far, after her death? When the matriarch met Esek's eyes again, Esek was suddenly certain she was thinking the same thing.

"Anything can be earned," said Alisiana.

It was all Esek could do not to crow her triumph. If something could be earned, then Esek would earn it—and Esek wanted *everything*. Everything the Treble held. Everything that could be acquired.

"I'll bring you its head," she promised.

Alisiana nodded briefly. Her response, when it came, was more threat than order. "Struck from its shoulders."

At that, Esek leaned forward again. She took her aunt's hand this time, and kissed it with passionate devotion, all the little bones shifting under fragile skin.

"Be *smart*, Esek," the matriarch warned.

Esek bowed her assent. When Alisiana gave a short nod of dismissal, she turned and left the room. The doctors were still standing outside, one of them with a fresh bandage on the side of their forehead. They shrank back from her, but she ignored them, sweeping down the hallway, toward the stairs. When she was out of sight from them, she melted into her detour, slipping down, not up. There was one more level, deep under the grounds of Verdant. A place for secret passages and hidden prisons and torture chambers they had used on their enemies for three hundred years. She knew exactly what room would house the Moonbacks' would-be assassin.

It would be the work of minutes to make the whole thing look like suicide.

CHAPTER NINE

1664

YEAR OF THE CRUX

Siinkai
Bei Continent
The Planet Teros

In the predawn, Jun wakes to learn Masar has secured them a ride from the innkeeper's niece, and he's given the village his warhorse to scrap for compensation. The machine's Trini-son steel frame *alone* is worth thousands, and the innkeeper's niece is driving an ancient ground shuttle sarcastically known as a warbunny—no defenses and built small. The hustler in Jun is offended on principle, but it's Masar's choice. They'll have money enough for hundreds of warhorses if this goes right.

In the bathroom, she turns on the shower and tries calling Liis again but gets no response, same as last night. She leaves a message, equal parts apologetic and easygoing. Tells her they have to zip down to the Cliffs for some equipment and after that she'll call again.

Hours later, there's still no word. Not even an acknowledgment. Something starts to wriggle in Jun's brain, pinging back and forth until she's generating enough anxiety to power the bunny twice over. Liis can be a grumpy fucker, but she's not petulant and she's not passive-aggressive. She ought to have responded by now.

"Who do you keep calling?"

Masar's voice startles her. He's sitting in the front passenger seat, Jun crammed in the back, and she doesn't know how he can even see her checking her comm. The innkeeper's niece, sporting a perpetually blasé look, glances at her in the rearview.

"I'm not calling anyone."

"You did this morning." Masar turns around to glare at her. "And last night." Jun scowls, refusing to answer, and his look sharpens. "I'm a fairly laid-back person. But when I start to think my partner is keeping secrets from me, I—"

"*Partner* is a stretch. And you made calls last night, too. Don't think I didn't notice." He doesn't relent, and she rolls her eyes. "Look, I've got family in the Ma'kess System and she's not answering my comms. That's it, all right? *Relax.*"

Masar looks taken aback. "*You* have family?"

"Why the fuck shouldn't I have family?"

"I dunno, you just seem like—"

"What, you think I'm some kind of intergalactic loner criminal who's sprung out of nowhere with no family?"

"Kata's *tit*, don't be so dramatic, I was only—"

"Might be the blocks won't let your comm through."

The Jeveni teenager interrupts with all the arch composure of someone used to rolling her eyes at her parents. Jun and Masar stop, looking at her. She can't be older than seventeen and she's a fascinating mix of Jeveni tradition and modern fashion. The jet studs in her ears and nose are pure Jeveni. The black twists of her hair are a Katish fashion. She's wearing a black band around her left forearm, which usually signifies mourning but has become a macabre affectation among Makessn teenagers in recent years. It goes great with her silver eyeliner, drawn out in whorls on her cheeks that proudly accentuate her Jeveni tattoo. Her clothes are all hand-me-downs, but there's something proud in her tilted chin. What must it be like for Jeveni kids to grow up in backwater villages cut off from most of the Treble? Jun feels a flicker of affinity.

Masar repeats, "The *blocks*?"

"She means the casting net blockers. Cities have started throwing them up in the past twenty-four hours, to stop protesters being able to collaborate. It's a good thought, kid, but the blocks aren't quite up to the challenge of *me*."

The girl shrugs. She's been chewing a mint reed all morning, insolent and cool. "Then she's probably mad at you. Give her space. Get her a present. It'll wash, yeah?"

All said with typical teenage bravado.

"Maybe I'm talking about my ma," Jun says.

Another shrug. "Nobody sweats over their comm like that unless it's a sweetheart involved. Just saying."

Masar's face splits with a grin, and Jun barely stifles her own amusement. She leans forward, gesturing at the black band on the girl's forearm.

"Why do you kids wear that shit?" she asks.

The girl flicks her a look in the rearview mirror. It's assessing. Like maybe Jun doesn't deserve to know the fashion logics of today's youth.

"My cousin was on *The Wild Run*. The ship with all the casters."

If it were possible to drop into the earth and never reemerge, Jun would. Her whole body turns heavy with shame, and the tightening along Masar's jaw, the way he looks away from them and out the window—he's clearly as embarrassed for her as she is for herself.

"I heard about that," says Jun. She hasn't had much time to follow the caster forums still discussing the attack, but most of it is depressingly unsympathetic. *Why were so many Jeveni traveling together? Why did they break the law by gathering in those numbers? A tragedy, yes, but—*

Only a few people have challenged the pirate attack story, positing that it was actually Kindom retaliation for the trouble in the factories. If that's true, Jun determines to prove it. Just as soon as she's got some time on her hands.

"I'm so sorry it happened. Sorry for your loss."

The teenager shrugs, as if Jun's apology is another embarrassment. Shit if it isn't. Masar, apparently well versed in how not to make an ass of himself, says, "May the barren flourish."

"May the barren flourish," agrees the girl. Then she points at an upcoming road sign. "Ten miles to the first Siinkai exits."

Relieved, Jun looks out the window. Sure enough, the weedy countryside is starting to give way to developed plots of land, and on the road ahead she can already see the sprawling breadth of the coastal city of Siinkai. The Cliffs, however, are a distant structure, built into the sheet of rocky outcropping on the city's southern flank.

"Don't go into the city itself," Jun instructs. "Take the Noor Ma exit and follow the highway southeast till we're out of the suburbs. I'll show you."

It's another forty-five minutes. Eventually the traffic thickens, then crawls as drivers fight over intersections and exits. The teenager is an adept driver, for all her country life, and she gets them through the worst of it, following Jun's directions to exit onto a nameless road that winds up into the soaring coastal cliffs.

Within minutes they are high enough to see the ocean beyond the city. It's an incomprehensibly blue and beautiful thing, shaming the interminable red glut of Bei continent's ordinary landscapes. The radiation shields actually reflect the ocean out here, which makes the air seem clearer and cleaner. As if Teros could actually be beautiful.

The road dead-ends in a dilapidated courtyard that abuts the cliff face. Wide stairways are carved into the rock, climbing upward toward a dozen towers of stone and the half-destroyed body of the abandoned palace that is the Silt Glow Cliffs. When Jun steps out of the warbunny, she's caught between equal impressions of grandeur and decay. In its heyday, the palace was a marvel of engineering, carved out of the very mountain, all its columns and arches and staircases of a single piece. Today, that master class of architecture and stonemasonry remains—but only in the east wing. The other wings are no more than broken sheets and collapsed rubble, bombed into obscurity during the civil war of 1512, which the Khen family only survived through Kindom intervention.

Masar leans into the warbunny's window, speaking to the teenager in Je. Jun switches on her translator bot, watching text scroll across her ocular.

"—stop anywhere. Get home to your uncle. I promised him."

"Yeah. Yeah."

"Are you going on pilgrimage?"

The kid hesitates, hems, picks at her thumbnail, and tosses the masticated mint reed out the window. "People say it's not safe to go. Lots of mobs at the docks, looking for Jeveni."

Masar frowns. After a moment he says hesitantly, "You've got a right to go."

She cocks an eyebrow at him. "What do you know about it? You don't live out here."

Masar looks taken aback, even wounded, but the girl only stares at him placidly. After a minute he sighs and gives her shoulder a tight squeeze. "All right. Take care of yourself."

"Yeah, yeah," she says, and Masar steps back.

"Stay safe, kid," Jun calls out in Teron.

The girl gives a dismissive wave. She brings the bunny around and zips back down the road. Jun watches Masar watch her go. From the bits of Je she's overheard, it doesn't seem like he walked into Fezn a stranger. He hasn't got the wheel tattoo, and even the ones who have assimilated wear the tattoo. So he can't be Jeveni himself. But what kind of pirate is friends with Jeveni separatists?

"Speaking of keeping secrets," she says.

He frowns at her. "What?"

But they don't have time to get into it. "Nothing. We should go."

She watches him absorb the cliff face and stairways above them. He has his giant shotgun gripped in one hand and makes no move to strap it to the holster on his back. Jun, aware that plenty of bandits could be watching for them from the cliffs, is suddenly grateful for his weapon, and his size. The swelling in his face from Captain Foxer's beating has gone down enough that he's got both eyes open now, and that doesn't hurt, either.

"Is there anything up there?" he asks doubtfully.

"The east wing," Jun replies, heading toward the appropriate staircase. "It was mostly guest quarters and a casino. The rebels ignored it to take out the main palace, and by the time they could have finished the whole thing off, cloaksaan had arrived. The Khens relocated to Trini-so. Worse climate, but fewer detractors. Perfect place to breed more murderers. All this was abandoned until the casters took over."

They climb for fifteen minutes. Jun flatters herself she does enough sparring with Liis to remain in relatively good shape, but by the time they reach the top she's dripping sweat and breathing hard. If she had her ship, they could have landed on the flight deck (the only surviving piece of the west wing) and walked from there. But *The Gunner* is still in Lo-Meek; the dockworkers have probably already sold it to settle her unpaid rental fee—and lined their damned pockets with the excess, those fuckers.

But now, standing on the flatlands that face the entrance to the east wing, there's at least the prospect of success.

Inside the dilapidated receiving room, the ground is unevenly tiled in white and gray stone, echoing what was once a mosaic of Teroton-teris. Intricately carved and crumbling columns support a shadowy mezzanine some fifteen feet above their heads, and there are moldering armchairs and couches scattered throughout the space, one or two occupied by figures that appear to be sleeping. Jun has no doubt they're armed and ready to spring. It's all just as she remembers.

Directly ahead, a large elevator shaft with no car spears the mezzanine and disappears into higher, unseen levels. There are no staircases.

It is the only way in or out. But it's guarded by a massive stone desk, and the single active figure in the room: an archivist.

At the sight of them, Masar looks suspiciously at Jun.

"What's an archivist doing in a caster den?" he demands.

Jun walks forward. "You're pretty naive for a pirate. Archivists *run* the Silt Glow Cliffs."

Masar follows her, muttering, "I always took archivists for respectable."

Jun shakes her head. "Yeah, well. Some of them can't afford to stay that way."

As for the archivist themself, they are hunched over the stone desk with insectile posture, hands dancing across what Jun knows to be a projected casting table. They wear the traditional white uniform, linen pants and tunic hanging loosely on a skinny frame. They've added elaborate goggles to the ensemble, and their hair, which most archivists keep short, tumbles down their shoulders and back in matted clumps. When Jun and Masar stand before them at last, she notices the rough green tattoos on their pale brown forearms, typical of the kind one gets in work colonies.

The archivist doesn't react to her approach, though of course they know she's there. After a moment, she knocks her knuckles on the desk. Its dense stone absorbs and mutes the sound, yet the archivist looks up with a start, buggy goggles ridiculous.

Jun bows over her hands. "Learner and Light. We need a casting room, tier seven or higher."

The archivist stares at her, as if they don't understand. Then, with measured movements, they pull off the goggles, blinking rapidly. There are heavy impressions around their eyes from where the goggles fit, and a sore on the bridge of their nose. She recognizes the glazed look in their stare. "Tech face," people call it. Like hypnosis or a dream. It takes them a moment to fully incorporate again. Only then do they give her a thorough perusal. Jun recognizes that look, too.

"You've brought a name, nah?" they ask.

Jun narrows her eyes. "Look at my face, friend. You've seen me before."

The archivist pouts their lower lip like a peevish child. "How should I know you? You—who disappear behind my goggles. You invisible thing. I can see you now."

Jun is familiar with the performative absurdity of archivists, who would prefer the world see them as shamans rather than glorified casters who come from money.

"Fine," Jun says. "Let me show you who I am."

She curls the fingers of her right hand, as if to grip a ball, and tosses it gently, underhand, into the orbit of the casting table. The archivist fumbles their goggles back into place, immediately running hands through the contents of her offering—a bit of code she wrote up last night, good for hacking several guardsaan casting hubs in Siinkai. The archivist's fingers pluck an invisible harp as they start to mutter and hum.

"Ah, you," they grumble. "Come upon us with your head covered, nah? Very shy. Try to make up for it with gifts." They sniff wetly. They stare at the space where she is standing, even though they can't see anything. With her Hood program enabled, she is utterly invisible. "So all right then, all right. Have a room, have a good room, tier eight. Good? Good. And a back door, as well?"

Jun thinks of her bank account, whose numbers she has always guarded like a dragon.

"There's no need to gouge me for—"

"Have a back door," they interrupt, something different in their voice. They flip up their goggles again, eyes bulbous and rheumy. "Everybody needs it, sometimes, the way out. The hunters are hunted, nah?"

A million tiny hairs stand up on Jun's body at once. For all their meaningless jabber, archivists do drop useful hints, sometimes. She leans closer.

"What have you seen?"

They make a silly gesture in the air, as if casting information for her review, but nothing appears, and their eyes remain locked on hers.

"Just a feeling. Just a whisper. Sunstep, Junian Graylore—or is it Jun Ironway?"

Jun flinches—makes very certain not to glance at Masar.

"What a non-face you have. Still, names catch on. Be safe, nah? Put your eyes on the back of your head, it's good, it's good, here we are!"

Behind the archivist, a car begins to descend the elevator shaft, dropping into place on the ground floor with a smoothness that belies the decrepitude of the Cliffs. Its doors open silently. The archivist bows them toward it with over-the-top solicitude, and Jun knows she won't get any more information from them. She homes in on the weight of the gun at her hip and takes reassurance from Masar beside her.

The last thing Jun sees before the elevator doors close is the hunched archivist, grinning wildly.

"Are they always that creepy?" asks Masar, as the car lifts upward.

Jun shakes her head distractedly. "Only when they want to be."

That name is burning in her thoughts: *Ironway Ironway Ironway.*

"I've been to the archivist's academy in Riin Kala. They all seemed like your average asocial scholars."

His mention of the academy only heightens Jun's unease. She makes a dismissive gesture, hoping he'll drop it, glad he didn't seem to notice what the archivist called her. Either that or the name meant nothing to him. And why should it?

"Living on the fringes makes everyone weird," she says.

The car halts on the eighth level of the palace. The doors open on darkness. In the courtyard below, they had brilliant sunshine and the ocean behind, but now they are enclosed in a shadowy stone tunnel. The average person would find this claustrophobic, but for the people who visit the Cliffs, it brings the comfort of all hiding places. The sensation of anonymity, however feigned. Jun's breaths come a little easier, and she scans the hall with purpose. There are doors on either side, all dark except for one about halfway down, frame lit gold.

She's there in moments, and a quick ocular scan snicks the door open.

It's a small room, but exactly what she hoped for. The casting table is state-of-the-art, with shadow lines connecting it to every major hub in the system, and enough processing power to manage anything Jun can throw at it. She shuts the door as soon as Masar is inside, gratified by the sound of the lock engaging, and by the hum of the working machinery. The only light comes from the monitors and console themselves, glowing gold like the door did.

Finally, she looks up at the ceiling. Masar follows her gaze and then whistles.

"Shit. I thought it was a metaphor or something."

It wasn't. The square outline of the escape hatch provides an unanticipated jolt. Not least because she has no idea where it leads. Jun drops her eyes back to the machinery in the room, breathing deeply.

"All right," she says to herself. "All right."

From that moment, it's as if Masar isn't even there. It's as if she's a swimmer, dropping into a deep lake. Jun wakes the casting table with an operatic sweep of her arms, using her own neural link like a lure that catches the flowing power of the Silt Glow Cliffs. Images flood the walls in flat and three-dimensional projections, turning the room into a cacophony of lights. First order of business is to sever the connection of any peeping eyes. She visions the spybot programs as so many amorphous ghosts in archivist white, lurking in corners. They are easily disbanded. She coaxes the contents of the memory coin out into the world, spreading them out on the operating table of her own mind. Every frame of the memory is obscured, strangled within the fragile netting of the encryption. But now, here, with an arsenal of illegal casting lines available to her, Jun can see so much more. The hack job Masar made of things appears to her now even balder and more corrupt, but with tender fingers she repairs the damaged code, tucking the images back into the repaired encryption. She must start everything from scratch.

The origin of the constraining net is obvious now—a program of limitless iterations that traces back to the fourteenth century. She visions it as a thousand-yard snake coiled into an armoring network, with fangs in every scale, sunk into the flesh of its target. Try to loosen them, and the fangs will lock on, and shred. They are all of a single mind, imbued with a knowledge of past attacks and parries. Nothing

that has ever been tried before will work. When Jun limns the boundaries, tests the defenses, touches a little too close to the nerve, she can
feel the code hiss its furious warning.

She discovers her advantage: The captor does not want to destroy its
captive.

Other encryptions will detonate at the barest hint of attack, incin-
erating what they shield with no regard for the lost contents. *This*
encryption is a rattler. How else did the coin survive Masar going at it
with an ax? The encryption showed him what his sloppy efforts were
doing and gave him a chance to back away. The solution, then, is not to
attack the fanged creature. The solution is to slip between its fangs and
become part of what it protects.

Jun blinks heavily, slipping out of the fugue in which she's been
working. She's conscious again of Masar, who leans in the corner,
his shotgun propped against the wall beside him. With massive arms
crossed over his chest, he looks *bored.*

"Welcome back. You've been twitching and mumbling to yourself
for half an hour."

"I may have found a solution, but I have to go back in. It'll take
longer this time."

Masar huffs in exasperation, then meets her eyes directly, speculatively.

"You're as creepy as the archivist when you do that, you know."

In this state, Jun feels a little drunk, a little disarmed, and maybe
that's why she admits with uncharacteristic honesty, "I trained to be an
archivist, once."

He looks at her without expression, wheels clearly turning.

"Didn't care to finish?"

Jun almost smiles. Through her mind flash images of the academy
halls in Riin Kala, and the casting labs as large and holy as temples.
But that way lie thoughts too dangerous to indulge, and she doesn't
want to distract herself from the work at hand.

"Didn't have the opportunity," she says, flippant. "You can't interrupt me. I'll be going deep this time."

He makes a gesture, as if to say, *Go on, then.*

Time loses all meaning. She adjusts her ocular to white out everything but the projections before her, dims her aural link until she's swimming in a cool and silent river. It's this, her disappearance into the code, that betrays her training as an archivist. Street casters are like mechanics, navigating casting technologies as machines separate from themselves. Archivists turn casting into a poem, where encryptions become insects, or stars, or kernels of sand; where the flow of information between a casting link and the wider net creates subterranean tunnels.

Jun makes herself a spelunker, a fox, a slipstream. She becomes a microorganism, approaching the fanged scales of her snakelike adversary, and crawling between its coils. She has no knowledge of the memory's contents beyond Lucos Alanye and a sphere of jevite. So, she images the sphere. She sees it as a chunk of the Black Ocean itself, polished and liquid. It has no stars—only threads of bloody viscera, caught in the creature's fangs.

It's fragile. Volatile. She'll never get it past the lattice cage it's caught in, but she can clone it, reproduce it into the little box she's brought with her. She sees Alisiana's hands, lifting the jevite out of the box—and then reverses the sequence, lowers it back in, pristine and untouched, not even fingerprints marring the surface. It exudes heat. It pulls with gravity. She compresses it between her open palms, feeling its very molecules condense—until it is a thumb-sized memory coin, easily tucked in a single pocket.

Getting out is harder than getting in. She can't make herself small again. All the weight and girth of the pilfered coin has spread her out and stretched her wide. She begins to feel the press of the snake's coils on her skin, and the prick of its fangs along her nerves. It flexes its clever body against her, and it's in this crucial, delicate moment—that something shoves her.

"Jun!"

The voice is an echoing warble. Her body jolts again and the encryption hisses. Around her, the fangs dig deeper.

"Jun, for fuck's sake!"

Shit, this is not *the time.* If she pulls out now, the net will shred the cloned memory right from her imagined pocket. It's already going into paroxysms. It'll detonate everything it touches and toss her back into the real world with nothing but empty screens and a fried memory coin.

"Jun!" something shouts at her.

She has only one more trick. She thinks of the warhorse with its protracting, infallible shield. She makes herself into a warhorse. She swathes herself in steel a half dozen inches thick, and before the encryption can blow them all to pieces, she lobs her own destructive code into the fray, and dives free just as the bomb goes off.

Her ocular resets. Her aural link switches on with a deafening crack. Masar stands over her, shaking her with a wild look, and the projections and the casting desk have all gone dark.

A bleating alarm shrieks at them.

"Evacuate," warn the Silt Glow Cliffs. "Evacuate. Kindom raid is imminent."

CHAPTER TEN

1664
YEAR OF THE CRUX

Siinkai
Bei Continent
The Planet Teros

They find the warhorse with a Jeveni smelter. They find the innkeeper who brought it to him. They learn his niece took two people south, to Siinkai.

Esek is unusually restrained. She doesn't kill anyone, not even to make a point. She does casually mention how easy it is to die on the highways of Bei province, to veer into a gulch, to never be seen again. She ponders aloud, how good a driver is this niece?

The innkeeper tells them where their quarry went: the Silt Glow Cliffs of Siinkai.

The shuttle flight from Fezn takes twenty minutes.

Chono wants to fly directly to the tarmac of the Cliffs. Esek wants to take their targets by surprise. Every moment feels an hour long as they disembark in a tourist district and commandeer transport from the local guardsaan, using a military access route that ascends the Cliffs from the west side. It takes an extra forty-five minutes, and beneath her carefully blank mask, Chono feels antsy, hyperaware of her blood and veins and the muscles of her heart. She feels eager, and reluctant, and these are strange bedfellows, not reassured by Esek's cheerful, unconcerned humming in the seat next to hers.

When they reach the Cliffs, Esek's seven novitiates are quick and silent as snakes. They discover and disarm every hidden marksaan with an easy precision Chono remembers being drilled into her under Esek's tutelage.

The archivist, though, knows they're coming. No chance at all the strange goggled person hasn't sent up an alarm.

"Where are they?" asks Esek, without explanation.

The archivist gestures behind themself as the elevator car arrives. Esek is already moving, but she points at the archivist and tells her novitiates, "Bring them with us."

Chono's heart is beating harder now, something quickening in her blood. The old training, the old ways. The old hunt. The *nearness* of Six...if in fact Six *is* nearby, in all their murderous elegance. To see them again, after all this time...

The elevator swallows them all, bears them upward, and she immediately reaches for her sidearm, releasing the safety and charging the clip while visions of sparring with her kinschool friend superimpose themselves onto brutal training sessions with Esek. For this is what Esek taught her to do. Search and destroy. It's what she's trained her current crop to do, as well, and their weapons are already drawn. The archivist, shoved into a corner with their goggles still in place, doesn't move, but seems to watch everything. Fifth floor. Sixth floor. Seventh...

Esek tells her novitiates, "I want them alive."

Chono looks at her, surprised. A moment later the elevator doors open on the eighth floor with an eerie warble. Esek flows forward, the novitiates flanking her like dark wings. The hall is empty, the only light a tepid glow leaking from intermittent fixtures in the ceiling. The carpet smells of damp, and there's an unnerving silence and stillness about the place. For a moment, Esek seems caught in that stillness, her bad ear tilted up, as if it hears things Chono can't.

"Clear all the rooms," Chono orders, stepping in front, and in the half-second pause that follows, Esek drops her chin in the barest permissive nod.

The novitiates break away from them like missiles launched from a warship, exploding against the doors with percussive claps as they shoot the lock pads off and shoulder in. Doors crunch and splinter open at their assault, soon accompanied by a call of "No target!" before the wave of destruction moves on. Chono follows in its wake, glancing into every small room as she passes, noting everything from monitors to beds to weapons racks, but no sign of the pirate or Sunstep. Or any person for that matter. The hallway ends some twenty feet away, in a solid rock face. There are only three doors left. Maybe they had time to get to the elevator? Escape to a lower level?

"Here!" someone shouts.

Chono bolts to the next door. A novitiate stands at the entryway, gun trained on an open hatch in the ceiling, where a retractable ladder dangles, disappearing into darkness above. Chono absorbs the rest of the room, the casting table, and the shoved-aside chair. Esek steps inside after her. Her eyes slide up to the hatch, then onto Chono.

Chono's about to grab the ladder and hoist herself up when two novitiates slip ahead, shimmying into the darkness with sidelong glances at her. She feels the strangest sensation, embarrassment—a cleric *never* goes first into danger.

But she can go third.

She sprints up the ladder, aware that more novitiates are behind her. They climb a good ten feet, ending up in a dark enclave with a separate narrow stone staircase. It can only lead to the roof. Esek hasn't followed them up, apparently content to explore the room below. But Chono has no such reserve. She bursts upon the stairs, four novitiates in tow, and sprints toward the door at the top.

The minute they reach the roof, shots go off.

Chono leaps back, into the cover of the stairwell. Bullets ricochet off the doorframe, and the novitiates return fire long enough for her to get a look at the wide, flat roof. There's a shuttle pad in the center, but no shuttle. A command center stands opposite from the stairway, some thirty feet away—a perfect shield. The gunfire ceases once Chono and the novitiates move out of range.

"You are firing on the Righteous Hand!" Chono bellows. "Put down your weapons and surrender, or you will die on this roof!"

More shots answer her—two different weapons. One has the concussive blast of a shotgun. The other must be a pistol, each pull of the trigger cracking through the air. The first is a pulsar weapon, the second sounds like bullets. If they have recharging clips and extra magazines, they could hold out for a while.

"Cover me," Chono orders.

Three of the novitiates set up a barrage of fire, pinning the target down. Chono charges the roof, gets about ten feet, and takes refuge behind a scorched boulder of debris no doubt left over from the Siinkai bombings over a century ago. No sooner has she found cover than another novitiate, short and fast, sprints across the roof—but not toward her. He flies directly at the command center. Chono shouts at him to fall back, but it's no use. The other novitiates continue their covering fire, and their small compatriot gets within six feet of the targets—

A shotgun blast lifts him off his feet. He crumples onto the ground in an ungainly tangle of limbs and blood splatter.

Chono sets her teeth angrily. She looks back at the stairwell, where the remaining novitiates crouch. She gestures at them to stay down, and speaks into her comm: "*Shuttle 3*, I need cover on the roof of the Cliffs now. Two shooters."

Their shuttle, still docked twenty miles away in the tourist sector, answers her, "Yes, Sa. We're en route to you now."

In the Black Ocean, a military shuttle could reach them in under a minute. Here, hamstrung by local air traffic, it'll have to move differently. Which means she has to keep her prey trapped while they wait. She looks back toward the stairway again, where five faces stare out at her now, all of them looking antsy. No sign of Esek. The Teron sun burns oppressively down on her, heat waves rippling across the roof.

Chono shouts, "We didn't come here to kill you. But *you* have murdered a novitiate of the Hands. Turn yourself in now. It's your only possible chance."

A beat of silence, then the sound of hushed voices, arguing. A perfect distraction—or so Esek's novitiates seem to think. Before Chono can stop them, two more sprint onto the roof, tearing toward the control station—

The pistol drops one of them like an anchor. The other manages to take cover behind another chunk of rock.

Someone calls out, "You send any more of those at us, and they'll get the same!"

The voice is deep, gruff, with a muddy Braemish accent.

"Masar Hawks," Chono answers. "We know who you are. Either you're the engine behind this debacle, or your companion is. Tell us which and we can make a deal."

The shotgun answers her, spraying stone chips off the boulder, very near her head. Chono looks at the stranded novitiate some fifteen feet away, and then to the stairwell again, where three of them squat out of range. She makes an urgent gesture but can't shake the feeling they're ignoring her. Their eyes are trained on the control panel like wolves sighting a deer.

"You have nowhere to go," she calls out to Masar. "You know what we want from you. Turn it over. If you don't, my incoming shuttle will destroy you."

"Fuck off."

A different voice. Venomous. It can only be Sunstep. Chono's nerves light up—and yet, the voice isn't familiar...

She glances back at the stairwell. Remarkably, the three novitiates are staying put. They have the upper hand. If these eager little fish will stand down, they can wait it out.

"What's your plan, Sunstep?" she asks. "We have control of the entire east wing. You're cornered. Is a simple memory coin worth so much? You'll never be able to profit from it, now."

In the answering silence, Chono has the distinct impression of someone sweltering. Enraged. This will make Sunstep dangerous, but also careless. More easily brought down. It doesn't seem right; this *person* doesn't seem right. And yet she finds herself testing the theory:

"Six?" Her own voice amazes her. There's something... *hopeful* in it. "Don't you recognize me?"

More silence, but this time Chono has no sense of its meaning. She takes another chance.

"Esek Nightfoot is here. She would very much like to talk to you."

The response is immediate and ferocious. A hail of shots rains from the control console. It's deafening, and when it breaks off, it's followed by a near scream—"Then tell her to come up here! Tell her to show me her fucking face and I'll blow it off!"

The stranded novitiate jumps up, bolting for the console and opening fire. There's a shout—Chono can't tell where it comes from. The novitiate crumples. The final trio spring to their feet.

"Stand down!" Chono thunders at them.

Before anyone can react, the unmistakable roar of an incoming ship reverberates across the roof. Chono's heart lifts—it got here faster than she hoped. She turns to find it coming up from behind her, guns out, inexplicably large for a Kindom—

That is *not* her shuttle.

Chono runs for it just as the ship opens fire, obliterating the rock behind her and kicking up enough stinging debris she can't tell yet if she's hit. A trail of bullets follows her as she sprints across the roof, diving into the safety of the stairwell as the ship alights on the shuttle pad. The novitiates are forced back as well, and the firing lets up as the shuttle hatch *whooshes* open. A figure appears inside it, but they are inconsequential compared to the massive rocket rifle they're hoisting onto their shoulder.

Chono grabs at the last novitiates, hurling them down the stairs as the first explosive strikes the doorway. The door flies off. Part of the roof caves in. There's a cracking, crashing sound, and a blow to the head—

When she wakes, she's sprawled on the ground with blood in her mouth and a ringing in her ears, the air around her split into strips of sunlight and smoke. She lies still for a moment, aware of the novitiates sprawled beside her. She assesses herself, the burning in her arm, the sting above her eye and in her mouth, the throbbing in her thigh. But there's no deep pain, no evidence of a serious injury.

"Burning One?"

The voice is distant. Chono winces, levering herself up on one arm and turning toward the sound. One of the novitiates' faces swims into view, filthy with dust.

"Sa, are you all right?"

Chono blinks for several moments. How much time has passed? She rocks herself up onto her knees. Something wet drips in her eyes and she smears it away, moving to stand.

"Sa, you should sit down," the novitiate says. There's a bad gash on his forehead, streaming blood.

Chono ignores him, turning toward the half-collapsed staircase. She grips the warped railing, hauling herself up through plumes of smoke until she's back on the roof.

The ship is gone. There's no sign of her shuttle in the sky, which means it's either gone after them or hasn't arrived yet. Chono, relieved to find her comm hasn't shorted, reaches out.

"*Shuttle 3*, where are you?"

The pilot's voice answers immediately, "Sa, we are two minutes out from your position."

Then hardly any time has passed. "A ship has fled the roof of the Cliffs. Pursue it and *force it down*. I want them *alive*; do you understand?"

There's a moment of crackling silence, before the pilot answers uncertainly. "Sa, I'm having trouble locating—"

"It's a battle shuttle," Chono interrupts. "It's big enough to appear on your scans."

"Sa, I'm scanning within a thirty-mile radius. There's nothing but commercial shuttles and taxi-pods—"

"It can't have gotten out of range yet. Find it!"

"Sa, my scans are completely clear."

The Hood program, of course.

For an irrational moment, Chono wants to argue, but then she sees the bodies on the roof. Into her comm she says, "Widen your search. Tell me when you've found something."

She breaks the cast and surveys the crumpled forms of the novitiates. Behind the control console, there's a spray of dark blood. Someone was hit, but there's no body. She looks down at her own thigh, where the pant leg is torn and a laceration bleeds sluggishly. In irritation she wipes more blood out of her eyes.

She returns inside with cautious, painful steps. The surviving novitiates appear all right, though one of them has a piece of something sticking out of her shoulder joint and she's gasping with pain. The one with the gashed forehead is helping her. Chono moves past all three and grips the ladder, not quite steadily. She limps down using one leg, grunting when she hits the ground.

She might as well have entered another world. Esek is sitting at the casting table, her chief novitiate standing behind her like a perched bird of prey. Together, they are staring at the archivist in the corner. All three are silent. If they know a rocket went off above them, they show no awareness of it. Esek looks up at her when she appears, surveying her with some interest.

"You look awful."

Chono doesn't mince words. "Both Masar Hawks and Sunstep escaped on an enemy ship, but one of them is injured. They have an accomplice, it seems. Our shuttle is having trouble locating the ship on scans. Most likely the ship is Hooded."

Esek clucks her tongue. "That's unfortunate."

Her unconcern is jarring. Chono says, "Three novitiates are dead. The rest are injured."

Esek frowns thoughtfully. She turns her head enough to give her chief novitiate a look, and he immediately vanishes up the ladder. Chono watches him until he's out of sight, then looks at Esek again. Esek once gave her a black eye for losing track of a pickpocket in the streets of Togol. Yet she looks relatively unaffected by their defeat, her attention fixed again on the statue-like archivist.

"This is Phinea Runback." Esek casts a simple ID record onto the dark wall. "They were a highly regarded tutor at the Riin Kala Academy of Archivists. And now look at them. The concierge of a caster playpen."

Despite the scorn in her words, Esek is smiling in a way that suggests admiration. The records on the wall describe a post-academy career riddled with casting heists, gambling debts, and work colony stints all over the Treble. By rights, Phinea Runback isn't an archivist at all anymore—just a street caster. Chono looks at them again, observing their sallow skin and the distinctly malnourished angles of their face.

She gestures at the goggles. "Take those off."

There's a pause, as if the archivist might be asleep behind their visual shield. Then, slowly, they lift the goggles up to rest on top of their head, like bizarre antennae. The deep grooves left behind are red and inflamed and if she looked more closely, Chono is sure she'd see scars. But their expression is perfectly serene, and vaguely curious.

Chono says, "You knew who we were looking for when we arrived. A caster called Sunstep."

Phinea Runback lifts one shoulder. "I know many casters, nah? Many names, many faces, many invisible people. You can see them, I can't. I can see them, you can't. Natural, nah, to know so many people?"

"I'm not asking about the others. I'm asking about Sunstep. She may also use the alias Junian Graylore. Has she been here before? Do you know her?"

The archivist looks offended, demanding, "Why shouldn't she come here? Fine place, this; best kind. Very useful, when you need it."

Esek chuckles. She puts her feet up on the casting table and folds her hands in her lap, eyes narrowed.

"Oh-ho," she says. "This is going to be bloody before it's over, isn't it, Sa?"

The archivist blanches, not as though they're afraid, but as though they find Esek's whole person rather unpleasant to look at.

"I am not bloody, am I? I am only answering questions."

At that moment, the ladder into the ceiling rattles, and the chief novitiate comes back down. Once on the ground, he faces Esek, hands clasped behind his back.

"Sonye, Navi, and Cors are dead. Fleetrock needs surgery on her shoulder, and Northcall has a concussion. Oxing is fine."

"Hmm." Esek gestures expansively at Chono. "What about your cleric, Rekiav? You have not considered her injuries, in your tally. What if she needs surgery, too?"

Rekiav's eyes slide toward Chono, giving her a cursory review. "Cleric Chono appears in no danger to me, Sa. I am more concerned about the targets who escaped her."

There is no mistaking his accusation, and at first Chono is too surprised by the brazenness of the insult to mind the insult itself. Brash young novitiates wanting to puff up their chests for their mentors—it's not unusual. And Esek always did inspire showmanship.

Ignoring him, she looks at Esek.

"Our best hope is to apprehend them before they can get off world. We should ground all flights to and from the planet."

Rekiav interjects, "The planetary border is in chaos with ships waiting on jump gate access. We can't ground them all. We have lost our advantage."

Chono looks at him again, aware he's staring at her with the hackles-raised intensity of a wolf preparing to fight. He's been Esek's chief novitiate for two years—a role Chono herself once held. He is tall and slimly muscular, tawny and blue-eyed and dark-haired: a paragon of Ma'kessn beauty standards. And Chono distrusts beauty.

She tells Esek, "They won't be able to cross through the radiation shields without taking the Hood off. We can alert the border hawks to fan out and search for a battle shuttle."

Esek shrugs. "So, do it."

"And recruit any local guardsaan pilots to assist."

"Esek Nightfoot does not need the help of gambler-worshipping *Terons*," says Rekiav. "We novitiates will track them down."

Chono ignores this dig at her planetary heritage, answering instead, "You have lost five novitiates to injury and death."

Esek adds, "You're forgetting yourself. That makes six."

"My kin are up to the challenge," Rekiav says.

Chono is tired of this.

"Your kin are in the staircase, licking their wounds. Go supervise their removal to the hospital. And extend my orders to the local guardsaan and warcrows."

To her amazement, he doesn't move. He goes on staring at her, a glitter of defiance in his eyes. It's so blatant, Chono thinks she may have misunderstood his intention at first. But then Esek laughs, and Chono remembers—she's among would-be cloaksaan, now. And has to treat them as such. A split second later, she has him by the throat, shoving his whole body up against the nearest wall.

"Now you've done it," Esek hums.

Chono's voice is perfectly calm. She doesn't even sound angry, though she is very angry. Angry that Esek's arrogant novitiate is making her do this. "If you think you would have been more successful on the roof, then maybe next time you'll instruct your kin not to throw themselves needlessly to their own deaths. Maybe you won't hide back here with your master like a bootlicking coward. You do not have to like me, Sa, nor respect me, but you *do* have to obey me. And if you won't, I will make you do it in the only language you apparently understand."

At least he has the sense not to fight back. She knows later, he'll tell himself he could have easily defeated her. But Chono is taller. She has twenty pounds of muscle on him. She pulls him away from the wall and shoves him into the ladder. He's already massaging his throat. It'll be bruised, in days to come—much like his ego. There's murder in his eyes and she wonders if he's about to do something unbelievably rash.

Esek says, "You're beaten, Rekiav. Take the loss with dignity and do as you're told."

This, at last, cuts his sails. He retreats up the ladder, sullen.

"That's the way," Esek tells Chono when he's gone. "You know you've got to make them afraid of you. Don't you discipline your own novitiates?"

Chono looks at her flatly. She is aware of Phinea Runback watching them, and this is not the time to dispute how they manage their novitiates. She faces the archivist directly.

"You warned them we were coming."

They shrug again, indifferent. "I am a housekeeper. I serve the ones in the house. It is right, nah?"

"You are a citizen of the Treble and beholden to the laws of the Kindom. We have the right to arrest you for what you've done. Whose housekeeper will you be, then?"

"Arrest me, and what? Then you have empty pockets, nah? Sunstep is a good guest, a clean guest, they cleaned up. No footprints even, left behind. No trace at all, and she is invisible. I cannot even see her, not with my goggles, not with my eyes. She is gone. You have nothing now. Arrest me, sure, please. Then, both our pockets are empty."

They are so unconcernedly rational, even in their irrational chatter, and Chono half admires such tranquility in the face of what will surely be a ten-year sentence, at least.

Esek grins, feet still up on the table. She opens her coat enough to reveal the jeweled handle of the bloodletter at her waist. Phinea Runback looks at the weapon, not with fear, but intrigue. Perhaps they are wondering why a cleric has a cloaksaan weapon. Perhaps they are merely lusting after the wealth of it.

"We are outmatched, I think," Esek says.

Chono half expects Esek to sail the blade right into the archivist's throat. Instead, she sighs. Takes her feet off the desk and stands, her coat settling gracefully closed over the knife. She steps up to the archivist, so they are face-to-face. Chono thinks of Captain Foxer, lunging with his last breath for a kill that would have made all his losses worth it. Archivists don't carry weapons. But Phinea Runback is not a real archivist anymore.

"Now," Esek says to them. "My kin cleric is right. We can arrest you, and you'll be squirreled away in some rotten work colony for the rest of your life. No goggles for you. No casting. No archivism, ever again. And then, yes. All our pockets will be empty. But do you know...I *like* the Silt Glow Cliffs. I like imagining disgraced archivists who have found second lives in these iniquitous places. So, if it's all the same to you, Learner and Light, I'd sooner fill your pockets than empty them."

Esek lifts her hand, and a new image casts upon the wall. It depicts a sum of marks, and a string of transfer credentials between the Kindom Bank and the Cliffs. It is a *surprisingly* high sum. Usually, Esek tries torture first. The archivist doesn't look directly at the casted image, but there's no doubt they see the numbers.

Esek continues, "I respect Sunstep enough to believe she left no trace of what she was doing here—that not even you could figure out what it was. But I don't need to know what she was doing. I need to know how to find her. Clearly you've worked with her before?"

A long, long pause. The archivist nods.

"How many aliases does she have?" asks Esek casually.

A mocking hum. "This is what you want in your pockets? Aliases? Ghost names? Vapor in the air—come and gone and useless, nah? I can give you vapor. Or I can give you a rock in the fist."

"Give me the rock, then," Esek says.

The archivist makes a popping sound with their lips, says, "I have a big rock. I have her *name*."

Esek's eyebrows lift in unconcealed excitement. She steps subtly closer, hungry.

"What is her name?"

Another grin, those teeth like shale crumbling off a roof.

"Ironway."

Chono's body locks with surprise. Esek, too, goes still.

This is a name they both know.

CHAPTER ELEVEN

1650

YEAR OF THE KINDLING

K-5 Station
Orbiting Kator

As far as Alisiana Nightfoot was concerned, all Esek's clerical duties now came second to the mission of finding Six. Esek didn't mind this, but such a mission required time and resources and information. In her current locale, the only information Esek had was that at some point the traitor Lucos Alanye had wandered his way into this little metalworking shop. What he'd wanted, what he'd bought, were a mystery to her, one of those details that Alisiana was keeping close. Yet somehow decades later Alanye's descendants had led Esek here, to this cluttered space with its glass cabinets full of trinkets and its faded carpet and its overstuffed ottoman—and its proprietors cowering before her.

Esek regarded the Ironway family with the curious remove of a bird-watcher. What *was* their relationship to Lucos Alanye? But more importantly, what was their relationship to Six?

Hosek Ironway, the matriarch of the family, stood in the center of the shop, the others gathered behind her. Esek's chief novitiate confirmed with a nod that it was all of them—all four generations, including the half-blind, arthritic Ricari Ironway. He was sitting on the ottoman. The youngest Ironway generation, three small children, sat around him. She gave them a long look, noticing how Hosek followed her gaze.

Esek tilted her head inquiringly. "What is it, Sa Ironway? You seem anxious."

Hosek swallowed. She was a short, squat woman, with muscular forearms and delicate hands, befitting her trade. She still wore her shop apron, smeared with the shavings of metalwork, some of which she'd accidentally rubbed on her cheek. The gray-silver smudge glittered like a body mod.

She said, "No, Burning One. We are honored by your presence."

"Are you? I had heard all your family were apostate."

Tension crackled across the shop like an electric charge. Even station dwellers were expected to genuflect for *some* god. Esek thought of the old riddle, and considered asking it—*Who is the Sixth God?*—but she was more interested in the reactions of the various family members, and what those reactions might tell her. Directly behind Hosek was another older woman, probably Hosek's wife. She looked pale and frightened. Then there were two men and a woman that must be Hosek's children, their faces ranging from stoic to nervous to angry. Around Ricari (himself notably opaque) the grandchildren were wide-eyed and silent. Novitiates circled them all.

Hosek said, "We are devoted to the Godfire and the Six Gods, Burning One. And to Makala, of course, fecund and—"

"—lovely, yes," interrupted Esek in a bored drawl. She looked around at the shop. "And what better place to celebrate that god than this sterile tomb of a station?"

Wisely, Hosek said nothing, but the son standing behind her had a face that gave all his feelings away. Esek zeroed in on him, curling her lip in pleasure. This one would misstep; she could feel the fury bubbling under his skin.

Hosek, no doubt sensing disaster, tried to divert Esek's attention.

"Burning One, your novitiates tell me you have concerns about the political alliances of my family. I don't know who has been lying about us, but we are Ma'kessn in origin, and the Nightfoots—"

"I'm not here as a Nightfoot," lied Esek. "I'm here as a Hand of the Kindom. We believe you are harboring a descendant of Lucos Alanye."

Suddenly Hosek was ashen. Her family, even the angry one, stood frozen behind her.

"Who would have said that about us?" asked Hosek, seeming amazed.

Esek smiled. "Perhaps I have received godly inspiration?"

No one said anything. Esek looked at her chief novitiate, nodding permission. He stepped up to Hosek and slammed his fist into her gut. She crumpled with a gagging sound. Her family cried out. Some moved to defend her and found themselves staring into the mouths of Kindom rifles. The small children were openly wailing now, and Esek spared a glance for them, watching old Ricari bury their faces against himself, murmuring comfort in their ears. Then she stepped forward, dropping into a squat beside Hosek, who was collapsed onto her knees and bent over, still choking.

"Breathe," Esek advised her. "Take deep breaths. That's right. In. Out. It will pass. Now, you must admit I'm being very reasonable. Usually when people lie to my face, I kill them. Or kill someone they love, at least. You have a lot of loved ones in this room, yes? How about, for every truth you tell me, I spare one of them. Doesn't that sound generous to you?"

"Burning One," Hosek gasped. "*Please.* I'll tell you whatever you want to know. My family has been loyal to the Kindom for generations. We would never—"

"Careful," Esek interrupted. "For every lie you tell, I'll take one of them from you."

"I don't want to lie to you, Sa, I swear. Ask me anything."

"Lucos Alanye had a son who lived on this station. Yes?"

Hosek nodded urgently. "Yes. Yes. But he left, decades ago. He took his daughter and granddaughters with him."

"All those are dead," said Esek. "I killed the granddaughters two months ago, on the To'sos Isles on Braemin. They were about the same age as your children."

Hosek breathed hard and stared at the ground. But Esek didn't have to look at her face or look around at the other faces in the room to see the impact of her words.

"They told me about you, about your family. You were friends with them, weren't you? Don't lie. I will kill the youngest one if you lie."

"She doesn't know anything about it!"

Esek looked up at the outcry. It was the angry son, grown desperate.

"Please, she never had anything to do with them!"

"Shut up, Coz!" the other man hissed.

Esek rose from her crouch. "Oh, no, Coz. Don't shut up. Not as you hope to live."

"My mother never had anything to do with the Alanyes. It was us." He gestured at himself and his siblings. "We were friends with his granddaughters. But we were just kids! We didn't know who they were. They changed their names. It was years after they left the station before anybody realized they were Alanyes. I swear we haven't spoken to them since! I—" His voice broke. "I didn't even know they were dead."

Esek approached the young man, taking him in from head to foot. He was small, but muscular. He was handsome. He had passion and courage in his eyes. She drew her gun and shot him in the head.

The shop filled with screams. Hosek's wife fainted. Their other son sprang to his brother, gathering the body up against him. The blood was everywhere. Hosek had sat up and was staring between Esek and her dead son, stunned and spattered red. She made a choked sound of denial.

"He—he obeyed you! He told you what he knew! He—"

"He lied," said Esek plainly, ignoring the cries around her, the sobbing of the small children and the man cradling his brother. "He said he hadn't spoken to the Alanyes since childhood, but they told me themselves how they kept in touch with him, for years. He lied. He knew. You all knew."

"But—"

"There is another Alanye descendant." Esek raised her voice above the sounds in the shop. "I don't know its name, or even what it looks like. I do know it visited its cousins on Braemin six months ago. I know the cousins gave it the names of family friends who might help it. A pious station family, with Ma'kessn origins, no less. Ironway." She tutted reproachfully. "Imagine my surprise, that such a family would harbor it. You must know that is forbidden, by the terms of Alanye's sentencing."

Hosek trembled all over. She stared up at Esek with an arresting combination of shock, horror, and utter bafflement. It was the bafflement that intrigued Esek. It looked so...genuine.

Then a new voice broke the silence. "My grandson told you the truth. Hosek does not know anything about the Alanyes."

Esek turned, watching as Ricari Ironway got slowly to his feet. The old man was gray, yet Esek detected no fear in him as he stepped forward. Two of her novitiates made to block him, but she waved them off, meeting the eldest Ironway halfway. When they were face-to-face, she observed the rheumy eyes, pale with cataracts. Ricari Ironway, unlike his descendants, was tall, and the arthritis that had clearly gnarled his hands had not, somehow, bent his back. He looked proud, standing before her, and while Esek knew her novitiates would gladly break his legs to humble him, she gave no command.

"Ricari." She drew the name out in a purr. "I researched you. Bit of an agitator in your youth, weren't you? But you also made all the jewelry for Alisiana Nightfoot's wedding."

"She wanted only metalwork. No jewels."

"An independent spirit." Esek smiled. "And not your only famous client. I'm told Lucos Alanye himself visited you once. What did he want?"

"He wanted to know how Caskori Nightfoot bought a jevite sphere from my mother."

Esek fell silent, amazed. *Caskori?* Alisiana's beloved uncle? What did *he* have to do with the mission on Jeve? Apparently a great deal—and now Esek understood one of the secrets Alisiana was trying to keep.

Esek asked, "Were you able to answer that question?"

"My mother had the sphere from a Jeveni, but she was a gambler. She sold it to Caskori so she could pay her debts. She was wrong to sell it. But she never knew its origins on Jeve. When Lucos Alanye came to ask her about it, she had no help for him."

"And you?" asked Esek. "Did *you* help him, Ricari?"

"I told him who gave her the jevite. That was the only information I had. If I could have helped him more, I wouldn't have. He had something bad in him. Ambition, but also, rot."

Esek snickered. "How poetic. I quite like a bit of rot, personally. But if you disliked him so much, why have you helped his progeny?" Esek pressed him. "That's what you're trying to tell me, isn't it? That your dear daughter knows nothing about the Alanyes, but *you* do? This latest Alanye, this young one—what do you know?"

This time Ricari's silence was confirmation. She stepped closer, whispering to him. "Tell me its name. Tell me its gender. Tell me if it's still on the station. I'll spare the rest of your family if you do."

To her amazement, Ricari chuckled. It was grim, and unafraid. "You don't intend to spare us. I know how it was, for the Alanye girls on Braemin. How you gathered them and their children up in one place, questioned them, and slaughtered them afterward."

Esek shrugged. "They were Alanyes. The Alanye name must not survive. *You* are an Ironway. Perhaps your family can do better. But only if you tell me where I can find who I'm looking for."

"The Alanyes had no friends to defend them on Braemin," said Ricari. "That is not the case, for my family. Our ghosts will come after you."

Esek's brows shot to her hairline. "You *are* reckless. I think I'll have to kill all the children, to teach you manners."

A cry went up from every corner. Only Ricari didn't make a sound, half-blind eyes fixed upon her. Esek looked toward the ottoman where the children still cowered, wondering where to start. But then her gaze slipped past them, landing on the workshop door at the back of the room. The workshop that she knew her novitiates had cleared before she came in. Yet there, half in shadow, stood a figure.

Time stopped. Esek couldn't make out the figure's face. But she knew. In that moment, she knew, and the knowledge went through her like a lightning strike, like the gods themselves had spoken.

The figure darted out of sight. And Esek followed.

"Burning One—" her chief novitiate said, startled.

"Keep them here. Kill anyone that moves!"

She burst into the workshop. Benches and tools were everywhere, the rough materials of the Ironway trade, crates and chairs and other detritus, but no sign of Six. She spun in a circle, looking around, desperate, and that's when she saw it: the curtain. It parted for her with a snap of fabric, spilling her into one of the long, narrow hallways that wended their way through the station. There, not thirty feet ahead of her, was the figure from the shop. She sprinted after it. She watched it run, memorizing its stride, its shaven head, its shape. She memorized its clothes—simple trousers and a sleeveless red shirt. Red. Perfect. Esek threw off her cumbersome coat, threw aside two stationers who got in her way, leapt over an overturned crate, certain its owner had deliberately tried to slow her down.

The hallway curved. For a moment she lost sight of Six, her heart stuttering. Then she saw it again, darting left, down a new hallway. Behind her, Esek heard gunfire, and wondered if the Ironways had tried to escape. She didn't care about that now. She turned left.

It was not a new hallway, after all, but an open square full of people. Esek cursed, but the space was not so dense that she couldn't spot her quarry. That red shirt was like a homing beacon. Six had not looked back once. She still hadn't seen its face, something she craved now with feral hunger. She watched Six flee the square through an open archway, and when she reached it, there were stairs, plummeting down into a lower level of the station.

Six had already reached the bottom, turning left again. But when Esek, too, reached the landing, she saw two paths, not one. They both branched left, but ran parallel to each other, sheathed in darkness. She heard a faint echo, and took the first hallway at a run.

Instantly, a door snapped shut behind her. She skidded to a halt, looking back at where the entrance had been. She looked forward, realizing with a plummet in her gut that this was not a hallway at all, but a long room. One wall, the wall that aligned with the second entryway, began to glow. It turned translucent—became a kind of screen. Esek knew where she was now: It was an interrogation box. She sucked her teeth, cursed, and spat onto the ground. Anyone on the outside would be able to see into the box, to see *her*—but all she would see were phantom shapes. A moment later, the figure appeared. Indistinct but unmistakable.

Neither of them moved. They watched each other through the wall. It had not been running from her, she realized, but leading her away. That red shirt. It had lured her into this trap, and though she had none of her novitiates with her, it might have a dozen friends nearby. Yet she wasn't afraid. She felt...elation.

"Well done," she said. The figure behind the wall did not answer, simply stared through at her. They were of a similar height. It was slender but not skinny. She imagined it was leanly muscular, like her. She tried to imagine its face but couldn't think how to age the child she'd met into what must be a youth of eighteen.

"What a long time it's been since we've seen each other," said Esek. "I'll admit, when I promised to forget you, I didn't anticipate you making yourself so memorable. Alisiana intercepted your little note. She seems to consider you a serious threat. You, and whatever secrets the Alanyes hold. She won't tell me what they are, but I've discovered this and that..."

The obvious invitation hung in the air, unanswered and unacknowledged. Was it a statue, on the other side of the partition? No, she could sense its life, its beating heart, its blood.

"I've had to go searching for you. I started at the Principes school—but all your records are lost. Strangest thing. No one even knows for sure where you were born. Some say Teros. Some say Kator. The secretary that sponsored you at school is dead. Indeed, anybody who might know of your past is dead, or at least missing. Granted, I killed some of them, but I didn't expect you to *erase* yourself. An...impressive strategy."

The figure still watched her, motionless. She imagined its eyes were locked on hers. She imagined a thread of tension, drawing tighter and tighter, that must eventually snap.

"I *did* find the pirate ship you escaped on. I even found the weapons merchant you worked for on North Avo. None of it was particularly useful. Maybe if you'd had the sense to stay away from your cousins, you'd still be in the wind. Not that you weren't careful. Before I killed them, they told me you wouldn't even give them a name. I've been calling you Six." She paused. "Did you ever take a real name?"

This time there was a change, a shift that made her draw her breath in anticipation. When it spoke, its voice was low and steady and delicious. "Six is fine."

She chuckled, as much from the delight of hearing it speak as from what it said.

"Did you ever pick a gender?"

It shifted again. "'They' will do."

The Katish pronoun. The one Chono had used for them, years ago, when she told Esek that Six had fled the kinschool.

"Tell me something then, Six. Out of curiosity, was the old man lying? Did Hosek know you were back?"

Six paused so long, Esek wondered if they had decided to play statue again. Finally, they said, "He was honest. My cousins told me if I was ever on K-5 station, Ricari Ironway would help me. For the love he bore their grandfather, Lucos Alanye's son. I came here to learn more. I was injured, and Coz was a doctor. He helped me, too. They did not involve Hosek, or anyone else."

She absorbed this, curious about Six's injury. What had happened? Were they injured, still? How hungry she felt, in that moment, to see the wound, the torn flesh, the bruising, and the blood.

"I did not think you would find my cousins."

Esek shrugged. "It was easy."

"It took you a year."

Her nostrils flared, but she didn't answer right away. Now that she had heard them say a few sentences, she was struck by the oddness of their voice. There was a...lilt to it. Something melodic. They spoke slowly. The consonants all dropped with a deliberate *plink*, like small stones into still water. Esek had traveled the entire Treble, and even beyond. She had heard many strange accents. Was this one a combination of all the places Six had lived? Or was it an affectation?

She said, "You've had a lead on me for some time, I grant you. But now you've brought disaster on your kin, and the Ironways—not to mention the four other families your cousins told you about. I've only visited the Ironways so far, but you must realize I'll have to obliterate the others, too. When you sent that note, when you decided to provoke me—did you understand the cost? Was it worth getting my attention?"

Six was silent for a moment.

"Where is Chono?" they asked.

At first Esek wondered how Six could possibly know that name. Even though they had known each other at the Principes school, Chono had been called Four then. But of course, the answer was perfectly simple: Six had been studying Esek, and everyone around her. It was enough to spark a little jealousy in her heart.

Six waited, silent, patient.

"I left her with my warkite," she said at last.

"From what I know, she is your best fighter. And very loyal. Why leave her behind?"

Esek stepped up to the wall. Six drifted a few steps. She followed them. They shadowed each other, pacing back and forth on either side. Esek wrestled with herself, so many excuses coming to mind. In the end, she found herself telling the truth.

"Chono wouldn't have liked this."

Six stopped. This time their strange, lilting voice held curiosity. "You shielded her."

Esek shrugged. "Chono is devout. She wants to be a cleric, and I haven't trained a cleric before. I can't very well break her spirit, can I?"

"Then you think she is weak," said Six. Esek did not think this, exactly—"sensitive" was the better word. "I remember her devotions. Does she still read prayers beautifully?"

"She does. It's annoying."

A low chuckle. "What a strange contrast she must be, to you."

"You don't think I'm devout, little fish? I am a cleric of the Godfire."

"You are devoted to Alisiana," Six corrected her. "You do not care about any of the rest of them. And your devotion to Alisiana is self-interested. You hope to take her place."

Esek paused. No one had ever dared suggest this to her. To hear it tossed before her, so casually, felt like the sort of invasion she was used to visiting on others. It was a strange sensation. Brightly she said, "What nonsense! I'm not in the female line."

"The female line is weak. Alisiana is the only strong one left. And she is old. Some say the family will not survive her death."

"And this concerns you, how?"

The shape on the other side of the wall shrugged. "Perhaps I would also like to see you replace her."

Esek felt a frisson of . . . something. Was it unease, or amazement?

"Why would *you* want that?"

A dramatic pause. Then—

"If I am to be your novitiate, how much better to serve the matriarch of a great family."

Esek hesitated in surprise, and then blurted a laugh. "You're telling me you still dream of being my novitiate?" When they didn't respond, her voice grew colder. "You *threatened* the head of my house. You're clearly seeking information that would hurt the Nightfoots. The families your cousins told you about—they aren't just people willing to shelter you. They're people who knew Lucos Alanye. Who know something about what happened when he was on Jeve. The Braemish ship you stowed away on? I know its captain was the jevite smuggler who got Alanye onto Jeve in the first place. That centenarian weapons merchant who you worked for on Kator? She was one of Alanye's lieutenants."

Six's shape nodded. "Yes. And where were they, when you found them?"

She paused, surprised, before admitting, "In the ground."

"Yes." The figure nodded again, like mockery. "I put them in the ground. It has been sixty-one years since the Jeveni Genocide. There are few people left who worked for Alanye. And I have put them in the ground."

Nonplussed, Esek's voice turned soft and skeptical. "Are you telling me you've been unearthing Lucos Alanye's secrets so you can...*protect* the Nightfoots?"

"I have done it to impress you. Is that not what you charged me to do?"

Esek could not remember the last time someone had surprised her like this. "You left your cousins alive. You left the Ironways alive. Does that mean they don't know anything...impressive?"

Six didn't respond. Esek licked her lips and spoke with a new urgency. "Your note shows Alisiana once favored Lucos Alanye. And I know now that he came here trying to find the source of a jevite sphere belonging to Caskori Nightfoot. What does that mean? Did Alisiana sponsor Alanye's mission? Did she *want* him to go to Jeve?"

Still silence. Esek raised her voice. "Tell me and I will make you my novitiate now. I'll hide your true identity from my aunt. I'll replace my chief novitiate with you."

In the answering pause, Esek hoped they were considering her offer. But their answer was strange. "I am not done impressing you yet, Burning One. But you *will* need a new chief novitiate. Chono, I think, will make the best choice."

Furious that they could deny her, she snapped, "What the fuck are you talking about?"

"Your current chief is dead. All the novitiates you brought into the Ironway shop are dead. My hired hands killed them as soon as I led you away."

Esek held perfectly still. Her mind raced. She remembered the sounds of gunfire. No, it couldn't be. No one would be so foolish as to attack a contingent of the Hand. And she had *five* novitiates in that room. They couldn't possibly have been routed by a gang of station rats.

"You will see for yourself in a few minutes," said Six. "I left the crew of your warkite alive. I wouldn't want you to be stranded."

Heat swept through Esek's body, more potent than the Godfire itself.

"*This* is how you impress me?" she hissed.

Six cocked their head to one side. "Of course. You murdered my cousins, though they were harmless. This is my response. Righteousness. Cleverness. Brutality."

Esek slammed her open palms on the translucent surface that divided them. She bared her teeth and snarled, "When I find you—"

"You are only angry because I have embarrassed you," Six interrupted, voice still lilting, like a ship rocked on gentle waters. "You did not love those novitiates. You do not love anything. You will forgive me."

"You took what is *mine*! You've stolen from me! I will *never* forgive that!"

"And how much did you steal from me?" Six asked.

Esek stepped back from the wall and sneered. "Good luck getting off this station. I'll shut down the docks. I'll have a battalion of cloaksaan here in two hours. All the Ironways' lives are forfeit now, and those other families, too."

Six cocked their head again. And then, to her furious amazement, they bowed.

"Please, Sa. Do your best. After all, you need to impress me, too."

Esek's mouth dropped open. But before she could think of a response, the lights in the ceiling and the wall ebbed, like a guttering candle. On impulse, she reached for her handgun, expecting an attack. But no. No attack. Instead, the lights blazed bright again. The door that had locked after her *snicked* open. And the wall, opaque once more, must mean Six had gone.

By the time she made it back to the Ironway shop, a troop of station patrolsaan had appeared, as well as the three novitiates she had left on her ship. Chono was there, and she stood amid the carnage with an expression as close to shock as Esek had seen her wear since the beginning. There were five dead novitiates on the shop floor, and two more Ironways: the second son, and Ricari. He had a bullet through the throat, and his cloudy eyes drifted to the side. Sometimes the dead wore expressions of disbelief or terror, but he did not, dignified even now.

With murder in her heart she shouted, "No one leaves this station! Find me every Ironway in the Treble. Distant relatives. Children gone at school. I want all of them."

"Yes, Sa," the novitiates answered, and broke apart to begin their work. Only Chono remained, watching Esek with those large gray eyes. All Esek could think was of her affiliation to Six, and it made her furious.

"What?!" she barked.

In the past, that tone had made Chono scatter. But her two years of training had already wrought a change in her, and now she absorbed the blunt force of Esek's anger composedly. She explained, "I can't leave the novitiates who have fallen, Sa. I have to wait vigil with them until the altarsaan arrive."

Of course. More religious pretensions. Esek took an aggressive step toward her, intending—she wasn't sure what. Maybe Six cared about Chono. Maybe if she killed Chono, it would hurt Six. But before she could follow this impulse, something crunched under her foot. She looked down. It was the sign that had hung over the shop, shot down in the carnage. The family glyph, a circle of gold with a footprint in the middle of it, had one of its toes shot off. This struck Esek as bizarrely funny, though she didn't laugh. Instead, she looked up at Chono again, and found her novitiate gazing at her with an expression of understanding that Esek had not anticipated.

"Was it Six?" Chono asked, seeming older than eighteen.

Esek locked her jaw, but couldn't contain it.

"Yes," she growled. "It was Six."

One day Capamame went down onto the First Planet so he could bathe in her rivers and fish in her seas. While he was fishing, Makala came down to the water, accompanied by some other gods. Ignoring the patient work of their little brother, they stripped the sea of fish, and gorged on their catch, and left the carcasses behind to stain the waves red. After they had gone away laughing, Capamame lay in wait. Soon, attracted by the blood, a great shark as big as an island came to feed. With powerful arms, Capamame took the shark into his net, and carried it back to Sajeven. And they feasted together for many nights, for Capamame, though ever so gentle, is also shrewd.

The Water Song, 5:5–9. Godtexts, pre-Treble

CHAPTER TWELVE

1664

YEAR OF THE CRUX

The Gunner
Orbiting Silt

Jun dreams of Great Gra, showing her how to clean the Som's Edge pistol. Everything is muscle memory for him, weathered hands moving instinctively—the hands of a lifelong artisan. His eyes, once the color of dark wheat, have turned milky with cataracts, but his mind is a razor.

"You're going to have to hide," he says.

She shakes her head no, feels pinpricks of terror on her skin. "No. I don't want to."

But he hands her the gun, all its clean lines gleaming. It's heavy in her hand, and her hand is heavy—like the rest of her, and she wakes in a fugue of memory.

A bed. Familiar, lumpy mattress. Quilted blanket caught around her waist. A single shelf against the wall, stacked with volumes of the peculiar Katish poetry Liis likes. The metal bulkhead above her has small embedded lights like stars, dimmed to a distant glow, as known to her as Liis's black cap, or the shop on K-5. *Home.*

She tries to sit up and all those warm feelings short out. Pain lances through her torso. She gasps, chokes, cursing all six of the gods and the Godfire twice. *Fuck*, her shoulder hurts. It's swathed in bandages and throbbing like a heartbeat. Her head is throbbing, too, a pain distinctly chemical, meaning Liis must have knocked her out with something. That tracks. The last thing she remembers is trying to fly *The Gunner* while blood ran down her arm, and Liis growling at her to "Lie down, damnit!" but she was too frantic with adrenaline to listen. Next thing, she'd blacked out. Liis always was the sort to carry sedatives on her.

Jun cranes her neck to look at her shoulder, though even that much movement sends frissons of icy fire through her nerves. The bandages are fresh and clean. She must have been lying here for hours. That means a lot of things, but most of all, they're not dead. Or caught, though the woman hunting them could be a hairsbreadth away for all she knows.

The woman hunting them.

Jun thinks of the tall, broad-shouldered cleric who led the attack on the roof. It's easy enough to access her ocular records, pinpoint a still frame, and then feed it through the public hubs. A moment later she's got an ID. Cleric Chono, the record states, no family name. Jun flits through the woman's biography until she finds the important piece: novitiate to Esek Nightfoot, 1648–1653.

When this Cleric Chono called her Six, Jun thought she must have been talking to Masar, but he showed no recognition. And then she spoke that other name, Esek's name, tossed down like a gauntlet.

Thinking of her now gives Jun the determination to throw her legs over the bedside and stand.

It goes poorly at first. She jostles her arm and nearly faints. There's a good thirty seconds of standing still and *willing* herself to remain conscious, before she finally makes it to the tiny bathroom in the corner. Sitting down to pee is harder than she expects. Splashing water on her face is harder still. She ignores the trembling in her fingers and the grayish face staring at her in the mirror, and weaves unsteadily back into the bedroom. Cleric Chono's hologram is still hanging where she left it, record pocked with commendations and, oddly, lacking any scandals but one. Jun peers curiously at a headline from a conspiracy website:

CLERIC MURDERS CLERIC ON QUIETUS. KINDOM HUSHES IT UP.

There's something vague about a sex crime, and the Khen family. Claims that Cleric Chono must have learned her murderous impulses from Esek Nightfoot. Jun stares at the cleric's solemn, unremarkable face, Teron in structure; fine inky black hair worn short; a squareness to her head and shoulders; eyes the color of station metal, with no overt glimmer of evil. Jun has always measured Hands by how many *civilians* they murder. Let them kill each other all they want. But there's no evidence in the logs that Chono has used her position to terrorize, even as Esek's novitiate.

So why is she helping Esek now?

Jun flicks the records away, still nauseated and unsteady. She notices for the first time the pneumatic injector on the bedside table, no doubt loaded with her next dose of tissue regenerator. She distinctly recalls seeing a chunk of her shoulder blown off when one of Esek's novitiates shot her on the roof. It'll take a minute to grow back. No wonder she's in so much pain. But that injector will have a sedative in it, and probably knock her out again, for hours. She turns away, limping toward the door to the bridge.

It's less than five feet but feels like a mile, and when she gets there, she has to muscle the door open with her good side. Except she doesn't seem to have a good side right now, and when the door gives, she falls forward.

Instantly, another body is there, slinging an arm around her.

"Gods, what are you doing?" Liis demands, pulling her out of the doorway. For a moment they're close to each other, Jun's nose pressed to Liis's throat, and she gets in one deep inhale of her skin, a green smell, slightly sweaty. Liis pulls back enough to cradle her face, check her eyes, and frown. "You should be in bed."

"And miss the party?" Jun looks at Masar. The ship's bridge is small, and he fills up a good chunk of it, sprawled on the mini sofa they keep in the back for catnaps. He sits up as soon as he sees her, brow knotted. "Get that look off your face," she mutters.

He rolls his eyes. "Come sit down, you damn fool."

She sinks into the command chair, barely having the energy to swivel toward them. Liis comes at her with a syrette of something, stabbing it into her uninjured collarbone.

"Fuck!" she cries. But already the cool relief of morpho starts to spread. She almost sobs with gratitude, but forces it down. "That better not knock me out. Seriously, what the fuck did you give me? I can barely walk."

"The blast burn went straight to the bone, Jun." Liis stands with muscled arms crossed over her chest, the seam of her prosthetic arm distinct against her bared bicep. She's not wearing her cap, and the short black twists of her hair are an attractive riot around her face— a momentary distraction for Jun, until Liis demands, "Do you not remember all the bleeding and screaming?"

Jun scowls. "I remember trying to get the Hood up on the ship."

Liis nods her concession. "You did that, too. You also lost two pints of blood. I had to take a transfusion from Hawks."

"Take is right," Masar pipes up. "Your girl here doesn't ask nicely. If I hadn't offered straight off, I think she would have strung me up and drained me dry."

He says it like it's a joke, but of course it isn't. Liis can be a little intense. A fact reinforced by the way she looks at Jun. "You're lucky you're a universal recipient."

Jun scoffs. Luck indeed. She changes the subject. "Where are we? How did we get through the planet shields without dropping the Hood? And how did *you* get from Ma'kess System to *here* with all the gates shut down? You've been ignoring my comms for two days!"

Liis presses her lips together in a line. Her eyes, dark as oil spills, hint at equal parts amusement and exasperation. She begins to count answers off on her fingers.

"We are orbiting the Silt moon, Hood on. You may be the genius, but I know how to run your programs, all right? We dropped the Hood long enough to get through the shields, and then raised it again. There are hundreds of ships out there right now. No one had a chance to even notice us before we disappeared. As for me, I stowed away on an essential supplies transport to Teros. I had to turn my neural link off until we docked in Lo-Meek."

Jun gawps at her. "You stowed away? Why the fuck did you do that?"

Liis raises an eyebrow feathered with silver scar tissue. "You know if I hadn't, you'd be dead, right?"

"They're cracking down on stowaways! They've got *cloaksaan* patrolling the ships!" That word, always so heavy between them, lands with force. Liis frowns. Jun barrels on, "If they had found you, you'd be—"

"I was not in danger of the Cloaksaan finding me," says Liis. She doesn't say, though her expression adds, *Or have you forgotten that most cloaksaan learned concealment from* me? Jun rolls her eyes at Liis's subtle version of bragging. "And anyway, do you think you're in a position to lecture me on recklessness?" Liis's low voice is cool as a Katish stream. "You risked your life for a godsdamned memory coin."

Jun fully intends to continue this argument—but the reminder of the coin jolts her. Suddenly her anger, the pain in her shoulder, her residual questions about the battle at the Cliffs all take a back seat. She glares at Masar, already on the verge of accusing him.

"The coin. Did you watch it?"

He snorts. "I *would* have. Except I didn't know if you'd broken the encryption or not."

Jun smiles, slow and self-satisfied. "I did."

At once he leans forward, eyes flaring with hungry hope. "Show me."

This time, Lucos Alanye's memories of the nameday party are crystalline, soaked in color and sound. Children laughing brightly; adults braying and raucous; the clinking of dishware and the soft *thump* as the hired acrobat lands a standing backflip, to oohs and aahs. A summer sun bleeds through the curtains, drenching everything in gold.

"Look at these people," says someone directly beside Alanye. "Do you think the Moonbacks will show up?"

"Keep your mouth shut," says Alanye, and Jun's breath catches at his voice, its growly affect—something he was known for.

"Som's ass! Being in charge has made you stuffy! I'm just trying to entertain myself."

"The heir to the Nightfoot dynasty is ten feet away," mutters Alanye, his own gaze fixed on the prim and stoic Alisiana. "And you're *bored*?"

The other guard grumbles, but says no more, and a shout goes up from the children as the acrobat spins and flips. Alisiana doesn't seem to have noticed. Then Caskori Nightfoot steps into view, transforming her somber expression to one of joy. The second guard whistles lowly.

"Fires! This just got interesting."

"Be quiet."

Caskori crouches beside his niece, returning her adoring smile as he holds out the gift. She withdraws the sphere of jevite, eyes widening in pretty delight. Jun half expects to hear Alanye gasp, but of course he doesn't. When he strides toward them, Jun imagines urgency in his steps, but there's no way to know—

"Excuse me, Saan." The two Nightfoots look up at him with twin expressions of annoyance, a common heritage in their noses and cheekbones. "I apologize for the interruption, but I'm instructed to scan all gifts. It will only take a moment."

He holds out his hand.

Caskori is a minor Nightfoot. He has no right to deny the matriarch's guardsaan, much as he may want to. Alisiana looks to her uncle for guidance, but when Caskori doesn't challenge Alanye, something flits across the child's face—the briefest, most potent flash of rage, that Jun had simply mistaken for a sulk the first time. It's there and gone in an instant, or else perhaps she weaves the feeling into a curse, depositing it on the jevite sphere, and into Alanye's hand.

"Thank you, Bright Daughter." Alanye lifts the sphere to his face, clearly scanning it with his ocular. Such scans take two seconds, maybe three. But he stares at it for ten. Jun strains for the sound of his heartbeat, *thump thump thumping* like her own.

"May I ask where you acquired this, Sa?" Alanye asks at last.

Caskori says peevishly, "From a metalsaan on K-5 station, off Kator. It's tenth-century jevite. An antique. Kata's tit, don't *smudge* it; it's worth more than your life."

Alanye doesn't react, though privately he must be disgusted at Caskori for not knowing the difference between antique jevite and jevite that's been recently mined. Those bright red veins in black stone are a dead giveaway. He returns the sphere to Alisiana. "Thank you, Saan."

"All right, then," snaps Caskori. "Get back to your post."

This is where the original memory ended. Which is part of why it startles Jun so much when a gun goes off. She jumps, and beside her, Masar leans sharply forward. On the cast, Caskori shouts. Alanye throws himself over Alisiana as the crack of a second shot echoes out and for several seconds it's hard to tell what's going on. There is screaming. Alanye gets back up, charging someone. Jun sees a face, a rictus of fury, and then there are more faces and arms and bodies as the guards tackle the shooter to the ground. Alanye snaps, "*Don't* kill him."

Over the cries of the partygoers, Jun hears the shooter sobbing something in a language she recognizes, but can't understand. She spins up her translator, and the words break off in a grunt. The shooter abruptly falls limp, the back of his head bloody from the ram of a rifle butt.

"Get him downstairs, now!"

"Lissy!" someone cries.

Alanye spins around. A throng of guardsaan have circled the heiress, and Caskori stands outside plaintively calling for her, like a puppy denied its mother.

"Lissy, are you hurt?!" he cries.

"The assassin is down," Alanye says.

They relax their circle. All around, the panicked guests are being cleared from the room, and Alanye is muttering orders into his comm as he watches the small figure emerge from her protection. Alisiana is pale but composed, her posture erect as she absorbs her surroundings. Though Caskori clearly wants to throw himself at her, she exudes such authority in that moment that he doesn't dare. Yes, here is the Alisiana Nightfoot who will lead her family for decades.

Alanye bows to her. "Bright Daughter. We have the shooter in custody and are taking him down to the prisons for interrogation. We will ascertain how he got a gun into this room. All entries in and out of the palace have been locked down. The guardsaan are searching your guests and everyone else on the grounds to be sure of no accomplices. My ocular shows you are uninjured, but I've sent for a doctor anyway."

"I'm fine," Alisiana says, clipped. "Someone should tell my mother. She's speaking with trade partners in the east wing."

"I've sent her a message as well."

Alisiana nods, assessing him with a cool frankness that seems out of place on a child. Her eyes drop, settling lower on his body. "You're bleeding."

The view weaves as Alanye looks down at himself, and there's a brief glimpse of something red before he looks up again.

"I'm all right, Sa. It's only a blast burn and my armor got most of it."

She continues staring at his injury. Then she looks back at the throne where she was seated before. She remarks, "My ocular suggests if you hadn't moved to cover me, I would have been shot in the head. And I haven't got any armor."

Caskori makes a sound of alarm. Alisiana, however, looks unperturbed. If anything, she seems to find the whole thing... interesting. This is probably the first time anyone has tried to assassinate her.

"I suppose you saved my life, then."

"It is our duty, Sa."

A dry smile touches the corner of the future matriarch's mouth. "You moved swiftly and efficiently, and you already have Verdant on lockdown. You appear to be the only one hurt, and you saved the life of the future matriarch of the Nightfoots. My mother will give you a commission for this if you want it." Then, after a moment's thought, "I'd better put a claim on you first, before she snatches you out from under me."

Alanye doesn't respond at first. Perhaps he, like Jun, is unnerved by the child's droll tone, by the sharpness in her bright eyes, all signifying the acumen and calculation of a seasoned political operative. She is like a tiny, deadly general.

Finally, Alanye says, "I'm at your service, Bright Daughter. With your permission I'd like to interrogate the shooter when he wakes."

"Of course."

"And you'll kill him after," says Caskori, reasserting himself with a waspish look. There's sweat on his purpled brow. "You'll execute him for this, do you understand? Get what you can and then *kill* him!"

There's a moment of silence. Alisiana looks at her uncle in a way Jun can't interpret, but which she doubts is impressed. Alanye finally responds, "I must do whatever the matriarch requests."

"You are mine now," Alisiana replies, her cold stare shifting from Caskori to Alanye with mechanical exactness. "I'm claiming you for my own guard. You'll do as I say, and I say my uncle is right. Find out if the man has family or friends here. They'll have to be eliminated, too. You have your orders, Sa...?" She trails off with a question in her gaze.

"Alanye," Alanye says.

"Alanye," she repeats, so the word sounds like an echo in the room. "You have your orders. Be sure to upload your ocular record before you go down to the prisons."

"Of course, Sa," says Alanye.

The projection ends.

In silence they stare at the empty air where the hologram hung mere moments ago. Jun replays the events with an archivist's rigor, trying to be dispassionate, but failing. She's not sure if what she's feeling is elation, or panic. This is . . . so much more than she bargained for.

She looks at Liis first, but her expression is far away. The burn scars on her jaw have whitened, the way they do when she grits her teeth. Lost in thought. Transported to her past life, when she, too, killed people—and their families. Jun hates the sight of it and tries to draw her back into the present.

"The assassin was the acrobat," she says.

Liis *hmms* but doesn't look at her.

Jun adds, "And the acrobat was a Jeveni." She looks at Masar, expecting some kind of reaction. He scrubs a hand down his face, which is pale. She prods him, "He was speaking Je. You must have understood him."

Liis swivels toward Masar. "You speak Je?"

He gives her a sidelong look. "Yes."

Liis casts her own link to the video file and, with a swift rotation of her wrist, rewinds to the moment when the acrobat wept and cursed in the grip of the guardsaan. The five-spoked wheel tattoo on his cheekbone is distinct. Liis asks Masar, "What's he saying?"

Jun is sure Liis has her own translator working, but she doesn't question the ask—even if it surprises her. Masar clears his throat, and translates, "Autonomy for Jeve. Death to thieves."

Liis regards him silently for a moment. Looking uncomfortable, Masar mutters, "Not much of an assassin, was he?"

"It was an impetuous move," Liis says. Her unblinking stare finally shifts to Jun. "When he saw the jevite sphere, he panicked. Death to thieves."

Yes. Like Alanye, the acrobat would have recognized what the sphere was, and what it meant. What it threatened. A renewal of the trade.

"Even if Alanye tortured him alone, there would be a cast recording of it," says Jun. "If Alisiana realized that there was still jevite on the moon, there's no way she could ignore that."

"It's not proof that the Nightfoots were involved in the genocide," says Liis.

"It's proof they were involved in Alanye's mission on Jeve," Jun retorts.

"It's not even that."

"It may as well be."

Liis lets out her breath, slow and even, her dark eyes fixed on the image of the acrobat's agonized face. "Yes. It may as well be."

Masar says, "No wonder Esek Nightfoot is after us."

At the mention of Esek, Jun's stomach swoops. After the genocide, the Jeveni were displaced from their moon and cut off from any means of self-determination. When Alisiana Nightfoot gave them work in her factories, she gilded her reputation for decades to come. Because while the citizens of the Treble may disdain the Jeveni, what happened on Jeve itself is considered the greatest atrocity of the millennium. It's taught in schools. Memorialized in art and law and literal stone. The entire Alanye family was *exiled* over it, and Lucos died in an alley. To be implicated in the Jeveni Genocide is to be cursed, by the Godfire and all its child gods.

Jun knows now why she's on the wrong end of this furious hunt. She even understands why an apparently righteous cleric like Chono is involved. Jun thought she was buying a coin that would simply *embarrass* the Nightfoots, provide leverage to their enemies, something sweet and scandalous that the Moonbacks or the Khens would pay well to control. But this coin...It would weaken the Nightfoots' already weak leadership, and make the already striking Jeveni revolt, and destabilize an unstable universe. Chaos, under the Kindom. Disunity, in the Treble.

It could finish the Nightfoots, once and for all.

And Jun has never seen herself as the type to burn down worlds, but something curls in her belly now, like hunger, like lust. To destroy the Nightfoots... to utterly *destroy* them—

"We should destroy it."

Jun's head jerks toward Liis, finds her standing with arms crossed and face blank.

"What?"

Liis's eyes are cold, the way she gets sometimes when she's wrestling her memories—or gearing up for a fight. "I know what you're thinking. You're thinking…sell it to the Moonbacks. Or sell it to the Khens. Let them tear the Nightfoots in half. Right?"

Jun rolls her shoulders back, a gesture that wakens her injury, sending little tendrils of pain like tree roots through her body. "Why shouldn't we?"

Liis shakes her head, like she can't believe Jun has to ask. The specter of her disapproval makes Jun tense. More pain. More blood, rushing through her veins. Adrenaline starting to quicken, like prey on the run.

"Do you really want to see another family rise in their wake? Would the Moonbacks or the Khens or even the Paiyes be any better than the Nightfoots? Because one of them will fill the hole that's left behind. And if not them, the Kindom."

This will be what Liis fears most of all: the Kindom's power, unchecked. Right now, the Hands may control the gates, but they don't control the sevite, nor the industries surrounding the sevite. That other, corrupt families monopolize those industries is cold comfort, but at least no one in the Treble controls *everything*. If the Nightfoots fell, and the Kindom managed to take over the sevite trade, then the very cloaks whom Liis once fled would become—what? Invincible? Nothing could terrify her more.

"Maybe it wouldn't happen like that," Jun says.

"How else could it *possibly* happen?"

Jun opens her mouth—and closes it. All the hunger for revenge that had sparked in her belly goes out, replaced by a curl of dread. She pictures Liis taking the coin. Grinding it to dust under her boot. Winking out not only Jun's revenge, but her payday. Something she *needs*.

"We're not destroying it," Jun says with borrowed confidence. "It's worth millions."

"It's worth nothing if Esek Nightfoot hunts us into the ground."

"All the more reason to cut her off at the knees!"

"A woman like that... You have to take a lot more than her knees."

That's true, but—

"I won't let you sell it to a First Family," Liis says. "Not something this powerful. We've got to have some standards."

"That's no better than protecting the Nightfoots."

A stubborn shrug. "It's what I can live with, Jun."

Then for a moment they are at an impasse, gazes locked and neither willing to bend. They've stood at cross-purposes before, but never with so much at stake. Jun swallows, surprised at the thick feeling of nausea rising up her throat. She feels a little dizzy, sweat breaking out on her forehead and back. The pain in her shoulder radiates outward.

And then, quietly, Masar tells them, "You don't have to sell it to a First Family."

They look at him together. He lifts his chin, defiant. "Sell it to me. Sell it to my buyer."

Taken off guard, Jun cocks her head. More pain, echoing down her spine. She ignores it. She thought his buyer *was* First Family.

"Who's your buyer, then?" Liis asks. "Terrorists?"

He glowers at her. "No. Not terrorists."

"So who?" Jun demands.

He hesitates, lips working, words caught between his teeth. And then—

"The Jeveni."

Jun waits for a longer sentence, for a delayed punch line. When none comes, she answers blankly, "What?"

Masar tells her, "I'm Jeveni, Jun. My buyer is a Jeveni collective."

Jun's head swivels toward Liis, expecting to see astonishment on her face, but her expression is flat, as if—

"You *knew*?"

Liis shrugs one shoulder, unperturbed. "I put it together a few minutes ago."

"Like hell you did, you—" She looks at Masar again. "You're *Jeveni*?"

His eyes harden. "You can stop saying it like it's a curse word, thanks."

"Fuck you, Masar, you've been lying to me since we—"

He stands abruptly. He's big as a house, and Liis's body flexes like a cat about to spring. "*I'm* the liar? I'm the liar, Jun *Ironway*?" Jun can only gape at him; he sneers. "Yeah, you think I didn't catch what that archivist called you? You think I don't know who the Ironways are? What happened on K-5? People said back then there was an Ironway kid who was at school in Riin Kala when it happened. That she disappeared right afterward. I assumed the Cloaksaan got you. But they didn't, did they? You must have run."

Run!

Jun blinks. The name Ironway travels down through her limbs, leaves her hot and weak. She has spent years concealing that name, sequestering it within herself. To hear it out of the archivist's mouth was like having armor stripped from her body. To hear Masar say it leaves her naked. And it doesn't help that he's right. If he's lied to her about his identity, it's no less than she's lied to him.

Inanely she says, "You don't have a tattoo." Like that's the fucking thing that matters. Masar looks coldly amused. "I thought they were considered holy, or—"

It's the wrong thing to say. His expression darkens. "Yes, they are holy. They mark belonging and devotion. But *you people* have turned them into a way to single us out. If I take mine off now and then so I can move in the Treble without getting slaughtered like that Jeveni acrobat, how is that different from a Hood program?"

Jun holds up her hands. "Fuck's sake, sorry! I—this is just a bit unexpected, okay? I'm not used to working with Jeveni. You tend to keep to yourselves. And I always sort of assumed you hated the rest of us."

He doesn't relax, watching her, and Jun is still irrationally mad at him for knowing she's an Ironway. What if he knows the truth about Liis, too? Jun can bear to have herself exposed, but *not* Liis.

Which reminds her—

She looks at Liis eagerly. "The Jeveni! They're not a First Family! You can't object to selling it to them! If anyone deserves to have the coin, then—"

Liis talks over her. "Is your buyer connected to the sevite factories? Information like this, it will hurt the trade. Could hurt the Jeveni in the process."

Masar narrows his eyes with nearly comic skepticism. Jun supposes it's not every day he runs into someone who shows concern for the well-being of the Jeveni. Especially now, when every other news cast Jun sees is about Treblen resentment of the coming Remembrance Day.

"My buyer has no intention of hurting their own people."

Jun says, "Then you'd use it in the labor negotiations. Right?"

It makes beautiful sense, actually. If the unions had this information, they could hold it over the Nightfoots. Get what they want, what they need—raise themselves above the role of feudal subjects and maybe even achieve some real power in the sevite trade. Yet the way Masar looks at her betrays nothing. Whatever the agenda of his buyer, he's not about to spill.

Jun redirects. "Okay. Then answer me this: Can your buyer afford to pay what it's worth? No offense, but the Jeveni aren't known for their riches."

Masar's smile is cool. "We can pay you enough to make it worth your while."

So, less than it's worth. But still—much more lucrative than dropping it out an airlock. She's about to ask for more specific numbers when Liis interrupts, sounding annoyed, "It is not a matter of money."

Masar and Jun look at her. Jun makes an incredulous sound.

"Why shouldn't it be?" Masar demands. "If we can pay you, why not—"

"The only reason we're alive is because we are Hooded and hiding. If we contact your buyer, we give Esek Nightfoot a potential lead. We put ourselves at risk again. And we put your buyer in her sights. You should consider that."

"It's considered," he answers. "Now let me tell you something *you* should consider."

"I'm listening," says Liis.

"No matter what you do—crush the coin, sell it to us—Esek Nightfoot will never stop. She's the kind that hunts to the death, and just because you destroy her family doesn't mean you'll destroy her."

Jun demands, "What's your point?"

"The money is one thing, but what you really need is protection. I've spoken to my people about it. They're ready to help you."

"Help us how?" asks Liis.

"Hide you. Hide you where you can't be found."

The words feel like a net, dropped on Jun's body. For a moment she doesn't react, taking too long to understand what he means. Then, pain spikes outward from her shoulder, a heavy throb answering in the base of her skull. She flinches and pushes back in her chair. A retreat, with nowhere to go. No, no, no, not that—

"Say more," Liis orders.

"No," Jun mutters, blinking fuzzily, dread coiling through her. Her throat feels tight. There's a buzzing in her ears. *Pull it together. Just fucking—pull it together!*

Masar says, "There's more to the Jeveni than sevite factory workers and poor isolationists. We've survived the violence of the Kindom, and of these systems, more creatively than even you could imagine. And that means knowing how to hide when we need to. My buyer wants to extend those services to you both."

"No." Jun says it again, louder this time, forcing her vision to clear. She stares at Masar and she hates him, just for saying those words. Irrational, uncontrollable hatred. "*No*," she hisses. "We're not hiding."

"Jun." Liis's voice has a warble to it, far away beyond the bounds of the fugue gathering around Jun, a feeling like suffocation. Jun watches

Liis make a placating gesture, *Easy, easy...* Jun swallows, staring at the ground and squeezing the armrests of her chair. Rage and terror wrestle each other for supremacy, rearing up against Masar's offer, and against the memory of Great Gra—

Run!

Masar sounds incredulous. "Am I missing something? You two are a couple of con artists. You must have had to go into hiding before."

"We have," says Liis, "but—"

"You're not sticking us in a hole somewhere," Jun growls.

"Jun, we have to think of our lives, here. We could at least—"

"No." Jun's mouth is dry, but sweat beads on her upper lip. She wipes it off and looks at Liis with eyes wide and dry and burning. "No."

Liis goes quiet, knowing better than to argue. But not about to concede, either. Liis is the one who fled the Brutal Hand when no cloak had ever done it before; she's the one who cauterized her own arm and spent ten months in an underground safe house; she knows, above anything, how to survive. She will do what's necessary to survive, without ego. Masar's offer to protect them must appeal to her, even as it repulses Jun. But she has never made Jun do something that Jun didn't agree to, and so after long moments her face settles with determination.

She looks at Masar. "Tell your buyer no. No deal."

And Jun knew she was going to say that, but the fury still soars through her like a hot wind. She grinds her teeth. "That's *not* what I said."

Liis is implacable, cold. "You can't have both."

"Oh yes I fucking can. If the Jeveni can pay us, then we're getting paid."

"We *can* pay you," Masar interjects. "And we can protect you. We—"

"We don't need your godsdamned protection," Jun snaps.

"We don't need his money, either."

"Of course we do!"

"Jun!" Liis's voice is like a slap, her oil-slick eyes fiery. "You need to calm down."

But Jun can't calm down. She feels like she's choking. Fire needles its way down her arm and through her chest, but it's not more power-ful than her determination.

"It's my coin, Liis. It's my choice."

Even as she says it, she knows the cardinal rule it breaks: partner-ship, in everything. Decisions, made together. Liis's nostrils flare.

"Are you really going to do this for the sake of *money*?"

Jun gapes at her, any guilt she feels evaporating at Liis's incompre-hensible words. What is she *talking* about? The money—it's not *money*, is it? Money is just the method, the key. It's the *lock* that matters, and the thing behind the lock, the thing she's been trying to get back to, all her life. How can Liis say the money doesn't matter when she of all people knows what the money is *for*? The *for* is what matters. What always *has* mattered. More than anything.

But Liis lands a killing blow—

"What good are you to your family if you lead Esek right to them?"

Jun feels it like thunder inside her skull. Her eyes burn, her body burns. The anger and disappointment in Liis's eyes are enough to crack her resolve—but not to break it.

"Give me time to think," she says, humiliated by the desperation in her own voice, by the pleading in her eyes, as she looks at Liis. Liis, who is beginning to melt around the edges, a halo obscuring the cor-ners of Jun's vision in concert with the spreading fire in her torso. She pushes it down. "We can find a way. I can—"

Liis shakes her head. There's pleading in her eyes, too. "It's too risky."

"What, you never want us to take a risk again?"

"A con knows when to cut and run, Jun. I want us to survive."

Jun leaps up. "I want more than that!"

No amount of surging adrenaline can prevent her body's response, prevent the agony that spreads out into every muscle and limb. She gasps, gags, has to brace herself on the command chair and fears for a moment her knees are going to buckle. A corona of pain pulses around her head, and beyond it she hears Liis's voice.

"You need your next dose."

Liis walks out of the room. By the time she comes back, Jun's vision has only barely cleared; she's breathing hard and drenched in sweat. She can see the pneumatic injector in Liis's hand, and the determined look on Liis's face. Jun holds up a hand.

"No. Just—just hold on."

"You're about to faint," Liis says flatly.

"I'm fine."

"You're not."

"We can't give up," Jun pleads. "We're *so* close, Liis. We can't just give up!"

"Let's talk about it when you're feeling better."

"No!" The whole right side of her body screams. She keeps herself upright by ferocious will alone. She's aware she sounds like a child, an irrational, reckless child, and in her thoughts, she *is* a child, the child that so many years ago—

Masar says cautiously, "Jun, you don't look well."

She blinks at him. Wonders how she didn't see it before. Wonders how a little thing like a tattoo stopped her from seeing him: another runaway, just like her.

Liis steps toward her slowly, holding her arms out at her sides, as if Jun were a wild animal that needs careful handling. Jun *feels* like a wild animal, a creature backed into a corner, who sees its liberty just out of reach, who snarls and thrashes—but can't get there.

"Okay, Jun," Liis says. "Okay. We'll talk about it, all right? Once you're feeling better, I promise, we can talk about it."

"Don't fucking patronize me," Jun snaps, even as her lover's soft voice acts like a tonic, lowering her defenses in spite of herself.

"I'm not," Liis murmurs. "I'm not."

Now they are standing right in front of each other, eyes level. Liis reaches out one cautious hand to touch her side, a gesture of appease-ment, of apology. Against her will, Jun softens. Against her will, this is what she wants—this tenderness, this warmth. To be alone with Liis and to feel, even for a moment, that she is safe...

In a flash, Liis pulls her shirt up, stabbing the injector right into her hip. It goes through her like a laser beam.

"Motherfucker!" she cries, jerking away, stumbling.

"Shit," Masar drawls.

Jun's legs turn to water underneath her, the potency of the sedative making sound and space contort. She's about to fall when she feels herself hoisted up into Liis's arms.

"You...*asshole*..." Jun mumbles.

And passes out.

CHAPTER THIRTEEN

1664

YEAR OF THE CRUX

The Makala Aet
The Black Ocean

Things seem to have gone awry on Teros," says Aver Paiye.

His tone is mild, even understanding. He looks at Chono without recrimination, but his expression is grave. Behind him on the casting view, Seti Moonback stands with arms crossed, blue eyes glittering. In a corner lurks the mammoth Medisogo. There's not a secretary to be seen, which is...odd. The Clever Hand usually helps keep the peace whenever the Brutal and the Righteous come together, but since this strange mission began, the Kindom star is missing one point. What was it Ilius said in Riin Kala? *When the Secretaries turn their backs, all law is lost.*

She pushes the thought aside, bowing her head to Paiye in acknowledgment.

"I take responsibility, Burning One."

Seti Moonback blurts a humorless laugh. Since Chono last saw her, she has adopted a female gendermark, but her sneering look is just the same. "That's very noble, but you're there as an adviser to Esek. *She's* the one who owes us an explanation."

Chono stands alone in the middle of her room on *The Makala Aet.* Everything around her is quiet but for the hum of the ship, and the casting view is large on the wall. Paiye and the rest appear slightly larger than life, and their gazes are angled down at her, as if she were a student again, studying Godtexts in the lecture hall.

Chono says, "Sunstep escaped both Lo-Meek and Siinkai because someone tipped them off that we were coming. We could hardly have anticipated that."

"Yes," says Moonback, flexing her fist so the knuckles crack. "Interesting twist, that. Obviously, the archivist helped them escape the Cliffs. But who spoke to Captain Foxer? If he hadn't pushed up his meeting with Sunstep, we could have caught them all in the act."

"Captain Foxer didn't know the identity of the person who warned him," says Chono. She adds after a moment, "My ocular recording showed you as much."

"Your ocular recording also showed Esek goading the captain into attacking her," says Moonback, her lip curling up, accentuating the long scar that wends through it like a ravine. "I noticed you fired off a shot yourself."

Aver Paiye sighs. "That's unfair, Seti. The pirate tried to attack Esek. Chono was only acting in defense of her kin cleric."

"Yes, of course. Cleric Chono is beyond reproach."

Moonback's stare is withering. Paiye sighs again. In his dark corner, Medisogo glowers.

"Chono, do you have *any* leads on where Sunstep has gone?"

Paiye's voice is gently entreating, but Chono says, "We don't."

Though . . . is that strictly true? They know about Jun Ironway. They know from genetic tracing that it was her blood, on the blue muslin scarf they found. Surely Jun Ironway is a lead, if nothing else?

Chono has not mentioned Jun Ironway, however. She withheld that piece of her ocular record from them. The archivist revealing Sunstep's true name.

She shoves it aside, speaking directly to Seti Moonback. "Quiet One, perhaps it would be better if the Cloaksaan took over this mission. Whatever the contents of the memory coin, it seems dangerous to risk recovering it by leaving the matter exclusively to me and Esek."

This is about as bold as she's willing to get, but what she doesn't say beats in her brain with accelerating force, *Why* did *you give this mission to us? What* possible *purpose does it serve, to test Esek in this way?*

The First Cloak and the First Cleric are silent. Moonback looks at her as if she detects the insubordination in her question but can't prove it. Paiye glances aside, conflicted. He is a man who makes age look handsome and refined, but right now the normally distinguished lines of his face are carved deep with distress. He meets Chono's eyes again and she's surprised by the hint of regret in them.

But neither person answers her question, nor even acknowledges it. Instead Paiye says, "Don't you think, Chono, that Esek's actions indicate a . . . disinterest in accomplishing this mission at all? It doesn't seem to me she has tried very hard to find Sunstep, or the coin. Why would she take such a lackadaisical attitude unless she's indifferent to our orders? Our authority? I can't help but think she *must* intend to renounce her vows and become the matriarch of the Nightfoots. Has she said as much to you?"

The changed direction briefly stymies Chono, but she recovers. "I'm afraid we haven't spoken about it at all, Sa. And she's been in her own cabin since we left Teros. I've had very little conversation with her."

A fact that continues to unsettle Chono, more than she wants to admit to herself.

"That's strange, isn't it?" Paiye asks. "Why would she spurn you now unless it's to avoid revealing her choice? Esek has always seemed hungry for company, in the past."

"Hungry for an audience," says Moonback.

"Esek often keeps her own counsel," Chono says, being very careful now. "And she often acts according to her whims. She plays games. I don't condone it, but the Kindom has always allowed her those eccentricities. It seems odd to expect her to be a different person now. If she intends to become the matriarch, she hasn't told me so."

Paiye's mouth twists. "The Treble is a powder keg. There are protests everywhere against the gate closures, and the labor strikes in the factories are nowhere near an end. Amid all of this, with so much capacity to effect change, Esek is indifferent. Godfire forbid such a feckless person should take control of one of the Treble's most powerful and influential houses."

Chono would like to defend her, but it's impossible. Esek *is* indifferent, to everything, unless her own benefit is clear. And she remembers what Esek said in the backstreets of Lo-Meek. *No one likes being left in the dark...* No doubt Esek's refusal to say what she will do is a power move, like everything else. Keep the Kindom in the dark—the better to ambush them, if she so chooses. But Esek is a strategist, and she may be willing to trade.

"First Cleric, perhaps if you were to confide in Esek about the contents of the memory coin, then she would—"

"Esek is a *cleric*," interrupts Paiye, sharper and colder than he has ever been with Chono. "She is obligated to obey me regardless of what I share with her about her mission. If I sometimes choose to withhold information, that is my right as the leader of our Hand. The Kindom cannot stand unless its people respect and obey it! That includes Esek. And you."

She says nothing. She considers all the ways she has disobeyed Paiye, all the secrets she has held for Esek. The truth about the Nightfoots and the Jeveni. The identity of a missing kinschool student with the power to expose it all. Fistfuls of coins, and all of them as dangerous to the sevite trade as whatever Paiye has chosen not to disclose.

I thought you trusted Paiye, Ilius said to her. But also, *I thought he trusted you*...

She bows her head in acquiescence. Paiye has every right to withhold information. Yet what flashes through her mind while her eyes are lowered is the face of Cleric Paan. Was he, was his reputation, something Paiye chose to withhold when he stationed Chono on Quietus?

She looks up again. "Sa, I didn't mean to imply I approve of Esek's actions. I trust your judgment, where this coin is concerned. I only hope—" She pauses, trying to convey submissiveness and respect. Wonders if she's acting. "I only hope we can all remember the events of the past year, and their impact on Cleric Nightfoot."

Seti Moonback jumps on this. "So impactful, she can purport to have no idea where Sunstep has gone."

Chono remains silent, impassive. Is there any way that Moonback knows Sunstep's true name after all? "Ironway" would mean nothing at first. But even shallow digging would lead the First Cloak to K-5 station.

And that could in turn lead her to Six.

Aver Paiye cuts through her thoughts. "The fact is, Chono, we learned more from the events in Siinkai than you may realize."

Chono doesn't react, but his words make dread pulse through her.

"Yes, you may not have a lead, but *we* do," Moonback says, casting an image into the air, a hologram of a woman, from the shoulders up. Her face is a map of battles, instantly captivating. "This is Liis Konye. Your ocular recorded her as the woman on the roof of the Cliffs, who appeared by battle shuttle. She is well-known to us in the Cloaksaan. Few defectors survive as long as she has."

Chono's head tilts. She's never heard of a cloaksaan defecting. "You're certain?"

Moonback's eyes narrow. She calls to her second, "Medisogo, are we certain?"

Medisogo's voice is ominously deep. "I would know Liis Konye's face anywhere. I trained with her at school. I nearly killed her when she defected. I had to content myself with taking off her arm."

The cloak's words seem half brag, half threat.

"Why did she defect?" Chono asks.

"Why does anyone defect from the Kindom?" Moonback scorns the question. "Cowardice. Disloyalty. A weak and self-interested character. She's appeared on our radar several times over the years, but we never connected her to Sunstep, until yesterday. I'm directing our entire casting network to finding her."

So, the cloaks will be involved after all. The matter is apparently too sensitive to leave entirely with Esek.

"Do I take it, then, that Esek and I have been recalled from this mission?" she asks.

Paiye shakes his head. "Not at all. We're simply offering you additional aid. I'm sure Esek won't ignore our intelligence, if we discover where Sunstep is before she does. Whoever catches her first—we insist on being there, for any preliminary interrogations."

"We'll make sure no one has a knife on them, this time," adds Moonback.

Chono ignores this. "Very well, Sa. Are there any new instructions for me?"

Paiye stares at her for several pensive moments, his expression unreadable, his seriousness redoubling the dread in Chono's chest.

"Your instructions, as ever, are to be her friend."

Chono does not outwardly react, but her anxiety becomes a tentacled thing, coiling down her spine. She can feel Seti Moonback watching her face, searching her for clues to her thoughts—and loyalties. Chono bows over her hands.

"I am the servant of the Godfire."

Paiye smiles his approval. Moonback wears a different kind of smile. Medisogo watches with unrelenting malevolence, and she's beginning to wonder what about her so obviously offends him.

"Gods keep you well, Cleric Chono," Paiye concludes.

The view goes dark.

Chono stands a moment, her composure during the call giving way to agitation. Esek's secrets. Paiye's secrets. All the Hands at odds, everyone withholding something from everyone else. How the fuck does she work like this? Chono pulls up her comms, shooting a message into the Black Ocean as rapidly as her thoughts will allow—

Any connection between the coin and a cloaksaan called Liis Konye?

It's the first time she's contacted Ilius since this began. She knows he would have reached out to her by now if he knew anything, but the quiet still frustrates her. If she must be the engine of this investigation, so be it. She needs information, and Ilius, at least, will answer her.

Chono checks the news hawkers: More protests. Talk of supply shortages across the systems. Surge pricing. A Jeveni run down and killed for trying to book transport to *The Risen Wave* for the Remembrance Day ceremonies. A Teron mother asks the camera, "Why should they get to travel in luxury while my children starve?!"

Chono warned Paiye this would happen. And he said, *I will take your thoughts to heart.*

She shuts the hawkers off. She bathes. Afterward, she stands for a long time at the bathroom's full-length mirror, regarding her tall and broad and boxlike body with clinical indifference. The deep laceration on her thigh is healing well, as is the blast burn on her forearm, signatures from the battle on the Cliffs. Her eyebrow and mouth are bruised, and that makes her think of the scarring on the cloaksaan defector's face. A cloaksaan defector. A person who simply . . . *left*. And lived.

Chono dresses, but when she tries to pray, it's all wrong. She's been good at praying since she was a child, the memorized verses flowing easily through her mind and from her lips. A comfort, to lose herself in their poetry. Tonight, though, she stumbles over crucial passages. She gets distracted wondering about the impacts of pre-Treble translations. What if everything the Godtexts say is misprint, misinterpretation, counterfeit? She remembers Six, arguing with the Godtexts teacher about his assertion that the Treble was the Godfire's gift to humankind. Six, a recalcitrant scholar who preferred the sparring court, argued that the Treble was no gift—it was simply composed of the only star systems their ancestors were arrogant enough to colonize. This went over badly.

A ping from her comms drags Chono back into the present. The message is obviously a transcription, and Ilius's excitable tone jars her out of grim thoughts:

> *Hello. Sorry. I'm not ignoring you. This coin is a bit of a nightmare, I'm afraid. Everybody has ideas but nobody has sources. It's like someone threw it out in the Black with a handful of rumors and said,* Come find me!
>
> *One thing I'm sure of: The dates are wrong. Original advertisement for the coin site 1589—the year of the genocide. But whatever your Sunstep is after, that's dated 1575. Which isn't a particularly interesting year, as far as I can tell. I'll dig deeper. Is it possible that someone advertised one coin and then sold another? Sorry, I'm just theorizing.*
>
> *Liis Konye. No connection. Is she connected? She killed seventeen cloaks ten years ago, so stay away from her.*
>
> *I'm still looking. Be careful.*

Chono sighs, considering. If the cloaksaan have an image that proves Liis Konye was on the roof, then clearly that information hasn't reached Ilius yet. Which means he may be behind her in this hunt.

Be careful, he said. Yes, she'll be careful. As careful as she dares.

She stands up, prayers unfinished, and dons her red coat. She heads for Esek's cabin.

The ship is just a warkite, small by Kindom standards, with only a hundred yards between her room and Esek's. Two novitiates stand guard, which is an utter waste of their time. Chono thinks of her own novitiates on Pippashap, studying their texts and working alongside the people of the water city. A sudden pang of homesickness echoes through her. She would like to be back on Pippashap. She would like to be speaking rites and offering counsel, and she'd like the chest in Ilius's vault to be with her instead. To hold and touch those few things in the Treble that are truly hers. Her longing for it feels almost rabid, like it's a limb that she stripped off herself. She wants it back.

The door to Esek's room slams open, and Chief Novitiate Rekiav comes out.

The young man looks harried. Disheveled. Chono's first thought is that he's been yelled at for something (a sport Esek always enjoyed). But then she notices the incorrectly buttoned shirt. The boots with loose laces. The lash of nail marks on his exposed collarbones.

When he sees Chono, he freezes. He steps aside in the hallway and lowers his eyes with far more deference than he showed her at the Cliffs.

"Burning One," he says.

Chono stares at him. There are bruises on his throat from when she grabbed him at Siinkai, but the nail marks are far more vivid.

What she feels in that moment is...nauseated. Coming up in Esek's cohort, many novitiates admitted how eagerly they would go to bed with their mentor if she asked. Chono had quailed at the thought that she might be expected to serve in that way again. But it soon became clear that Esek, though sexually voracious, never bedded her novitiates. It had brought Chono comfort, pride in her mentor, and certainty the Godfire had given her to an ethical, if eccentric, cleric. Not that those thoughts lasted long.

Under her stare, Rekiav shifts his loose boots and swallows hard.

"Is she available?" asks Chono at last.

He nods. "Yes, Sa, she's having dinner."

Chono looks at him, silent, measuring, and he stares back. The other two novitiates are starting to look nervous. What must they have overheard?

"On with your orders, then."

He darts away, pale and relieved. Chono approaches the door to Esek's cabin. She intends to knock, but at the last moment forgoes it completely, letting herself in unannounced.

Esek is seated at the table, her gnarled ear on display. She's fully clothed, except for the coat flung over a sofa arm. She's eating the meal before her with relish, knife and fork clinking on porcelain. When she sees Chono, she makes no mention of the absent knock, but smiles broadly and gestures her toward another chair.

"Sit. Sit. I'm famished. Have you eaten yet?"

Chono sits down rigidly.

"These cuts are exquisitely aged. You can taste the funk on them. I do love fermentation." Chono says nothing. Esek gives her a quizzical look. "Anything the matter?" Chono stares at her and finally Esek chuckles. "This is taciturn, even for you."

"What was Rekiav doing here?"

Esek frowns, slathering a hunk of bread with butter. "Reporting to me, of course. I've had him looking into Masar Hawks's stolen warhorse. I think we may be onto something, there."

"He was undressed."

Esek's brows shoot heavenward. "Well, that's a magic trick because when he closed the door after him, he was fully clothed."

"I mean he was..." Chono pauses. To her own horror, she's in danger of blushing. "He seemed to still be dressing himself."

Esek spears a few thin slices of meat, wrapping them around the tines of her fork and taking the whole bite into her mouth with a groan of pleasure. She chews and swallows. She sips from a glass of clear liquor, and puts it down again, and throughout all of this she does not stop looking Chono in the eye. At the end, she waves a finger.

"If it were anyone but you, Chono, I'd think this was jealousy."

"But it *is* me."

"If you must know, you roughing him up on Teros has left Rekiav very insecure. Sometimes, when my novitiates fear they've fallen out of my favor, they make ridiculous gestures. You did it sometimes, though of course your offerings weren't...carnal. But you see how pretty Rekiav is. He probably fucked half his kinschool. I think he thought he could use that advantage to regain my good graces. He was terribly embarrassed, when I told him to put his clothes back on."

Esek drops the eye contact to focus on ripping off a hunk of bread with her teeth, and moans again.

"Nothing like Katish butter. You should eat, Chono. You look pale. I don't care if the doctor's given you a clean bill. You're still recovering. Eat."

Esek pushes the platter of cuts and fruits and cheeses across the table. Chono, obedient on instinct, takes a cube of cheese and puts it in her mouth, chewing mechanically. It's hard and sharp and—can she believe what Esek has said? Her story certainly doesn't explain the nail marks. Is there any way to prove she's lying? What would Chono do, if she did prove it?

"Now," Esek says, apparently having decided the conversation is over. "You're not one for house calls—not unless you're delivering a message. What is it?"

Woodenly Chono relays her conversation with Paiye and Moonback. Esek seems interested in the deserter cloaksaan, amused by Medisogo's talk about the arm, but when Chono mentions that they'll now have Kindom assistance in finding Sunstep—

"Ha!" She stabs a slice of fruit, sliding it off the razor edge of the knife with her teeth. "That's cute of them."

"If they can use Liis Konye to track down Ironway, we shouldn't object."

"And we won't. But that doesn't mean our own investigation is over. I predict I'll have the whole thing figured out long before Seti Moonback does."

She goes on eating. Chono watches her. Listens to the sound of chewing and swallowing and drinking and all Esek's little noises of enjoyment. She can't stop thinking about the deserter cloaksaan. What moved Liis Konye to abandon her oaths? How did she end up helping Jun Ironway escape Siinkai? Is Liis hired muscle? Or something more?

"If you have ideas for how to track them down, you should tell our kin what they are."

Esek shows her teeth. "But *you'll* tell them. When you report our actions afterward." Chono folds her hands on the table in a gesture that belies the tension in her body. Esek waves her fork at her. "Don't worry, Chono. I don't mind it. I know you're obligated by duty. And your own infernal righteousness."

"You're talking as if the Kindom are a separate entity from us. But they *are* us. The work we do is for the protection of the Treble, not ourselves. We share that mission with all Hands of the Kindom. Unless, that is, you no longer consider yourself a Hand."

Esek stops eating. It's as if a mechanical toy has been shut off and for a moment the silence feels deafening. Then Esek looks at her, her bright eyes conveying not anger, but surprise, even curiosity, and behind all of that, something dangerous. She puts down her fork, but keeps the knife in hand, twirling it between two fingers as she regards Chono.

"Do you believe that?" she asks. "Peace, under the Kindom? Unity, in the Treble, et cetera?"

Chono balks. The chest in Ilius's vault seems to rattle. "Do you doubt it?"

A bark of laughter. "Nice deflection. But I can see you're very agitated tonight, Chono. What has Paiye been telling you? Go on, say what you feel."

Chono, still unnerved by Esek's question, and by her own answer, clears her throat. "Paiye wants to know whether you'll accept the matriarchy. He thinks your actions so far prove you intend to renounce the Kindom."

Esek nods pensively. She points at Chono with the knife.

"And what do you think?"

Chono hesitates, but she's not afraid of Esek. Not in the way she used to be. Perhaps, she's afraid in a new way.

"I don't think you're thinking about that decision at all. I think you're behaving as you always have, pursuing the same goal you've always pursued. The Kindom has set you a test, but you're not interested in the test. You're only trying to find Six."

Esek lifts her sculpted eyebrows but has no rejoinder. No denials and no confirmations. The dead air of that silence is stifling.

Chono asks, "Why haven't we talked about Six?"

A clearing of the throat. A twirl of the knife. "Because there's no proof Six is involved in any of this."

Chono is silent. Bewildered. In years past, Esek has grabbed any excuse to connect Six to even the most unlikely events of their lives. The liquor could run out, and Esek would blame it on Six. At the slightest provocation, she'd be off on some new lead, sniffing the ground for tracks.

"I know time has passed. You and I are...changed. But there was a time when you confided in me about Six."

"Because we had things to talk about."

"And we don't, now?"

"Not unless you're keeping letters from me."

Goose bumps flood down Chono's arms, thankfully concealed beneath her coat. *Yes, the letters...*

The first time Six sent a letter to Esek, Alisiana Nightfoot intercepted it.

Not discouraged, Six found a different way to get their messages to Esek: through Chono. A chocolate shop in Trini-so started sending Chono a monthly box of sweets—a subscription that she had apparently purchased for herself. Once a year or so, the box included an extra gift, some new piece of evidence that proved Alisiana Nightfoot's involvement in the Jeveni Genocide. If Esek had intended to keep the truth from Chono, Six removed the option. They wove Chono into their rivalry with Esek, whether Chono wanted it or not.

And now, years later, Chono is still woven in, still bound to Esek and Six both. Still wondering why Esek hasn't killed her for knowing these Nightfoot secrets.

"No," Chono says at last. "No new letters."

But this was not Esek's wording, was it? She had said, *Unless you're keeping letters from me.* That is a more dangerous question, and for a split second Esek stares at her in a way that terrifies Chono. Could Esek know about the chest in the vault?

"Well." Esek shrugs. "I suppose there's nothing to discuss, then, is there?"

Chono breathes through her nose, the only hint at her feelings. "I thought perhaps you would trust me again, someday."

"I trust you as far as I trust any of my kin."

Esek's ability to hurt her is apparently just as potent as it always was. Even after everything. Esek must realize how hard she's hit, because she rolls her eyes.

"All right, don't look so heartbroken. You're a cleric. I hate clerics. Didn't I tell you how it would be, when I sent you off to become one?"

"You told me I would never be yours again."

Esek pauses at this, cocks her head as if listening to the memory.

"Hmm. I forgot that part."

"If becoming a cleric did make me so untrustworthy, don't you think I would have betrayed you before now? Told our kin cleric about Six? About the things that happened on K-5? The things that happened at Soye's Reach?"

"Yes, I've often wondered about that. Are you proposing that you are still my creature?"

Chono clears her throat, flexing against that phrase. "I'm proposing that if we agree Six is involved in this, we work together to stop whatever they're doing."

Esek sets down the knife, but with an exaggerated thoughtfulness.

"Tell me why you think Six is involved."

It is so much like being her student again. She did this sort of thing all the time, back then. Asked a question, and waited for her novitiates to make an argument. Provide evidence. Convince her.

"You've been hunting Six for more than fifteen years. They've been your singular obsession for as long as I've known you. And you've been theirs for just as long."

Esek's slow smile is predatory. "A complicated dance, to be sure."

"Six has spent much of that time collecting secrets about your family. Taunting you with them. Telling you enough to make you keep hunting them, but never revealing what they plan to do with those secrets. And now we have this person, Jun Ironway—and we know that Six saved her family from you, and probably saved Jun as well. Maybe Jun feels indebted to Six, works for them. She's running around with a secret that could hurt your family—just the sort of secret Six would want. It can't be a coincidence. Even if it was, there's no way you would treat it as such. There is no way you aren't viewing this as Six's work."

Esek parries, "Jun Ironway wasn't on K-5 when we went there. She may have escaped the Cloaksaan on her own power. There's no proof she is under Six's protection."

"But somebody warned Saxis Foxer we were coming. Six is the only one who would have done—"

"That was me," Esek says.

Chono stops. It's as if Esek has spoken in some language her translator doesn't recognize.

"What?"

Esek looks at her with a muted smile. She meets Chono's bafflement with curiosity, interest—desire.

"I said...I am the one who warned Foxer. I warned the archivist as well."

Repetition doesn't make the words any better. Chono's mouth opens and closes. Her mind turns back to the roof of the Silt Glow Cliffs, to the sprawled bodies of the novitiates.

"We lost people at Siinkai," she says.

"My novitiates were reckless," Esek replies.

"Half of Foxer's crew was killed by those marshals."

"*That* is on the marshals."

"Esek—how—why would you—"

"I didn't want to catch them." A shrug. "I still don't. Not yet."

"*Why?*"

"Because I'm hoping they'll lead us to a more important target."

Realization dawns, and the cold feeling in Chono only spreads. Of course. Of course this is Esek's plan. Esek the strategist. Esek the merciless. Esek, always willing to sacrifice whatever was needed in her pursuit of Six.

"Oh, Chono." Esek draws her name out in a long, low sigh. She's still watching her with that curious, hungry expression. Her hand slides across the table to toy again with the dinner knife. Chono watches her fingers. "Look at you struggle. Look at you think. We're back to this again, aren't we? Me, doing some horrific thing. And you, forced to decide. Do you see now why I haven't confided in you, my old friend? Do you see the *mercy* in it? Now what will you do? Betray me to our *kin*?" She emphasizes the last word, all mockery.

Chono stands up. Esek watches her, anticipation in every line of her sharp-angled body.

"You've been lying to me," Chono says—ashamed at once of the asinine words.

Esek shrugs. "Everyone is lying to you. Or do you still think the Kindom really knows what's on that memory coin? They are as in the dark as us, and twice as frightened."

Taken aback, confused, Chono ignores the obvious deflection.

"You're testing me."

"Everything is a test."

Yes, that's true. From the first time she saw Esek, everything has been a test.

"You must be confident in the outcome," Chono says. "If I report what you've done to the First Cleric, it'll be grounds to arrest you on treason."

Esek chuckles. "Yes, and we'd go down together, wouldn't we? Or haven't you just admitted all the things you keep secret from them, for my sake? We are both traitors to the Kindom. Remember, you were *at* Soye's Reach. You joined the Clerisy after the massacre on K-5 and never said what happened there. Don't pretend you carry my secrets for *my* sake alone."

Chono flinches. Esek smiles again, but it's not mocking. It's grim, and keen, and it implicates Chono in a long trail of bloodshed, some righteous, and some...despicable. She feels ill. She moves toward the door to the cabin. Has a fleeting thought that she probably shouldn't turn her back to Esek.

"I've asked the captain to dally here for a while."

She stops. Esek lets the silence hang a moment. Stringing Chono along.

"I'm waiting on some information that may be of use to us. Take some time to yourself. But do let me know if you plan to turn us over to the Cloaksaan for all our many crimes."

Chono doesn't respond, simply opens the door and steps out into the cold hallway, where the two novitiates stand, staring straight ahead. Chono wonders what crimes Esek has dragged them into since fishing them from their schools.

"Cleric Nightfoot doesn't need an honor guard. Go get some rest."

They don't move. She may as well be invisible. Everything they do is at their mentor's behest, and no one will distract them. She heads back to her own cabin. Over and over, she feels something tickling the back of her neck. As if Esek's very spirit is tracking her movements, reminding her that she will never truly be free.

In her own cabin, she stares around herself at the constraining walls. The beautiful prison. Rebellion surges in her, overwhelming and probably foolish, but for once she doesn't question herself. Her instructions to Ilius are only a sentence long:

Send me the chest.

We will have a game, a drinker's game, full of revelry and risks.
We will turn the plates of the worlds to tiles, and spin the sun on our
wrist.
We will tell tales that only hustlers know, and sing to their babies at
night.
We will fight and steal and drink and fuck and live till Som takes
our life.
    The Songs of Terotonteris, 22:12–15. Godtexts, pre-Treble

CHAPTER FOURTEEN

1653

YEAR OF THE FLIGHT

Soye's Reach
North Avo Continent
The Planet Kator

The room was warm and heavy with the smell of sex, and Esek was lying naked but awake. She held a glass of praevi, a bright and rosy amber that she sipped from pensively. The young man dozed beside her, and it was a bad sign when a knock on the door didn't wake him. She'd enjoyed the sex. It was a good way to pass the time. He, on the other hand, had clearly been transported, crying out at a volume that put Esek in mind of clerics, not cloaksaan. His was not the temperament of someone who could go unnoticed. She considered punishing him for staying asleep. She could take off a toe, maybe? It would teach him to never drop his guard. Not like he couldn't have it replaced.

There was a second knock, firm but not demanding (so typically Chono). Ah, Chono. Chono was not the type who would scream during sex. Did Chono even *have* sex? Esek had never heard of it happening, but then, Chono had her secretive side and might have simply hidden it from her.

She called out, "Enter," and Chono did, eyes dutifully cast away from the bed.

"They're here," Chono said.

Esek's heart thumped. The glee and anticipation that flooded her were better than any orgasm. She swallowed her drink and leapt up, kicking the young man in the process. He came awake, gurgling with confusion as she reached for her clothes.

"How do you know?" she demanded.

Chono still looked away from her. "Four figures in similar dress approached by both roads all within ten minutes of one another."

"But none of them will be Six."

"No, they're obvious decoys."

"And our insider?" asked Esek, finishing up with her pants and shirt and reaching for her boots. "Has she seen them yet?"

"No."

The young cloaksaan in the bed sat up, rubbing his bruised leg and muttering, "You mean you haven't even sighted them? There's no proof they're even here."

Esek finished with her second boot, standing up straight again. She spun elegantly on one foot, and cracked the back of her hand against his face so hard his lip split open. He cried out, falling back.

"How many years have you been a cloaksaan?" asked Esek pleasantly. "A year? Two years?" From her periphery she saw Chono holding out her coat for her. She swept it on, watching the young cloak bleed. "I'm about to send this one off to be a cleric, and in ten years I promise she'll still be a better cloaksaan than you. Make sure to clean things up before you go. I don't want blood on my sheets." He groaned in pain. "Gods keep you well."

She went out into the hallway with Chono behind her. They walked swiftly toward the elevator, which would lift them out of the barracks and toward the command center on the ground level. This camouflaged Cloaksaan outpost, austere and economically built, all metal gangways and stone walls carved from the mountain, was typical of the Brutal Hand. Dark, and dry, and full of serious purpose. An isolated point of Kindom authority, hidden in the frozen wilderness. The cloaks who lived here were like so many black beetles scuttling underground. Up on the surface, it was all ice cliffs and rock, the forests of North Avo ever green and draped in a muffling snow. They were three hundred miles from the nearest town, but Soye's Reach was only fifteen miles away. That hunting lodge, built into the cliffs, was as close to civilization as one got in the North Avon wilderness. And Esek planned to make of it a bear trap.

The elevator hummed as they ascended. Esek said, "You'd better watch out while you're here. That boy will tell everyone you're to be a cleric. It'll make you a target for pranks."

Chono stared straight ahead as they rose three, four, five floors.

"Tonight is going to be the first jewel in your crown, Chono," Esek went on. "I can feel it. You'll go off and be righteous next week, but you'll carry this victory forever."

The doors opened. They stepped into the command center to the unnerving quiet of cloaksaan at work. Even when they were busy, cloaksaan were quiet. Three of them sat before casting stations, filling the air with a dozen internal views of the lodge. Two of them were extracting the data from these views and conducting wordless conversations with operatives outside and inside Soye's Reach. Another cloaksaan stood monitoring it all, his pauldron appliquéd with the rank of a commandant. He observed her entrance with a tight smile that, for a cloaksaan, looked downright warm. Honestly, blank-faced Chono had the *perfect* temperament to be a Brutal Hand—why must she insist on being religious?

"Burning One," said the commandant.

His name was Yorus Inye. He had been one of her first novitiates, and he'd climbed the ranks of his Hand with a flint-eyed ambition Esek credited herself for teaching him. She liked him and had helped him place his bastard child with a respectable family two years ago. It had saved him some embarrassment with his superiors, and Esek sensed his gratitude whenever she spoke to him. She was not one to ignore an advantage, and that included cultivating loyalties. There were whispers that he might be in line for First Cloak, presiding over the Silver Keep. How delicious it would be, to have such a person in her debt. To even, perhaps, wheedle the location of the keep out of him and empower her family in new ways.

She came to stand alongside him. They surveyed the wash of views in the air, some showing the interior of the lodge, some showing the white blanket of North Avo, cut apart with the slivers of trees. "Anyone suspicious?" she asked.

Commandant Inye's tight smile edged toward a sneer. He gestured at the casting views.

"It's Soye's Reach, Burning One. They're all suspicious."

Yes. This was an essential component of the trap Esek had laid. Six had a penchant for criminals, for underworlds, for places off the beaten path. In the three years following their reunion on K-5 station, Six had used the fruits of those proclivities to send Esek several gifts (Chono an unwilling pack mule). And all of those gifts were tracked to criminal and insurgent organizations. Soye's Reach, with its rotating guest list of poachers, isolationists, and former convicts, was exactly the sort of place Six would choose for one of their business dealings.

"Where are the decoys?"

Chono pointed them out. They were, as she had noted, similarly dressed but otherwise nondescript, bundled heavily for the weather and taking up various positions. One was at the front desk, negotiating for a room with the proprietor. One was at the bar, a square of thick oak countertops and shelves overstuffed with bottles and flasks. Two had sat down to play tiles in the gambling hall, surrounded by other rickety tables and inebriated gamblers; everything looked sticky and fetid and alive, and the operatives themselves fit in well. Indeed, there was nothing to connect them to one another, besides one detail: The hoods of their coats were up.

In one corner of the gambling hall, another figure sat in a booth, smoking. This was Yorus Inye's plant—a convict whom they had delivered from a work colony in exchange for fronting the sale of some Nightfoot records. Just a little bit of correspondence, linking Alanye to a Nightfoot guardsaan. Not much, perhaps, but enough to attract Six. Or so Esek had gambled.

She scoured the room for something, anything, familiar. She crossed her arms and uncrossed them, shifting restlessly. Commandant Inye glanced at her sidelong.

"I assure you, Burning One, my cloaks are up to this task."

"I don't think anyone is up to the task of Six," muttered Esek. Then, placatingly, she added, "I'm sure you've only picked your best. I'd still rather I was with them."

Chono's eyes never ceased their calculated roaming of the various casting views. "You are too recognizable, Sa."

Esek scowled. Would she miss Chono's *ceaseless* logic and composure? It was one of the most annoying things about her. And yet Esek, arrogant though she knew herself to be, couldn't deny Chono's value to her. How her stoicism and practicality so effortlessly countered Esek's recklessness. Even Six might not have made a better chief novitiate than Chono. Six, after all, was a bloody and merciless creature, who killed almost as whimsically as Esek did.

Indeed, since K-5 and the run-in with the Ironway family, Esek was convinced Six's kills were all explicit answers to her own. Esek found a one-time crewsaan of Six's, interrogated them, and left their body in the stairwell of a housing project. A week later, one of Esek's novitiates turned up with his throat cut in the courtyard of a temple. Last year, Esek had tracked down a clerk who stole records from Sorek Nightfoot's private vaults, and sold them to Six. Esek broke every bone in that clerk's body and deposited them at the bottom of a lake. Not two weeks later, a secretary who had always been sympathetic to Esek's financial interests was shot in a bathhouse.

"Don't worry, Sa," said the commandant, snapping Esek back into the present. "My people have strict orders not to kill the target. You'll have that pleasure yourself."

The lines of Chono's brown coat swayed, indicating a slight rebalancing of her weight that Esek recognized very well. Poor Chono. It wasn't her fault Six produced complicated feelings in her. Esek herself had never had any need for friends, but she abstractly recognized it was difficult for Chono to know her one-time companion must die for the threat they posed. Why, even Esek sometimes bucked against the necessity. She often wondered—could she do it? When she finally had Six in front of her, vulnerable to her, would she be able to put that fire out? A fire that had filled her life with heat.

"Perhaps you should say a prayer, Chono," Esek said.

Inye chuckled, glancing at Chono. "Still reciting the beatitudes left and right?"

Esek chuckled back. "She makes the Godtexts sound like she wrote them."

Esek knew how uncomfortable this made Chono. After a moment her novitiate asked in her usual wooden voice, "What would you have me pray for, Sa?"

"Why, for victory!" Esek exclaimed. "For the demise of a terrorist! For the survival of the Nightfoot family! For the glory of the Kindom."

There was a beat of silence.

"The Prayer for War's End," Chono suggested.

"Ugh." Esek rolled her eyes. "You take the fun out of everything. Gods know what the clerics will do with you!"

Chono said, "Decoy one is moving."

Sure enough, the one who had been at the bar approached Inye's contact in her corner booth. Esek honestly couldn't remember the contact's name, but Chono reached into one of the nearest casting clouds, plucking at an aural link. "Stay calm, Devye."

Devye. All right, good. Devye watched the decoy approach her with slightly widened eyes. When they reached the booth, they sat down and cast back their hood—a man, mouth stretched in a flirtatious smile. He had brought a bottle from the bar and two glasses and began to pour. His voice was low and throaty and his flirtatious smile soon turned to flirtatious offers. Devye, a ratty little Katish shit stain who probably hadn't been laid in years, looked equal parts confused and terrified.

"Decoy two is moving," said Chono.

With a room key in hand, the second of the unknown figures left the lodge proprietor and went up the staircase to the row of rooms on the mezzanine floor. Esek watched them go inside Room 3, their hood still pulled up. In the gambling hall, the final two decoys were behaving normally, laying bets at the tile tables, while the people around them smoked and drank and hollered.

Suddenly, Devye received a comm.

"Link that through," Commandant Inye ordered.

A voice flooded the command center.

"If you'd like to accept my colleague's invitation, leave the package in the booth and follow him up to Room 3. You'll be paid there."

It was not Six's voice.

Devye paled. "That wasn't the deal."

"Have we got views on Room 3?" demanded Esek.

The cloaks at the casting stations were working furiously. Chono said, "We *did*."

"They appear not to be working," someone admitted.

Esek's pulse fluttered with excitement.

The voice on the comm told Devye, "We've had to adjust our plans."

"Do *not* leave the booth," ordered Chono into Devye's ear.

"I—I—I didn't agree to this. You said you'd meet me here, second booth from the back, between four and six. I've been here. Where are you?"

"If you don't go to Room 3, the deal's off."

The man sitting with Devye leaned closer, his smile dripping sex. "Don't make me kill you, sweetheart."

"They must be bluffing," said Inye.

Esek shook her head. "No. They're testing to see if it's a trap." She snatched the aural link from Chono, ordering, "Go with him. We'll cover you."

Chono looked at her. "If Six has any idea this is a trap, they'll kill her as soon as they get into Room 3. She's only safe if she stays in the booth."

"I don't give a shit about her safety. Where is the warhawk?"

"*The Katanye Four* is in position," Inye said.

Esek felt Chono watching her again. "Warhawk?" she repeated.

"Last resort," Esek said, as Devye gingerly rose from the booth and followed her leering seducer toward the staircase.

For several moments no one spoke, everything in a holding pattern as Devye went up the stairs like a woman walking toward the gallows.

"Commandant Inye," Chono said. "How many people are currently in the lodge?"

Esek sighed, aware of Inye glancing between her and Chono.

"Based on our last count? Two hundred and seventeen. All enemies of the Kindom."

There was a beat of silence. Chono looked at the commandant. "Living on the outskirts does not automatically make you an enemy of the Kindom."

"And being one of Sa Nightfoot's novitiates does not make you a military authority, *Cleric* Chono."

Esek clucked, "Now, now. Let's not resort to name-calling, Inye." With as much placation as she could muster in herself, she told Chono, "It is a *last* resort."

Inye turned his head, dismissing Chono altogether, and spoke into his comm, "Take up position near the booth."

"No, take the booth itself. I want to see what happens."

Immediately, three disguised cloaks at the bar carried their drinks toward the abandoned booth. They laughed and jostled each other, performing a state of mild drunkenness that no actor could fault. When they sat, one of them made a show of finding Devye's abandoned satchel. Looking incredulous, he pawed through it like a thief. It contained nothing but laminate records, which no drunk would have found interesting. He dropped the satchel on the floor by his feet, and he and his compatriots went on laughing and drinking.

By now, Devye had gone into Room 3. The aural link broke like a twig snapping. Inye's caster cloaksaan worked swiftly, silently, trying to restore it. Esek's heart was a drum.

"Tell the proprietor to send fresh sheets to the room," Chono ordered.

Esek said, "No. It'll be too suspicious."

The two gambler decoys stood up simultaneously. One of them went to a different table. One of them headed toward the stairs. Esek was so distracted with watching their movements, it was Chono who redirected her attention with a sharp "Look."

Someone had approached the cloaksaan in the booth. Someone… Esek had not even noticed in the crowded gambling hall. They were tall. Narrowly built. They had a hood on, and when they approached the booth, the cloaksaan's oculars passed back an image of a person with a scarf obscuring the majority of their face. Only their eyes, and a bit of warm brown skin, came through. The eyes were a vibrant purple, which could only be mods. A retinal scan brought back nothing. The mods must have blockers in them.

"Excuse me," said the figure to the gamblers. "But that satchel belongs to me."

At the sound of the voice, heat flooded Esek's veins. Potent as arousal. Searing as rage. She would know that voice anywhere. Beside her, Chono's body tightened like a bow. The three cloaksaan, still working their performance beautifully, jeered at Six. One asked, "Oh yeah? Why'd you leave it here, then?"

Six did not reach for the satchel. They stood poised and serene before the three cloaksaan. "Perhaps one of you could hand it to me?"

Commandant Inye must have caught on to the way Esek stared at Six, because he asked, "Is it them?"

Esek sucked her teeth. Her mouth was wet with saliva.

"Yes," she murmured.

"Then we should take them into—"

"Not yet," Chono interrupted. "It's some kind of trap. Don't move yet."

Esek didn't bother looking at Inye, but she could feel the outrage rolling off him.

"Esek, tell your fucking novitiate not to give orders in—"

"Shut up!" Esek snarled.

She stepped closer to the casting view. She stared into the sliver of Six's face. It wasn't enough. It would never be enough until she'd stripped their mask away.

The cloaksaan in the booth were still laughing. "You want it so bad? Pick it up!"

It was classic bully behavior. If Six bent forward, they would kick the satchel out of reach. But Six did not bend forward. They said, "I wonder if you could tell me something. It is a simple question. Who is the Sixth God?"

Static spread down Esek's limbs. The three cloaksaan cackled and one said, "What the fuck? Asshole, get out of here, we're drinking."

"Surely Commandant Inye would say Kata? Do you agree?"

Inye stepped aggressively toward Esek. "We have to take them now, while we have the advantage."

Chono said, "We don't have the advantage. Six wouldn't be doing this if we had the advantage."

Esek knew she was right. More than that, she knew her carefully orchestrated trap was being turned on her with an elegance she would have admired, if she weren't the one in the noose.

"Tell the warhawk to arm its missiles," Esek said.

Inye gave the order. A flurry of activity began on the casting views, including a glimpse of the warhawk outside the planet Kator's atmosphere, readying its guns for a killing blow.

In the hunting lodge, one of Inye's cloaks told Six crossly, "I don't know if you're drunk or what, but get your face out of here before I break it."

"But my face is of such interest. To some, anyway."

More static in Esek's body, like lightning strikes stamped on a night sky.

"Burning One, talk to them," Chono urged. "They know you're watching. They want to talk to you. We don't need to kill a roomful of innocent—"

"None of these people are innocent," said Inye.

"Your cloaks are in there. So is Devye. We promised to protect her."

"My cloaks are prepared to die for the Kindom."

Chono's voice rose barely a decibel. "None of this was sanctioned by the Kindom."

Inye made a furious sound. Chono stepped closer to Esek, urging her, "You can't mean to do this. You can't mean to kill them like this. Not after everything."

Esek looked at her slowly, surprised by the barely contained vehemence in Chono's voice. Their eyes locked for what felt like a small eternity, but couldn't be more than moments. Yet it was long enough for Esek to see the breadth of Chono's knowledge. For years she had known that Chono understood her family's crimes, the things Six stood to reveal about them. For years Esek had weighed that point of vulnerability against Chono's fidelity, and concluded that she could trust her. But suddenly she saw that her chief novitiate was more insightful even than she had realized. Chono knew more than *why* Esek was hunting Six. Chono knew that Esek *wanted* Six. She knew how deep and ravenous her longing for Six was, and that even direct orders from Alisiana might not be enough to force her to kill this fish she'd been hunting so long.

Distantly Esek realized—she would have to kill Chono. She would have to kill her favorite novitiate, not because Chono carried secrets about the Nightfoots, but because Chono knew the strength of Six's grip on Esek herself. For this unbearable crime, Esek would have to kill her.

And Esek saw the moment that Chono realized it, too.

In her long career, Esek had seen many people grasp that they were about to die. She'd seen the sudden panic and horror and denial. But

Chono's eyes betrayed no such feelings. Hers took on a gleam that married resignation to resolve.

Esek's hand slid toward the bloodletter. She could make it quick. Not painless, but qui—

"Commandant!" someone cried.

Esek whirled back toward the screens in time to see over a dozen gamblers stand up. It was simultaneous. Synchronized. They threw off their heavy coats to reveal shaved heads and red sleeveless shirts. Esek's breath caught. The same uniform Six had worn on K-5. And under their coats, there was more than that red taunting flag. There were guns. They drew in tandem, and one of them began to shout about a robbery.

Screams went up in the lodge. Patrons darted under tables. Others tried to draw their own weapons, and were picked off by Six's crew. Seven cloaksaan, spread throughout the lodge, moved for a killing strike. The three in the booth dropped all pretense and drew on Six, but from within their own coat Six pulled two daggers with blades as long as Esek's forearm. The first move slit the nearest cloaksaan's throat open. The second sailed a knife into another's chest. Six leapt onto the table as the final cloaksaan managed to aim his gun—and they drove the first blade down through his eye and into his skull.

It happened in the space of two seconds, three. Esek watched in amazement as gunfire erupted in the lodge. Inye shouted orders and Chono called her name and Six jumped off the table and grabbed the satchel on the ground, running toward the bar. Esek knew, from the lodge's blueprints, that there was a trapdoor behind the bar that led to a cellar. The cellar had a service tunnel. They had cloaksaan guarding that tunnel's exit. But Six would certainly know that, too—

"Esek, *don't!*" Chono pleaded.

But she'd sworn to Alisiana. Sworn it knowing that her whole fate, all her ambitions, rested on success. *I'll bring you its head.*

Struck from its shoulders...

"Fire!" Esek cried, spittle flying from her mouth. "Fire on the lodge, fire!!"

"*Katanye Four*, open fire," said Inye into the comm. "Open fire now!"

On one of the casting views, the quiet black of space surrounding the warhawk was disturbed by four missiles loosed upon North Avo. Two, three, four seconds passed. Esek watched Six, vaulting a table, landing on the bar, dropping down behind it—

Eight seconds, nine seconds, ten—

They would be in the cellar now.

Fifteen seconds, sixteen seconds, seventeen—

Even from fifteen miles away, the impact of the missile strike was deafening. The command center rattled. All the views of the lodge's interior went black. One of the casters provided a new view of the North Avon wilderness, and the cliffside called Soye's Reach: The lodge was gone. Plumes of black smoke rose off the mountain like the emissions of a volcano. Whole trees and sheets of rock plunged off the cliffside into the ravines below. Fires overpowered the blanketing snows, and smoldered in the surrounding forest. Even if Six had made it to the tunnel—the tunnel itself was no more.

It became very quiet in the command center. Esek could hear her own heartbeat. She was aware she was breathing hard, elated, ecstatic—but she also felt ill. And it was not only a physical sensation. Not just nausea and ringing ears and the beginnings of a headache in the front of her skull. It was something deeper than that. Something she couldn't name, and hated.

She looked at Chono, who was not moving at all, who was hardly even breathing. Would she shave her head for Six, as mourning Terons did? Would she grieve? Was *that* the feeling in Esek's chest? *Grief?*

"A direct hit," said Inye, his voice far away. "There's nothing left."

Nothing left...No, of course not. With missiles like that, there wouldn't be bodies. Just ash and the occasional knuckle bone...

Esek ordered, "Send a recovery team. To be sure."

Commandant Inye did not argue. This kind of thoroughness was the Cloaksaan way. It's what she had trained him to do. What she would have trained Six to do.

Esek turned her back on all of it. She went out of the room. She bypassed the elevator and took the stairs, jogging down toward the barracks level. The metal slats rattled under her feet. Behind her, she could feel and hear Chono keeping step. Loyal, loyal Chono. And what of Esek's own loyalty? Hadn't she proved it now, to Alisiana? Hadn't she done everything that could be asked of her?

I have done it to impress you. Is that not what you charged me to do?

She reached the door to her chamber at a near run, throwing it open.

The boy was still in her bed.

The sound of the door crashing open woke him from a doze. He sat up, eyes wide. Esek stared at him, momentarily confused. His mouth had stopped bleeding, but there was a rusty stain on the bedspread, and he was still naked, carefree as a child.

A red haze descended on her. He turned gray before her eyes. He made an abortive motion, as if to get up—but it was too late. Esek had him by the hair in an instant. It was thick, and made a perfect hand-hold. She yanked him out of the bed and threw him against the wall. His head cracked against concrete, his terrified eyes fuzzing.

"Esek!" someone cried.

But the bloodletter was already in her hand. She snarled through her teeth. She drove it up, through his ribs. She felt the bones give, felt the hard muscle of the heart as her blade went through it. He gasped, choked, shuddered in a useless attempt at resistance. She twisted the blade and blood poured out of him like a geyser. It spilled hot over her hand and arm and onto the front of her body, which was close to his. A horrible stench filled the room as his bowels released. He made one last, whimpering sound of confusion, and Esek watched his eyes change. Even after he went limp, she held him against the wall, panting, her whole body coiled. Then with a shove she stepped back from him.

He collapsed in a twisted heap, leaving smears of blood and excrement on the wall. Esek stood looking at him. She felt far from her body. Far from what she'd done, and also, totally indifferent to it. Slowly, she turned around.

Chono stood in the doorway, white as a corpse. For once her feelings were completely transparent. Horror had transformed her face into a stranger's, and she didn't move, didn't breathe. She was like a statue. Esek thought of their moment in the command center, when this had so nearly become Chono's fate. Was it her fate, still? She would not be helpless. Not like the dead cloaksaan on the ground. Chono would fight back.

Esek swallowed. Very slowly, the trembling rage that had consumed her body began to leak out of her. She felt control come back to her, like a cloak slipped over her shoulders. They stared at each other. It seemed to go on for hours.

Esek's voice was a rasp. "I think it's good you are going away to be a cleric, Chono. I think, otherwise, I might end up killing you. And I wouldn't have you dead. Not now."

Still, Chono didn't move. She didn't speak. Her hands were under her brown coat, within reach of her gun. Esek nodded approvingly. She wiped a hand against her forehead, which was damp with sweat, and now gore.

"Find me water, and something to eat. I think…I need to sit down."

CHAPTER FIFTEEN

1664

YEAR OF THE CRUX

The Gunner
Orbiting Silt

This time, she wakes like a gun going off. A cry catches in her throat, and her body, filmed with sweat, locks up. She lies shivering, gasping at the light-speckled bulkhead above her that warps and tunnels like a journey through a jump gate.

It's happened before. She's an old hand at this now. *Breathe,* she tells herself, imagining it is Liis's voice. *Breathe.* It's only after what feels like hours of trembling effort that she remembers to *exhale* as well as inhale, and oxygen floods her brain. It takes minutes more to get her heart rate under control. To get the feeling back in her fingers and toes.

Why does this still happen? It was more than ten years ago. Sometimes it feels like the whole Treble has flooded the space between her and that day when Great Gra's message came through on her comm. Until moments like this, when it might as well be happening all over again, her ocular pinging an alert:

sunstep
sunstep
sunstep

She remembers blinking at the words. The family glyph, a footprint in a circle of gold—rendered as a code word. She'd squinted, not even aware her hearing had started to fuzz, her heartbeat quickening—all behind a veil of confusion and disbelief. It was in that baffled state that the fourth message appeared:

RUN!

And she had. And she had never stopped.

Jun's throat is parched. She moves her arm and finds the searing agony has retreated to a deep ache. The second dose appears to have done its job. She considers sitting up but decides against it, lies motionless, staring at the ceiling and thinking of the near hysteria that gripped her before Liis jammed the injector into her hip. That fucker.

A sound of voices through the wall piques her interest. No, one voice. A bass rumble that must be Masar. Masar the Jeveni. Masar with the buyer. The buyer who wants to *hide* her. Jun casts a line into the ship's cockpit, and hears—

"—known a lot of casters. My friend Woon used to talk about Sunstep like she's a fucking miracle worker." The remark meets with Liis's implacable silence. Apparently undeterred, Masar asks, "Is it true she wrote her Hood program when she was fifteen?" He whistles low.

"Fuck. That's almost impressive enough to make up for her being such an asshole."

"She's not an asshole," mutters Liis. Adds, "Not in a bad way. A little single-minded sometimes, but—"

Masar huffs. "You think I'm not used to having people reject an idea just because it comes from a Jeveni? She clearly doesn't think we're capable of protecting you."

Jun's body tightens. Liis says, "It's not about the Jeveni. It's about the idea of hiding itself."

For a moment Jun thinks she's going to say more, just spill Jun's secrets on the cabin floor, but to her relief, Liis goes silent again.

Finally, doubtfully, Masar says, "Well, at least she's not all or nothing, like you. She's still willing to work with me. You should talk to my buyer. He'll change her mind about the protection, I swear it."

"He won't change her mind."

"Then *you* change her mind. *You* aren't opposed to our help. She'll listen to you."

"I don't want this deal at all. I don't work with strangers."

Masar grumbles, "She must have been a stranger to you once. You don't know her from the womb."

Liis says nothing, and this time a smile twitches at Jun's mouth. He's got her there. The first time Liis saved her life, they were very much strangers. Jun had seriously misjudged a con she was running in a casting lab, pilfering credit off three Teron blockheads who turned out to be savvier than she anticipated. They cornered her in an alley behind the lab, and as the second and third blows landed, Jun finally realized she had made a miscalculation. She supposes they would have killed her if not for the sudden arrival of a stocky, ferocious hurricane of a woman who left them all unconscious in the muck and took Jun with her. Patched her up in a tiny dark room cluttered with spices and weapons and books of poetry.

As introductions go, it was memorable. And quite outside Liis's usual wheelhouse.

But Liis didn't open up to her right away, didn't want to work with her, didn't trust her. It took months of "accidental" run-ins and gifts of information and occasional, blistering sex before Jun persuaded her to partner up on a job. Since then, they have only ever worked with well-established contacts, people Jun knows from the casting net or Liis knows from her years of surviving under the radar. When Masar offered protection on behalf of his buyer, and Liis seemed open to it, Jun was frankly shocked. But what can it mean, except that Liis doesn't think they can protect themselves? Not this time.

Masar says, "I think you know you can trust us." Liis doesn't respond, and if he was wrong, she would say so. Which means she *does* believe they can trust the Jeveni. But she won't say it outright, and in her silence Masar blusters on, "I saved Jun's life. Twice. I mean, Som's *ass*. I'm pretty good with this shotgun, and I've got a hundred pounds on both of you. Don't you think if I'd wanted to take you two out, I would have done it by now?"

Liis drawls, "Congratulations on having a big gun, but please believe me when I say that killing you would be about as easy for me as picking the wings off a fly."

Jun smirks. There is something so obnoxiously *attractive* about Liis's moments of arrogance and swagger. Moments when the cloaksaan in her shows its deadly face.

But that word—cloaksaan—triggers an internal flinch. It pulls Jun back in time, into memories she can never control. Sometimes she'll see a dark shape in a doorway, or a dark coat on a stranger, and find herself returned to the academy library in Riin Kala, the Six Gods painting the ceiling overhead. Her alarm going off. Monsters in the foyer. She remembers the head archivist, flanked by cloaksaan, calling her name—but Ricari's warning had already come, and Jun was already out of the room. She found a window. Shimmied down an escape ladder onto the alley floor, catching her calf on a ragged piece of metal during the descent. Wet blood ran down her leg. She made it to the safe house, panting and faint. It was only a twelve-by-twelve flat squeezed between a hundred others in the slum town of Barter Street, half a mile from the academy. She did her best to clean the wound and seal it with suture gel, sobbing and shaking the entire time. She kept the lights off in the flat so no one would notice her arrival.

And then, she passed out.

Over the cast, Masar says, "It's Jun's coin to barter. When she wakes up, I'm taking my lead from her." Liis doesn't reply. Suddenly petulant, he adds, "My buyer will change your minds. Give them a chance to change your minds."

Liis says, low and emotionless, "Jun would rather Esek kill us than have to hide."

Jun's stomach twists at the words, a combination of dread and guilt, and that uncanny feeling she still gets sometimes, when Liis proves how well she knows her. Especially the wretched parts of her.

This time, Masar doesn't have a retort, and the air goes dead. Jun cuts the casting line. She lies staring at the bulkhead, listening to the low hum of the ship. A moment later, the door to the cabin opens. Jun closes her eyes, feigns sleep, doesn't want to talk right now—

The door closes with a definitive hiss. "I know you're faking."

Fucking former cloaksaan.

Jun sits up. Liis watches her solemnly. She looks tired and worried and it pricks Jun with regret over all she's put her through in the past week. Liis says, "You look like shit."

Such a romantic.

"You should probably have more painkillers." Liis brandishes one of the morpho syrettes.

Jun notices she's holding it in her right hand rather than her left; she's got her left arm subtly cradled against her side—a sure indication it's sore.

"Sure you don't need that yourself?" she asks.

"I'm fine."

"Let me look at your arm."

Liis scowls. "I've got to shower. Here."

She tosses the syrette across the bed, and Jun manages to catch it, though not without wincing. She watches Liis go into the bathroom and shut the door. The shower turns on. Jun uncaps the syrette and jabs it into her own neck, gritting her teeth through the initial pain, and then collapsing back against the mattress as floaty relief takes its place. For a moment, all she can feel is drugged and grateful. But that blessing turns on her, becomes like a key unlocking all her mental defenses...

Run. Run. Run.

That word in her mind is like a fishhook, dragging her back through the waters of time. She remembers Ricari, his voice, his hands, his lined and weary face.

Always have an escape plan. Have two, he said before she left K-5 to start school on Ma'kess.

If you get the signal, don't question it. Just go.

Keep this gun clean. Keep it on you at all times.

Go to the safe house. Stay there until I can come and get you. If I can't, I'll send word.

The old memories pull her under, like the vacuum of space, like an ocean of code. The fact is, she did everything he told her to do. She kept her gun clean and she made her contingencies and she listened when his warning came. She went to the safe house and waited. And she still nearly died. Later she would realize the wound in her leg became infected right away, that bit of rusty escape ladder introducing a hundred years of city grime directly into her veins. She spent two days in a fever fugue. The flat was stocked with water pouches and dried mealpacks and even antibiotics, but she got sick so quickly she didn't touch any of it, and she was too frightened and too delirious to seek help. How sepsis didn't get her is a miracle—

Except it's not a miracle at all. Because the next time she was truly conscious, she realized someone else was sitting in the room. And it wasn't Great Gra.

A cloaksaan, she thought, but was too weak and miserable to care. Distantly, she noticed an IV in her arm, connected to a bag of some liquid that hung from the bedpost. Was the cloaksaan poisoning her? Weren't they famous for doing cruel, creepy shit like that?

"Good," said a voice, very quiet and calm, as she had always imagined cloaksaan sounded. "Your fever broke an hour ago."

Jun realized her leg no longer felt like it was on fire. In fact, she had the sense it had been wrapped properly, though she couldn't quite sit up and look. She blinked—her vision was fuzzy. The figure in the chair was half-shadowed, but she could tell after a moment that they were not wearing the black uniform of a cloaksaan. There was no pauldron with its three-pointed Kindom star against a blazing sun. There was no bloodletter at their waist. Jun tried to talk but her mouth was too dry. The figure gestured at something.

"Drink that."

Only then did she realize there was a water pouch on her chest. She tore the foil corner with weak, trembling fingers, and began to suck desperately, guzzling, and then squeezing out every last drop until the pouch fell from her hands and she was panting from exhaustion.

"I admit," said the person in the chair, "I did not expect you to escape. The Cloaksaan must be very embarrassed."

They had a strange voice, a strange accent, that reminded her of a game of tiles. They spoke each word like it was a game piece they were delicately placing on a table, one after the other, in a perfect line. Their face was still shrouded, but Jun had an impression of them as tall and lean. Their head, she thought, was shaved. Their hands, resting on their knees, were gloved.

"Who are you?" Jun croaked.

"A friend of your Great Gra."

Jun stared. She was better trained than to take them at their word.

"What's your name?" she asked, with a haughtiness that might not have been smart.

"It is not safe for me to give you a name."

"Then how do I know you're Gra's friend?"

"Because I knew I could find you here. He has had this safe house since before you or I were born."

Jun knew this was pretty airtight, but she was unwilling to concede it. "I don't know who you are. Gra told me to come here and wait for *him*."

"I know," said the figure in the chair. "But he could not come."

Fear pooled in Jun's stomach. It dried out her mouth again, as if she'd never tasted the water. Her fingers twitched. But she forced herself to ask the question they had clearly come to answer. "Where is he?"

Then the stranger told her a story that would take her hours to understand. Maybe years. They described a confrontation in the family shop. A cleric called Esek Nightfoot, who shot her uncle Coz in the head. The stranger explained that two other members of her family had been killed. Her second uncle, Misek, and Ricari. Jun's own parents had died when she was very young. She remembers them with a fuzzy tenderness, but at heart, she was Ricari's child.

"My cousins—what—what about my cousins? What about Bene?"

Her voice was raw. She wasn't crying because the adrenaline of disbelief had choked out all other bodily responses. She wanted to sit up, jump up, scream—but she couldn't move.

The stranger said, "Alive. As are your grandmothers, and your aunt."

Jun had never been particularly close to these women. Knowing they were alive brought her relief, but it didn't even nick the shell of grief growing over her now. Her cousins were safe—that was the most important thing. She thought of Bene. He had the same dark wheat eyes as Ricari. He was just a sweet and good-natured kid, always following her around, always wanting to *be* her. And now his father was dead...

"Was it because of Gra?" she asked, thinking maybe if she asked questions, if she kept talking, she could hold the wall of horror and grief at bay a little longer. "Was it because he used to speak against the Kindom?"

Granted, that was over fifty years ago, when Gra was a young man living in Riin Kala and heading up protests against cloaksaan terrorization and corrupt secretaries. Maybe they decided to finally make an example of him? Maybe they—

"This had nothing to do with Ricari's political past. This was the action of a single cleric, working outside the purview of the Kindom."

Jun was too stunned to speak.

The stranger went on, "Cleric Nightfoot's true purpose is to protect the interests of her family. She will kill anyone if it helps her to get what she wants."

Jun blurted, "But that's wrong!"

Instantly, she flushed in humiliation, realizing how absurd, how naive she sounded. The stranger was silent, a silence Jun couldn't read. Was it an indictment of her foolishness? Was it agreement? Was it simply indifference to the outburst of a child? Jun's eyes burned suddenly with unshed tears, first of embarrassment, and then, an all-consuming rage. The kind that burrows and takes root and spreads its filaments through every vein and nerve, till it becomes an underlying code that will dictate everything that comes next. Her tears went away. A dark resolve descended.

"We have money. Ricari put away enough to start over." She nodded, feeling the beginnings of a plan. "We can relocate. The frontier stations in Teros System are completely off the grid. We'll go there. I'm a caster—I can make all of us new identities, and so long as we lie low for a few—"

"The money is all gone," interrupted the stranger. "The Kindom seized your family assets. They have put out statements that the Ironways are a terrorist cell. That you slaughtered a contingent of novitiates. Your family's names and faces are all over the Treble now. I have had to separate them into two groups and place them with protectors."

Jun's heart and stomach dropped out of her body.

"Protectors?" she whispered. Her fingers were cold. Her limbs were numb.

"People I trust," they said, and said no more.

Jun swallowed over and over. She flexed her fingers, trying to get feeling back into them.

"For how long?" she asked.

They said nothing. This was an answer. Jun's ears started to ring. Even in the darkness of the room, her vision went white.

The stranger said, "I promised your grandmi I would bring you to her, if you lived. You will not be well enough to travel until tomorrow at the earliest."

Those words managed to break through her descending panic. Sharply she said, "No!"

As before, the person in the chair was silent, and as before, Jun heard the sheer *ridiculousness* of her words. What other option did she have? Where could she go that this Esek Nightfoot wouldn't find her? She had nothing. She was *fourteen*. She was wanted in the Treble. Her grandmothers must be desperate to get her back, and she was desperate to hold her little cousins and know they were safe.

But they weren't safe. They were destitute. Dependent on protectors they didn't know. Separated from one another, probably forever. That would kill Hosek, who cared about nothing but her family. And what about Jun's cousins? They would grow up in hiding. Bene always wanted to go to the academy, like her. But that would never happen now. Isolation. Exile. They would never have anything that was their own. They would never even have freedom. Refugees. *Outcasts*.

No. *No.* Jun couldn't stand it. Wouldn't allow it. With all the fever and ferocity of youth, she set her fate in that moment.

"Take me somewhere else."

After a pause, the stranger said, "Nowhere else is safe."

"I don't care. I'm not going to disappear down a hole. I'll go out on my own. I'll survive on my own, until I have money. Until I can make us free again."

Another pregnant silence.

"If I let you do that, I will be breaking my word to your family. To Ricari."

She had a sense then that the stranger was angry. Or at least, feeling something very strongly. Were they angry at her? Somehow, she didn't think so. She took a gamble.

"Would *you* let yourself be carted off like this? If someone killed *your* family, would you run away and hide forever?"

A long, stifling pause. Then, the stranger let out a breath, which was the most human thing they had done so far. They leaned forward. Their face came out of the shadows. The first thing Jun noticed was their Katish gendermark. It was very pale, as of someone who did not want to be gendered from a distance. It was a slightly taboo assignation, one Jun had only seen once or twice. The rest of the stranger's face was ordinary. But the dark eyes were so intense that Jun shrank back.

"I cannot be your protector. I cannot take you as an apprentice. If I do not deliver you to your family, I will have to abandon you somewhere. You will probably be found. You will probably be killed. You may be tortured first."

Jun fought to control her expression. She felt cold and sweaty with fear.

"If you accept those odds, then I will take you wherever you want to go. I will give you what I can. But after that, I will have to forget you. You may not survive. Indeed, to survive, you will have to be...extraordinary." They paused on the word. It was like a door coaxing Jun to step through. "Do you understand, Jun Ironway? Is it truly what you want?"

In that moment, Jun's future split into two paths. The stranger was letting her choose, and whatever choice she made, it would be her responsibility alone. This was both an act of deepest respect, and utmost cruelty. Years later, Jun wonders what would have happened if the stranger had responded to their encounter differently. What if they had treated her words as the bravado of a grief-stricken teenager? What if they had been patient, and won her over slowly to the more rational decision? What if—

"Jun?"

She looks up to find Liis standing next to her. She didn't even hear the shower go off, much less the door opening. Liis is looking at her with a furrowed brow. She's wearing loose shorts and a bandeau around her breasts. A long, thick scar wends down her rib cage, carving a tract through blue-black skin.

"Are you all right?"

Jun blinks, as if blinking were a switch that could flick her from one time back to the present. Slowly, cautious of her still aching body, she puts her legs over the side of the bed and stands up. Liis watches her.

Jun tests out the strength in her legs, walking to the bathroom to get a drink from the tap. To her surprise, she's not dizzy at all.

It's when she turns back, looking at Liis across the room, that she asks quietly, "Do you think I was wrong, to never make contact with them?"

Liis thinks about it for several moments. "Knowing where they are, knowing they're safe, is the most important thing. Making contact before we were ready could have put them at risk."

Jun smiles, but it's pained. Before they were ready... They've had this conversation before. It took her five years to find her grandmothers and Bene in a small mining town on the coast of N'braekos, Braemin; two more to learn her aunt had died of fever on a farm station orbiting Quietus, but was survived by Jun's younger cousins, the twins. Yes, they are safe. Trapped in poor communities with no way out, but safe. Bringing them together again, accruing enough fortune to keep them close and protect them—that motivation has driven her hardest. For years, nothing else mattered to her. Then she met Liis, and things were different after that. Liis signed on to her mission. Liis gave her partnership and watched her back. Liis brought trust into her life. Liis is powerfully strong, and achingly brave—and so much smarter than Jun.

Which reminds her.

"How did you know Masar was a Jeveni?"

Liis rubs the back of her neck with her right hand, like she's debating whether to answer. Then she gestures at her face. "The Braemish tattoos. They don't cover the spot where the Jeveni tattoo should be. That spot is smooth."

Jun rolls her eyes. "You cloaksaan freak."

"*Also*...he speaks Je. You may have taken that news in stride, but the fact is it's nearly impossible for non-natives to learn Je. It's composed almost entirely of tonal variation and idioms. The acrobat said, 'Wide tunnels in our rock. Kill the oxygen snatchers.'"

"What the fuck?" says Jun.

"But Masar translated it as, 'Autonomy for Jeve. Death to thieves.'"

"My own ocular did the same," Jun argues.

"That's because *your* language translator is more sophisticated than anything a Braemish pirate would have had on his own ocular. Because *your* translator was programmed by *you*. You caster freak."

"Well, if you're so smart, tell me: Why shouldn't we sell this coin to the people who have more right than anyone to know what the Night-foots did?"

Liis glowers. "Is this your play? We're risking our lives to work with the Jeveni out of a sense of justice? In that case, why don't we just give it to them and be done with it?"

"Well, let's not be rash—"

"Haven't I kept you alive all these years? How do you think I did that?"

"I like to think we've kept each other alive, thanks," Jun shoots back. "And we have taken plenty of risks to get what we want. Everything we do is a risk. Maybe we haven't been this exposed before, but—"

"Fine," Liis snaps. "Then sell it to them. And let them pay us in a currency we can use."

Jun closes her mouth. This impasse, again. Liis watches with troubled eyes. Jun thinks of the dark eyes of the stranger in Great Gra's safe house. She thinks about Bene's dark wheat eyes, full of terror as Esek's novitiates killed his father. She thinks of Bene, forced into hiding—

"Everything I've done has been so we can get to the frontier stations. So that we *don't* have to hide. How can you ask me to—"

"You think it's weakness," Liis interrupts. She moves toward Jun, till they are standing in front of each other, of a height but otherwise opposites—Liis muscular and compact, dark-skinned and dark-eyed; Jun skinny and pale brown and so much less remarkable. "You know that's all I've been doing for ten years, right? Hiding from the Cloaksaan. Hiding from that life. Do you think I'm weak, Jun?"

Jun's stomach churns with acid. Angrily she reminds her, "I've *never* called you that."

"And yet if I'm not weak for hiding, why would you be weak for—"

"Because I had that chance," Jun snaps. "I had the chance to hide away with my family, and I said no. If I do it now, then all this time was for nothing. I might as well have gone with them in the beginning! Instead, I broke my own heart to try to find a better way. And for what? So the Jeveni can put me in a hovel somewhere?"

Liis sighs. "So, it's this again? You still blame yourself."

"I—"

"You were a child. You made a decision. None of them died because of you. You have to forgive yourself. And you have to look past your fear and your stubbornness and do what's needed. That is survival, Jun. And you don't need me to tell you so."

She walks away. Jun watches, silent. She eats up the sight of her: her short wrestler's legs and her strong shoulders and her stomach cut with muscle and scars. A body wrought from survival, and regret.

Sitting on the bed, Liis uncaps the jar of oil she uses at night. It's a plant-based medicine from the Katish village where Liis was born. It's the green smell that suffuses her. She slowly rubs it into her knee joints, then the elbow and wrist of her right arm. Her left arm, seamed below the bicep, is pulled against her body in a posture that might look defensive to someone else, but which Jun recognizes as pain.

"Is it hurting?" Jun asks. "Why have you still got it on? Give it to me."

Liis does nothing for long seconds. Then she sets the jar of oil down. With a practiced movement of her right hand, she disconnects the arm at the bio port; there's a sucking sound, and a click. Jun holds out her hand for it, and Liis passes it over with a mutter of annoyance. The arm is soft and warm in Jun's hands, with a supple give of muscle and flesh under skin perfectly matched to Liis's. Jun finds Liis's backpack next to the bed and pulls out the supplies pouch. She goes to the room's small table and turns on the lamp. Sitting down, she rolls out the pouch of tools and holds the arm under the light. She uses a tip of live wire to test the reaction in each fingertip, as well as the crook of the elbow. She sprays a disinfectant into the connector and carefully examines the interior under penlight. Several ports emerge from behind a thin membrane, behind which the muscle and fat and bone of Liis's cybernetic arm regulate their own blood flow and nervous system.

"I'm going to clean these plugs," she says without looking up. "And you need a new connector for the brachial artery."

Liis doesn't answer. Jun sets to work, methodical in her treatment of the arm. Not for the first time she feels a shiver of anger, that Liis must make do with a prosthetic. A very high-end prosthetic, yes, but a prosthetic, nonetheless. It requires lots of maintenance. It's more painful. It squeaks sometimes in a way she knows makes Liis's skin crawl. But she lives with it, because the upgrades are so expensive.

"I want to buy you a body mod," Jun says.

Liis narrows her eyes. "Why?"

"I want you to have a real arm. Something that won't hurt like this. If we go into hiding, we won't have access to high-end medical. You'll never get the arm."

Finally Liis answers, her voice flat but not cold, "I won't get one if I'm dead, either."

"Gods*damnit*, Liis. Work with me here!"

"I *will* work with you," Liis retorts. "I'll go meet this buyer." But before Jun can get excited, she adds sharply, "*If* you agree to hear their *whole* offer." Jun grimaces. "Those are my terms. Take it or leave it."

They stare each other down for long moments. This is the nature of their partnership. Negotiation and argument, compromise and devotion.

Blinking rapidly, embarrassed by the sudden burn of tears in her eyes, she focuses on the prosthetic arm. She uses a disinfectant swab to carefully oil the valves. Then, she injects a needle into its median vein, extracts a sample onto a slide, and examines it under her magnifier.

"I want to get you a new sleeve cap. It'll help with the chafing. And I'm putting this in the regenerator for the night. The platelet count is low."

"Fine," Liis mutters.

"Fine," Jun retorts.

Jun slips the arm into its regenerator sleeve. She goes to Liis and gently fits the cap onto her exposed upper arm, checking for hints of inflammation first. For all its muscle and scars, Liis's skin is always unexpectedly soft. Jun can smell the clean green warmth of her, and she wants to bury her face in that warmth. To be delivered of all her cares. For a little while.

Instead she asks, "Are you still in pain?"

"No," Liis says. She's such a liar.

"If we agree to hide, I may never see my family again."

"You don't know that. You don't know anything until we talk to them."

Jun nods. Two years ago, Grandmi Keena, Hosek's wife, died of a treatable illness. How much longer before Hosek is dead, too? Bene works a dangerous job in the copper mines. The twins are scraping by on a farm station with bad air filtration. Every day, Jun feels that she is running out of time, running out of chances. And now she must face an even worse possibility—

"If we don't hide, I may lead Esek right to them."

Liis has the generosity not to jump on this. She is quiet, letting Jun feel the unwelcome truth.

Jun recalls the day she boarded a freighter in the wake of the stranger's purposeful step, and disembarked on Kator, in a factory town in north Dunta. Carrion birds wheeled overhead and plumes of smoke smudged a pale skyline with purple and black, and Jun had nothing to her name but a small bag and a credit coin with five thousand plae on it. The stranger looked at her one last time, and gave her a final chance to go with them. To be returned to her family. But she didn't take that chance. The stranger, half annoyed, half impressed, had said, "You will be on your own. That is safest, for now. But not everyone can bear it. If you decide you want something different, find outsiders, like yourself. Casters, criminals—the Treble's rejected ones. Be smart. Learn to run. Learn to fight. Learn who to trust."

So she had. But ever since that day Jun has wondered if she was wrong—stubborn and foolish and rash. She has wondered if she is, herself, fundamentally *wrong*, somehow.

Only Liis has ever quelled that fear.

Jun shyly touches one of the twists of Liis's hair. "I'll listen to their offer... their whole offer." Liis's eyes glint with cautious satisfaction, and it would be irritating if she didn't look so beautiful right now. So incongruously vulnerable. Jun runs a thumb across her eyebrow, adding cautiously, "I was thinking that... maybe... you should let me go with Masar on my own. You know, lie low, just until I—"

Suddenly, there is an arm winding around her waist. She finds herself pulled forward, pulled close, onto the bed, knees either side of Liis's hips. She makes an *oofing* sound, tries to balance—and stops. She can feel the hardness under Liis's shorts, the straps on her thighs and across her hips. A white-hot bolt of hunger goes through Jun, even as she tries to right herself in the face of this... unexpected turn. When did Liis even put it on?

"Really?" she asks.

Liis looks up at her with solemn eyes, lips parted, arm tightening around her. She nudges her hips upward and Jun groans. Liis runs a thumb over the injection site on Jun's hip.

"How are you feeling?" she asks.

To be honest, everything hurts. But she doesn't give a shit. Liis is the feeling of home. Her shoulders flex when Jun rests her hands on them; she tips her head back to look at Jun, exposing the column of her throat like an offering. Jun puts her mouth on her burn-scarred jaw, biting possessively, and Liis's whole composed, powerful body shudders.

They're economical, removing only what they have to, and careful with each other. They use the oil from Liis's jar, a bloom of life between them. When Jun finally sinks down, it punches a moan out of them both. Jun shivers and holds still, staring Liis in the eyes and unable to speak. Not needing to speak—a silence that brings reprieve. Then, they're moving. Steady, strong; a bright tension strung between them. Liis slides a hand up into Jun's hair, fingers tightening, and when they kiss, it's with rabid hunger. Their mouths shift and press and slide, molten.

Long, exquisite minutes get eaten up in the push and pull, and Jun—Jun has never found anything, in all the systems, as perfect as this. Yes, she'll plan. Yes, she'll scheme—but not without Liis. Nothing, without Liis. Her eyes slip shut, and the hand in her hair tightens.

"Look at me," Liis breathes. "Look at me."

She opens her eyes, obeying. Her fingers dig into Liis's back, nails pricking as their pace increases, as their breathing deepens. Her shoulder hurts, her hip throbs, but the burn of it only makes every other sensation sharper, deeper. Sweat breaks out across her skin, pooling at the small of her back and between her shoulder blades. She watches the same bead across Liis's collarbones and hairline and breasts.

"Let's lie down," Jun gasps, wanting to give more.

Liis growls, "No. You first."

That offer, that permission, spears through her. She moves faster. Liis's hand releases her hair to grab her hip, and then her ass, urging her on. Jun darts a hand between her own legs, moving frantically, and everything sharpens inside her. It gathers, and gathers—and breaks—flinging her headlong into shuddering, clenching pleasure. She shouts, burying her face against Liis's neck, overwhelmed by the low sounds of encouragement in her ear. They carry her all the way through, until finally Liis falls back on the bed, Jun collapsing on top of her.

"You think I'm letting you out of my sight now?" Liis says breathlessly. "I've got your back forever."

The sound Jun makes is a laugh and sob together, and as the last tendrils curl through her, she uses her arms and legs to grip Liis as tight as she can, as tight as she's ever gripped anything, in all the years since she fled Riin Kala under a stranger's wing.

CHAPTER SIXTEEN

1664

YEAR OF THE CRUX

The Makala Aet
The Black Ocean

Chono is lying in bed when a knock sounds on the door. She climbs up, body stiff, the impacts of the Silt Glow Cliffs disaster still telling on her. At the door, one of Esek's novitiates is holding a courier container.

"Forgive me, Sa. Were you asleep?"

"No," Chono mutters. Though she should be asleep. It's 1:00 a.m. local time in Lo-Meek. It's 4:00 a.m. standard system time. But on Pippashap it's already noon, and Chono, little sleep as she's gotten in the past few days, hasn't acclimated yet. She's been staring at the ceiling for the past two hours, imagining her novitiates preparing a meal for the fishersaan. Sticky rice and steamed fish with vegetables. Maybe a tea cake to go with it, shaped to resemble the round-cheeked Capamame.

The novitiate says, "We rendezvoused with a courier shuttle, Burning One. This has arrived for you from Riin Kala."

Chono, realizing what it is, goes momentarily still. She feels a surge of equal parts relief and deep uncertainty, but she doesn't let it show. "Oh, yes. Put it in here."

After the novitiate has gone, Chono stands a moment staring at the container on the table. When she finally opens it, looking cautiously inside, she half expects a monster to leap from within. She slides the chest out of its protective casing, which triggers a holographic message to unspool in the air. Not his voice this time, but his handwriting:

I hope you wanting it back has nothing to do with a failure of trust. But it may be just as well. Certain illustrious secretaries got wind that I was investigating this Sunstep thing, and I've been told categorically to drop it. Whatever is going on out there, my kin don't want me involved. I've got to go quiet for a while.

I have nothing valuable to offer you. No proof of what the coin contains, or why it was advertised, or how you can get it back. But there is something dreadful about this hunt of yours, and all the Kindom's interest in it. Something . . . miasmic. If I thought you could be guided by me, I would say to walk away while you still can.

And I know now why you think Liis Konye is involved. I hope you weren't badly hurt in Siinkai. I hope you won't let Esek be the death of you. But I suppose there's no use in my saying it, Mysterious Chono.

Good luck, and may Kata's Many protect you.

Chono stares at the message for long moments, every emotion from irritation to surprise to regret moving through her. There's something weary and resolved in Ilius's tone, not his usual excitement. The old nickname sounds like defeat. And that he's being stonewalled by the secretaries recalls her own questions about why the Clever Hand has been missing from this operation since the beginning. She wants to write him back. To say, *I'm sorry for my secrets. I'm sorry for all the things I never told you.* But what would it serve? The chest doesn't just keep secrets in. It keeps other people out.

She gently sweeps the message from the air, focusing on the chest itself. She looks at it for a long time. She doesn't even realize she has inserted the combination until the lid lifts and—

Letters. Soft as silk under her fingertips. There are several dozen of them, haphazardly stacked, not a one folded up and all of them crinkling together like music. The words spill before her eyes, slide into her veins with the ease of hypodermic needles. Sentences she has read a thousand times, and which now come at her in bursts: *I see you visited Teros again. Find anything interesting on Braemin? Do you enjoy the sweets? You always loved sweets. Does Esek mock you for your prayers? Does Esek appreciate your intrepidness?*

Does Esek like the presents I send her?

Oddly enough, what she thinks of first is Lucos Alanye and the various coins Six has sent them over the years: the memories and the video journals, and the increasing desperation of a man whose high ambitions hit a deadly ceiling. When Chono thinks of Alanye, she thinks of someone small-minded and ill-equipped—a very good soldier and guardsaan, but a poor political operative. And yet, he's Six's forefather. Six's origin story.

There in the letters, she reads: *I once said I was Kindom in my heart. I am not. I have a different kind of heart. So do you, Chono.*

Another knock on the door makes her jerk.

She slams the chest shut and barely has time to step away from the table before Esek strides in. She peruses Chono critically, and Chono's veins run with ice.

"It's the middle of the night. Have you slept at all?" Esek demands.

In the end it is discipline, self-control, and *practice* that allow her to answer as steadily as ever. "I slept a little."

Esek frowns. "Well, you look awful. You'd better sleep more, after this."

"Yes, Burning One."

A low chuckle. "Ah. So, we are back to formalities, are we? I reveal one little treason, and now you're as guarded as a female on her menarche."

Chono merely looks at her. Esek grins. She goes to the untouched bar in the corner of Chono's room and pours two drinks. "If you're not going to sleep, you should have some of this. It's not praevi, but it's got a stimulant in it. Can't have you passing out from exhaustion."

Through Chono's mind skitter the words and phrases of a hundred letters. She surprises Esek and herself by walking to the bar and accepting the outstretched glass. It's the same clear liquor Esek was drinking last night, and it bites its way down, icy and bright. Esek is still regarding her.

"You're dressed," she says.

Chono glances down at herself. Besides her red coat and sidearm, she's wearing the same clothes from last night, rumpled now. Esek, as always, looks immaculate. Beautiful in a hypnotically serpentine way, her umber eyes tracking Chono.

Esek declares, "The hunt is back on!"

She tosses back her shot of liquor, gesturing with the bottle at Chono's empty glass. Unthinking, Chono allows her to refill it, but she doesn't drink.

"You mean you think you've found Jun Ironway?" asks Chono.

"Even better!" Esek cries. "I've found out where the warhorse came from."

Chono gives her a blank look. She feels . . . slow. Distracted. As if Esek were speaking another language and her translator hasn't caught up yet.

"Warhorse, Sa?"

"Yes, yes—tell me, Chono: Ever heard of the Ar'tec Collective?"

"You mean the work colony on Ar'tec Island?"

"I *mean* . . . the work colony that, unbeknownst to the average citizen, operates entirely under the control of its prisoners, communicates exclusively via AI interface, and runs factories that, among other things, build toys for the Cloaksaan. Including this one."

She flexes her fingers and casts an image into the air—a three-dimensional, rotating schematic of a warhorse. Chono, who is still processing Esek's claims about Ar'tec, stares at the schematic without speaking. When she faces Esek again, the older cleric looks as excited as a child.

"In case you're wondering, this is the warhorse Masar Hawks traded to the Jeveni innkeeper in Fezn. I traced the schematic to Ar'tec and told them to give me everything they knew about what happened to it. They sold it to a mercenary broker."

Chono looks from the schematic to Esek again. "Why haven't you reported them?"

Esek gives her a condescending look. "My dear Chono, Kindom vendors do this sort of thing all the—"

"I'm aware," interrupts Chono with a sharpness that makes Esek's eyebrows shoot up. "I'm not *amazed* that such illegal transactions occur; I'm amazed you are tacitly enabling them."

Esek whistles. "My. Feeling *spirited*, aren't we?"

Now, instead of ice, it is heat that creeps up the back of Chono's neck.

"Let's save the lectures for now," Esek goes on. "As I was saying, they sent me all the information they have. It's quite useful stuff. Let me show you."

Esek rotates her wrist and replaces the warhorse schematic with a glut of text, documents, diagrams, and faces—including Masar Hawks. It all moves too fast for Chono to process what she's seeing. This is probably Esek's design.

"What we have here...is an impressively complicated game of cups." Esek looks at Chono with one of her rakish smiles. "It all started at the end of last year, right around when the sacking at Verdant happened. The warhorse got bandied about with alacrity, first one ship, then another. Lost to pirates. Regained by traders. Disappeared from the public record. But in the end, it was sold to a fellow in Lo-Meek called Saboshi, who has an old, professional acquaintance with Masar Hawks. But Sa Hawks is a middling pirate, you may say. And all these machinations suggest something bigger at work. Think like a secretary, Chono. What would a secretary ask?"

Chono pauses, unprepared to play a part in Esek's theater. After a moment she says flatly, "A secretary would ask who paid for it."

"Very good! That's where these come in." She points at some ledgers floating amid the other holograms in the air. "When Saboshi took ownership of the warhorse, he didn't pay for it. Instead, his bank shows a deposit of twice the warhorse's value. Where did the money come from?" Masar Hawks's profile momentarily takes center stage. "From Hawks. But how does our middling pirate get that kind of cash? Here we have another game of cups. Money bouncing between accounts, flung from planet to planet. All going back to one place."

Esek rotates her hand, and a new face swims to the forefront, a man. He is Jeveni, slender and dark-haired, something vividly clever in his pale eyes.

"Nikkelo sen Rieve," says Esek grandly. "An isolationist by birth, a collector by trade. *He* is the one who transferred the money to Saboshi. But, even more important, he is the one who arranged the purchase of the warhorse from Ar'tec. He's run these deals before. Weapons, mostly, but also casting equipment and the occasional ship. Our Ar'tec contacts were kind enough to direct us to mountains of evidence against Sa Rieve." Data begins to flow like a waterfall down the casting view. "It appears his machinations can be traced all over the Treble, to all kinds of organizations as shady as the Ar'tec Collective."

Chono watches the data on the screen: star map coordinates and company brands and credit deposits and withdrawals, all occurring over a time span of twenty years. But there is a glaring omission.

"Who funds him?"

"I thought you'd never ask!" From amid the crowd springs a featureless outline of a person in profile. "All of sen Rieve's purchases are traceable to one entity. And not only weapons, by the way. His employer has a taste for historical artifacts."

Does Esek like the presents I send her?

"Artifacts?" Chono repeats.

"Mm-hmm. It seems Nikkelo sen Rieve has negotiated with hundreds of archivists over the years. He's acquired dozens of historical records. So, what do we have before us, Chono? A link between Masar Hawks and sen Rieve's mysterious, nameless employer, who appears to have a great deal of interest . . . in uncovering the past."

Chono considers this. In the heyday of their hunt for Six, Esek often ranted about their solitariness—the fact that they only worked with others when it was necessary to complete one of their escapades. Like the firefight on K-5. And the disaster of Soye's Reach. Esek always believed Six could not have survived this long, nor accomplished all they did, without at least one consistent confidant. Could Nikkelo sen Rieve be that person? That missing link in the picture of Six's life?

Esek claps her hands, looking delighted with herself. "So, you see, it's a matter of tracking down sen Rieve. He's no doubt commissioned Hawks to locate the coin, and will rendezvous with them soon— before moving on to his employer. I've already got my fish scouring the casting net. Once we have *him* . . . we have his employer."

Chono absorbs this, still silent. They have tried to track Six through their associates before—and failed. Six, always one step ahead. Six, always just out of reach. So why does Chono feel such a strange anxiety, now? Why does the prospect of finding Nikkelo sen Rieve, finding Jun Ironway, finding, somehow, a route to Six—make her light up with nerves? This is an old game. Chono played it for years, before leaving Esek's household. Is she not prepared to play it now? Now, when the whole Treble is in uproar, and Six may threaten it more than ever?

Her silence has not escaped Esek, whose expression suddenly hardens. She regards Chono narrowly, demanding, "What's the matter with you?"

Chono doesn't answer her, and Esek's eyes begin to flit about the room, as if looking for some sign. When she lands on the chest on the table, Chono feels her throat close. There was no chance to hide it, before Esek barged into the room. Hardly time to shut the lid, to reengage the lock. For a moment the silence in the room feels like a glacier—hard, massive, icy. Then Esek looks at her, reads her in an instant, and moves toward the table. She picks up the chest in both hands. Chono holds her body perfectly still, maintains her implacable facade, but she is reminded of strangers in the dark, stripping her naked, touching her body without permission and without regard.

"What's this?" Esek asks, turning the chest this way and that, as if she can prize it open.

Chono says indifferently, "It's one of my personal effects."

Esek meets her eyes. She gives the chest a little shake, testing Chono's response. Chono remains impassive. No sound emanates from the chest.

"I never noticed it before," says Esek. "What other 'effects' are you hiding, Chono?"

Chono doesn't respond, and Esek's fishing falls flat. Carelessly, Esek drops the chest back on the table, the weight of it making a gunshot sound. Chono wishes suddenly that the chest was her own heart, that she could secret it in her body, a place no unwelcome fingers could touch.

"I take it you expect me to conceal the crimes of the Ar'tec Collective, just as you intend to conceal them?" she asks Esek in a flat voice.

Esek chuckles, but it's humorless. "I thought we had discussed this. If I am *already* a traitor to the Kindom, so are you. We may as well make the best of it."

At this, Chono's lips turn in the barest of smiles, but it's bitter. She feels hot, sweaty, *dirty*.

"So you think I'm content to remain one? A traitor?"

"Content? No, I'd never use that word to describe you. *Consistent*. That's a better word for you. All these years you've known that I was hunting Six and killing people to do it and all these years you've known my family's crimes, and did you ever tell the Kindom? Did you ever betray me? No. So why shouldn't you carry on protecting me, as you always have?"

"You're assuming I did all that to protect you," Chono shoots back, reacting without thought, without caution.

Esek raises a slow eyebrow, intrigued. "Then what *did* you do it for?" she murmurs.

Chono doesn't answer. Can't answer. Esek watches her, and it's one of those rare instances when she's not smirking, not sneering. She raises a hand to her head and touches the grotesque scarring of her ear. It's subtle enough one could mistake it for pressing aside some errant coil of hair, but Esek's tight crown of braids is impeccable.

She heaves a sigh. "Do you know why *I* think you've done it?" she asks mockingly. Chono doesn't answer. Esek's look turns viperous. "For the same reason you killed Cleric Paan."

It's like having her legs taken out from under her by the unexpected sweep of a stave. It's as if the chest on the table has exploded shrapnel everywhere, each letter a razor blade.

"What?"

"The old man who was raping children," says Esek lightly, as if Chono doesn't know who she means. As if Chono's whole body hasn't clenched with fury and fear at the mention of him. "The one you slaughtered. Brutally done, from what I heard."

Does Esek appreciate your intrepidness?

"Why, you could have cut his throat and had it over with! You could have broken his neck. I taught you how. But no. You *beat* him to death." She whistles. Nausea tightens Chono's throat. "I keep wondering, why did you kill him like that? Why take the law into your hands? Didn't you tell the Clerisy what was happening?"

"Of course I did."

"And what did they do?"

Chono's mouth closes. Esek nods at her, knowingly. Her lip curls back.

"Nothing, right? They did nothing. And you knew they would

do nothing. When you caught him at it, you could have trussed him up. You could have submitted an ocular recording proving what he'd done. They would have had to at least remove him. But you knew they wouldn't kill him. Wouldn't even put him in a work colony—not a cleric! You knew those children wouldn't get the justice they were owed. So, you did it yourself. For them. Just as I did it for you when I rescued you on Kator."

Chono takes a step back from her.

"Don't talk about that," she says, and her voice sounds distant and dangerous.

Esek looks back at Chono with a sinister smile; it goes through her like an X-ray, seeing every part of her.

"You were always so devout. You always believed, so deeply, in the justice of the gods. In the mission of the Kindom, to make that justice manifest. Even after what your masters did to you..." A shiver rolls down Chono's spine, and she's convinced Esek can see its progress— that it's a chord she wants to pluck with her fingers. "For the longest time, I thought you were in denial. That that's how you survived it all—how you justified your vows. You told yourself the Kindom didn't know you had corrupt teachers who sold your body for favors. Then I came along and rescued you, and it must have fit the narrative in your head. 'See? Here comes a righteous cleric, and as soon as she learns what is happening, she rescues me, and slays my monsters.' That must be why you've loved me so much."

"Come to the point, Esek."

Esek's smile twists like a knife going in. She takes two, three steps closer to Chono, until they are an arm's length apart.

"But you know the truth now, don't you, Chono? The Kindom knew. The Kindom *always* knows. It let you suffer for the same reason it let the children on Pippashap suffer: To protect itself. To maintain its own order. So, a year ago, you did what I did: You took vengeance into your own hands. You decided your loyalty to the Kindom...has limits. Like mine."

This is too much. Chono doesn't even try to stifle the anger in her retort. "Your disloyalty is rooted in your own self-interest. What *I* did was to protect people. It is *not* the same. And don't insult me by pretending you care about the abuse of children. You've made it clear many times that you'd as soon see me whored out as help me if I wasn't going to be useful to you."

Esek pauses, considering.

"And you don't think all the work you've done with me has been a kind of whoring, Chono?"

The shiver down her spine pulls taut, and snaps. Chono's arm moves like a whip, her closed fist cracking against Esek's face. Esek reels, stumbles. She hits the table and barely grabs it in time to keep from falling. Hot air spills between Chono's teeth and through her nostrils as she watches Esek hunch over, cradling the side of her face. Seconds get eaten up in the sound of their heavy breathing. Esek spits blood onto the floor, and that crescent starburst on the white rug makes Chono realize, in a stomach-plummeting shock, what she's done.

Her cocked fist drops. Her eyes widen. Esek spits more blood onto the carpet. Then, all at once, she's pulling herself upright. She wipes a hand across her bloody mouth, and charges at Chono—Chono, who is still too stunned at her own actions to react, to defend herself, to anticipate the lunging knife—

But Esek doesn't stab her. Doesn't tackle her. No. Esek grabs the back of her head, yanking her close, pressing their foreheads together. It is more intimate than anything Chono has ever experienced.

"*Yes*, Chono!" Esek hisses between her teeth. "*Yes!*"

Only now does Chono realize how hard she's breathing, almost hyperventilating, and Esek's breath is hot on her face.

"Don't let anyone disrespect you! Not me. Not Six. Not anyone. If they do, fight them. Kill them if you have to, but you are not the plaything of your masters. Don't you understand how I've survived all this time? Do you know how many people have wished I would die? But I *refused* to submit, to be small, to retreat."

Chono remains motionless, still stunned at the anger that exploded out of her. She, who has made her well-known, constant calm a bulwark against the darker feelings inside her. She feels confused, and a little frightened, and still angry underneath it all. So furiously, overpoweringly *angry* at all she has seen—

Esek lets go of her, stepping away.

"I want you to *survive*, Chono," she growls. The corner of her mouth and cheekbone are red, swelling. "Our Kindom grinds its people into dust. So be like me. Be like Six—be whatever you need to be. But *survive!*"

Chono doesn't respond. Any comparison of the violence Esek and Six have experienced from the Kindom feels...grotesque.

The silence is crushing. All at once, Esek turns away. She heads for the door, clearly finished. It's this abrupt departure that startles words out of Chono's throat.

"What about Nikkelo sen Rieve?"

Esek pauses at the door but doesn't look back.

"We find him," she says. "We follow him. We follow him straight to his employer."

Chono swallows.

"To Six," she says. Not a question.

This time Esek does look at her, a look as bright as the Godfire.

"That's our mission, isn't it?" she asks. "Hasn't it always been our mission?"

Our mission. Our mission.

"And we will not tell our kin about it?" asks Chono.

A cool look. Esek says with undisguised contempt, "Not if we want to *succeed.*"

Chono stares back at her, not answering. After a moment, the older cleric turns away. The door closes behind her.

The chest sits on the table.

The blood soaks into the carpet.

Chono looks down at her knuckles, which are already bruised. In a kind of fugue, she goes to the chest, enters the combination, and stares into the pile of letters. Her hand moves, sifting through them, knowing them as much by sight as touch, until she finds the one she's looking for, so worn that it's translucent. She reads—

I am sorry it is so long since I wrote you. I have been very busy refusing to die.

There were four hundred people living in Soye's Reach, including the surrounding homesteads. Many children died, which I know will matter to you. You and I are both guilty in this. But we are not the guiltiest parties. I will have such a revenge, Chono. Gods grant you are not burned up in the process.

I enclose a gift for Esek, if you will be my courier again. Do you still do her bidding? Do you still follow in her footsteps like a shadow? If she catches me someday, and brings the ax down on my head, will you mirror her?

The letter ends. Abrupt, like all the letters. Chono puts it back and closes the chest and listens to the snick of the lock engaging, as loud in her ears as the crack of her fist on Esek's jaw, or the strike of a missile in the Katish wilderness.

Chono breathes in. She breathes out. She casts a comm directly to the temple at Riin Cosas. Within minutes, Aver Paiye appears before her, dressed in his evening robe. It's nine o'clock in that part of Ma'kess. He frowns, clearly surprised to see her.

"Dear Chono! What is it?"

She breathes in. She breathes out.

"Forgive the late hour, Burning One. I have news regarding Sunstep's location."

CHAPTER SEVENTEEN

1658

YEAR OF THE SLEEPWALK

Xa Cosas
Ka'Braevi Continent
The Planet Braemin

Esek arrived back at the villa grounds to find a cleric prostrating themself before an icon to the Godfire. It was unexpected enough that she stopped in her tracks, taking in the scene with curiosity. Everywhere upon the grounds were tropical trees and wildflower hedges, stamped against the uniquely cyan-colored skies of Braemin, shot through with cottony clouds. Among this vibrancy and color, the Godfire icon was obnoxiously large, a sun like an eyeball, emitting flares. Inanimate, it seemed nonetheless to be alive, caught in the sunlight and burning. Kneeling there, the cleric looked small as a child, and Esek couldn't help imagining the icon was about to open itself in a maw, and devour them.

As she often did, Esek thought of Chono. Chono would probably welcome being devoured. What did Chono want, but to be the foodstuff of her gods? She was too mild a person to have gained a reputation in the Clerisy since their separation, but whenever Esek did hear about her former novitiate, it was always the same thing: solemn, righteous, humble—and loved. This was the part that surprised Esek most. Apparently, wherever Chono went she was loved. Oh, not among her kin, of course, for she baffled and annoyed them. But among her *parishioners*, among the people she served. It was the strangest thing. Chono had never even been *likable*, so stony-faced and untalkative, from the beginning, and the people had always liked their clerics charismatic. She must have changed in the past five years, to have jumped all the way to lovable. Not to mention the rumors that Aver Paiye himself knew her and respected her. How lofty.

But thinking of Chono irritated Esek. It was too beautiful a day, on too beautiful a planet, for that. She resumed her stroll up the path to the villa gates, assuming the cleric must be from town and come to pay respects.

She was about ten feet from the icon when the cleric dropped their prayerful hands and rose to their feet—and Esek stopped short again. That height. Those shoulders. The square shape of them. When they faced her, with that always masked expression, Esek already knew—

"Chono," she said.

The young cleric bowed over her hands. "Hello, Burning One."

Esek huffed, then shook her head, then chuckled. Of *course* the little shit was still going to call her "Burning One." Never mind they were equals now. She looked Chono over, trying to get a sense of her. She seemed a little thinner than Esek remembered. Not unhealthy, but lean, like a winter fox. Esek trained her novitiates to maintain bulk through a regimen of high-protein diets and strenuous exercise, because it was best that cloaksaan look big enough to break your neck. Apparently Chono had let some of that regimen go, though she was still broad in the shoulders. She was still ugly, too. Poor Chono.

"How'd you know I was here?" Esek asked, a little miffed. She'd come to Braemin to be left alone, to enjoy herself. Then it occurred to her. "Wait. Let me guess. You heard about the library?"

Chono inclined her head. "It was very generous of you, Sa."

Esek sighed. When she arrived on Braemin two weeks ago, it was to learn that the local village had been hard hit by a recent storm, and their library destroyed. The libraries managed most of the education of the young people in this part of Braemin, and it had annoyed Esek to think of her favorite vacation haunt debilitated by something as obnoxious as a storm. So she'd thrown some money at it, and the repairs were already underway. It must have gotten out that she was responsible.

"Yes, well," drawled Esek. "You know me. Woman of the people."

Chono's smile was tight and awkward and the silence between them stretched. Growing impatient, Esek glanced back toward the wooden staircase that led to the beach, a thousand miles of white sand and oceans only a little bluer than the sky. A Braemish servant was standing back, encumbered with Esek's coat and shoes.

"You," she snapped. "Take those things inside."

The Braem went immediately. When Esek faced Chono again, she saw her novitiate's eyes cutting back to her—she had been watching the young woman walk away. Admiring her, perhaps? She was a pretty thing, and scantily dressed.

"Would you like an introduction?"

Chono blinked once.

"No, thank you, Sa."

"Clerics aren't supposed to be celibate, Chono. Sex is one of the blessings we confer."

Chono paused again, her eyes like storm clouds. "I'm not looking for a lover, Sa."

Esek snorted. Of course, if Chono did take a lover, it wouldn't be a servant. Wouldn't be someone vulnerable to her. Chono had too much honor for that. Esek thought of the last time they were together at Soye's Reach, when Esek had not only taken a junior cloaksaan to bed, but murdered him afterward. No, not exactly honorable. What a trial that had been. Commandant Inye was very upset about it. Esek had left the Cloaksaan outpost soon after, trailed by wisps of smoke and flame that wrote elegies to Six on the air. With each month that followed, with each year that no more messages came, Esek's confidence in the mission's success grew. Chono's sweet-box subscription ended. The matter was closed. They had found no bodies in the tunnel under Soye's Reach; they hardly even found a tunnel. And while she didn't get the satisfaction of standing over Six's corpse, she did have a report that finally mollified Alisiana. Not that any rewards had come of it.

Esek said, "Well. I suppose you're here for some reason. Let's talk inside."

Two novitiates held the villa gates open for them. Chono followed her.

Inside the manor house, they were confronted with a depth of reds and purples, and art and tapestry. Though Esek liked the local color of Braemin, she preferred her dwellings to reflect strictly Ma'kessn styles. Arched doorframes and gilded moldings. The ceiling of the vaulted foyer bore a mural of the Childbirths of Makala. Braems might worship Som, but in this Nightfoot house, Makala was the Sixth God.

A delicious smell wafted in from the kitchen on the right, and up the winding staircase straight ahead, her private suite boasted the luxuries she'd had little of these past months. For once, she needn't rely on her novitiates to wait on her, for a quintet of career servants stood against the wall. Braemish servants were always beautiful; it was a prerequisite of the work, and Esek homed in on one of them: a neatly cut beard and high cheekbones and eyes like the sky. He came forward with a wet cloth, and knelt and washed her feet of the white sand that crusted them. When he was done, he gave her shoes, and she stepped into them, balancing with a hand on his pretty head.

Perhaps she'd engage in another dishonorable tryst, later. This was something else about Braemish servants; they were always available for sex.

With that pleasant thought, she turned toward the dining room, calling over her shoulder, "Have dinner with me, Chono. We can catch up."

"I would be very happy to, Sa. But first, I believe we should speak in private."

Esek stopped at the threshold to the dining room. She turned, looking her former novitiate in the face again. Chono's seriousness held a note of caution Esek had not noticed before.

"What *are* you doing here?" Esek asked. "I know I never trained you to announce yourself before showing up somewhere, but surely your kin clerics have filled in the gaps?"

"I'm not here in an official capacity."

The succinctness of this made something crawl up the back of Esek's neck.

"Oh no?"

"I think you'll understand after we talk."

Esek stared at her for long moments, hoping to bully more information out of her with the gravity of her stare. This had always been effective in the past, but to Esek's surprise, Chono met the move, unblinking. It was Esek who gave in.

"Fine. Let's go upstairs."

They went up the spiraling staircase, Chono a step behind her. The private suite was lit with glowing spheres hung on cables. It gave the room an intimate mood. The bed was turned down and the bar was stocked. Balcony doors stood open, letting in a cool, salty breeze, and the view of the beaches and the Clev Sea was unparalleled, miles of coastland to the north and south.

"Not bad, is it, Chono?" Esek went to the bar and found a decanter of praevi. She poured out two glasses and turned to offer one to the young cleric. "You know my family owns the temple. If you ever want to borrow this villa, let me know."

A barb lurked in her generosity. Esek knew how much it upset Chono to hear people talk about owning temples. But Chono seemed to barely have heard her. Now they were alone, she accepted the tumbler of praevi only to set it down on the bar top. She went to the balcony doors and pulled them closed, drawing the curtains. Esek watched her in amazement and mounting unease.

"Som's ass, Chono. What is going on?"

In answer, Chono came back to the bar, standing only a few feet away. She reached into the inner pocket of her brilliant red coat (it suited her surprisingly well) and pulled out an envelope. She set it on the bar top. Chono's name and an address were scrawled across it in a bold, black, instantly familiar script.

A shiver went up Esek's spine and into her skull, blood vessels constricting, heart beating hard enough she could hear the *wub wub wubbing* of it. This was...not possible.

"Where did you get this?" she asked.

"It came to me by local post." Chono gestured to a marking on the envelope, dated five days ago, and boasting the by-now-familiar origin: Dewbreak, Jeve.

Esek's breathing became slightly shallow. Her fingers twitched. She wanted to grab the envelope. She wanted to rip it open with her teeth. And yet, she couldn't move.

"No sweets this time," she observed, finally meeting Chono's stare. "What's in it?"

Chono paused for several moments. "It's something you should look at."

Esek almost laughed, but she didn't want to sound like a strangled bird, and right now, that's how she felt. Strangled. But was the feeling horrible? Was it pleasurable? Was it exciting? Esek couldn't tell. She glanced at the glass of praevi she was still holding and tossed the rest of it down her throat. Then, in a burst of resolve, she grabbed the envelope and tore it open.

A single memory coin spilled onto the bar top. She picked it up gingerly, as if it might be an explosive. A quick ocular scan demonstrated that it contained no kill ware, yet when she slotted it into her neural port, she still felt a bit like someone throwing themself into a lake full of gaba sharks.

She cast a view into the air between her and Chono, a translucent hologram through which she could see her former novitiate's face. Immediately, a different face appeared in the air.

It was Lucos Alanye.

For a split second, she didn't recognize him. She was used to the few public records, pictures of him in his guardsaan uniform, a steely-eyed and handsome Katishsaan in the prime of health. Now he looked rough, his long face as haggard as a horse that's been run too hard, his hair overgrown, uneven, and his narrow dark eyes slightly red-rimmed. He looked exhausted. Esek had very little interest in him beyond the fact he had spawned her nemesis, but now she felt a curl of contempt. He sat at a desk, shoulders hunched forward. The room behind him was dim, but Esek could detect a window that looked out on a gray world. When he spoke, he coughed, as if he'd been breathing dust.

"This is...Nine Month, Five, 1581, Year of the Glass. The second anniversary of my arrival on Jeve. The flu seems to have run its course since my last entry. My med upgrades got me through the worst of it, but two of my crew died. Gus ben Roq says they have a flu like this every couple of years. It's to do with the filtration system, and leftover toxicity from the mining operations. The engineers here are top rate, but they can't build a state-of-the-art filtration system without supplies, and they're too poor to order the supplies, so..." He trailed off, clearly exasperated, and rubbed his hand down patchy stubble. "They're fuck-ing stubborn. And indifferent. In the beginning they accepted the gifts I brought, but I think now they were just being polite. They aren't even using the upgraded casting hubs, and the hydroponics equip-ment must be in storage somewhere. I don't know how they haven't all starved to death."

Esek poured another glass of praevi, sipping this time. The irratio-nality of an uncivilized, extinct population was of no interest to her, and she found the idea of Alanye *caring* for the Jeveni and their rotten lives not only disingenuous, but maudlin.

Alanye spoke on, "I keep getting messages from Verdant, pressure to confirm the jevite is here, but what am I supposed to do? The Jeveni act like they don't even know what jevite is. Even when I show them the seam on the map, they claim it's just the ruins of a tapped-out mine, and I can't get to the seam myself to confirm anything, because they're always watching me."

Esek sipped her drink. "He's a whiny little bitch, isn't he?"

"I've had a message from Sorek this morning," Alanye went on. Esek's ears perked up at the name of Alisiana's one-time second-in-command. On the casting view, Alanye read from a projection in the air. *"My family has already invested a great deal of money in this project. Enclosed are the receipts for supplies, travel arrangements, and salaries for you and your ten surveyors. As a businessaan, I recognize different investments require different amounts of time to pay out. But I am not ultimately the last word on our decisions. If she does not have a satisfactory answer by the end of Nine Month, she will want a personal audience with you. And I can't promise the outcome of that meeting."* Alanye stopped, and looked at the camera again, lips compressing in a tense smile. "That's not subtle," he muttered.

No, thought Esek. *Not subtle at all.* Fuck *you,* Six.

Alanye sighed a deep, rib-creaking sigh. "I've gone over the math a dozen times. If I'm right about the seam, it's half a mile wide, no more than a quarter mile deep. Maybe two miles long? But three-quarters of it will be ordinary rock. Based on variations of depth and purity modeled on historical jevite seams, miners would be lucky to pull ten, eleven thousand cubic feet of pure jevite. After expenses, the Nightfoots could probably bring in a profit of forty or forty-five million over five years..."

"Forty million!" Esek blurted, looking through the hologram at Chono. "This Katish mongrel thinks my family would go to all this trouble for forty million ingots? Fuck's sake, even a hundred years ago they could make three times that value in sevite every year!"

Chono didn't answer. Alanye said, "If I bring those numbers to Sorek, with no real proof? Fires. Alisiana will have my hand cut off. That kind of money is small change to the Nightfoots. I'd be better off claiming I found nothing and just... resolving to a life of debt slavery."

He stopped talking. He looked away from the camera. He had the hunted look of a person who has laid an incredible bet and sees the odds dwindling. In his silence, Esek grew impatient, but then at the last he breathed in. Like his soul was returning to his body. He sat up straighter and stared into the viewport with sudden, steely resolve.

"If we missed one seam, we missed others. Everything about them says they're hiding something, and it's not a few thousand cubic feet of jevite. It's more. It has to be more."

He stood, stepping abruptly away from the camera. He was tall, she realized, as tall as her, and lean in a way that reminded her of the figure she chased through the hallways on K-5. All at once he turned to the camera again, stepping closer in a surge of determination.

"The first thing I've got to do is send the other surveyors away. Ten was a bad idea to begin with—it made me look like a conqueror the second I arrived. And now two of them are dead I've got a good excuse to send the rest home. But I'll stay on. If I can lower their defenses... embed myself with them, somehow, then it's only a matter of time before I learn more. I'll tell Sorek to stop paying me; I'll offer him double interest on what they've already spent. I'll—"

He paused. He sounded on the edge of hysterical, and Esek narrowed her eyes suspiciously. Which is when Six's message delivered its final, devastating blow.

"Alisiana saw something in me." He seemed to be willing his viewer to believe this—challenging them to prove him wrong. "She wouldn't have funded me if she didn't have faith. I've just got to convince her... to keep faith a little longer."

The image of Alanye—dark-eyed, hawkish, mouth set in a viciously determined line—disappeared the moment his sentence ended. But Esek had no chance to process the indictment in those words, because no sooner had he gone than a new image appeared on the screen. And a new person stared out at her.

She knew it was Six, not because she could see their face, but because she couldn't. They were wearing a traditional Sajeven mask, five eyes high on the forehead. A voice came from behind the mask, and Esek would know it anywhere.

"Hello, Chono. Or is it Esek? I admit, my message changes depending on who is there."

They paused. The wall behind them was black. A light shone from above, draping them in shadows and gold. Sajeven's mask, with its warm, crinkled eyes, was too harmless an image. Unbefitting this scheming creature. Then again, Sajeven was known for her secrets, too.

"If it is you, Chono, and you have not decided whether to take this to your master, then let it remind you of who your master is."

Esek glared through the hologram at Chono, who did not meet her eyes.

"If, in spite of this proof, you *have* delivered it—and I know you will, Chono; your sense of duty is too deeply ingrained—in that case, I address myself to you, Esek. It has been some time, and I could not resist this opportunity to speak with you. I have had to watch you from afar for years. Lately, I make a pastime of studying your face. I have no face, you see. Or . . . not one you would remember. But give me time."

Esek swallowed the last of the praevi in a burning gulp. Her skin was hot all over, and there was a ringing in her ears. Six went on. "I admit, when I learned you were laying a trap for me on Soye's Reach, I never dreamed you would raze the lodge. I would have done things so differently. But what good is self-recrimination? I would rather discuss my latest gift."

Esek wanted to reach through the cast and strangle them.

"As you know," they said, "this recording is from the very beginning of Alanye's sojourn with the Dewbreak Jeveni. It would appear he persuaded Alisiana to give him more time. How impressive, to be able to persuade her of anything. I wonder, will you be as persuasive, when you urge her to give you a second chance to stop me?"

Esek tightened her fingers around the praevi glass.

"I am still looking for ways to impress you. I make strides every hour. Someday, I think, you and I will have a long talk, and I will tell you all the secrets I have unearthed. I will tell you everything, Esek Nightfoot. I will be your most *valuable* novitiate of all. For now, picture me watching you.

"And, Chono—if by some strange shift in character you choose to keep my gift to yourself, then know this: I am watching you, too. And I am...as I ever was."

Then, silence. And Six sitting there as if the recording would never end. As if they would simply go on like that forever, a loathsome presence. Esek's lip curled back. There was something perverse about the Sajeven mask. About being spoken to through the mask, its five eyes portending a range of vision she couldn't match. The silence made her livid. She growled, and the growl rose to a shriek at the end. She snatched her hand into a fist, vanishing the hologram from the air, and then she hurled her empty glass at the wall. The thick tumbler broke at the edges and fell in pieces to the carpeted floor, but there was no satisfying shatter.

Now, without the casting view between them, Esek could read the unease in Chono's tightened muscles and unblinking eyes.

"Did you debate whether to bring it to me?" Esek demanded.

Chono's pause might have simply been the drawing of a breath, but its weight suggested otherwise. "Not after I watched it."

Esek had wondered if Chono would admit to watching it first rather than bringing it directly to her. But of course she admitted it. Dutybound, honest Chono. Chono, who had known for years about this Nightfoot complicity in the Jeveni Genocide, and for whom each new piece of evidence must hit like a bullet, rending her further apart. Yet she'd stayed the course. She was loyal, through all of it. Before, Esek had credited this to the fact that Chono was her novitiate, and novitiates were like dogs to their masters. But now? What drove Chono now?

"Well." Esek clapped. "You've delivered it. Are we to resume our old pattern of hunt and be hunted?"

Chono grimaced, but it came and went with a blink.

"I'm stationed this month with the Paiye family, at their estate on Sikata Leen. I'm to oversee a wedding in three days."

Esek snorted her amusement. Of course Chono would pull that kind of job. But three days was a drop in the bucket of the weeks and months and years they'd spent pursuing Six. Esek had some pull when it came to clerical assignments. She could get Chono transferred to her. Esek would need someone to share the—

"After that, I'm to join the First Cleric in Riin Cosas."

Esek's thoughts stuttered to a halt. She stared at Chono, unblinking. Chono held the gaze for two, three beats, and then glanced away.

"Sa Paiye wants me to train in Riin Cosas. I'm sure you can understand that I...can't refuse. If I do well, he'll take me on a tour of the Treble in 1661. It would be a great honor."

"A great honor," Esek repeated. She let the silence hang over Chono's head like an ax. Yes, it was a great honor. The type of honor reserved for someone the First Cleric expected to fly high in the Righteous Hand. Something buzzed in Esek's ears, vicious as hornets in the Braemish jungle. She barked a laugh, and Chono's slight shift in stance was as good as a flinch. "Well, then. I suppose Six and I will have to continue as a twosome."

"There's another choice, Sa."

"Really? And what's that?"

"You could stop."

Esek raised her eyebrows so high she felt momentarily light-headed. Had she drunk too much? "I'm under an obligation from my matriarch to—"

"Tell her to hire mercenaries. They might be luckier. You're too close to this to—"

"I'm not giving Six to fucking *mercenaries*," Esek snarled, a hot rage skittering across her limbs at the idea.

"You're a cleric, Sa. You're a member of the Kindom. Perhaps this is not a mission for a cleric. Even a cleric such as you."

It was the most absurd thing Esek had ever heard. After all these years, did Chono really understand so little? What a fool she was, to think that Esek's standing as a cleric so much as scratched the importance of her standing as a Nightfoot! And to admit defeat to Alisiana! It was impossible, horrifying, not to be borne. Esek barely withstood the impulse to strike her. The hornets in her head sang, and she wanted to tear and scratch and burn. She wanted to *kill* Chono, in that moment, just as she had at Soye's Reach. There was no way Chono couldn't see it in her face. The young cleric shifted her stance, a subtle preparation for attack.

In the end, she found the perfect blow. "I should have left you to be traded around by your kinschool. I'm sure servicing Paiye will be right up your alley."

Her reward was that rare thing: Chono, unable to hide her reaction. Her jaw slackened, lips parting. She blinked so rapidly, Esek thought she might be about to cry, and if she did, gods and fire, Esek *would* kill her. But she didn't cry, only grew pale and small as a wounded child. The sight was disgusting.

"Get out," Esek sneered. "You're no use to me."

In the pause that followed, Esek briefly thought Chono would resist. Maybe apologize. Maybe beg for another chance, as plenty of novitiates had begged before. But then, the young cleric was turning from her, making for the door with stiff, measured steps. Esek turned her back, refusing to watch the coward leave. When the door *snicked* shut, she flung herself through the balcony doors, striding out to the railing as if she could leap into flight. There on the coast she saw the construction of the library underway, heard the ring of hammers across the beach, and the Braems singing a workday song. The bright sun was beginning to melt across the sea. Reds and oranges spread in smudgy clouds against the horizon, like blood spilled in water. Next time she wouldn't trust a bomb, no matter whether it leveled a lodge, or a continent. Next time, she would bite out Six's throat, and drink till they were a husk at her feet.

Sing to the holy Sajeven,
barren in her womb.
Warm devotion, ceaseless kind.
Wheel that turns the worlds.
Let the dry riverbed and the bare rock sing out,
"I, too, am beloved of the gods."

Words of Sajeven, 1:1–6. Godtexts, pre-Treble

CHAPTER EIGHTEEN

1664

YEAR OF THE CRUX

The Gunner
Orbiting Silt

W hat kind of a fucking name is *The Happy Jaunt*?" Jun mutters. The ship on approach is a simple merchant vessel that's seen better days. Its guns are perfunctory, its hull stained with the scorch marks of too many planetary entries, its engines recognizably out-dated. Calling it a "happy" anything seems misplaced.

"You're one to talk," Masar retorts. "You call your ship *The Gunner*."

"That was Liis's idea."

Liis looks at her sharply. "I thought you liked that name."

Jun clears her throat. "Baby, of *course* I do—"

Luckily, one of their perimeter alarms goes off, drawing all their attention. Jun shuts it off but makes no other move. The chances that a Jeveni ship is going to attack them are admittedly slim, but stranger things have happened in the Black Ocean.

"Are you gonna drop the Hood or not?" asks Masar.

"Are you gonna shut up and let me work?" she shoots back.

They've been at each other's throats ever since she kicked him awake six hours ago. As soon as she told him she wanted to meet his buyer, he turned skeptical, wary, looking at Liis with narrowed eyes.

"Don't tell me the sex changed your mind. I'll never respect you again."

Jun sneered, but Liis was unaffected. She looked at Jun, eyebrow raised in expectation, and finally, irritably, Jun said, "We'll...consider hiding."

Masar was surprised, and then pleased, which only irritated her more.

"I said 'consider' it. You know, your buyer doesn't know us very well." She gestured importantly at herself and Liis. "We've done some shit. You may not want to hunker down with us."

"The shit you've done is exactly why we're working together," Masar replied. "And as for you"—he looked at Liis—"we already know you're a cloaksaan."

Icy fire traveled down Jun's spine, and her hackles went up in a rush. *"What?"*

Liis, though, showed no surprise, and said after a moment, "Former cloaksaan."

Jun was not so sanguine. Her adrenaline surged, and panic came with it. What if the Jeveni tried to take revenge on Liis for the crimes of the Cloaksaan? What if they tried to sell her to the Kindom? What if—

"Would you relax?" grumbled Masar. "We're all in this together. Partners."

This did not fix things for Jun. "If you put her in danger, I'll cut your fucking throat."

Masar rolled his eyes. "You couldn't even reach my throat."

So yeah. Things have been a little tense.

"Their guns are cold," Liis observes, pulling her black cap over her curls. "Even if they made a move on us, we'd be able to Hood ourselves before they had a chance."

Masar huffs. "They're not going to make a move on you. Kata's tit, Jun, either lower the Hood and let's do this, or—"

"Shut up," Jun snaps, trying to conceal her nerves. She flicks a glance at Liis, and gets a barely perceptible nod. "Lowering the Hood. Opening comm."

It never fails to give her a little hit of satisfaction, imagining her ship materializing on scans, coming out of nowhere. The legendary Sunstep, displaying her grandeur. Well, she better hope she's not making a mistake, because grandeur won't save them now.

"*Happy Jaunt*, this is *The Gunner*. Please respond."

Hardly a moment passes before the views on the command panel alight. Jun has refrained from transmitting her own image, yet to her surprise the other ship takes a different tack.

As soon as the figure appears, Jun realizes she was expecting something different, someone…rangier, maybe? A rebel warrior, like Masar. But the man before her wears the fine tailored jacket of a businessaan. There's an emerald scarf gathered at his throat, and a mourning band on his upper arm. Black rings adorn his fingers and a black pearl dangles from one of his ears. He has a short, well-kept beard, and a streak of white crests his dark hair like a wave. He's beautiful, and elegant, and he greets her with an artless smile.

"Sa Ironway." Even his voice is pretty—low and melodic. "My name is Nikkelo sen Rieve. Would you believe, I've been looking forward to meeting you for quite some time?"

Wrong-footed, Jun doesn't know what to say. It's bad enough hearing him use her name, but it's worse not knowing exactly what he means. Has he wanted to meet Sunstep for quite some time? Or Jun Ironway? And if it's the latter, what does that signal about the breadth of the Jeveni's knowledge? Beside her, Liis shifts her stance, weight redistributing an inch closer to Jun's body, which is the same as if she were telling her, *Stay calm*.

"I suppose Sunstep has her fan base," Jun says, a test.

Nikkelo smiles again. His eyes are a pale blue, like ice, and yet they crinkle warmly.

"Yes, and well deserved. I was recently reviewing that con you ran against the Paiye household in fifty-eight. I have to ask—how did you get around the banking certifications? I've robbed a few people in my time and I never could have penetrated those firewalls."

Jun's eyebrows hike up.

"Are you trying to *flatter* me?"

His answering smile is all bright teeth and humor. "What's a little flattery between business partners, Sa Ironway?"

"We're not partners yet."

He tilts his head to the side. He must be in his forties, but his face has a slim youthfulness, the forehead surprisingly smooth for someone who works in the dangerous corners of the Black Ocean. "I didn't mean to make you uncomfortable. The fact is I am as much an admirer of your family as your casting career. Surely your Great Gra Ricari told you all the work he did to protect the Jeveni living in Riin Kala fifty years ago? Many of us owe him our lives."

Jun flounders again, startled and unnerved. Yes, she knows about Ricari's life as a political agitator on Ma'kess. The details, however— well, Grandmi Hosek never liked him to talk about it in front of the kids, and—

In the vacuum of her silence, Nikkelo sen Rieve frowns. "I seem to have made you uncomfortable again. What a start we're having! But even for a criminal, I'm afraid I have an innate compulsion toward honesty. Sajeven permit it doesn't get me killed! But I want to be transparent with you, Jun Ironway. My people hold your family in high regard."

If he means this to comfort her, it has the opposite effect. Her family is alive because the stranger from Riin Kala hid them—made their Ironway names invisible, untraceable. If this Jeveni businessaan knows who and where the Ironways are, that is a sign of vulnerability. Jun thinks of Bene. Of Hosek and the twins—all of them exposed. Unsafe.

"Jun." Liis's voice is so low, she almost doesn't hear it. There's a rushing in her ears, drowning out all sound, and it's the touch of Liis's fingers to the small of her back that jolts her back into place. She blinks rapidly. She stares at Nikkelo sen Rieve, who is still frowning in a perplexed way, clearly confused by her silence.

His friendliness, his warmth—what if it's an act, designed to disarm her? This mention of her family—what if he's revealing leverage? Threatening them? She cuts a glance toward Masar, who looks at her earnestly. She thinks in that moment he knows her fears, and wants to reassure her, but she doesn't give him a chance.

"I'd rather not discuss my family," she says woodenly. "I assume Masar told you about the memory coin?"

Nikkelo sen Rieve looks into the camera as if he can see her after all, as if he is assessing her and learning her, and it's unsettling. "He has. Do you have a price in mind?"

"I thought I would let you make an offer first," Jun replies.

A dry smile. "Perhaps you think the Jeveni cannot afford to pay you what it's worth?"

Jun has certainly considered that. "I wouldn't presume."

This time he chuckles. "It's a reasonable assumption. But I hope you will allow me to defend my own negotiating power."

"Your ship is ancient," she observes. "That doesn't make your negotiating power look very attractive. You couldn't afford something from this century?"

She's goading him, trying to see if he'll reveal something she can use. Negotiating a simple coin sale is one thing, but negotiating a protection contract, and knowing that he knows who Liis is, is something else. She needs to get the measure of him, to see if this affable exterior is legit, or just a veneer over something deadly. To her annoyance, he looks amused. Suddenly he reaches up to his ear and withdraws the dangling earring. He holds it up between thumb and pointer finger.

"Do you know what this is?" he asks.

Jun squints. The pearl is no bigger than one of her fingernails, jet black but also—her chest thumps—threaded with scarlet.

Holy shit. It's not a pearl at all. And the gems on his rings—

Nikkelo speaks into her silence. "Masar tells me you're as scrawny as a back-alley cat." Jun's nostrils flare; she hurls a glare at Masar. "But you and I know, don't we, Jun Ironway, that sometimes the scrawny things, the damaged things, are much more than they seem."

The injury in Jun's shoulder twinges, a remnant of what she survived on the Silt Glow Cliffs, an echo of what she survived as a child, in that miserable safe house, far from home.

"One alley cat to another," says Nikkelo. "I think you'd better come aboard."

He meets them in the landing bay, two armed guards in tow. Liis stares at them fixedly, watching for one wrong move. But Masar marches right up to Nikkelo sen Rieve, all open smile. They don't bow to each other, but rather clasp arms.

"You survive again," Nikkelo remarks.

"The barren flourish," beams Masar. He turns to Jun and Liis. "Let's do this formally. May I present my buyer, Nikkelo sen Rieve."

"Nikkelo is fine. In my culture, place names are a rare formality."

Masar gestures at Jun. "You've met this one." And then at Liis. "And this is—"

"Liis Konye. Yes. The former cloaksaan."

Liis is as unreactive as a statue, but Jun flinches, fingers buzzing with the instinct to draw her gun. Nikkelo looks at her kindly. "There's no reason for concern. Even if Masar hadn't told me about Sa Konye, I've intercepted Cloaksaan intelligence connecting a renegade cloaksaan to the battle on Siinkai." He turns to Liis again. "Your former kin are looking for you."

Liis says dryly, "They always are."

"You'll find I'm a thorough operator. I have to be. I know a lot about you, Sa Konye. I know about the Teron village that your battalion burned down eleven years ago. I know how you tried to stop it, and how you lost your arm defending those villagers from your own kin. That was a very un-cloaksaan thing to do."

Liis considers this. Jun can read the subtle tension in her, the way she flexes the hand of her bionic arm, like she needs to remind herself that it's there.

"The Cloaksaan agreed," she says.

Nikkelo nods. "Everyone on this ship is a fugitive from the Kindom. I wager some of us have darker secrets even than you. Now please. Come with me."

He turns his back on them and walks toward the landing bay exit. Masar goes next. The guardsaan regard Jun and Liis impassively, and after a moment, Jun steps forward. Liis follows in her wake.

They leave the bay. In the outer hall, Jun realizes how old and decrepit a ship *The Happy Jaunt* really is. Her shoes clack against plastic grate work, cracked at the edges. The ceiling runs with old cables and pipes. Time has pocked and dimpled the sheet metal walls. She takes it all in, memorizing the route, counting the steps. Within two minutes, they reach a short staircase and follow Nikkelo out onto a landing that overlooks the ship's bridge. Three Jeveni are standing around the navigation table, where a star map plots a course to the nearest jump gate.

Nikkelo takes them along the landing toward a door on the opposite side, and then into what is obviously a captain's cabin. True to the humble ship itself, the cabin is small, cramped, with a battered desk and a couple of equally battered chairs. There are books stacked in haphazard towers, and a suit hanging from a hook in the corner. There's a painting on one wall that depicts the sooty flatlands of a moonscape, with a dome city glaring gold in the distance. Nikkelo goes to the chair behind the desk, gesturing to the other chairs as he sits down.

"Please, please. Make yourselves comfortable."

Liis and Jun hesitate, watching the two guardsaan that have followed them into the cabin. Nikkelo, noticing their hesitation, glances at the guardsaan in an unreadable way. Jun can practically hear a low hum coming off Liis, like a tuning fork. But then, to Jun's surprise, the guardsaan step out, closing the door after them. Masar leans his back against the wall, arms crossed.

Now that they are all situated, Nikkelo smiles around at each of them, his gaze stopping on Jun. He tilts his head sideways, contemplative. She tongues the corner of her mouth and narrows her eyes at him.

"And do I?" she asks.

He frowns. "Do you what?"

She leans back in her chair, affecting indolence.

"Remind you of a back-alley cat?"

Masar snorts. Nikkelo grins, and holds an open hand out to her, like someone inviting a musician to play their instrument.

"Would you like to show me the coin?"

Jun looks at Liis, needing one last assertion of support. Liis nods once, curt, and Jun turns back to Nikkelo. The coin is already slotted into her neural link, and its encryption is rock solid. Even if he cut it out of her, he'd never be able to open it. But once she shows him what she's got, there'll be a rebalance of power. Jun just has to make sure it rebalances in her favor.

She bumps the memory into a panoramic view on the cabin wall. Once again, Lucos Alanye gazes across the room at the diminutive Alisiana Nightfoot.

Nikkelo watches the scene silently, his expression giving away nothing but avid concentration. Jun has run through the coin two, three dozen times. She's memorized every frame. She pretends to watch it now, when really she watches him.

On the view, Alanye asks for permission to interrogate the Jeveni acrobat. When Caskori demands that Alanye execute him afterward, Masar shifts off the wall, standing straight again. A moment later, the icy Alisiana tells him, "Find out if the man has family or friends here. They'll have to be eliminated, too."

A few more seconds, and the memory ends, leaving the wall dark. Nikkelo is barely even blinking, mind clearly at work. It seems forever before he faces them again. This time, he looks at Masar.

"Is there any chance Alanye didn't carry out his orders?" he asks.

This is... not what Jun expected.

Taken aback, she looks at Masar, who is shaking his head soberly.

"The local media reported that Sool ben Leight was killed in an assassination attempt. Collateral damage. His family disappeared a day later. This is as much proof as we'll ever have, short of bodies."

"It'd be better if we had bodies."

"I know." Masar sighs. "I tried. Nightfoots cremate everything."

Nikkelo nods. Jun's eyes dart back and forth between them, baffled.

"I'm sorry, what is going on?"

Nikkelo is once again gazing distantly at the wall. Jun isn't sure how she expected him to react to the memory coin, but this is—

"I apologize," he says after a moment, dragging his eyes back to her. His smile seems forced now. "This coin is very valuable, and you and Masar are to be commended for finding it. We can offer you a good price. Probably not as much as it's worth, no, but still a good price."

Jun looks at him, silent. Ordinarily, all she would care about is the sum he can offer—but now she keeps turning over the words between him and Masar. *Sool ben Leight... It'd be better if we had bodies*—what does that mean?

Liis steps closer to the desk. "The bodies you're referring to. You mean the Jeveni acrobat and his family?"

Nikkelo heaves a weary sigh. "Yes, I do."

Jun looks at Masar, startled to find he's got one hand rubbing the back of his neck, eyes down. "What is this?" she asks. Masar is silent. "That coin practically proves the Nightfoots helped *eradicate* your moon. And all you care about is the *assassin*?"

Nikkelo makes the first sign of irritation he's shown yet, eyes flicking toward the ceiling. "Sa Ironway, I don't need a memory coin to prove to me the Nightfoots were involved in the destruction of Jeve. We knew that already. Masar's mission has always been of a different sort."

Jun gawps. "His mission? What *mission*?"

Neither of them answers. Jun looks at Liis, who catches her eye for a second and lifts a finger against her crossed arms—a signal to wait.

Nikkelo says, "I realize my behavior confuses you. Let me try to explain."

"Yeah, that'd be fucking great."

Masar snaps, "*Shut up*, Jun."

"Please," Nikkelo says, with a reproving look for Masar, and an appealing look for Jun. "Yes. Masar had a mission. It's a mission rooted in the very history this coin unveils. When the universe has tried to erase your people, Sa Ironway, it takes great collaboration, great dedication, to keep what remains of you alive. A hundred thousand Jeveni survived the genocide on our moon, and we had lived a long time on our own terms. Our government didn't seek Kindom sanction. Our people didn't worship the Godfire. The Treble viewed us as strangers and malcontents. We were given a choice: either assimilate, preferably as workers for the Nightfoots, or divide our communities into tiny, unthreatening numbers. Many of us assimilated. Many of us starved or were killed. Many simply disappeared. There are whole lines of our descendants who we've lost to the march of this century. But in the past few decades, we have fought hard to track those people down. More often than not, we end up at a gravestone. That's the mission to which Masar has dedicated his life. That is the mission that sent him after this memory coin."

Jun recalls the early years after her flight from Riin Kala. She was young, foolish, and without resources. She wanted to know where her family was, to know they were safe, even if she refused to join them—but her search hit dead end after dead end. And all the while she dreaded where that search would ultimately take her.

Masar says, "I wasn't looking for a connection between the Nightfoots and Alanye, Jun. Local records said Sool ben Leight was killed. I learned there was a coin out there, something that had gotten loose after the attack on Verdant, that might show how he died. *That's* what I was after when I teamed up with you. All of this..." He gestures at the air around him, encompassing their whole situation. "I didn't know about any of it."

The pain in his eyes is acute, full of sincerity. It's disorienting, this reconfiguration of his motives. He never wanted money—just to know the fate of one Jeveni and his family. So in his own way, he has been as single-minded as Jun. Both of them, trying to find the ones who are lost.

"How long have you been doing this?"

He raises his head, proud. "Since I was seventeen. In nine years I've tracked down dozens of our people. Sool ben Leight and his family were my last assignment."

"May the barren flourish," says Nikkelo, in Je.

"May the barren flourish," echoes Masar.

Liis murmurs, "Kata's Many protect them."

The Katish blessing is a small sun flaming out between Jun's ribs. And yet—

"Why did you bring me aboard this ship?" Jun looks at Nikkelo and he looks back. "If all you wanted was to know what happened to the acrobat, now you know. Masar has known for days. You don't need the coin, do you?"

Nikkelo regards her for several moments, contemplative. Then he gestures as though weighing two comparable stones.

"Do we need the coin? For our records, yes. For its own sake, for what it proves about the Nightfoots? No. But my compatriots and I believe in paying people for their work."

Jun narrows her eyes. "Compatriots?"

He shrugs, smiling dryly. "You didn't think I worked alone, did you?"

"I thought maybe you were with the sevite factory unions," Jun admits. She looks him up and down. "But I don't think it's that. And a single collective of Jeveni isolationists wouldn't have the capital to fund this kind of operation. Who are you, really?"

Nikkelo appears both amused and impressed. "We are the ones who believe there is always a better world." At Jun's skepticism, he smiles openly. "Sa Ironway, have you ever heard of the Wheel?"

Up from long-forgotten hours in the K-5 schoolroom emerge vague memories. A lesson on dead civilizations. The star systems from which their ancestors fled to Ma'kess; the Dustrow family that tried and failed to colonize a planet outside the Treble; and, of course—the Jeveni and their destroyed moon. This last piece blooms with the richest detail. A crayon drawing of a five-spoked wheel, each spoke decorated: a crooked Tree and a round gray Stone, a streak of blue that meant the River, and a yellow circle for the Star, and trying with wavy gray and blue lines to depict the Gale.

Seeing recognition in her eyes, Nikkelo nods his approval. But Jun says, inanely, "There is no Jeveni government anymore. The Anti-Patriation Act—"

"It's true, any time we tried to make a public stand, we were squashed by legal and . . . violent measures." Jun notices a subtle tightening in Liis's body. "The Jeveni have a long history of keeping our traditions alive in secret—a history that far predates the Jeveni Genocide. Even when we were jevite miners, our overseers distrusted us and tried to squash our culture. We have always known we can't count on the wider Treble to protect us. That is what the Wheel is for. Five elected representatives of the Jeveni, who work together to defend our people. I am called the River. My role, historically, is to manage matters of business, trade, and defense. Hence my work with Masar and the other collectors. Hence my interest in you."

Jun is still processing the idea that the Jeveni survivors have maintained some kind of secret government, but at this she frowns, confused. Before she can say anything, Liis asks, "What do you mean, your interest in her?"

Nikkelo looks at Masar, and Masar shrugs.

"Well," says Nikkelo. "The fact is, Sa Konye, that this operation changed for us as soon as we knew that Masar had made contact with the caster Sunstep." He looks at Jun. "Masar tells me that you are resistant to our offers of protection. But perhaps I should clarify the meaning of that offer. We don't simply want to protect you. We want you to work for us."

Jun's eyebrows hit her hairline. "I'm a private contractor."

He chuckles. "Yes, I'm sure. But you have come into our lives at a time when we need you, very much."

Liis shifts restlessly, like she's trying to decide whether Jun is about to get kidnapped and how many noses she should break to discourage the attempt. This time it's Jun who catches her eye, who lifts her pointer finger in a subtle *Wait.*

"Need me how?"

"My role is to help protect the Jeveni." He spreads his hands apart on the desk, as if to show her the breadth of the opportunity. "That includes not only finding them, but giving them what they need to survive. Call me a . . . talent scout. You are an unmistakable talent, Sa Ironway, and I would be a fool to ignore the good you might do for my people."

"*What* good?"

"Right now, across the Treble, tens of thousands of Jeveni are making the jump to Jeve's orbit. Some at great risk to themselves and their families. They do it because they know when they arrive, *The Risen Wave* will be there. For the first time in twenty-five years, we have dispensation to gather as one people—assimilationists and isolationists—on the very generation ship that first entered Ma'kess's orbit seventeen hundred years ago. This is a holy experience for us. For the next forty-eight hours, we will have independent run of the generation ship, and freedom from Kindom oversight. We will gather the best of our resources—not just the Wheel, but our engineers and scientists and artists and priests. We'll celebrate who we are, and everything the Treble has failed to take from us. But there will be a terrible gap, in our numbers."

Instantly Jun's thoughts flit to the moment in the snack shop on Lo-Meek, the harrowing news bulletin. Liis says, "You mean *The Wild Run.* The casters who died in a pirate attack."

Nikkelo nods somberly. Masar mutters, "It was no pirate attack."

"Who, then?" Liis demands. "The Kindom?"

"Why would the Kindom assassinate your casters?" asks Jun.

Masar and Nikkelo look at each other, and something passes between them.

"We can't prove that they did," Nikkelo says. "But regardless of why or how it happened, the fact is that a month ago, we had an entire corps of experienced casters, a resource of inexplicable value to us. Now, our corps is down to thirty."

Masar whispers a prayer. Jun, too, feels an impulse to pray. So many lives snuffed out.

Nikkelo says, "Those casters represented the best of our technical minds, at a time when we need those minds more than ever. Rebuilding a casting corps that will be equal to the days ahead means we cannot afford to ignore the gift Sajeven lays at our feet."

He looks at her meaningfully. Jun's eyes widen. "Are you saying you want me to join your casting corps?"

This time, Nikkelo sen Rieve smiles a real smile, full of fire. "Sa Ironway, no. I'm saying I want you to lead it."

CHAPTER NINETEEN

1664

YEAR OF THE CRUX

The Makala Aet
The Black Ocean

Chono's hand hurts.

Bruises have already developed along her knuckles; when she flexes her fingers, a deep ache radiates through her. There's a pulse of heat, a pulse of memory—hands broken and covered in blood, Cleric Paan motionless at her feet. She nearly gags. She tries to think of other fights. Like when the kinschool master made them spar for Esek's entertainment. Getting a blow across her jaw that zipped pain through her. Watching the bruises multiply on Six. Suddenly that's all she can think about: the murals of color that covered their face and body more than twenty years ago.

When Chono steps onto the bridge of *The Makala Aet*, the first thing she sees is Esek, and the purple-and-black bloom spreading from her mouth to her cheekbone. Their eyes meet for the first time since the events in Chono's cabin. Esek grins, almost feral. Esek likes the bruising, wears it with pleasure and pride. For a moment, Chono wishes she had stayed in her room. Then she thinks of the chest on her table. She imagines herself, laid out on the floor, buried under Six's letters—a terrifying thought that is still somehow less terrifying than Esek's grin. The knowledge of what Chono has done (everything she's done) makes it hard to stand in the same room as her former mentor.

But a Teron jump gate has relayed the arrival and passage of a ship associated with Nikkelo sen Rieve, which has jumped to Jeve's orbit. Esek is like a dog on the hunt, eager to follow. It's possible Jun Ironway is mere minutes from being in their grasp . . .

The captain of *The Makala Aet* stands before a glut of holographic views hanging in the center of the bridge. He greets Chono with a bow over his hands, his eyes flicking to the bruises across her knuckles. "Good day, Sa. We've confirmed with the Teron 3 jump gate that a ship called *The Happy Jaunt* passed through an hour ago. Nikkelo sen Rieve was on the manifest."

"No mention of extra passengers, of course, but that's to be expected," says Esek.

"If they're in Jeve's orbit, there will be a lot of traffic on the other side," Chono remarks.

"The Jeveni ships are only now starting to dock with *The Risen Wave*," says Esek. "We'll be able to find them before they go aboard. Then, it's a matter of following in their footsteps. But there's no time to waste. Are we ready to jump?"

"Yes, Sa," says the captain.

"Then let's go."

Chono watches her take her seat. The captain broadcasts their intention to the gate, and the navigators set a course. Esek has already strapped herself in when she notices Chono. She raises an eyebrow.

"Have you ever tried to jump without strapping yourself in? Easiest way in the world to break your neck."

Chono hesitates. Sweat begins to prickle at the small of her back. Her hands are damp, and her knuckles twinge.

"We don't know that Nikkelo sen Rieve found them."

"But we do know he jumped into Silt's orbit and back out of it in a three-hour period," Esek retorts impatiently. "Sounds like a pickup to me."

"It could be a diversion."

"Diversion? Kata's *tit*, Chono, they've got no idea we've even heard of sen Rieve. Now strap your ass down so we can get out of here. Captain, ready when you are."

Chono sits down, the impulse to obey Esek deeply ingrained. Will she ever overcome it? Even when all the bridges are burned? She focuses on keeping her pulse steady, willing the flush to recede from her neck. She knows Esek is watching her but she pulls on her harness and buckles it tight across her chest and hips and doesn't look up. Doesn't even look when the jump gate lurches into view. The captain queries navigation, and there's a back-and-forth exchange. An emergency light bathes the bridge in red, and an alarm goes up across the warkite, warning everyone of the impending jump.

Esek is still watching her. She would know the feeling anywhere, of those eyes assessing her. Chono doesn't dare look at her.

"Coordinates locked," says navigation. "Gate is clear. Crossing in five... four... three... two—"

The force of the jump slams Chono back in her seat, throws her head against the cushioned headrest, and with her eyes lifted, she sees her— staring across the bridge as it shakes and rattles. Esek, still watching.

Chono closes her eyes against the sight, against the mounting pressure and turbulence. It's like they're in the throat of a snake constricting tighter and tighter and trying to shake them loose at the same time. Her stomach drops. Her skull throbs. She feels a wave of nausea cresting in the back of her throat and then—

They're through.

Through, and looking out over a broad swath of ships-littered space. Hundreds of Jeveni transports, arrived for the pilgrimage. The curve of Jeve's gray-black form is cast in the light of the Ma'kessn sun. But more than the moon itself, it's the breadth and girth of *The Risen Wave* that immediately dominates Chono's attention. The generation ship is huge. Against its glittering mass, the fleet of civilian ships look like little garden birds swooping around a treetop.

Esek whistles. "Look at that."

The Makala Aet's bridge has gradually stopped shuddering, and no sooner does it still than the older cleric tosses aside her harness and stands up, steady as ever. By the time Chono and the other crew members have gotten out of their own seats, Esek is standing right in front of the holographic views, eyes swallowing everything. Chono, feeling mostly steady, approaches from the other side of the bridge, but keeps a few feet between her and Esek.

"Have you ever seen one before?" asks Esek. "A generation ship?"

She shakes her head. Ordinarily the remaining generation ships of their ancestors are berthed at a research station in the far limits of the Teros System. In the early centuries, inter-Treble wars destroyed much of the artifacts of pre-Treble civilization. But the generation ships survived. Now they are meticulously maintained, kept like museums. Ilius has been there. He described it to her once, hands animated, face lit up with an eagerness that endeared her. But now, for the first time, she truly understands. And stands amazed.

The Risen Wave is a leviathan, with a long torpedo-shaped body, its thrusters like sharp, fixed wings, its hull like the breastplate of a mighty warrior. Chono stares at it, this ship that's bigger than Riin Kala. Big enough to host the tens of thousands of Jeveni who will gather to it for their Remembrance Day celebrations. They will find it modernized and pristine, a museum piece made commercial, with shops and residences and amenities. A ship that, if it wanted, could soar away from here. Chono imagines herself on its bridge, charting a course—out. Out, into the limitlessness of the Black, into the exquisite possibility of…somewhere else.

"You seem anxious, Chono."

Esek's voice is closer than she expects. She's come and stood right next to her, and though they are of a height, Chono feels as if the cleric towers over her, an all-consuming presence. Like *The Risen Wave* itself.

"Don't tell me you're still upset about that row in your cabin?"

Chono flexes her hand. She stares at the generation ship.

"I almost broke your jaw."

"You didn't. Believe me, I've had my jaw broken before."

Chono shakes her head. She barely conceals a surge of annoyance. Now that she's overcome her initial reaction to the generation ship, her eyes are scanning the views, searching.

"We need to identify sen Rieve's ship."

The captain answers, "We're scanning now, Burning One. We should have them in—"

"Captain, there's a message incoming. Kindom warfalcon."

Chono's heart stutters as the view changes, homing in on the stern of *The Risen Wave*, and on the unmistakable shape of the falcon approaching them. The captain makes a startled sound.

"That is Seti Moonback's command ship. Patch it through now."

In moments the view changes again, replaced with the interior of a captain's cabin. There, standing with clasped hands, is Seti Moonback. Medisogo is a long shadow behind her. Esek doesn't give the captain of *The Makala Aet* time to offer formal greetings.

"Seti! Well, I'll be damned. Changed genders again, have you? I didn't think someone of your caliber stooped to chaperoning Remembrance Day. You'll scare all these poor Jeveni to pieces, lurking in that ship of yours."

"Hello, Esek. Up to your usual machinations, I'm sure."

"What else is life for?"

The First Cloak smiles, eyes glittering. She looks at Esek the way

Esek looks at people she wants to fuck. It's not lust, but rather the hunger of conquest. Chono's stomach turns.

Moonback says, "I imagine you're looking for *The Happy Jaunt*?"

Chono doesn't think anyone but her could recognize the significance of Esek's half-blink pause. Cheerfully she asks, "Oh, are you onto it, too?"

"We are," says Moonback with a coolness that frosts the sweat off Chono's neck.

"I thought you were working the Liis Konye angle? You know, tracking your little runaway cloaksaan. Did that not pan out?"

Esek's voice is droll, mocking, but Moonback doesn't rise to it. Suddenly, the view bifurcates, becoming a dual screen that reveals another room. Another person. Aver Paiye.

"Hello, children."

Esek laughs. "My, my. Brutality *and* righteousness. Now all we need are our clever secretaries, and we'll have a proper trio. I see you're casting from your office in Riin Cosas. Didn't you want to join us in the Black?"

Paiye replies, "No. I'm an old man. I've learned to know my place."

Chono flexes her hand again, using the pain like an anchor to her own body. Esek looks as unperturbed as ever, and with a curl of unease Chono realizes she'll never know if Esek anticipated this. She's about to say something, to try to breach the tension, when a comm pings in her ocular. She feeds the message to her aural link, not sure what she's expecting, but—

"Chono. Where are you? Listen to me." Ilius's voice is sharp, urgent. "I've just seen something. It's a contract kill, for Esek."

Chono's eyes flit to her mentor. They flit from her to Moonback. To Paiye.

"Are you with her?" Ilius's message demands. "Chono. You have to get away from her. I don't know where the contract comes from, but I think it's real. Please, tell me you're getting this message."

Before she can even think to answer, Paiye's mild voice is saying, "I'm surprised to see you, Esek. When we learned how Masar Hawks acquired his warhorse, I assumed you could not possibly have the information yourself. Otherwise you would have told us about it, in keeping with your oaths as a Hand. Yet...here you are."

Esek chuckles. "Well, to be honest, I didn't know if the intelligence was good. And I have to protect my sources, sometimes. Which makes me wonder—what are *your* sources? Why, how in the worlds did *you* track down Nikkelo sen Rieve?"

Moonback smiles witheringly. "You are one cleric pretending to be a cloaksaan. I have an entire arsenal of intelligence operatives at my fingertips. Can it really surprise you that we discovered this Jeveni terrorist?"

"Terrorist, is he? I thought he was a smuggler. What an upgrade!"

"Any person who acts against the interest of the Kindom is a terrorist," says Aver Paiye, his normally gentle tone taking on a note of rabidity. He stares at Esek with unmistakable malice, and Chono feels more of that frost creeping over her skin. "This is known, from the Godtexts."

"Is it? I had always thought we added that bit later on. Chono would know. Chono, is it true the Godtexts say anyone who defies the Kindom is a terrorist? Don't the Godtexts predate the Kindom? What do you think?"

Chono, still reeling from Ilius's message, isn't prepared to have so many eyes suddenly focused on her—to say nothing of *The Makala Aet*'s captain and his bridge crew, who all look wary and confused. But they're mere pawns in this bigger game Esek is playing, and that thought gives Chono back her control. She doesn't answer Ilius's message. She doesn't answer Esek. She looks directly at Seti Moonback.

"Where is *The Happy Jaunt* now?"

Moonback curls her lip, clearly holding Chono in as much contempt as Esek. "They're preparing to board *The Risen Wave*."

"You...haven't taken the ship into custody?"

Aver Paiye says, "We didn't want the spectacle. With so many Jeveni in one place, and so much unrest in the Treble, we feared there might be chaos if we tried to take the ship like that. More importantly, we have reason to believe Nikkelo sen Rieve isn't working alone. He's a collector, which means his efforts to accrue this memory coin are doubtless on behalf of someone else. Finding that person is as important to us as finding the coin itself."

Chono can't think what to say; her mind is a hornet's nest and her pulse thunders in her ears. This is—this is not—

"If they're boarding *The Risen Wave*, it may only be to obscure their tracks," says Esek.

"Which is why *we* will board the generation ship, and tail them," replies Moonback.

"Is that legal?" Chono asks.

Everyone stares at her. She clears her throat.

"According to the terms of the Jeveni dispensation, they're permitted to hold the ship without Kindom oversight for two—"

"Law-abiding Jeveni will have no objection to us boarding the ship," interrupts Seti Moonback. "If they did, it would be grounds enough to question their lawfulness, would it not?"

This is... terrifying logic. Illegal logic. *When the Secretaries turn their backs, all law is lost.* Ilius would stop this. If he were here, he would make these people obey the law. Then she remembers his message from yesterday: *Whatever is going on out there, my kin don't want me involved.*

What if the Secretaries *chose* to turn their backs? Not only on what's happening here—but on a kill order for Esek...?

"Go on, Cleric Chono," Paiye says. "We value your insight."

She's not sure they do. She feels Esek's eyes on her, hot as a forge licking blisters across her skin. The First Cloak's glare is contrastingly icy. It is not safe to defend Jeveni autonomy right now. But she has to do *something*.

"I think we may be underestimating Liis Konye."

This is clearly the last thing anyone expects her to say, and the silence of their surprise gives her room to breathe, to regroup.

"I've reviewed her records extensively since we learned of her involvement. By all accounts she was among the most dangerous cloaksaan in the Hand's history. Sa Medisogo himself can attest to this."

Medisogo has been a malevolent statue in the background until now. He looks at Chono hatefully. "She bled like anyone."

"Perhaps. But if she is with Nikkelo sen Rieve, it will be next to impossible for you to tail them without her knowing it. How else could she have survived all these years?"

Seti Moonback curls her lip. "We have been tracking her since she abandoned—"

"Her showing up on your radar from time to time is one thing." Chono hardly believes the sharpness of her own voice. "But the Cloaksaan would never let one of their own go rogue without trying to capture them. I imagine you've attempted to hunt her before, and failed." Moonback's scarred lip quirks viciously. But she doesn't argue. Chono addresses Paiye this time. "If you want any chance of capturing the memory coin, tracking them through a ship the size of a city in hopes they'll lead you to their buyer is a fool's errand. You're much better off capturing them when they disembark, before Liis Konye has a chance to realize you're there."

"The buyer is a very important target for us, Chono," says the First Cleric solemnly.

"You'll have the memory coin, and Nikkelo sen Rieve. The Brutal Hand shouldn't have any trouble persuading him to give up his contacts."

Beside her, Esek makes a little sound that might be a chuckle. Grim but impressed. Medisogo glowers, his shoulders high and tight like he wants to throw himself through the casting view and grab Chono's throat. As for Moonback, she looks irritated...but not unconvinced. Her eyes cut toward Aver Paiye.

"What do you think?" the First Cleric asks.

The First Cloak grunts, and shrugs. "Your pet cleric isn't wrong. Liis Konye was the best cloaksaan of her generation. If we try to tail her, it's possible we'll lose them in the crowds. If we board *The Risen Wave* via the captain's dock, we can make our way down to the civilian bays and arrest them as soon as they make port."

Paiye nods, contemplative, before looking at Chono again.

"Having studied Liis Konye...do you think we can take them in the civilian bay?"

In truth, Chono suspects both Konye and Ironway could probably disappear into thin air with a circle of cloaksaan bearing down on them. Chono doesn't care if they do, but in terms of convincing Paiye—

"Send me down to the ship." Esek's voice draws every stare in the room. "There's always a risk they'll slip away even as we close in on them. But Sunstep and I have history. If they see me, they won't be able to stop themself from taking a swing. Putting themself out in the open."

"I wasn't aware of such history," says Paiye, with a glance at Chono.

Because Chono kept this part to herself. In Paiye's glance, she sees him realize the same.

Esek shrugs. "I didn't know of it myself, until recently. But we've got to use everything we have, haven't we? Anyway, this is *my* mission. You told me to recover the memory coin and prove my loyalty to the Righteous Hand. You ought to let me do it."

Chono expects them to laugh at the idea, to reject her outright. But Moonback answers right away. "I have no objection to you joining my cloaks on *The Risen Wave*."

The words send a shiver down Chono's spine. And then comes Aver Paiye's voice—

"Nor do I. It is, as you say, your mission."

The throb in Chono's hand intensifies. She glances between Esek and Seti Moonback. Sees a savage promise pass between them. Thinks how easy it is, in a firefight, for the wrong person to get hit...

Chono says, "I'll go as well."

Aver Paiye looks at her sharply, startled. "Why is that necessary?"

"Why, we're partners!" Esek claps a hand on Chono's shoulder, leaves it there a moment, and squeezes hard enough to bruise. "We ought to finish the race together!"

Paiye says, "This will be dangerous, Cleric Chono. I would prefer you remain aboard *The Makala Aet*."

"You summoned me from Pippashap to assist Cleric Nightfoot. This is my mission, too. I must be allowed to complete it."

The pause that follows can't be more than two or three seconds, but in its silence, a private message flits across her ocular. Not from Ilius this time:

Don't do this. Esek is a traitor.

And: *She is working with Jeveni terrorists.*
And: *If you go to that ship, I can't protect you.*

Each word sears Chono's retinas, flooding her with adrenaline that she is forced to contain. She can feel her heart in her chest, a vicious drum as she casts a message back to Paiye:

I'm sorry.

Paiye stares at her, unblinking. In that stare is their entire history: meeting him for the first time at Riin Cosas; officiating his nephew's wedding; their two-year tour of the Treble. All the ways she gained his favor and served his interests. Yet now, she chooses to defy him, for Esek—whom she has betrayed. When their stare breaks, Chono knows that something else has broken, some bond that cannot be repaired.

"Very well," says the First Cleric, voice flat with resignation.

Seti Moonback says, "Medisogo will meet you both on the captain's dock in half an hour. And he won't wait for you. See that you're punctual."

With that, the First Cloak's image vanishes from the screen. Aver Paiye hesitates a moment, before offering a simple, "Gods keep you well, children."

Then he, too, has disappeared. Esek Nightfoot doesn't wait on ceremony.

"Bring us around the ship," she orders the captain. "We'll take one of your warcrows."

The captain frowns. "Our crows don't accommodate more than two people. What about your novitiates?"

"Well, as the First Cleric said, this will be dangerous. My novitiates are staying here."

Chono doesn't know if this is mercy or cruelty. Her eyes dart toward Rekiav, who is standing in the back of the bridge. He looks shocked at first, and then ashamed and wounded, like a kicked dog. Chono remembers being Esek's chief novitiate. How would she have reacted, to Esek leaving her behind at an hour like this? To knowing that her master was going into battle, and didn't want her there? It would have devastated her.

And now? Would it devastate her now, to be left behind?

The captain still looks confused, but he nods. "Very well, Burning One."

Esek glances at Chono, a summons. They leave the bridge together, walking straight past Rekiav. Esek doesn't even look at him, though he's clearly desperate for an explanation. Chono tries to catch his eye, wanting to impart some comfort. No comfort is welcome. He looks at her with a flash of hatred. She is his usurper, the one who has stolen Esek's favor from him.

But what does it even mean, to be Esek's favorite? Esek, who has only wanted one thing, for as long as Chono has known her?

She follows her former mentor through the doors, keeping a double arm's length between them without immediately realizing it. She expects Esek to make a brisk path to the stairs that will lead them down a few flights to the landing bay. But to Chono's disquiet, Esek turns instead into one of the elevators off the bridge. Chono has no choice but to follow. The doors slide shut, enclosing them in a small, silent space, and as the car begins to descend, Chono tells herself, *It'll only take twenty seconds to reach the bay . . .*

They're five seconds in when Esek hums, "So . . . you *did* betray me."

Ten seconds. Any fantasy Chono may have entertained that Esek wouldn't realize who told the Kindom about sen Rieve evaporates.

Fifteen seconds.

Like a striking snake, Esek's hand darts out, slamming against the emergency brake. The car jolts to a halt. Chono throws up her arm, blocking the first of Esek's blows on instinct, heart leaping into her throat with the burn of adrenaline. She grabs at Esek's shoulders, wrestling her against the wall of the car. She's bigger than Esek through the shoulders. For a moment she thinks she may have her in a grip—until an excruciating pain explodes in her side. Esek's knee, driving up into her kidney. Chono gags, chills breaking out over her body as she manages to slam an elbow into Esek's solar plexus, only half aware of her choking sound as she staggers back. Chono forces herself to stand up straight, sweat stinging her eyes as she grits her teeth against the burn in her lower side. She's *almost* ready for Esek's charge, for the flurry of fists that suddenly clouds her vision—but not quite. Something snaps Chono's head back like a slingshot. She doesn't even know which punch hit her, only that her ears are ringing, her face is on fire, and she's collapsed against something solid. It must be the wall. It must be—why can't she—there's—

And then, the fury of the fight comes to a vibrating standstill, with the pricking pressure of a blade at Chono's throat.

It takes her a few seconds to get her bearings, still dizzy from the force of Esek's punch, still throbbing all along her side where Esek kneed her. Esek's body is pressed close to her now, and the bloodletter fits snugly against Chono's jugular. Chono knows better than to try to kick her off. She's seen people try that before, seen the arc of blood Esek took with her. Chono makes herself still, even as she pants and swallows and feels the blade move with her throat. She looks Esek in the eyes, sees the vicious gleam, and knows that her survival is long odds.

"Now," Esek whispers. "Seti has put us on a bit of a clock, if you'll recall, so I think we had better get straight to the point, hmm?"

"Esek—"

"Shh-shh-shh—" A terrifying coo. "Don't defend yourself. You took a side. Have the courage of your convictions."

Chono can't help it. This close to death, all her masks have fallen, and she makes a sound that is half snarl, half laugh. There's a wetness on her throat; she can feel it trickling down into the collar of her shirt; she can feel the sharp sting of a shallow graze, and she hisses, "You don't know anything about my convictions."

"I'm starting to get that impression," Esek agrees. She drops her eyes from Chono's, staring at the place where her bloodletter has lived up to its name. "At first it all made sense. You knew I was a traitor, and so you betrayed me to the Kindom. Like a good little cleric. I was disappointed, of course, but not...confused. Except then the strangest thing happened, Chono." She looks into her eyes again. "It didn't go your way."

Chono grits her teeth against a wave of nausea. It's either pain or Esek's words, or both. She isn't sure she's ever seen Esek's eyes this close up. Their golden fire is foreign and familiar at the same time. She doesn't answer Esek's declaration, but Esek doesn't need her to.

"When you realized they hadn't taken the ship into custody, gods, you were as transparent as I've ever seen you. You told them about sen Rieve, knowing they would track him down, but you thought they would arrest him en route. You never expected them to take a page from my book and tail him to his master instead."

Suddenly, Chono is furious. "*Get off* me, Esek," she snarls.

Esek only presses closer, like a lover. Chono can feel the heat of her breath. "You don't want to find Six anymore, do you? That's why you betrayed me to our kin. That's why you convinced Moonback and Paiye to arrest sen Rieve and torture him for information. Even though you and I both know that would never work. It's as if...you're protecting Six. But that couldn't be right, could it, Chono? Six, a terrorist and a murderer. Six, a danger to the Kindom itself. Why would you protect them? Whose creature are you, Cleric Chono? Six's, or mine?"

Chono doesn't answer. It occurs to her that she could say what Ilius told her. She could warn Esek about the hit, and prove her loyalty again. But those words won't come. Instead—

"If you're going to kill me, do it before someone wonders where we've gone."

Esek's lip curls. And then, suddenly, she steps back.

She cleans the bloodletter on her sleeve and sheathes it.

She releases the emergency brake on the elevator.

She watches Chono as the car reaches a soft landing in the ship's bay, doors slipping open to reveal the mechanics already preparing a warcrow.

She tilts her head to one side, like a curious bird, like an alien being, like a phantom in the dark. Then she smiles. It's grim. It's excited. It's beautiful and horrible at once.

"I think you must be your own creature, Chono," she murmurs, and steps out of the elevator car, striding with purpose toward her next move.

CHAPTER TWENTY

1662

YEAR OF THE FISHHOOKS

Miirvek
Sevres Continent
The Planet Ma'kess

The doorsaan outside her building looked sweaty and pale. Not an uncommon reaction to Esek's arrival, she found, but it still pricked her interest. She was in a fantastically good mood this evening, and the prospect of fucking with the staff pleased her.

"Sa Nightfoot," the doorsaan greeted, his voice pitched a little high as he opened the door into the building foyer. "Welcome home. It's been too long."

Esek winked at him. "Four months. So happy to be missed."

Miirvek was a small city in the Sevres riverlands, tucked in the join of two major tributaries and surrounded by forests. Its population rarely encountered important Kindom players like Esek.

The doorsaan replied with a nervous smile, standing back to let her enter. She made sure to brush against him as she passed, and reveled in his tight-drawn breath. Across the foyer, a tenant saw her; their eyes widened, and they cut a retreat through the nearest hallway. Esek grinned and strode toward the elevator.

Inside, she withdrew a coin case from her pocket and held it up under the light like she was searching a diamond for flaws. She smiled, pleased, not only by the coin itself, but by what it represented. Six had sent her several memory coins since their reemergence in '58, including the memory of a nameday party that was particularly damning. But in sending that coin, Six had made their first mistake. The coin had markers that led Esek to a warehouse in Kriistura, a trove of Six's collected treasures, and so now she had this new coin, as valuable as a jevite seam. And for once, she had the drop on Six. It wouldn't be long now. Not at all.

A great day, Esek thought, as the elevator delivered her to the top floor of the apartment building, and she looked up to find—

There were cloaksaan at the door.

Her first thought was an assassination attempt, and she hummed inside with rising excitement. But the cloaksaan stood as sentries, not attackers, and so in some disappointment she let that thought go. Her mind shifted to the nervous doorsaan, who must have known, but chose not to tell her. When Esek leased the apartment five years ago, the building manager had assured her absolute privacy, protection, and staff loyalty. Well. This was what you got for choosing to live a little off the grid, and *rent*.

She strolled to her door, and stood a moment looking back and forth at the figures on either side of it, who gazed forward without offering an explanation. Unblinking fuckers.

"Is someone dead in my apartment?"

The one on the right looked at her placidly. "No, Burning One."

Neither wore any expression. Oh, how they reminded her of Chono! But Chono was somewhere on Teros, accompanying First Cleric Aver Paiye on his Kindom tour, and no doubt reciting her beatitudes daily, to the rapture of any congregant who heard her. Waste. So much waste in Esek's career.

She came back to herself, remembering her recent triumph. She turned her nose up at the cloaksaan and scornfully asked, "Am I allowed into my own apartment, then?"

The one on the left gripped the door handle and swung it open without comment. That door was locked with a combination hand-print and ocular key. Only the building manager could have let them in. Another nail in that coffin.

Esek went inside, half expecting to be ambushed from behind. Might be fun, at least? But instead the door shut after her. Now she stood in her elegant sitting room, with its stark wooden floorboards and chaise lounge of sea elk leather, and fifteenth-century battlefield paintings by the Braemish artist Mitri Lioning, who had a gift for communicating war's beautiful savagery. Recessed lamps made the white walls glow. The low round coffee table lay stacked with the mail she had left behind four months ago. And Alisiana Nightfoot stood in the room.

They regarded each other like actors in a play, each waiting for the other to say her line. Esek went first, "I didn't know you were traveling by cloaksaan these days, Auntie."

She should have known, though. She should have guessed. There had been three assassination attempts in the past year. Setting Alisiana up with cloaksaan bodyguards was a smart move on behalf of the Kin-dom, who must, of course, protect the sevite industry. And Alisiana *was* the sevite industry, her descendants having proved no more capa-ble of taking her place now than when she and Esek last spoke about it. Esek remained the only natural choice, the only living Nightfoot with the ferocity to keep the family aloft. Yet no one had told her about this latest move to drape her aunt in cloaksaan. It rankled her.

Esek asked, "Do they make good company?"

This time Alisiana released a tight chuff of—not amusement. No, she looked far from amused. She looked old, and tired. Hard to square her, sometimes, with the vibrant woman she had been for most of her life, a legend in the Treble for her beauty and iron-fisted power.

"You're looking well," said Esek.

Alisiana gave her a slow perusal. "You look thin."

Esek snorted. "I'm hale and hearty." Then she shrugged. "I was up in Kriistura. They are terrible hosts. I suppose they didn't feed me well."

Indeed, the Moonbacks and their ancillaries had watched Esek hawkishly all the time she was in their territory, and Esek took great pleasure in their suspicion and coldness and inability to arrest her for anything. Fucking Moonbacks. So transparent.

Alisiana said, "And now you've come back to your playhouse."

A chortle. "Even you have properties off the beaten path."

"I don't *rent apartments*. It's six months since you were home, and before that, a year. I begin to think you're avoiding me."

Esek paused. She would have to move carefully through whatever minefield had been laid for her. "All you ever have to do is call. Coming to this hovel is clearly beneath you."

"I wanted to catch you out," Alisiana admitted.

"Perhaps if there weren't *cloaksaan* at my door, you would have."

"I've gotten what I wanted, though."

She gestured to the leather chaise. Only then did Esek notice a slim tech purse lying there, open to reveal two rows of memory coin slots. Six were occupied. She felt both amusement and grudging admiration for the old woman. She'd debated bringing the purse with her, but it felt too risky, going among the Kriisturan Moonbacks with so much dynamite in her pocket. In the end, the coins stayed behind, secreted within what should have been an impenetrable safe behind the nearest painting by Lioning. In the painting, thirty warriors fought a battalion of Moonback soldiers, whom they were aptly slaughtering in an event known, and here immortalized, as *The Wrath of the Nightfoots*. Those warriors had nothing on Alisiana, who waited in vibrating silence for Esek to acknowledge the purse.

"Have you watched them?"

A viperous smile curled the matriarch's lips. "I have."

Esek nodded. Shrugged. "Well, then, you know what they are. The rantings of a mass murderer. Even if the information got out, do you think we couldn't prove it was all fabricated?"

Alisiana's teeth were pearlescent. She asked, "Is that your plan? These memories hit the market, and we simply dismiss them as lies? You think we could survive that scandal? That the Kindom would *let* us survive that scandal?"

"We still have no reason to believe Six ever intends to sell the—"

"And what about the sixth coin?"

Rage had drained the color out of Alisiana's face; she looked ashy and terrifying.

"Do you intend to argue *that* coin is a fabrication as well? Do you think the people of the Treble will *believe* us if we say I never took Lucos Alanye as my personal bodyguard? Never consorted with the murderer of the Jeveni?"

Esek scoffed. "The people of the Treble don't give a shit about the Jeveni."

"But they *do* give a shit about *themselves*," retorted Alisiana. "They give a shit about believing in their own righteousness, in telling themselves the genocide was a bridge too far. In demanding a Treble where such things are not permitted. We have *capitalized* on that mythology, Esek. The Kindom grants us exorbitant tax breaks for employing the Jeveni—if our link to Alanye gets out, the Kindom will use it to crush us! And that includes *you*!"

Her voice rose at the end, becoming both louder, and more animal, like some Braemish jungle cat snarling from a treetop. Of course it was the recording of the nameday party that upset Alisiana most. The only coin in the pack where her face appeared. She was a child, yes—but already formidable. And already implicated in mass murder. Alisiana had been brilliant, over the years, at insulating herself from these kinds of exposures. Now, at the end of her life, of her reign, it was all in jeopardy. Esek didn't tend to spend much time thinking about other people's emotions, but even she could appreciate the complexity of what Alisiana must be feeling. Too bad she couldn't uncomplicate things. The success in Kriistura was exquisite, yes—but it had added spiky new layers to everything.

Finally, Esek said, "I'm gaining on Six, Alisiana. I think they might even be—"

"It."

Esek broke off. Her aunt continued. "You are still searching for *it*. *It* was never released from its kinschool, so *it* has no gender. No humanity. *It* is an insect I set you to exterminate more than ten years ago. And not only have you failed to do so, but you have concealed from me the full extent of its effort. This...*parasite* has spent years stockpiling evidence, hoarding like a vermin, and yet you talk of it with respect in your voice!"

Esek frowned, annoyed. This was all very melodramatic. She might hate Six religiously but she still preferred to think of them as a person. More satisfying to kill them, if they were.

Alisiana wasn't done.

"What's worse—you've spent the past ten years sniffing around me like a bitch in heat. Slavering for a shot at my place. Fancying yourself my natural heir. And lying to me all the time! Why should I give a useless girl like you so much power?! When you can't even squash one miserable insect?"

Esek was too startled, at first, to be angry. No one had ever insulted her like this before. She had killed people for half as much.

"Are you trying to hurt my feelings, Riin Matri?" she murmured, and wondered if Alisiana really thought she could push her as far as she wanted. That Esek would let her get away with everything...simply because she was the matriarch.

Alisiana sneered. "I don't need to hurt your feelings to ruin you. And this *is* your ruin, do you understand? *All* of this is down to *you*, Esek. Your petty cruelty has created a monster bent on destroying us.

What do you think will happen, if I tell other members of our family about these coins and your part in bringing them to light? I could cast your name onto an assassination list like *that*"—she snapped—"and no one in our family would think to help you!"

Esek's brows flew up. What a way to spin the blame. Of course, Esek had never been naive enough to think Alisiana's determination to preserve the Nightfoot name corresponded to a determination to preserve individual Nightfoots. She had given Esek over to the Kindom to become a Hand, and given her over to the clerics to become righteous, because she viewed Esek as one of her tools. But Esek had never been any such thing, and for that reason, Esek laughed.

Alisiana's fury took on a note of disbelief, utter bafflement that someone could laugh at her and expect to live. Her fingers extended like claws.

Esek didn't laugh again, but she did smile, and walk away. The sitting room adjoined the kitchen, the two divided by a paper wall with a sliding door. The height of Ma'kessn fashion, the doomed building manager had told her. She left the slider open, and the lights in the kitchen came on at her arrival, spilling a warm glow over countertops and appliances of artisanal make and pristine condition, given she never used them. It looked like the cleaner bot had been doing its job nicely. Esek nodded in satisfaction, and then called over her shoulder—

"Drink, Auntie?"

Without waiting, she poured two glasses of praevi, aware that Alisiana preferred wine. She turned to find her aunt standing in the doorway, and it gratified Esek that some of her fury had faded into wariness. Perhaps she finally understood that Esek might be about to kill her? Poison her, even? Esek took a sip from each glass, a dramatic performance, and then held one out to her. Grimacing, Alisiana came into the kitchen and accepted the glass, wiping the rim with her sleeve. Esek gestured grandly to the serving table.

"Please, sit. Would you like something to eat? I think I have crackers somewhere."

Alisiana didn't drink or sit, simply watched Esek with calculating eyes. Esek took a drink from her own glass and dropped carelessly into one of the chairs at the table. She sighed with pleasure and ran her fingers lovingly against the neural port behind her ear.

"I've got something to show you," she announced, and flicked a view into the air.

It was not one of Lucos Alanye's video logs. No, this, like the name-day party, was one of his memories. He was sitting at a long table. Across from him was Sorek Nightfoot, the executor of all Alisiana's business dealings, looking surly and sunken-eyed. It had taken Esek very little work to discover that the events of the memory occurred six months before the genocide on Jeve. Sorek's presence in a room with Lucos Alanye was catastrophic all on its own. But Sorek was shunted to the side. It was Alisiana who took pride of place at the table.

And sitting next to her, three secretaries of the Clever Hand.

Esek wanted to look at Alisiana now—wanted to drink up her shock. It made no sense that this coin existed. The moment Alanye came among these people they would have forced him to deactivate his neural link and his ocular. Certainly, Alisiana wouldn't have been there otherwise, cautious snake that she was. And yet somehow, he'd found a way to record the events anyway.

One of the secretaries was taking notes on a projected writing tab. Another secretary, blond and thin, dictated for his benefit. The third secretary watched Alanye closely.

"Today is Three Month, Five, 1589, Year of the Steeltrap. Thank you for agreeing to meet with us last minute, Sa Alanye. You know who we are, do you not?"

As if the appliqués on their white tippets didn't give it away—high-ranking and dangerous.

"I do, Prudent One," Alanye said. He spoke in his affected growly voice, like a child pretending at adulthood.

"Good." The blond secretary nodded perfunctorily. He was not looking at Alanye, but shuffling between holographic files in the air, their contents invisible. "Sa Nightfoot has relayed to us all your records of your time on Jeve. In return for her cooperation, we are conceding her right to negotiate for access to the jevite seam, and we are also conceding your right to operate as her liaison in these matters. It's not our interest to interfere with a business venture, legally undertaken. What we want is to…expedite your work."

Again, Alanye didn't answer right away, but his head did turn the slightest degree toward Alisiana, before shifting back to the blond secretary. "My progress has kept entirely to the agreement I made with Sa Nightfoot in 1581. I'm on track to have the entire breadth of the jevite seam charted by the nine-year mark, and a contract with the Jeveni by 1591."

The third secretary, a woman of vibrant auburn hair, leaned toward her compatriots and murmured something. The first secretary scribbled on his tablet. The blond secretary said, "Yes, I appreciate your surprise. However, there are…new factors in play."

The third secretary spoke. "Other parties in the Treble may have caught wind of your activities on Jeve."

She watched him to read his reaction. After a moment, Alanye said, "This is news to me."

"Yes. It would be, as it has all stayed very quiet…for now. However, I think you can't help but sympathize with our concern."

Her voice was annoying to Esek, who had always liked secretaries least of all the Hands, even when they proved vicious. But she had to admit the auburn-haired woman had gravitas, and in that moment, she was directing it all on Lucos Alanye with the force of a laser beam. There was no way he didn't realize they were suspicious of him.

"More people on Jeve would threaten everything I've spent the past ten years working toward," Alanye said. "The last thing I want is for powerful families to squabble over the seam. But the work I've been doing is very delicate, and if I rush now—"

"What we fear, Sa Alanye, isn't a squabble, so much as outright war." This from the blond secretary, who was still not looking directly at him, but pawing through holographic files. "The reports you've shared with Sa Nightfoot indicate a seam worth several trillion ingots. A vast improvement from your original projections. Can you explain that discrepancy?"

Alanye paused, and said, "My original projections were based on aerial photographs. I made friends with the right people. Once I got access to the seam itself, my surveys proved it was ten miles deep. That's…a lot deeper than most seams."

The blond secretary nodded, thoughtful, and said briskly, "Well. It could take twenty years to mine. You have already been there ten. This operation grows and grows, and we secretaries like concision."

All their hemming and hawing to the contrary, Esek thought, beginning to be bored. She took another drink, dared a glance at Alisiana— who stared without expression as her past unspooled before her, in all its travesty. The secretaries spoke a few minutes more, outlining a new timeline for Alanye, as well as certain checks and balances that made Esek's eyes roll back. The auburn secretary explained that Alanye would not communicate directly with Alisiana anymore; at this point Esek perked up again.

Alanye asked Alisiana, "Is this what you want, Riin Matri?"

"I am a servant of the Godfire," replied Alisiana with a touch of a drawl.

"And I am *your* servant," Alanye reminded her.

The young matriarch's eyes turned to slits. Alisiana, a mere twenty-five, looked as delicate and beautiful as a poisonous flower.

"Are you really?" she asked.

"Of course. I—"

"And yet, I hear parenthood changes a person."

Esek wished she could see Alanye's face. He always looked so maudlin and weary in his wretched little video logs, but this! Oh-ho, this must be doing *something* to his face. His silence alone must signal Alisiana had the better of him, and when her pretty eyes glittered with malice, they could have been the razor edge of an ax, kissing the back of his neck.

"You've been there ten years, Alanye. I don't begrudge any person getting their needs met. Even if it is with some...native slut who lives like an ogre."

That was Esek's favorite part. It took all her self-control not to hoot with delight. That kind of vehemence spoke to more than disdain, but to jealousy. When Esek had first heard it, she overflowed with juvenile imaginings (Alisiana and Alanye had been lovers; Alisiana had loved him in secret; Alisiana had a fetish for Jeveni women—or ogres), but after the fourth viewing she concluded it was nothing so lascivious. It was only that, after taking Alanye as her personal guard, Alisiana had come to view him as hers, the way she viewed Esek as hers. And she was a vicious, jealous thing by nature, who could not tolerate her ancillaries to do anything without her permission. Even go to bed with someone.

Alisiana went on. "I don't even begrudge you getting her pregnant a few times. But I do wonder why you sent the children to Kator. Why would you hide them from me, unless you feared I might use them against you? And why would I do that, unless you were preparing to give me a reason?"

"That's enough," said Alisiana suddenly. Alisiana in the present. Alisiana old and wrinkled all over, her smallness become fragility, but her eyes still as magnificent as ever.

Esek vanished the memory from the air. All the important parts had happened already, and she supposed Alisiana remembered the rest. Her not-so-subtle threats to eradicate his family. The secretaries' insistence that Alanye extract a contract within the month. Alanye's silence, because he was a beaten man. None of it was half as interesting to Esek as the knowledge that Six themself was descended of a Jeveni woman, but she supposed that wouldn't matter to Alisiana—who suddenly picked up the glass she had discarded and tossed the liquor back like a true credit to the Nightfoots. She began to slowly walk the length of the kitchen, a tiger pacing. Her expression was hard to read, distant. Finally, she stopped, and looked at Esek.

"When did it send you that one?" she asked.

"Oh, they didn't," replied Esek brightly, swallowing the last measure of liquor and refilling both glasses. "That's what I was doing up in Kriis-tura. Six made a mistake, you see. The most recent coin they sent, the one of the nameday party—it held a clue, to where it had come from. I tracked it to a storage facility up north. Found quite a few artifacts, in fact. All the original coins and documents they've been sending me over the years were there." Alisiana looked up sharply, a wild light in her eyes, and Esek grinned. "Yes. Well, don't get too excited. They undoubtedly have copies, which are just as damning to us. But Six is a collector. A hoarding vermin, as you said. When they discover their prizes gone, it will infuriate them."

It had half surprised Esek, not to find Six waiting there for her. But though they'd left quite a lot of booby traps to guard their stash, they themself were absent from the storage facility and neighboring town. She had dreamed of a showdown. But that would have to be deferred.

Esek went on, "That's where I found this seventh coin. Most of what was there I'd seen before, but not that one. No doubt Six had been planning to send it to me next. It'll drive them to fits, not having that chance. Sweet revenge, wouldn't you say? And as for the coin itself—imagine if these secrets fell into the wrong hands? I mean, we're not the only ones who fooled the Treble by pretending to rescue the Jeveni. The Kindom makes such *theater* out of decrying the genocide and pro-tecting its survivors. How will it explain *this*?"

Alisiana looked at Esek as if she were seeing her for the first time. Esek swallowed down the sight of it, greedy, because she knew that while Alisiana would never admit it, she was impressed. Angry too. Incensed at having her past stripped naked in front of her. But also, definitely... impressed.

"Tell me something." Esek's voice was as smooth as the praevi sliding down her throat. "Did Alanye even *instigate* the bombing on Jeve?"

"Alanye was a fool," said Alisiana waspishly. "He was a glutton and a schemer and didn't have the brains to follow up on those schemes. He lost control of the situation and got what he deserved."

Esek raised an eyebrow. "So . . . it *wasn't* his idea?"

Alisiana stared at her for some time, face pinched. This was the crucial moment. Would she confide, or conceal? All Esek's future rested on her response, and yet she sipped her drink, composed as she'd ever been.

"It was mine," Alisiana said. And then, after a pause, "It was the Kindom's execution."

Esek's smile was slow, feline. "Was it really?"

"The jevite seam was probably worth twice as much as what that secretary described. We were looking at a resurgence of the jevite trade, and all the war that came with it. The Kindom rules through a myth of solidarity. It tells the people that great families are united in their devotion to the Godfire. The renewed fight over Jeve would quickly prove the limits of the Kindom's control. It would be far less expensive, and far less deadly, to pay me off for my stake, and destroy the seam."

"Two million people died on Jeve," Esek remarked.

"A hundred million would have died, in the course of a war. The Kindom's actions were calculated, and practical. The least death, at the least cost."

Esek felt a visceral delight at this logic. Amorality couched in utilitarian ethics. Murder defended as mercy. "I wonder why you've been so worried about what the Kindom would do to us if this information got out. They can hardly push the blame onto us, can they?"

"I didn't know this coin existed. Until now I thought all the evidence of the Kindom's involvement was in the possession of the Kindom."

"You didn't keep anything yourself? No insurance policy?"

The old woman glowered. "I had plenty of insurance. But I trusted the wrong person. Cloaksaan infiltrated my inner circle fifty years ago. They destroyed all the evidence I had."

Now that Esek thought of it, hadn't Alisiana intimated this in the past? *I've had snakes in my garden before. Spies and traitors even in my own family.*

Who could it be? Oh, this story got better and better.

"To think," said Esek dreamily, gazing up at her ceiling as if it were a field of stars, "you've gone from an empty arsenal, to the possession of a Kindom-killer. Isn't it incredible, how fortunes can spin?"

"This 'Kindom-killer' of yours would kill our family, too. I can't use it against them without exposing us."

"And they can't ruin us without us in turn ruining them."

Alisiana looked at her quizzically. "If the Jeveni discover our place, and the Kindom's place, in this massacre, they could abandon the factories. It would devastate the trade. It would devastate the Treble."

"Yes, all the more reason for the Kindom to keep us happy, don't you think?"

"And that's what you would do? Even if you realized it would not save us, you would unleash these secrets and watch the Treble's very foundations of law and order shake apart? Simply for revenge?"

The very thought of it made Esek's blood heat. Quietly she answered, "Auntie, if I was drowning, I would use my last strength to pull my enemy under with me. If I was burning alive, I would run into their arms like a lover. If I was bleeding to death, I would bite out their throat. I am not one to die with dignity and temperance. I will be vindictive and selfish to my last breath. Just as you would be."

The matriarch's nostrils flared. It might have been horror, or pleasure, or both—horror and pleasure sharing so many characteristics, for the two of them. For now more than ever Esek knew she and Alisiana were the same. They had different trappings. But they were the same. And this was why Alisiana would have to name Esek as her heir—because no one else in their family had the temperament to orchestrate the massacre of two million people, and march through the bodies afterward, and make ingots out of the blood.

Suddenly Alisiana exhaled. "It's all very well, you looking forward to a monstrous death. But I would rather we survive. I would rather this whole thing had never been a problem to begin with. And the fact remains, all of that is still down to *you* and your ridiculous feud with that creature."

"And *I* will resolve it."

Alisiana narrowed her eyes. "You've said that for years."

"I've made mistakes for years. Oh yes, I can admit it now. When I laid my last trap for Six, I made mistakes. I used insufficient bait. Worst of all, I pretended Six and I didn't both know exactly what was happening on Soye's Reach. Now I see it's impossible to trap them by pretending it isn't a trap. So, I won't. They know I stole their pretty things up north. Now I'm going to wave all the trinkets under their nose and invite them to come and take them back."

Alisiana looked suspicious. "Invite them *where?*"

Esek shrugged pleasantly. "Why, to Verdant, of course. How else to seduce them but with a genuine challenge?" Alisiana's shoulders tensed, though she controlled her reaction otherwise. Esek could hardly blame her for wanting to keep Verdant safe. Esek, on the other hand, longed for a fight on home turf. "Come, Auntie, I know it's uncouth, bringing the rats inside—but you and I both realize that we will never be safe from Six until we've stomped them out. We can't do that unless we trap them. To trap them, we need to offer something we know they want. No, I don't mean the coins, Auntie. I mean me."

The old woman sniffed. "You?"

"Of course. I have been their primary focus their entire life. They want to impress me. They may want to kill me. At the very least they want my acknowledgment, but I wouldn't give them that last time. That was my fatal error at Soye's Reach. Leaving the killing blow to someone else. Refusing to meet them face to face. That is our *only* chance. Otherwise, this will go on and on and on. If you think I'm wrong, say it, but I know you don't. There's no time left for half measures. No one else in our family can solve this problem. No one else but me can eliminate this threat. *Accept that.* And let me work."

Alisiana tilted her head up and looked aside, and the loose flesh of her throat and around her chin was repulsive. Esek barely contained her grimace of distaste. Then at last the old woman looked at her with eyes so sharp and intelligent, she might have been the twenty-five-year-old beauty again.

"Tell me your plan," she said.

Esek's blood sang. She could almost *taste* Six's death.

"I intend to. But first, let's discuss how soon you can change the terms of your will."

Behold the devouring Som, who eats up the dead and leaves the living to thrive. If one day Som slept, they would make a misery of life—suffering without relief; old age unending. Give to Som their holy book, to write each name after every meal. To say, "This one, too, was eaten into their rest." Praise Som for the salvation of their tireless appetite. Yet, though you can't help running, have no fear. For Som flies.

The Book of Deaths, 1:1–3. Godtexts, pre-Treble

CHAPTER TWENTY-ONE

1664

YEAR OF THE CRUX

The Happy Jaunt
Orbiting Jeve

Liis is tense, and that worries Jun more than anything. She hasn't changed positions since they jumped to Jeve's orbit. She stands before the casting screens like a hunting hawk, scanning the sea of ships against the mammoth bulk of *The Risen Wave*, and if what she's looking for is out there, Jun knows she'll see it. But Jun isn't exactly sure what she'd be seeing.

Nikkelo warned them the First Cloak's command falcon would be in orbit, a reminder to the congregating Jeveni that Kindom order still hangs over them, even if they get a few hours of independence. The smattering of warkites and smaller warhawks are as expected, their menacing shapes flitting among the Jeveni ships that await their turn to dock. No, it isn't the *presence* of the Kindom, exactly, that signals trouble.

Liis is looking for something else. Something that may be invisible to all but her.

Navigation says, "About ten percent of our ships have docked with *The Risen Wave*, Sa. We're next in line. Bay 7."

Nikkelo nods. He's still in his jump seat, though he's unstrapped the buckles and folded his hands in his lap. The jevite rings gleam on his long-fingered hands. *He would make a great pickpocket*, Jun thinks.

Masar comes to stand by Jun, though he's watching Liis. "She knows if they were going to attack us, they'd have done it already, right?"

"You have absolutely no evidence for that," Liis says.

The Happy Jaunt's approach to Bay 7 feels glacial. The bay doors open like a maw and swallow the ship ahead of theirs, just as the other dozen bays are swallowing other vessels up and down the flank of the generation ship. Ten minutes of silence later, and then it's their turn to slip between its teeth. Bay 7 accommodates mostly shuttles, and the passengers from the ship ahead of theirs have already disembarked and disappeared. Docking personnel in lightweight space suits and gravity boots stand waiting for them to begin the landing procedure, which turns out to be remarkably graceful given the ship's age and bulk. Jun still has to brace against the wall to keep from falling when they set down. Liis, of course, never loses her balance, eyes scanning the dock. Seconds tick by like minutes. Navigation exchanges words with the bay chief, voices bouncing off the bridge before signing off. Liis turns toward Nikkelo sen Rieve.

"Those are cloaksaan."

The River looks at her silently for a moment. He rises, coming to stand beside her, to stare out at the line of station hands awaiting their disembarkation. Nothing about them hints to Jun that they are cloaks. But Liis is never wrong about this sort of thing.

"Kindom aren't allowed on the ship for two days. The Secretaries have it all written into law." Nikkelo says this, not as if he's arguing, but simply relaying additional information.

The bay doors close, allowing pressurization and the flow of oxygen into the bay. The dock workers leave their helmets on.

"Those are cloaksaan," repeats Liis, without emotion—how easily she slips into her cloaksaan mold, that ancient mask she carved in blood and horror.

Nikkelo nods slowly, pensive. Suddenly his head cocks, listening, and Jun knows there's been some kind of signal on his ocular. His expression changes, barely. A new set to the jaw, meaning unclear.

"What is it?" Masar asks.

Nikkelo is silent. Then, finally, he tugs the pristine cuffs of his shirt. He smooths his jacket and adjusts his rings, all slowly, all with the care of a man who values appearances. Only then, put to rights, does he answer.

"Sa Konye is right. It's a trap. Esek Nightfoot is here, with several cloaksaan battalions."

Chills run down Jun's spine. "And your people waited till we were *on the ship* to tell us this?"

Nikkelo gives her a droll look.

"We always knew this might happen, Sa Ironway. We planned for it. Masar—you'll have to use the engine room hatch." As he speaks, the other members of the crew leave their stations, moving to different parts of the bridge. Nikkelo goes on, "Take the service tunnel as far as Ketch Market and catch the train to the military district. From there it's a straight shot to the bridge. The Wheel are holding command there."

"Are there cloaksaan in the military district?" asks Masar.

"We don't know yet," says Nikkelo. "We don't think so." All around, the crew members are reaching into cabinets along the walls, pulling out weapons. Other Jeveni Jun hasn't seen yet come onto the bridge, accepting the guns. Nikkelo asks, "Do you need a map?"

Masar's face is grim. "I've got it memorized."

"Excuse me, but can I get an explanation here?"

Nikkelo replies, "You're in danger. You need to go with Masar now. He'll take you the rest of the way."

Jun watches the Jeveni around her arm up. "And you're gonna, what? Stage a last stand?"

Liis tells Nikkelo, "You'll have no chance against them."

Nikkelo nods, accepting a handgun from one of his crew and sliding it into a holster under his arm, hidden beneath his jacket. He looks at Liis, his expression preternaturally calm. "Please remember, Sa, I am an excellent negotiator, and very good at stalling. They'll arrest me, yes—but it'll give you time to get away. And my people will free me."

"Then why all the guns?" Liis tosses back.

This time he smiles. "Well...there's no harm in preparedness, is there?"

Liis's chin tips in the barest nod of acquiescence. Jun isn't so sanguine. "Hold on. If there's some kind of escape route, why don't you come with us?"

As if in answer, the communication officer says, "You're being asked to disembark, Sa."

Nikkelo gives Jun an ironic look. "Called out by name. I'm sorry, if I don't go, it'll raise their suspicions. Go with Masar, *please*. You have no idea how valuable you are to us now."

Masar reaches for Jun's arm. She shakes him off, holding Nikkelo's gaze.

"Because I'm some genius caster? My life doesn't matter more than yours."

The River nods, pondering. "No. But our lives are ours to use," he murmurs, and then leans subtly closer. "Please, Sa Ironway. Use it well."

Jun wills him to say more, to offer some explanation, but Nikkelo just looks at her, determined. Liis touches her elbow. Only then does Jun turn away with a growl of frustration.

They move fast, taking a winding metal staircase into the belly of the ship. Armed Jeveni pass them, moving in the opposite direction—one clasps arms with Masar in passing. There are far more than Jun ever guessed were on board. When they reach the engine room, it's already abandoned, but Masar heads straight to the center and grabs a handle on the floor. They find themselves staring down at another hatch, one set in the bay floor itself. Masar opens this as well, and then they are all shimmying down a narrow ladder. No sooner has Jun grabbed its rails than she hears the unmistakable whoosh of *The Happy Jaunt*'s disembarkation doors. By the time they've climbed down into the service tunnel, she is already casting a line.

It takes her mere seconds to connect with Bay 7's camera grid, a half dozen views made available to her in an instant. She funnels the signal to her ocular, the images superimposed over the tunnel sprawling before her. She selects a camera, and watches Nikkelo stroll down the gangplank as the bay's interior doors open. Nine cloaksaan appear in all their black regalia, led by one that Jun would know anywhere. Her throat closes in panic.

"What is it?" Liis asks at her side.

Jun doesn't answer, simply casts the same signal to Liis's ocular, and then Liis, too, can see him: Vas Sivas Medisogo. Whatever his presence makes Liis feel, it doesn't show on her face, but Jun can hardly stop herself glancing at her lover's prosthetic arm.

"Keep going," Liis says.

She does, but not before noticing the cleric called Chono coming up behind Medisogo. Jun recalls her brief research on this tall and solemn person, known for temperance, for mercy, and for being just. Her presence can only be a good sign, can only aid Nikkelo.

But right behind her comes Esek Nightfoot.

Masar starts to jog, leading them down the dark and abandoned service tunnel. Jun practically runs to keep up with him. But she has spent a lifetime learning how to be in two places at once, and now she may as well be standing next to Nikkelo as the troop of Kindom Hands approach him.

Nikkelo bows over his hands, looking relaxed and friendly.

"Quiet One," he says to Medisogo. He bows to the clerics next, pausing at the sight of them. Jun thinks he must be taken aback by their faces, freshly bruised, and—Jun zooms in—is that a cut on Cleric Chono's *throat*? Nikkelo continues, "Burning Ones. Blessed Remembrance Day. How may I be of service?"

Esek, predictably, speaks first.

"Yes, gods keep you well. I suppose you know what we're here about?"

"I'm afraid not," says Nikkelo, eyes sweeping over the three clutches of cloaksaan, before flicking toward the station hands who Liis recognized as three clutches more. That's two-thirds of a battalion. It is *staggering* overkill. "I've never seen so many Hands of the Kindom take an interest in Remembrance Day. I can only assume something very serious has happened."

"This way," Masar calls back to them.

They cut to the right, into a much narrower tunnel that reminds Jun of sewage pathways she's fled down in capers past. Liis at her back is a liquid presence, spread out and suffusing everything in her tireless search for a threat. On her ocular, Jun switches views so she can focus on Medisogo, an oversized block of a man, half battering ram, all malice.

"You are Nikkelo sen Rieve, are you not?" he asks. Jun shivers at the resonating bass of his voice. She adjusts the audio, watches him stare at Nikkelo unblinkingly. He may not be human enough to blink.

But Esek clears her throat, forestalling Nikkelo's answer. Jun switches camera angles again, and Esek says, "There's no need for us to be coy with each other. We believe you have three passengers we're looking for. A pirate called Masar Hawks. A former cloaksaan called Liis Konye. And a caster who goes by the handle Sunstep."

Nikkelo smooths his hair, as if it's not already immaculate. "What a roster. But you must know I am Jeveni. And only Jeveni are allowed aboard *The Risen Wave* today. If I brought outsiders onto this ship, it would be a betrayal of my people."

Esek chuckles richly. For a moment all Jun can do is *stare* at her. Stare at the *longness* of her—her legs and arms and throat and even the bloodletter glinting on her belt. Stare at the burning umber of her eyes and the totally unexpected deformity of her left ear below a crown of coiled black hair.

"We're two blocks from the market," Masar says, glancing back at them. Jun sees his ocular glint, sees the sallowness of his skin, and realizes he is watching the same thing she is. "Keep up," he grits out, and faces forward again.

Then it is the second cleric, Chono, who speaks. "If you're saying they're not on your ship, I assume you're prepared for us to search for them?"

Nikkelo looks at her pensively, perhaps wondering about the mottled purple blooming like a flower around her eye. "This seems like a disproportionate response to a couple of criminals, even if one is a former cloaksaan." He looks at Medisogo. "I know as well as you that the Kindom doesn't send whole battalions after street thugs. Or am I wrong that the rest of your battalion is behind that door?"

Medisogo looks at him as if the past two minutes haven't even happened.

"Are you Nikkelo sen Rieve?" he asks again. And adds, "Also known as the River?"

Jun's stomach drops. Ahead of her, Masar staggers to a halt. He looks back—the expression on his face is horrified. He glances down the path they've been walking, and then back again, his body vibrating, his hands closing into fists. Jun can almost see it happening: Masar, bolting back the way they came. Racing toward his River. Liis makes a low sound of question, clearly as prepared to go back and fight as he is, and Jun palms the butt of the Som's Edge, ready to draw. But a moment later, Masar blanches. His neck tenses, like an animal about to wrench against a lead. Then, snarling, he turns, and carries forward. Jun and Liis rush after him. On her ocular, Jun homes in on the clerics, sees Chono look at Medisogo in surprise. Watches Esek briefly close her eyes, lips pressing together. Swings around to Nikkelo again, and sees him smile the cool smile of the untouchable.

"May the barren flourish," he murmurs.

Everything seems to hang in a kind of impenetrable stillness, like the heart of the Black Ocean itself. Jun pans out, trying to see it all at once. But what happens next is so fast, so ferocious, it's only later that she'll piece together anything resembling a chronology.

Nikkelo reaches for his gun.

Esek Nightfoot shouts.

Cleric Chono steps forward.

And Medisogo shoots him in the head.

In the service tunnel, Masar stumbles.

The power of the shot lifts Nikkelo off his feet, like a doll flung away. It drops him onto the bay floor, a supernova of blood and brain matter and crooked limbs.

Masar makes a sound—a terrible, animal sound that rings in Jun's skull.

Medisogo smoothly turns his gun on Esek Nightfoot, even as she draws her gun on him.

They leap in opposite directions, shots going off.

Medisogo is hit, thrown down, body sliding across the hard surface of the bay.

Esek grabs Chono's arm, yanking her back, already shooting at the other cloaksaan.

"Now!" someone shouts, unseen. "Now! Now! Now!"

From within *The Happy Jaunt*, gunfire erupts like thunder, spraying the bay as Nikkelo's loyal crew unleash their fury and their grief.

But the cloaksaan scatter, like tiles flung on a game board, like birds taking flight. They slip behind transports, behind shuttles, behind the strange mechanical detritus of the landing bay. They weave around corners and angles, stalking *The Happy Jaunt* and ducking under its fire.

They'll find a way inside the ship, Jun knows it. They'll kill everyone.

"What do we do?" she cries. "What do we do?"

They have all stopped still in the service tunnel, right under a hatch marked KETCH MARKET. Masar's eyes are wide and stunned, his chest heaving with horrified breaths. Liis puts a hand on his shoulder and shakes him, not cruel, but hard. He wrenches away from her. He looks at her like he thinks she's Medisogo—like he'll kill her just for standing there.

"Masar," Jun whispers, shocked by the brokenness of her own voice.

"We have to move," says Liis. "Masar. We have to move."

He blinks rapidly, the rawness of his pain filling the hallway. Suddenly he bends at the waist, pushing a fist into his forehead and screaming like a wounded bear. Shivers race down Jun's spine as she remembers the stranger in Riin Kala, their expressionless murmur, *Ricari is dead*— and hadn't a scream been caught in her throat, too? When the foundation of the world collapses, what can you do but scream?

Liis says, "We have to move, *now.*"

Masar stands up, flushed and wild-eyed, before all his pain transmutes into determination. "Yes," he gasps. "Yes, we have to move."

A flash of red in Jun's ocular draws her sharply back to the scene in the bay, where Esek Nightfoot emerges from behind a stack of shipping crates against the wall. She fires on the cloaksaan, unhesitating, unshaken, her red coat like a flame enveloping her. There's no manic energy in her face, as Jun has seen before in footage of her fighting. No, her face is cold and her eyes are flints and she picks off one, two, three cloaks—before slipping back into hiding behind the shuttle. Jun snatches for a new camera angle. Now she can see Esek's shelter, where Cleric Chono is facing a wall—no, a *door*. A door out of the bay. She is huddled over it, clearly attempting to cast her way through the locks, but to no avail. Her face is corpse pale, but she doesn't stop trying.

Two clutches of cloaksaan abandon their assault on *The Happy Jaunt*, redirecting toward Esek's last stand.

Masar grabs for the ladder in the ceiling, hauling it down.

Cleric Chono grapples with the door's command codes, shouting something at Esek.

Masar starts up the ladder, and Liis pushes Jun to follow him.

The cloaksaan flow closer, like a slow-gathering, unstoppable wave.

Jun watches Cleric Chono; Jun imagines she can feel the rising panic in this woman, this stranger who she knows only through stories of good works, of those she has served, of those who have loved her. Of those she has saved as she now, clearly, needs to be saved.

The cloaksaan are moments away.

Jun wants Esek to die. Wants her gunned down and torn apart and *dead dead dead*—like Ricari.

But Cleric Chono...

Jun doesn't question herself. She scours and slams her way through the bay's meager securities. She disarms the door as easily as breaking a twig, watches Chono practically fall through it, and feels Liis's presence behind her, following her up through the hatch in the ceiling and out—into open air.

The wide-openness of Ketch Market assaults her senses. It's huge and, to a station-born brat like her, bizarrely terrifying. The ceiling is as high as five ordinary station decks. Buildings and lampposts and trees line the street as if they were in a city on a planet. Jun knew in a roundabout way that *The Risen Wave* has been maintained all these centuries as a museum piece, a tourist trap, at its berth in Teros System. But she never expected anything this grand, nor the ways the Jeveni have made it their own. Everywhere the colors and imagery of Sajeven adorn market stalls and windows and banners, and everywhere Jeveni walk in cheerful groups, completely unaware of the carnage on their doorstep.

The train station (a *working* train station!) is directly across the market square, tracks disappearing into a tunnel, train cars collecting passengers.

"The next train leaves in two minutes," Masar croaks. "Come on."

But Liis says, "Wait."

She is looking out over the crowd, her brow furrowed.

Jun tries to see what Liis can see, but it's a garble of colors and people and *things*. Masar says something about hurrying, but Liis ignores him, and Jun looks where Liis looks and there, in line for a food vendor, a man in a black shirt. She sees it: eyes that flick toward them, and a five-spoked wheel tattoo that looks...wrong.

Liis moves—the shot hits anyway.

Its cracking report pierces all the chatter of the Jeveni crowd. Liis's prosthetic sprays artificial blood like a spigot, sprays wires and sparks and gore onto the wall behind them as screams go up in the market. Masar swings his shotgun off his back. Jun throws her body at Liis, propelling her into cover behind the nearest stall; the second shot misses them both. Neither shot came from the cloak in the black shirt. There are others—how many others?

They hit the ground hard. The screaming is louder than before, and the sound of the fleeing crowd sends vibrations through the floor as Jun scrabbles desperately at Liis's clothes. Her sleeve is all but ripped off; the arm hangs limp, destroyed. Under her shirt, the bandeau around her breasts is shredded and her side is singed red with contact burns. Jun can't tell if the blood is all from the prosthetic or not.

"I'm fine," grits Liis. "Let me up."

Jun's fingers shake as she starts working on the damaged ports holding the dead arm locked to Liis's body. Masar, crouched beside them, scans the false sky overhead.

"Stay down," he orders, and stands, and fires.

Twice. Three times. Not into the crowd but into great streetlamps that line the market and spray glass and sparks through the air, billowing smoke and small flames. Within moments, the unmistakable odor of extinguisher mist floods the market, and right after comes the mist itself, cloying, sticky, snuffing out any hint of fire—and creating a gray veil over everything.

"Follow me," Masar says.

The arm comes off with a wet, sucking sound. They leave it where it falls, scrambling to their feet and rushing through the mist toward the train station. They're on the platform when Liis draws her gun, spins, and shoots a cloaksaan who is not three feet from Jun's back. Jun shouts mindlessly, watching him hit the ground and disappear in the wave of mist as they rush on.

They hear the train set off from the station in a rumble of engines and shrieking whistles. Jun is vaguely aware of its shape vanishing into the mist when they reach the platform, but immediately a new train appears. It's a gigantic double-decker affair, empty, anticipating passengers, but the silence in the mist means that the Jeveni who weren't on the first train must have fled the market by other means. Jun knows that when the mist clears, it will just be them on the platform, perfect targets.

They make a run for it toward the front of the train, some fifteen cars ahead. Liis is breathing hard, and not from exertion—she *is* hurt. When they reach the lead car and climb on, it's into an extravagantly upholstered cabin of benches and curtained windows and glittering chandeliers hanging overhead. Jun makes Liis sit down; she calls to Masar, "How long before we leave the station?"

Masar hurries down to the door connecting this car to the next, gazing through the window and checking the lock.

"Hold on," he says.

He starts speaking rapidly into his comm in Je. Jun knows she ought to at least set up an ocular text translation but she's too focused on the damaged port close to Liis's shoulder, where the arm wrenched out. Red bruising has already begun to marble the skin, and the contact burns on Liis's side are beaded with blood and plasma. There's internal bleeding from the impact of the blast, but she can't tell how serious it is.

"Put your arm up," Jun orders, and when Liis obeys, she pulls her shirt up high enough to probe for broken ribs. Liis grunts, which is practically a scream coming from her, and the knowledge that she's in pain makes Jun furious.

"We're not safe here," Liis says.

"No shit," mutters Jun.

"How many are out there?"

Jun finds an aerial view of the market, and casts it into the air between them. The mist is clearing, but it takes Jun several moments to identify the dark shapes slinking down the street, like wandering ghosts drawing ever closer.

"Can you get this train to move?" Liis asks, voice tight.

Jun hurls herself into the net like a skydiver, spreading her arms wide and growing her fingers into ropes that reach and wrap and snatch at the complex system powering the train, that winds its cars in loops and spirals all over *The Risen Wave*. She slips between the matrices that bracket the train's security system—

And slams into a brick wall marked with the Kindom star.

"Fuck," she hisses.

"What is it?" Masar asks. He's no longer speaking into his comm, but approaching them from the opposite end of the car.

"The Kindom has control of the train system. They've got it in a stranglehold."

He says, "I know. My people are trying to break it, but there are casters fortifying it in real time. Can you get through?"

She *can* get through. She can build a bomb in her mind as subtle and sophisticated and devastating as the cloaksaan themselves, and shatter the brick wall and fling herself into the cockpit of this fucking train—but it'll take *time*. She glances at the aerial view of the market. The cloaksaan have reached the train, but they haven't boarded it.

"I need five minutes," says Jun, already working, furious and ferocious as she weaves together the pieces of her arsenal.

"We don't have five minutes," Liis murmurs, as more cloaksaan appear within the view Jun has created.

"Three minutes," Jun amends through her teeth, forcing herself to go deeper into the cast, to let the voices and the people around her fade. Even so, she's peripherally aware of Liis shaking her head, of Liis looking at the spiral staircase leading to the second deck of the train. From one of the holsters on her person, Liis withdraws a short baton, and flicks her wrist. Jun hears the sound, a musical *shiiiing* as a two-foot blade protracts.

"Do you have reinforcements coming?" Liis's distant voice demands.

Masar says, "Yes."

But even Jun, two-thirds submerged in the net, can hear what he doesn't say: Those reinforcements are no closer than Jun's access to the train. Some unspoken conversation occurs between Liis and Masar, and Jun doesn't have the time to pay attention to it, until suddenly Masar is calling her name, sharp as a gunshot.

In her mindscape, Jun has cast a net over every security system on *The Risen Wave* and is mining her catch for tiny sharp things that will help her break through the Kindom's brick wall. Blearily she looks at Masar, makes a questioning sound. He says, "When you're through, you have to get to the military station. All right? It's not even fifteen minutes away. People will be waiting for you there."

His eyes are fierce. Confused, disoriented, Jun can't quite parse his meaning.

"Do you understand?" he asks.

She mumbles, "What?"

Then Liis is squatting down in front of her, looking straight into her eyes.

"Keep going," she tells her. "Don't wait."

Still half in fugue, Jun suddenly recalls the first time they met. An alley behind the casino, where the trio of men cornering Jun found themselves abruptly laid out like felled trees. And over their sprawled and groaning bodies, Jun looked into Liis's oil-brown eyes for the first time, and saw whole galaxies.

Realization strikes. Masar has his orders. Liis has her mission. And both are keeping Jun alive.

"Liis—" she starts, horror choking off her voice.

But then Liis has a hand on the back of her neck. She reels her in, kissing her hard. It's not passion. It's *devotion*. It's promise and history. In the muddy background, far outside the circle that is them, always them, *just* them, Jun hears Masar climbing up the spiral staircase, boots clanking on metal as he goes for higher ground. He will draw the cloaksaan's attention away from the front car, she realizes. Draw it onto himself. He'll throw everything he has at the Brutal Hands, and slaughter all he can before they get to him—and Liis will do the same.

Liis pulls back, the pressure of her mouth leaving a brand behind.

"I love you," she says, and darts for the stairs.

CHAPTER TWENTY-TWO

1664

YEAR OF THE CRUX

The Risen Wave
Orbiting Jeve

Chono has cast a fourth comm at Aver Paiye when Esek growls, "He won't answer."

They've thrown off their red coats, and all in black they walk with sidearms drawn. Esek keeps looking back the way they've come, her expression more serious than Chono is used to. They're in some kind of neighborhood, the houses preserved as museum pieces, the street an immaculate, empty portal to the age of their ancestors. A block away, the street opens into a market, and there are signs pointing toward a train station.

She casts another message:

Cloak Medisogo has attempted to assassinate Cleric Esek Nightfoot. First Cleric, as you serve the Godfire, please respond.

She doesn't expect him to answer any more than Esek does. She sends the comm on instinct, a protocol trained into her over twenty years. But even if a corner of her, the last shreds of her naivety, hope Paiye knew nothing about the hit on Esek—his refusal to respond to her messages now is damning. This is why he didn't want her to join Esek on *The Risen Wave*. He knew she would not stand by for the assassination of her former mentor. He knew Medisogo would have to kill her, as well.

Why did Nikkelo sen Rieve draw on him? Why did he provoke a cloaksaan—

"Because the Kindom knew who he was," says Esek. "And he didn't want them to use him to get to the Wheel."

Chono hadn't realized she asked the question out loud. Esek's answer makes no sense.

"The Wheel is defunct."

"And yet, the River ran with blood."

"There is no Jeveni government," Chono shoots back, like an obstinate child.

"Certainly none that enjoys the sanction of the Kindom. Which would make them, and all who followed them, criminals before the law."

Chono follows a step behind Esek, who is walking quickly, purposefully down the street of anachronistic houses and alien-looking greenery. It's bizarre, a perfect complement to their circumstances, for even in her most confused moments, Chono never could have anticipated aligning with Esek against Kindom Hands. Yet it appears following her old mentor is another ingrained instinct. Only now does she think to demand, "Where are we going?"

Esek looks over her shoulder. Despite her grimness, her body is loose, relaxed. This is her element. "The train station."

"Why the train station?"

"Because it'll take us to the Wheel."

Chono's nostrils flare. Sweat has dripped into the cut on her throat, turning it to a line of needle-sharp fire. She finds her lauded emotional control fracturing, a brutal crack down the center of her.

"I thought we were looking for Six."

Esek glances at her, amused. "I thought you were trying to *stop us* looking for Six." She glances sharply behind them, then—"Come here, quick."

She pulls Chono into an alley between two of the houses, crowding back into the shadows. They watch the street, and after a few seconds a clutch of cloaksaan stalk past. Chono doesn't know where they came from, how Esek knew they were coming. They move in the direction of the train station, and Chono wonders if this changes Esek's plan at all. Seconds pass in silence as they keep cover. No one else walks by.

Chono says, "They must have had battalions aboard already."

Esek grunts agreement. "Yes, I suspect trotting out *The Risen Wave* despite the jump gate embargo was a ruse, to get the Wheel in one place and capture them. Not a bad strategy."

"It's the sort of thing you would do to Six," says Chono, listening for more sounds on the street, startled when gunfire goes up in the distance—three booming rifle shots.

Esek looks toward the sound. She murmurs distractedly, "Yes, though it never worked."

Hearing Esek admit it—Esek, who never admits defeat—sends anger bolting through her. "But you did it anyway. Over and over. That's all we've ever done, Esek. Chase Six, and fail."

She expects Esek to bristle, to erupt, but instead the cleric laughs, turning away from the sounds of the gunfire to scoff at Chono.

"My, my. You're honest all of a sudden."

"You almost killed me an hour ago. You've killed at least three cloaksaan, and you shot Medisogo, and none of it has stopped me following you. We're both going to die on this ship. I'm not sure there's a better time for honesty."

Esek's look turns sharp. She says in exasperation, "I wasn't *really* going to kill you. And we're not going to die, not this late in the game. I...forbid it."

It's such a ridiculous, pompous, perfectly Esek thing to say that Chono nearly laughs, but gunfire cuts her off again. Esek's body coils, waiting, listening. It's either moments or minutes that they stand suspended, watching for signs of more cloaksaan in the street. Then, seeming to reach a decision all at once, Esek bolts from the alley. Instinct prevails, and Chono follows, both of them forgoing stealth for speed. The market can't be more than a hundred yards away. They run forty. Sixty. Seventy-five. Suddenly there is more gunfire. And more guns: the unmistakable, weighty crack of a shotgun Chono recognizes from the roof of the Silt Glow Cliffs—answered at once by a rain of cloaksaan fire.

They break upon a market that is dark and filmy with dissipating mist. Chono can smell the acrid extinguishing agent, and underneath it, the smoke of fires it put out. A train of maybe twenty cars occupies the station on the opposite side of the market, and two dozen cloaksaan are firing on it in bursts. Even at a distance, Chono sees one of the cloaks lifted off their feet by the force of a shotgun blast (she thinks of Nikkelo sen Rieve, dropping dead) and only then does she locate the shooter. They're on the second level of one of the train's center cars, flitting from one shot-out window to the next. It's unclear whether they are trying to aim at the cloaks, or simply keep them at bay with scattershot. Whatever they're doing, it won't be long before a cloaksaan picks them off.

The shotgun fires again. Chono says, "That's Masar Hawks. I recognize the gun."

Esek takes her at her word, nodding, muttering, "Then Sunstep is with him. Gods, why hasn't she got that train moving? It's nothing to her to hack a transport!" Chono is silent. Maybe Jun Ironway is dead. But Esek doesn't seem to think so. "She'll have it soon, and she'll be headed to the Wheel. We've got to get on that train." Chono's shoulders tighten instantly, and Esek, seeing it, chuckles. "Oh, Chono.

What are you going to do now? Help me reach them before the Kin-dom does? Or kill me so I can't get any closer to Six?"

The cloaksaan are tightening their ranks again, zeroing in on one of the cars, and it's been whole seconds since any rifle shots. They're close enough they'll be able to board in moments—and that is when it appears. Something the cloaksaan can't see at all from their position: a new figure, *running* across the roof of the train car. *Leaping* from the roof of the train car. Landing upon them, amid them, like a bird of prey that dives, and doesn't miss.

For a bizarre moment, Chono is certain it's Six. Who else but Six could move like that? That murderous elegance. That flurry of blows and kicks and what looks to be some kind of blade, edge catching the light with every violent swipe. Who else but Six could lay out three, four cloaksaan on their own, in what seems like mere seconds, but—

No. Because Six has two arms and—gods—this person only has one! And Six is tall, and this person is short, and Six is slim like a knife edge, and this person is a muscular, compact one-armed *explosive*, ripping through the glut of cloaksaan like they were nothing but kin-school children. For a split second Chono thinks she is going to watch Liis Konye single-handedly butcher nearly twenty cloaks.

"Fuck," says Esek beside her.

But no one can take down that many Brutal Hands on their own. A blow to Liis Konye's truncated arm nearly buckles her. The cloaks re-form, a wound knitting itself together, a united, multiplying cancer. They hit her again.

Six blows to win.

Liis Konye goes down on one knee. The crowd surges, an indomitable tide. It will swallow her entire, it will devour as Som devours.

Like a volcano, Konye erupts with a fresh round of swinging, furious violence. Two cloaks are flung back, nearly decapitated by that arcing blade. But their kin don't retreat. They converge, they knock her down, and that small, remarkable fighter disappears within them.

Chono starts to run.

This is another ingrained instinct—to go to the fight, to give of her body, to be the instrument of her gods. And some part of her still looks out on the scene and sees, not the one-armed warrior with her spinning blade, but *Six*. Six, fighting to the death. Six, alone in the melee. Six, with no one to stand beside them. And the part of her that sees Six knows with sudden ferocious certainty that Liis Konye didn't abandon her oaths out of cowardice. Liis Konye doesn't fight these cloaksaan now out of some impulse toward chaos. No, something else, something righteous, is what drives her. And isn't that something Chono understands? Isn't Chono the one who killed the old cleric on Pippashap? Who caught him in the act and slaughtered him with her bare hands? Even though it meant killing one of her own, she did it. She could not look away. She was haunted by the beatitudes in her heart.

And now Esek is running beside her, and Esek is urging her to *stop, just stop!* But it doesn't matter. She didn't need Esek on Pippashap, and she doesn't need Esek now, and she can't be thirty feet away from the outer edges of the cloaksaan mob when something hits her so hard her whole body is thrown back onto the ground.

Her head must crack onto the concrete underneath. She must pass out for a moment, or else die, maybe. How else to explain the sudden fuzzy sensation of familiarity, of being back in her old kinschool on Principes? Don't the Godtexts say death will be a return to all that matters most? A return to the core of oneself? But perfected. Untouchable.

That must be why she's suddenly in the kitchens of the old school. She's not alone. There, standing over the gigantic hearth, is Six. But the child Six, who she remembers so well. They look up at her. They lean over a pot on the hearth and their dark face seems to float in a cloud of steam: a round face, a slightly crooked mouth, a broad nose, and tall forehead. Their eyes, always a deep, cool brown, meet hers, and they're scowling. They were always *scowling*. She goes and stands next to them by the hearth. They both have to stand on step stools to reach. She looks down into the pot and sees a jump gate glittering like a sphere of mercury. Six has a big spoon, and stirs in concentric circles.

"What are you making?" Chono asks.

Six drops black-and-red chips of raw jevite into the pot. "I am making a death for Esek Nightfoot. When I drink it, Esek Nightfoot will die."

To Chono, either dreaming or dead, this makes a kind of pure sense such as nothing has ever made to her before, and she feels relief, joy, and no fear.

"Why did you never answer my letters?" asks Six, gazing into the pot.

Chono flinches, and far away, on the table in her warkite cabin, the locked chest rattles and groans. The last time she touched the letters, they were in that chest. Hoarded. Concealed. Now, suddenly, her pocket is heavy. She can feel the letters there.

"I never knew how to reach you. And your letters were mostly for Esek."

Six says, "My letters were for you. Even the ones I wrote to Esek were for you. I know you could not write me back. But you did read them, yes?"

"Yes," Chono promises. The letters in her pocket have begun to burn through her clothes, melting into her skin, scarring her with secret words.

"Well." Six lifts out a draught of the potion, eyeing it. It steams and gurgles, an unmistakable poison. "When you wake up, you will have to write to me."

They bring their crooked mouth to the lip of the spoon, and drink it down in a shrieking, burning, smoking rush that fills the room with darkness, and then bright white light that burns her eyes and forces them open and—

Chono is lying down. The ground is moving.

She's staring up and it's not the cavernous space of Ketch Market she sees but a glittering chandelier that swings with the movement of the room around her. Someone is kneeling next to her and cursing and moving their hands, and something is being pressed into her chest. Chono gags on her own scream.

"That's right, godsdamn you, wake up!" snarls Esek. "I told you we weren't going to die and I *fucking* meant it!"

Chono's body is trembling as hard as the room around her. The pain is incredible, radiating out from her chest as if she were the one who swallowed Six's jump gate draught.

"What—oh, gods—what happened?"

"Be quiet," Esek snaps, still moving too fast to follow, still doing... something to Chono, even as she mutters to herself, "This medic bag is practically empty. Gods, what's the point of putting medic bags on these cars if they're going to be empty?! Hold on, the painkillers are coming."

Instantly a rush of coolness floods her body. It's so acute, it feels so good, that she gasps, all her pain melting into relief. But the first high subsides moments later, leaving her dizzy and nauseated.

"What happened?" she mumbles again.

"You mean while you were flying to the rescue like a martyr? A squad of Jeveni fighters showed up in the market. One of them shot you."

This feels... intangible. Surely, she would have noticed? Or couldn't she see anything but the figure of Six—no, *Liis Konye*, disappearing under a mob?

Esek goes on, "Medisogo was there, too. The bastard survived wherever it was I shot him. I had to throw a *grenade* at him this time. I barely got you onto the train before it took off. You're fucking heavy."

Chono giggles. She actually *giggles*. Esek's look is scathing. *I'm in trouble*, thinks Chono, and giggles again.

"Am I dying?"

"No, you are not."

But there's a note in Esek's voice she's never heard before. It sounds like panic. Chono fights through the weird heaviness, forces down the impulse to laugh, blinks hard and determined, and says with something like her usual stoicism, "I'm not wearing armor. If I was shot in the chest, it probably struck my lungs or heart."

Esek says angrily, "You'd be dead already. Hold still. I've flooded your body with coagulants and I'm about to inject you with suture bots."

Chono considers this, frowning, like it's a particularly obtuse bit of Godtext. "Aren't suture bots meant for external wounds?" she asks fuzzily.

"Yes, but these are about to get a promotion. Look, there's no anesthetic in this damn kit, and I don't think the painkillers will stop you feeling it. I've got to sit you up first. Are you ready?"

Without waiting for an answer, Esek grabs her under the arms and hauls her up. Even with the painkillers it's terrible. She tries hard not to scream but bites her tongue instead, and then her mouth is full of warm, coppery blood, which must be the same flavor as the potion Six made in her dream...

"It's all right," Esek tells her. "Take a breath."

Dizzy and faint, Chono peers around, finally putting the pieces together. Her back is braced against the rocking wall of the train car, and she can see a door down the aisle of seats, leading to the next car. Esek is kneeling next to her, doing something indecipherable again.

"I'm going to inject the bots now."

Almost pensively Chono says, "I feel cold. That means I'm bleeding to death."

"No, you're not, because I'm already transfusing you."

Chono blinks in perplexity—forces herself to focus on Esek, who she only now realizes has one of her arms raised and a tube coming out of the crook of her elbow, flowing...somewhere.

"Really?" Chono says.

Instead of answering, Esek jams something into her chest. At first all Chono can feel is an intense pressure. Then she starts screaming.

"It's all right!" Esek shouts, and to Chono it sounds like an echo chamber and feels like a javelin through her brain. "It's all right, it'll pass in a minute! Chono—*fuck!*—I'll give you more of the drug. Hold on. It's all right!"

When that icy rush comes again, it's not enough to stamp out the immolating pain in her chest—but it does blunt it enough that she stops screaming. She makes a sound, a choked sob, and feels wetness on her face. She can't remember the last time she cried. It would have been while she was still a student. Maybe when one of the people who bought her left her naked in a bed. Or maybe not even then. Maybe the last time Chono cried was when Esek visited Principes and cast her curse on Six.

By horrible degrees the pain lessens—probably the surgical bots shooting her nerves through with paralytics even as they create new agony, cauterizing and sewing and burrowing. Even when the pain is no longer threatening to burn her mind out of her skull, Chono can't stop weeping. It makes her so angry she blurts out, "Six wrote to me."

Through all the sensory overload of her body trying to die, Chono senses Esek go still beside her. It feels like whole minutes pass, but it's probably only seconds before Esek says, "I know."

"They wrote me a lot. Probably twenty letters in the past decade."

"I know."

This makes Chono furious again. "How could you know?"

"You thought I didn't?" She's still holding her arm up, and now when Chono squints she can see the red blood flowing through the tube. She can see Esek has formed a fist, clenching and unclenching.

"Don't give me too much," Chono mumbles.

"The med kit is monitoring me. I won't give too much."

For a moment neither of them says anything. The train is still rocking, its deep mechanical hum like a lullaby. Chono can't remember if any of her parents ever sang her lullabies. At school, Six's breathing was a lullaby, slow and deep when they woke her from nightmares.

Chono says dully, "You didn't know. If you'd known, you would have killed me."

Esek chuckles. "Yes, I can...see why you'd think that."

Another few seconds of silence. Chono says, "I never told you. I thought you'd be jealous. Aren't you jealous?"

"That's a complicated question."

Chono blinks, disoriented, observing, "You're trying to save my life. You seem to be working very hard at it."

Esek opens and closes her fist. Chono looks at this in fascination. She looks at her mutilated ear, struck for what is probably the thousandth time by Esek's horrible marriage of ugliness and beauty.

"I won't be able to stop you now," she mutters. "I won't be able to stop you killing Six."

"It's cute you think Six needs your protection."

"Don't kill them." Chono is on the verge of weeping again. The pain is like a thousand gripping, tearing talons, but it's no worse than the future she imagines. "Please don't kill them."

Esek ignores her. She's staring down the length of the car when suddenly she reaches for the tube in her arm. She pulls it out, and for a second Chono thinks she's decided to let her die, but then Esek gets to her feet. She's not entirely steady (she did give too much) and has to lean against the nearest train seat as she stanches the bleeding in her arm. She's still staring down the length of the car and now Chono recognizes the sharp look on her face, of one predator sensing another.

"What is it?"

"Be quiet," Esek says. A pause, and then she calls out, "I know you're there. You won't get the drop on me. Come in here and neither of us will have to shoot the other."

For a few seconds nothing happens. Then the door to the next car bangs open. A woman appears, pointing a handgun directly at Esek's head. Esek holds her hands palm outward on either side of her, and doesn't draw her weapon. Chono squints at the woman. She carries the gun like someone who knows what she's doing.

"Throw down your weapons." She advances slowly.

Esek says, "I don't think you want me unarmed, Jun Ironway."

"Throw them down!"

The woman is wild-eyed and disheveled. She's got a film of grayish extinguisher mist all over her, and what are either sweat or tear tracks streaming down her face. She grips the gun like it's her last handhold on a sheer mountain cliff. Esek does not throw down her weapons. Jun Ironway glances away from her long enough to eye Chono. For a moment, their gazes catch, and hold. Chono hasn't been this close to her before, hasn't ever actually *seen* her, before. She's struck by how *young* she is, how skinny—and how fearless. A station brat, through and through.

"What happened to her?" Jun demands.

Esek, hands still held out in as nonthreatening a gesture as Chono has ever seen, says blandly, "She was shot. I am trying to keep her alive until we get to the next station."

"The next station?" Jun Ironway sneers. "There are Jeveni at the next station. You know what they'll do when they see the great Esek Nightfoot? They're going to pump you full of bullets."

"I would prefer it did not come to that," says Esek, her voice low and composed, none of its usual acerbity.

"Maybe I'll do it for them!" Jun Ironway's voice is high-pitched. She sounds hysterical, and she keeps blinking fat teardrops out of red-rimmed eyes. "Maybe I'll do it for my Great Gra! Remember him?!"

"Yes, Jun Ironway, I remember your Great Gra."

"Shut up! Just—fucking *shut up!*"

Remarkably, Esek *does* shut up. No goading words or looks. No sudden, deadly draw of the handgun or bloodletter. They stand at an impasse for several moments, until Chono, feeling a little drunk, asks, "Do you know Six?"

The caster gives her a baffled look. Esek blows a breath out through her nostrils. She's still leaning for support against the train seat, and she looks a little pale, Chono realizes. She definitely gave too much blood.

"Who the hell is Six?" Jun asks.

Esek looks at Chono, face inscrutable, then answers Jun. "Your Riin Kala rescuer, by another name."

Jun stares. She steps farther into the car, aiming all the more sharply at Esek's head.

"How the *hell* do you know about that?"

Esek says in that same steady voice, "It is not actually important right now, and I—"

"I'll fucking decide whether it's import—"

"Sa Ironway." Esek's voice is a boom of thunder, her gentleness evaporating. The young caster flinches, and Esek tells her, "There are things happening here that you, that neither of you"—a glance at Chono—"understand. And believe me, I would like very much to explain them. I have spent years wanting to explain them to *someone*. But right now, my friend is badly injured. I am trying to keep her alive. Could you *please* refrain from shooting me until I can get her to the medics at the next station?"

Jun looks stunned. Chono wonders how long she has anticipated this meeting, and how brutally unexpected it's been so far. Esek doesn't wait for her to give permission. She squats down in front of Chono. She pulls a palm-sized monitor out of the med kit and looks at it, her face hardening. She reaches for the tube.

"I am going to give you more," she mutters.

"Esek—"

"Do not argue with me. I can give you more."

"Esek, I just realized..." Chono trails off. She feels fuzzy. She feels cold. She can't feel the pain from the suture bots anymore and she thinks that might be very bad.

"What?" Esek asks, sliding the needle at the end of the tube back into her vein, not even wincing. Behind her, Jun Ironway stands like a statue, gun still drawn, but lifeless-looking now.

"Esek," Chono murmurs. "We don't have the same blood type." Esek's blood type is rare, as rare as she is. And Chono is not a universal recipient. "Esek, why is the kit letting you give me blood...if we're not the same type?"

Esek stops. Esek looks slowly up at her again. Their eyes meet. Esek doesn't say a word, and Chono feels dizzy dizzy dizzy...

For when you die, you shall return to that which matters most, to that which is the core of yourself. And you will see what you are, laid out before you as a banquet. In your death, you will eat the fruits of your life, and whatever ripens them shall ripen your death—either with joy, or regret. And your loves and your hates will gather to you, and you will dine with them at the long table of your life. And thus is all death a return.

Words of Sajeven, 11:3–7. Godtexts, pre-Treble

CHAPTER TWENTY-THREE

1663

YEAR OF THE TRICK

Verdant Estate
Sevres Continent
The Planet Ma'kess

If someone did not turn off that *fucking* alarm, Esek was going to kill them. Everywhere she looked, lights flickered, smoke curled, people ran, and that alarm kept on blaring.

Months of waiting for Six to make their move, to spring the trap, and now, this. She had laid so many snares outside the estate grounds, from bombs to her very own novitiates, all her intelligence suggesting that Six planned a solitary stealth attack. Well, so much for that. Now her birds of prey were out of reach. And the Nightfoot guardsaan had rushed the east wing. And Alisiana was dead. Esek stood alone in the dining hall.

She was a quarter mile from the ruins of the security command center on the opposite side of the estate. That's where the aerial assault had struck, blowing out the communication center and the holo fence, cutting off their ability to signal for help, and leaving way for a ground attack. Ten shiploads of Braems had stormed Verdant. The dining hall looked like a hurricane had gone through it, its thirty-foot table the only object left standing. Chairs were overturned—broken glass and dishware scattered the ground, but it appeared the most expensive cutlery was gone. The statue of Ri'in Nightfoot lay on its side with its head broken off and rolled several feet away, the jewels that had adorned its throat and fingers gouged free. Priceless paintings had been yanked off the walls, canvases stripped from the frames and carried off. Though the bulk of the pirate army had gone through this wing and moved east, Esek had caught one of them, a straggler, trying to take Alisiana's portrait.

She stood over his body now. She was aware of her own chest rising and falling with each breath, sweat in her hairline and streaming down her back. She still held the bloodletter she'd used on him: one slice through the lower abdomen, one across the throat, and when he was on the ground, she'd stabbed him so hard his chest caved in. His intestines lay pooled around her, and she was covered in his blood. She blinked the sweat from her eyes, then threw her head back and shouted into the air, "You think you can do this?! You think you can come into *my house* and do this?!"

She was practically screaming, as if her voice could drown out the tireless alarm. Her plan had been *perfect*. Even Alisiana had said so. She'd laid enough traps that even a mouse could trip them; she'd lurked in wait for Six like a river monster, patient, listening for the faintest ripple in the water. Her bait was unparalleled. Her contingencies numerous. When Six slunk into Verdant like a shadow, Esek would turn on the floodlights and drop every net.

She'd expected subtlety. Finesse. Instead, she got a battering ram.

Esek stormed out of the dining hall, entering the foyer in time to see another pirate jogging down the nearest ornate staircase. He had a bag of goods slung over his shoulder, and when he saw her, there was no recognition in his face.

"Do you know who I am?!" she thundered at him.

He went for his own weapon, but her bloodletter was already flying. It struck him in the throat, throwing him onto his back on the last couple of steps. She flowed forward like Som themself, drawing her sidearm and emptying the magazine into him. She wrenched the blade free, turning at a sound of gunfire. She did not run, but stalked down the hallway, dripping gore.

"You *fucking* people know who I am."

Within two minutes she had found a knot of four Verdant guard-saan. They were taking cover behind a giant fountain in the atrium that separated this wing from the next. From her position, Esek saw a group of pirates advancing into the atrium on the other side, fir-ing on the fountain. There were ten of them. Her guardsaan returned fire, but they would soon be overrun. No one had noticed her yet. She fired on the Braems, taking out three with sniper precision before they cottoned on to her. She ducked behind one of the room's decorative columns. The pirates rained fire on her; shards of the column sprayed past her head, and with a kind of brutal and furious glee she plotted her response.

For days Esek had been walking around armed to the teeth, antici-pating Six. Her old protégé, Commandant Inye, had sent her a pack-age of marble-sized crowd-killer grenades a year ago, and she felt like killing quite a few crowds right now. She glanced at her useless guard-saan, signaled them, and they at least had the courage to open fire on the pirates. All right. Good. With gritted teeth Esek slipped around the column long enough to fling her activated grenade. It felt a bit like rock-skipping, and no sooner had she taken cover again than the explosive went off in a very pleasing crack of violence.

When Esek stepped out to view her handiwork, the Braems were in pieces, though not all had died. They lay in the wreckage of the grenade, groaning and shaking and crying out in panicked agony. She advanced, picking each survivor off with quick shots to the head. When she got to the last one, her magazine was empty again. Teeth bared, she drew the bloodletter for the third time. The pirate's leg was almost severed at the knee. She stepped on the flimsy connective tissue and for a moment his screaming overpowered that incessant alarm. Then she knelt and grabbed him by the hair, yanking his head back. She carved so deeply through his throat that she nearly decapitated him, and still it didn't feel like enough. His dying agony wasn't enough. The waterfall of his carotid artery *wasn't enough*. She wanted to reach through the gap she'd left and pull his heart out. She wanted to leave such a carnage that the Treble itself would heave with nightmares for a thousand years.

Her home. Her legacy. Her inheritance—despoiled by fucking Braems. She would kill every one of them. And when she found Six (for of course, all of this was Six), gods, *killing* them would be the last act in many acts of exquisite revenge.

She wiped her blade on her pant leg but it was little use. Her pant leg was soaked red already. She reloaded her empty gun and checked to make sure the second was in reach, tucked into a holster under her armpit. When she turned, the four Verdant guardsaan had climbed out from behind their hiding place. They were wide-eyed and gray, and one of them had an injured arm. They stared at her, at the scene around her, in something between awe and terror.

"Burning One," said the ranking guard, a captain. "You—you shouldn't be here."

Esek replied, "My home is under attack. I fully intend to defend it."

She was about to say more when a sound behind them made her draw and whirl—but it was only another guard. He flung up his hands and Esek sneered.

"Where are you coming from?"

The guard stammered, "The—the shuttle pad. Sa, what are you doing here? All your family are evacuating."

"All my family are cowards. I'm going to the tower to retrieve Alisiana's ashes. I'll go to the shuttle pad after."

She was already planning to turn and leave, but something in the guard's expression stopped her. He looked confused, and then blanched with fear.

"What?" she snapped.

He swallowed convulsively, saying, "Sa, the tower is on fire."

Esek looked at him. That...did not make sense. The tower was full of valuables. The pirates wouldn't burn it down before stripping it of every last possible bounty, and there hadn't been time for that yet. Esek's eyes darted toward the atrium's ten-foot double doors, the ones that led out onto the grounds of the estate and directly faced the tower. Alisiana's tower. Through the doors, all elaborate crystal, there glittered refracting shards of orange and gold and red.

"Return to the shuttle pad," Esek ordered the guardsaan icily. "All of you."

She turned to go, but the captain said, "Sa, you can't! You must come with us."

"I'll follow," Esek replied, already moving.

Suddenly, inexplicably, a hand was on her arm. "Burning One, I insist that you—"

Esek looked at the hand, then into the captain's eyes. He realized his mistake too late. Carving out the pirate's throat had only banked her fury. Now it roared to life again. She grabbed the captain's suddenly nerveless hand, breaking it at the wrist. She struck him squarely twice, three times. He crumpled, and she kicked him hard, in the gut and then the kidney.

"Do not!" she snarled. "Ever!" Another kick. "Touch me!"

He was unconscious, blood spilling from his broken face. Esek looked up to find the other guardsaan standing back from her, looking between her and the man on the ground. They were ready to piss themselves. What good were fighters like this? At least the Braems had a gift for viciousness. No wonder they'd railroaded her estate so easily.

"Take this shit sack to the landing pad and make sure the rest of my family evacuates." This time, no one stopped her when she turned to go. "And turn off that *fucking* alarm!"

She reached the crystal doors within seconds, shoving them open to the stunning vision of Verdant at nightfall, and Alisiana's tower burning at its top like a candle. Esek stared. The flame was crawling downward, engulfing the lower levels. If the tower itself didn't buckle and collapse, Esek predicted another hour at most before the fire reached the foundation, and then the underground rooms. But in that moment, with that peak of blazing flame against the night sky, she thought of Chono calling her Burning One—and she almost laughed.

The tower was a hundred yards away. She ran for it. She smelled the night air and the fresh green breadth of Verdant, and she smelled the black smoke spreading out in suffocating waves. Her lungs burned by the time she reached the tower doors, panting as she took off her ruined gloves and coat. In the end, she ripped off her shirt as well, leaving her in blood-stiffened trousers and the sweat-soaked undershirt. She had no armor on. But something told her Six wouldn't, either.

She flew inside, gun drawn, thinking for some reason they'd be waiting for her in the foyer. Instead, she met an unexpected and unnerving stillness. The west wing's blaring alarm had not followed her here, and the foyer was silent. Sevite torches glowed dimly in their sconces. Artwork hung untouched on the walls; cupboards stood unbroken. The tower's spiral staircase gleamed with fresh polish. Not even the smoke from the fire had reached this level yet.

Esek didn't put her gun away. She started down the staircase with slow, measured steps, not making a sound. Here the lights were dim, too. Esek listened for *everything*. She kept going until she reached the temple level, and the hall to Alisiana's chamber. There were no signs of life, of movement.

She glanced into the temple, which was dark except for the shape of the icon to Makala—her large body oiled to a shine. She knelt on hands and knees, vulva on display, her son Praed crowning. For a moment, Esek considered going into the temple. Searching its corners.

But the thought of Alisiana's ashes prevented her. She continued down the dusky hall.

The matriarch's bedroom was not dark. The clerics who had delivered her final ceremony had set the sconces blazing in an homage to the Godfire, to whom they sent Alisiana's soul through chanting prayers. It was customary to keep the lights like this for at least a year after a matriarch's death so the Godfire would shine brilliantly down on her ashes. After the darkness of the larger estate and the tower itself, this bright room made Esek flinch.

She looked around. The bed still stood resplendent where it always had, its posts swathed with silk curtains. The rugs were clean and shiny with gold thread. The Nightfoot portraits hung untouched, including the small painting of Caskori Nightfoot by the bed. The plinth in the corner still displayed that little box Esek had never opened, and it was closed now, its secret retained. In fact, the room was exactly as it had ever been. Even Alisiana was here, though only as a sphere filled with ashes, sitting in the center of the giant bed.

For a moment, she thought her suspicions must be wrong. The missile that blew up Verdant's security command center must have flung fiery debris onto the tower. The pirates had not gotten here yet, and probably wouldn't come now that the place was on fire. Six was somewhere else, or maybe they'd never shown up at all. Maybe none of this had ever had anything to do with Six in the first place. Alisiana's death had weakened Esek's family. Maybe the pirates saw a chance to attack a wounded predator. One thing was sure: If she lingered here, she'd never get out of Verdant, and burning alive struck her as undignified.

Run, a voice whispered in her head. In hilarity she realized it was Chono's voice again, like an oft-ignored conscience bleating for attention. *Take the ashes and go. There's nothing else here for you.*

Yes. For once, Esek would listen to Chono. She went to the bed, picking up the sphere of ashes with one hand, fully intending to dart out of the room again. She didn't know why her eyes flitted to the plinth a second time. Nostalgia, perhaps, for Alisiana's secrets? Or her investigative instincts, to look and look again? Whatever it was, this time, when her eyes landed on the plinth in the corner, a wave of ice broke over her.

Behind it, half-shadowed and leaning in the corner, was a stave.

As if someone had breathed a sinister wind down the hall, she felt them behind her. There was no sound, but of course there wouldn't be. Esek waited a moment, even though she knew it was dangerous to leave her back to them. She had to gather herself—the excitement flooding through her felt like drunkenness. When she was sure she could control the gleeful laughter and vibrant rage bubbling up, she turned.

They stood two or three feet outside the doorway. With Alisiana's room so bright, and the receiving room dark, they were a shadowy shape. But a shape she thought she recognized. Tall. Lean. They seemed to be wearing some kind of coat, and holding something, too. Delight zipped through Esek as she realized it was a stave. They did not advance, and she thought of the years, gods, *years* she'd spent waiting to see their face.

Esek grounded her stance. She spread her arms out, still gripping Alisiana's ashes in one hand, and her sidearm in the other.

"Why so shy?" she demanded. There was no response from the figure in the dark. "I've only ever tolerated one shy novitiate, and you're no Chono, are you? How can you be my novitiate if you're shy?"

They took one step closer to the doorway, but Esek still couldn't see their face. She dropped her arms and tossed Alisiana's orb of ashes back on the bed. She holstered her sidearm in a show of good faith, and shrugged.

"You've done it, all right? I told you to do something extraordinary. I told you to impress me. Well, you have. Alisiana is dead. I will be the matriarch of the Nightfoots now. Forget being a novitiate. I want you for my right hand."

Another pause. Then a voice murmured, "My eye is on a different prize."

Esek smiled nastily. The voice was quiet, and somehow different from the voice in the coin recordings, yet she still recognized it. She wanted to hurt them.

"You'll never get your coins back, you fool. I've scattered them all over Verdant like salt. Your Braemish pets won't find them. Even if they did, they're encrypted beyond anything you could break."

The figure paused, and said, "That's not the prize I meant."

This was tiresome. Esek beckoned with curling fingers.

"Stop being so melodramatic. Come inside and say hello."

They stepped forward, stopping just outside the glow of the bedroom lights. Their coat swayed against their shins. The stave was like a brutal extension of their right arm.

Ever since Chono's fateful delivery on Braemin, Six's gifts to Esek had always come with a personal addendum. A recording of some kind, ranging from monologue to missive. In all of these, Six had worn the clay mask of Sajeven. But not now. Now, there would be no hiding of faces. They stepped forward, out of the obscuring shadows, and showed themself at last.

"Hello, Esek."

At first, Esek didn't understand what she was looking at. She thought it was a trick of the light. If not that, it must be a hallucination. But even the most grotesque and bizarre hallucination would have seemed realer to her than this. Something went through her that she had never felt before, like a phantom blade between the ribs. She couldn't name the feeling, couldn't even properly describe it to herself, it was so foreign. It flew into her on dark wings, and brought clarity as sharp as a looking glass. She was not hallucinating.

Stood before her, she saw herself.

And not a mere approximation, as some sycophants had attempted over the years. This person looked *exactly* like her, from the shape of their eyebrows to the coils of their hair to the lines of their throat and the subtle curve of their hips under the cleric's coat they wore. Somehow, they'd even managed the subtleties of her *age*, though there were over ten years between them. Esek had seen stunning body mods before. She thought of cousin Torek on Praediis, whose servants were modified to look like clones. She thought of gangs she'd interrogated, who approximated one another as a con tactic. She thought of Ev Nightfoot, the little fool who modded herself to look like Alisiana. Very good work. But nothing… nothing near as exquisite as what Esek saw now.

"Hello, Six," she said.

And drew her bloodletter, hurling it straight at the creature's face.

Six moved the stave with expert grace, striking the blade midspin. It flew right, hitting the nearest wall with a *thunk* and landing on the ground. Esek chuckled. She began to move, not toward them, but around the breadth of Alisiana's bed, putting it between them. Six stepped farther into the room, drifting the opposite direction. They watched her with a little smirk she'd been perfecting since she was five. Their umber eyes glittered with mockery and hunger. This time, Esek laughed outright.

"Damn, you're good-looking!" she declared. She waved a hand at Six's tall, lithe frame. "Is this what you've been doing? How long did it take?"

"Years," Six admitted. Their voice was perfect. Smooth, cool, a little gravelly. The way they *moved* was perfect. All catlike poise and rippling energy, all confidence and threat. "It'll please you to know the explosion on Soye's Reach fucked me up pretty bad. Having your face burned off is the perfect opportunity to remake yourself."

Esek *was* pleased. "The face is one thing. But the height, the build! How did you do it?"

Six said, as if they were discussing house renovations, "I was lucky. Our builds are similar. The leg lengthening procedure was minor. My shoulders and hips took more time."

Esek asked, "What about your cunt? Have you got one of those? Won't be able to pass yourself as me without one."

Six grinned, showing their incisors. "I'll be fine."

"And is this really what you've been working on all this time? It takes admiration to an incredibly creepy level, you know. I thought you wanted to be a cloaksaan! You can't go unnoticed looking like that! And the Treble's not big enough for both of us."

"It won't have to be."

The dark-winged thing in Esek's chest fluttered, but she scoffed. "So you want to take my place. *That's* how you choose to impress me?"

Six smiled softly. For a moment they didn't look like her at all. "Oh, Esek. I moved on from impressing you so very long ago."

Esek paused at the head of Alisiana's bed, standing beside the nightstand with the little picture of Caskori on it.

"I hate to break it to you, sweetheart, but none of this implies you've moved on."

"I don't mean I no longer care about impressing you. Impressing you has been the most impactful mission of my life." They tilted their head in the acerbic, querying way Esek often did. "Have I succeeded?"

She chuckled. "Oh-ho... Beyond my wildest dreams."

She reached into the nightstand drawer, drawing out a hunting knife Alisiana had always kept there. It had belonged to Caskori (as if he were ever any kind of hunter). Esek flipped it in her hand and threw it, fast and accurate as an arrow. This time Six slipped left. It struck the wall behind them, embedding itself in thick wood. By the time Esek drew her gun, Six was already leaping onto the bed between them, spinning their stave in a wide arc. Esek barely avoided being struck in the head, but the blow against her shoulder sent her sprawling, gun knocked from her hand. Pain went through her in a shock wave as she hit the ground. Six did not advance on her, but got down from the bed and bent over to pick up the gun. As Esek watched, seething, they deftly took it apart and threw its different pieces across the room.

"I brought you a stave for a reason." They nodded toward the corner. "Six blows to win."

"I'm going to blow a hole in your head," said Esek, getting to her feet.

She drew her second gun from the holster under her arm, but wasn't fast enough. Six struck it out of her hand. Esek glared at the weapon on the ground, the barrel split. With a growl she stalked over to the corner, kicking down the plinth in a rage. The box cracked on the floor; a pale black sphere with faint pink striations rolled across the ground, but Esek ignored it, grabbing the discarded stave. She whirled on Six, who had put some space between them again. Their eyes— *Esek*'s eyes—were bright.

Esek sneered. "With everything between us, with everything we could discuss right now, you want to resort to an old kinschool *game*?"

"You like games," said Six lightly, with a gesture Esek recognized as her own. "That's two blows for me. None for you."

Esek's lip curled back. "No. You struck the gun but not me. Body contact only. One to zero."

Six laughed merrily. "I knew you'd find this fun. You're a narcissist. You must have wondered before what it's like to fight yourself."

"I've wondered what it's like to fuck me, too. Should we try that?"

A thoughtful hum.

"I don't think we'll have time."

Esek turned the stave in her hands, feeling its weight. She made a habit of training in all kinds of weapons, wanting as much facility in hand-to-hand combat as knife or gunplay, but it had been a while since she'd used a stave. Six, she imagined, practiced daily. But they weren't advancing on her. Weren't even in a combat pose. They watched her, waiting for the perfect moment. Esek's eyes flicked across the room, to where her bloodletter lay on the ground. Six smiled grimly at her.

"If you cheat again, you'll be sorry."

Esek huffed with laughter, and attacked, moving so fast Six couldn't hide their flinch of surprise. She whirled the stave like it was her own arm, a ferocious strength infusing her. She might not have used the weapon recently, but she had muscle memory, and she had years of experience, and this was *her* fucking house and *her* fucking body.

Wood cracked against wood as loud as any gun's report. The shock waves reverberated down Esek's arms. She felt and heard the whistling breeze of each strike. No foam toys for them, no, no. A proper strike to the head with one of these would crush your skull. And Esek was going to *beat* Six to death.

They crashed into each other like competing riptides. Same height, same build, same musculature—and same determination. While Six might have her body, they did not have a lifetime of using that body to fight. Within moments Esek was crowding them back like the little ingrate they were, adrenaline pumping through her with each vicious blow, until she had caught them in the side hard enough they grunted, and tripped away from her.

Esek didn't advance. If Six wanted to play the cocky shit, then she could meet them smirk for smirk. And so she stood, breathing through her nostrils, and watched them recover their stance. Watched, with great satisfaction, as they shrugged off the cumbersome cleric's coat. Esek could practically *smell* their adrenal glands in action, could *taste* the pain receptors in their torso.

"That's one to one," Esek said.

Six came at her again.

The force of their assault was dizzyingly precise; it threw Esek into a defensive stance before she could fully get her bearings. Six drove her across the room, pushed her harder and harder. Even through the exertion of trying to keep pace, Esek could only marvel at how abruptly they'd changed their technique. Esek had always been a no-holds-barred, knock-down, drag-out fighter, and Six had shown moments ago a facility for that same style. But now they used their stolen body in a way that was clearly, utterly their own. Less blunt, less brutal—more elegant, like a dancer. They were technically *pristine*, as they'd been at the kinschool. They fought how Chono prayed: with reverence for the particulars of form and function, and when Esek tried to overpower them by crowding close, all she saw was a whirl of spinning wood before the stave cracked against her shin.

They broke away from each other, Esek limping.

"Two to one," Six said.

Esek gritted her teeth, walking off the throb in her leg. They were both breathing hard. She could see Six was hurting from that blow to the side. They were sweaty and disheveled and it made Esek unhappily aware of how she must look right now. Six must have seen her expression because they bared their teeth in a grimace-grin.

"Don't sulk. You brought this on yourself. Luring me here with my own cache of coins. I'm surprised at you, Esek. Did you actually think

I made a mistake, leaving that clue on the nameday coin? Don't you realize, I planted the cache in Kriistura?"

Esek stopped moving. She remembered arriving at the archival hall in Kriistura half convinced she'd find Six waiting for her. Instead, she found their stash. She found proof of Kindom atrocities. She snatched them up and flew away, unpursued, and never considered—

"You're fucking with me," she accused.

Six shook their head. They'd begun rotating the stave between their hands, slow, lazy turns.

"I was curious if I could make you go where I wanted. Puppeteer you, let's call it. And then, of course, you tried to puppeteer me. Even though Soye's Reach failed so badly."

"Not *so* badly. I burned your face off."

"That's true. I thought you were too obsessed with killing me yourself to blow up the whole mountain. I learned from that mistake. Not so sure you have, though. I mean, look at where we are."

Esek managed to cling to her composure. She said in a tight voice, "You've always been such a stealthy shit. Who'd have thought you'd land on me with a whole Braemish fleet?"

"Who'd have thought you'd underestimate me so much? Don't you remember K-5 station?"

Having that loss hurled at her was a bridge too far. Instead of attacking, Esek pulled all the rage she felt into a knot inside her, feeding it with flames and poison, preparing it for a volley that would kill Six where they stood.

"Do you know what I do remember, Six? I remember what it was like to kill Ricari Ironway's grandson. I remember what it was like to torture your cousins to death on Braemin. They all died so *brutally*, especially the teenagers. What were you thinking, going to them like you did? If I hadn't thought they might know where you were, I'd have left them alone. As it is, they died *terribly*. And it was because of you."

She wasn't sure this kind of goading would work. She wasn't even sure Six *cared* about their dead relatives, let alone the Ironways. Yet all at once they surged toward her. Now Esek got a taste of their strength.

They were *incredibly* strong, maybe as strong as Chono. They pummeled her with blows, sent shock waves down the stave into her hands and wrists and elbows. It was like trying to stand against a storm. There was no option but to drop back.

Esek used it. She let them move her in a circuit around the room. Every step was a retreat. Every blow a defense. It was not how Esek liked to fight, but through her panting breaths and close calls she watched in glee how Six's focus became so intent upon striking her, they lost focus altogether. Even enraged, Six was not a brawler. But Esek was. With a shift of footwork, she stopped retreating—held her ground. Six's momentum carried them toward her, and with a quick duck under a broad sweep, Esek punched them in the face.

They staggered back, nose like a spigot of blood. Esek gave no quarter. Crowding in, shoving back, thrashing Six with strikes until she'd breached their defenses. She struck their legs out from under them as easy as picking the wings off a fly. She tried to follow through with a finishing blow to the head, but they rolled clear. No matter. Esek had made it to her bloodletter, which she snatched off the ground, ready for a *real* close-up brawl.

Hands were suddenly in her hair, grabbing the thick coils and wrenching her neck. She knew what was coming a half instant before Six struck her head so hard against the wall her legs turned to water beneath her. She dropped to her knees. Her vision swam; nausea rose from her toes to her throat. She fell onto her back, disoriented and groaning, only for Six to straddle her waist. Their face was a mask of dark blood. The little fucker had her bloodletter and then—

She felt a pain like she had never felt before. Fire engulfed the side of her head. She *roared*. Six had gotten off of her and it didn't matter. She clutched at her head, hot blood pouring down her hand and her neck, nerves overpowered with a white-hot agony. She looked up to find Six standing over her, something dangling from between their fingers. She didn't understand what it was, until they threw it on the ground, directly in her line of sight. Then she knew. She roared again, in pain, but also black fury.

Six said, "I told you not to cheat."

Esek watched them spit blood on the ground. They sheathed her bloodletter in their own belt, and wiped their face with a bloody hand, creating only more smears of dirt and gore.

They said, "Only stave blows count. We're tied, two to two. Now get up."

Esek did. She had her stave in one hand, the other still clamped to her butchered ear. The pain was so extraordinary, it fascinated her.

With a scream, she flew at them. She left her ear to bleed and burn and clot, her hands slippery but still gripping the stave firm. Six absorbed her barrage of strikes and spins with perfect counterstrikes. They let her drive them back, maybe thinking they'd lure her into a trap as she'd lured them. But anger had never made her a careless fighter. On the contrary, it made her more dangerous. Six moved with elegant symmetry and practiced control, but they weren't prepared for her own animal ferocity. At least they were clever enough to protect their head, but no matter. She got them twice: in the shoulder, then the forearm. That last made them cry out in shock and anguish, and she would have gone for another swing, except they managed a last-ditch blow straight into her gut.

Esek doubled over, vomiting onto the pretty carpet. Six stumbled back, finally bracing their back against the nearest wall. Esek had never seen her own face in the throes of agony before. She saw it now, and felt viciously glad, even as she spat bile onto the puddle of sick. She straightened up, tried to advance, and stumbled sideways. In the end she had to catch herself on one of the posts of Alisiana's bed. She and Six watched each other, and suddenly she was laughing. She laughed for several moments and had to spit more bile out.

"You little *shit*," she snarled, and laughed some more. "Do you know how little you had to do, to become my novitiate?" Six didn't answer. They were still cradling their arm. Esek waved her free hand in the air, as if to encompass all their lost opportunities. "Do you know how fickle, how distractible, how *easily pleased* I am? I gave you a rule, and all your life has been about following the rule to excess. Doing

something *extraordinary*! You fucking fool! You could have done anything! You could have spied on the Secretaries. Stolen secrets from my
cleric kin. You could have killed one of my enemies among the Moonbacks. Fuck, if you were this hard up for drama, you could have killed
one of my Nightfoot rivals! I'd have called you my own blood, if you'd
done that. Ha!"

She gagged a little, spit some more, looked up at the ceiling, and
listened to the blood pounding in her mutilated ear. The lights were
bright and fuzzy. It was hard to breathe. That blow to the stomach had
gotten her ribs as well. This was going to be a fucking pain to heal from.

"I did," said Six.

She looked at them again. All pretense of Esek's facial expressions,
her mannerism, were suddenly gone from their face. Their eyes held
none of Esek's wild energy. They met her gaze coldly.

"I did all of those things," they said. "I spied on all three Hands
and was never caught. I killed a number of Moonbacks. I killed
Paiyes. And Khens." Their voice had changed, too. Still Esek's, but the
inflection—it was the way they had talked on K-5. That…distinct,
peculiar accent. "I killed Nightfoots, too, Esek." A cold smile. "And
not just any rival. The greatest rival of them all. The door that stood in
your way. The door that stood in mine."

Esek stared at them, unblinking. They stared back.

"Do you know what she admitted, before she died?" murmured
Six. Esek didn't move. Didn't breathe. "She admitted she was sorry…
about the massacre of the Jeveni. Even though it was her idea, she said
she never wanted it to happen. She said she was wrong to suggest it.
Can you imagine it, Esek? Alisiana Nightfoot on her death bed…
showing regret."

They stood up from the wall. They still kept one arm cradled to
their chest, but with the other they gripped the stave. Esek swallowed
convulsively, throat raw. There was no confusing what Six meant. No
avoiding the thing that somewhere, under layers of denial, she had
wondered. Now, the confirmation left her momentarily frozen. It was
not exactly shock, or grief. It was more of that unnameable emotion

she'd felt before. It was also anger, of an entirely deeper character than she'd experienced before. Less riotous, more bone-chilling. She managed to stand up straight again, letting go of the bedpost. She saw the sphere of Alisiana's ashes in her periphery. She said in a low, poisonous voice, "Alisiana was mine."

She didn't add what she really meant: *Mine to protect. Mine to keep. Mine to kill.*

But Six knew. They tilted their head like a bird. "You think everything is yours."

This time, they were *both* sloppy. Esek was woozy, nauseated, but Six only had one arm. They limped and thrust and grappled their way from one end of the room and back. Esek tried a dozen times to get their injured arm again, but they protected themself well. Esek, over-eager, got too close, and Six brought the butt of the stave down on her foot. She howled, swung wide, and missed, but suddenly they were close to each other. She kneed them in the groin. They doubled over, and finally Esek got her hands on their injured forearm, squeezing and twisting as hard as she could. Six made the same sound she had made, when they cut her ear off. The animal shriek was like music, exquisite, until Six reared back, and head-butted her.

She stumbled away, fell, landed on her ass, and sat there, stunned. Her ear was still bleeding. She could feel the wetness, all down her neck and shoulder. Dazedly she realized that Six, too, had stumbled and dropped, their back against the wall. Their skin had gone so gray they looked like a corpse, and the angle of their forearm was wrong, bowed in the center. Esek wanted to get up, to tackle them. She thought she could probably win, if she did it now. Only she couldn't get up. And there was a smell in the air.

Smoke, she realized, looking at the ceiling. She remembered suddenly that the tower was on fire. She was underground. There were escape tunnels, yes, but not if the tower collapsed. How long had she and Six been in this room? It felt like hours. She needed to get up, to go. Fuck this game. Where was her gun? She could put the pieces back together—

But she couldn't get up, too disoriented, too weak.

"What's the score?" she muttered. "Four to four, I think..."

Six clearly wasn't listening. "I have thought a lot about it, actually." Their voice was a little faint. "What you did to my cousins..."

"*Gods*, are you still on that?"

"After it happened, I spent weeks trying to understand why. And then I realized...it was not *you* who killed them. Not of your own volition, that is. You were ordered to. By Alisiana. Alisiana was the one who feared me and my name and my relatives. And why would she fear us...unless we could hurt her somehow?"

Esek sneered, "Congratulations. You solved the mystery! And now you're going to suffocate to death in my house. And I won't be joining you."

She tried to stand up, got as far as her knees, and toppled sideways again. This was getting embarrassing.

"Discovering your family was complicit in what happened on Jeve," mused Six, "that was almost...easy. Alanye was not a clever man, and your aunt was a fool to work with him. He left clues everywhere. I simply had to find them. I admit, I did not anticipate the Kindom's involvement. To think, I wanted to be a Brutal Hand once. When it was the Hands who slaughtered the Jeveni. Who slaughtered my people."

Esek groaned in exasperation. "For fuck's sake, would you *shut up*?! What do you want, an award? Do you honestly think this is the first genocide the Kindom ever committed?" She made a cackling sound, half mockery, half pain. Six watched her as she got onto her knees and then, with monumental effort, her feet. "Those Jeveni were sitting on a seam worth trillions," she said. "It was only a matter of time before the other families found out and we all went to war over it. The Kindom made a choice. Eradicate the jevite. Nobody goes to war. Millions of lives saved. Simple! And now you want me to ooh and aah over you because you learned this Big, Dark Secret." She crowed in mockery, felt dizzy, braced herself against one of the nightstands. "Well, *fuck* the Jeveni! And fuck Jeve, too. Do you know what will happen if the truth gets out? *Nothing!* A little shock and outrage, maybe. The people will call for change. They'll raise new memorials and demand some token payouts for the Jeveni descendants. Will the Kindom suffer? Sure, at first. But they'll make acts of contrition. They'll change up their leadership. They'll promise to *never* do it again." She giggled scornfully at the thought. "And *then*—everything will go back to being what it was before! Because no one actually cares about you or your fucking mongrel people. They *pretend* to care, because it's fashionable, but they disdain the Jeveni as much as they ever have. And they'll forget about this." Six only looked at her, silent. "That's what order means, little fish! Storms may trouble the water, but no one can defeat an ocean! So, either you learn to ride the waves, or you drown!" She panted, knees weakening for a brief moment. "Alisiana chose to ride. Alanye drowned. That's how this story ends."

Six was up, too. They staggered into each other, swings wide and messy and yet Six still managed to slip to the right and crack their stave against Esek's side. But the blow lacked force, and when Esek cried out, it was less pain than propulsion, throwing her forward. She grabbed Six's shoulders, punched them in the stomach. They doubled over, and Esek clasped her fists to strike them across their jaw, throwing them flat onto the ground.

Esek stumbled away from them, toward the place where they'd thrown the pieces of her gun. She bent to pick one up before dizziness dropped her to her knees, shuffling forward and reaching for the others. With weak fingers she began shoving it back together. Behind her, she could hear Six muttering to themself. She glanced over her shoulder. They were trying to get their knees under them, face planted in the carpet. She struggled to her feet, racking the gun at last. She almost dropped it. She spun back around, ready to fire—

And staggered back from a blow she didn't understand.

Six was kneeling several feet away. They hadn't touched her. Yet somehow, she was thrown back, toppling against the bed. Confused, she looked down to find something protruding from her chest. It took her several moments to understand: It was the hilt of her bloodletter. She looked at Six again, stunned. They stared back at her. With their face covered in blood and saliva, they might as well have been wearing a mask. She couldn't even tell anymore that they looked like her.

Six stood up. Esek wanted to shoot them but she had dropped the gun. She thought about trying to pick it up again, but there was a weakness in her now that she had never felt before. A kind of watery, distant feeling, and her limbs seemed empty. She used what strength she had to brace against the bed and keep upright, but her knees started trembling. She blinked rapidly, watching as her little fish approached, swimming toward her through air gone murky with smoke.

Esek didn't understand.

She understood perfectly.

Then they stood before her. They were breathing hard. She could smell their sweat. Their eyes—her eyes—looked a little fuzzy, and a blood vessel had burst in one of them, creating a blotch of red.

She waited for them to say something, but they didn't. They watched her with a strange expression. She could feel the wetness on her chest, and when she breathed, the knife moved, stunning her with pain. Her legs started to buckle, and suddenly Six moved forward, using their good arm to grab Esek around the waist. They helped her into a sitting position against the bed. They didn't attack, but they knelt close; now their faces were only a few inches apart, Six using their own lagging strength to prop her up. It was so strange. It was so intimate. Perhaps the most intimate thing Esek had ever experienced, she realized.

"What will you do?" she whispered, because it was suddenly a very important question. She *had* to know. She was so . . . curious.

Six grabbed the bloodletter, yanking it out of her. Esek screamed, but it was a weak sound, full of gurgles and a viscous coppery taste in her mouth.

"I will give the ocean to the Jeveni," Six said.

Esek frowned, confused. It didn't make any sense.

"How?" she asked.

Her voice was a weak whisper. There was a numb feeling, spreading outward. Blood dribbled from her mouth and Six wiped it away with a thumb. Tenderly.

"By being you."

When Esek only stared at them in blank incomprehension, Six heaved a deep sigh.

"I must thank you," they said. "If not for you, I would have become some cloaksaan in the crowd. I would have never discovered who I was. I would have never found...purpose."

This gave Esek the energy to cackle, which turned to a bloody cough.

"Purpose," she sneered. "Yes, a fine purpose you've chosen. Now you'll spend your life having to convince everyone you're me—the person you hate. I'm going to fucking *haunt* you, Six, I swear it. Even when you're dead, my ghost will come after you. I'll haunt you into the ground—"

She broke off, coughing more. The pain was strange now. Terrible, but also, far away. Six only looked at her, and she couldn't stand the serenity of that look.

They said, "All our evils give something back."

She snarled at them, "How long before your charade fails? You'll never fool everyone. You'll *never* fool Chono!"

"Ah, yes, Chono," murmured Six. "Our one...shared friend."

Esek's vision swam. She blinked to clear it. She wanted to get up! To strike! To fight! No, no, no, this was not how she would go! She would not give up her stake in this life! She would not die knowing Six would take everything that was hers—Chono included. *Get up!* she snarled at herself. *Get up!*

"You never deserved Chono's loyalty," Six said, with something new in their voice: scorn. "You never earned her devotion. I'll have to bury that, too."

Esek shuddered. She opened her mouth, moved her lips, no sound escaping. Six leaned slightly closer, and when Esek kept trying, weakly, to speak, they brought their face alongside hers, the better to hear her last words. She could see their throat, sweaty and blood-streaked. She could hear the pulse in their carotid artery. She could hear Chono's voice, murmuring rites. How *beautiful* Chono's voice had always been.

How deeply Chono always seemed to feel . . . *everything*. For all her sto-icism, for all Esek's contrasting loudness of life, it was Chono who flared like a meteor now. Esek blinked. Esek focused on that throat so near to her own. She had one last statement to make.

Esek moved like a snake in its death throes. Her first shot was true. She sank her teeth into the meat of Six's ear, clamping down and rip-ping with all her might.

Six reared back, screaming. They fell onto their back, grabbing fran-tically at the side of their face. Esek spit the chunk of ear from her mouth, Six's blood mixing with her own as she cackled wetly. It was funny. In the end it was all so *funny*. Six's cries sounded far away. She saw their writhing from the end of a long tunnel. Something bright and immutable and terrifying came to her then, a lightning-flash premonition.

But her laughter drowned it out.

CHAPTER TWENTY-FOUR

1664

YEAR OF THE CRUX

The Risen Wave
Orbiting Jeve

Jun has spent years imagining a final showdown with Esek Night-foot. Even in her fantasies, she knew she probably wouldn't survive it, so she always pictured unexpected disruptions, interventions, *surprises*, that gave her the upper hand.

Now, standing in this train car and watching—them?—crouch next to a probably dying Cleric Chono, she thinks the surprise must be a hoax. There's no way she misheard what this...person has said to Chono, and there's no way Chono is faking the look of blank shock on her blood-drained face. Which means either it's true, or Esek Night-foot is fucking with both of them. Something Esek Nightfoot is quite capable of doing.

Apparently, Jun isn't the only one to consider this.

"You're lying," Chono says. Her voice is a harsh whisper, and Jun wouldn't even be able to hear it except, to her own surprise, she's stepped up close to them, disarmed by her own confusion and shock, lured to their small knot of confidence like an insect seeking light. Chono says again, "You're lying," and this time she sounds raw, strained, caught on the cusp of a sob.

"You know I am not," says this—this *not* Esek. "I believe you may even have suspected this for some time."

They don't sound anything like Esek, Jun suddenly realizes. In fact, they sound like—

"*You*," Jun whispers.

For the first time since their confession, they look around at her. It's hard not to flinch at the blaze of those eyes, the exquisite symmetry of that bone structure, the mouth with its natural, cruel curve. They look *nothing* like the stranger from the safe house.

"You may call me Six," they tell her.

"Six," whispers Chono, her eyes wide and white-rimmed.

When Six turns to look at her again, Chono looks back with a mix-ture of longing and horror that makes Jun's stomach clench, sure she is witnessing something that does not belong to her. But then the cleric starts breathing harder than she was before, a new, sweaty pallor on her face. On instinct Jun casts out toward the medical kit, pulling up the array of her vitals. She's losing blood, and yet her heart rate has skyrocketed—a deadly combination. Jun locates a swarm of suture bots in her chest, which are struggling with a tear in her major artery.

"You need to sedate her," Jun says.

"This kit is practically empty. I have already given her the strongest drug."

"She's built like a freighter; give her more."

Six growls, "There *is* no more."

Jun holsters Great Gra's gun, pulling her satchel out of her inner pocket and crouching beside the two clerics (*no... the* one *cleric*). She unrolls the satchel and finds a syrette of morpho, twice the dose of what Liis gave her on *The Gunner*. She holds the syrette out to Six, who looks at it for a moment, and then looks her in the eye.

"If this hurts her, I will kill you."

"For fuck's sake," Jun mutters, and jams the syrette into Chono's shoulder.

The cleric passes out instantly, eyes rolling back. Esek—*Six*—catches her lolling head gently, and Jun sees the tourniquet around their elbow. Up close, there's a sheen of sweat on Six's body; they look slightly pale, even weak. Did they really survive a fight to the death with Esek Nightfoot, only to *exsanguinate* themself trying to save this woman?

Of course they did, murmurs a voice in Jun's head. *Wouldn't you? Wouldn't Liis?*

"You should sit down," says Jun flatly, standing up again and walking a few steps away. The thought of Liis drains the life out of her. She checks her various casting projects. "We should reach the next station in... less than five minutes. Let's see if the Jeveni believe your story, or shoot you first."

"I can handle the Jeveni," says Six in a cold voice.

"All right, well. Like I said. Five minutes."

Then, as if to mock her, the train comes to a sudden, screeching halt.

It throws her across the car—the nearest seat rams into her torso so hard it takes the wind out of her. She manages to get herself upright again, throwing out a dozen different lines, casting for an explanation to how she lost her grip on the train.

"Jun?" a voice crackles over the train's intercom. Jun's head snaps up, staring into the nearest speaker. "Jun, can you hear me?"

She establishes a comm link with the flick of her wrist. "Masar?"

"Oh, thank gods. We thought you were dead!"

"How the *fuck* did you take control of my train?"

"That's why I thought you were dead! Or at least—I don't know—distracted?"

Fair.

"Where's Liis?"

"I don't know. My people got to Ketch Market but—it was a blood-bath. We think we've routed most of the cloaksaan, but we can't be sure. The Wheel only managed to get control of the train when—"

"Why?" snaps Jun, her whole body vibrating with equal parts hope and despair. If he hasn't seen Liis's body, then maybe... "*Why* did they take the train? I'm five minutes from the military station and I—"

"Jun, Esek Nightfoot is on the train! We saw her and that other cleric boarding!"

Jun stops. Her eyes roll heavenward. She breathes in slowly and lets it out, and turns to look at Six. They watch her with still features, eyes fathomlessly deep, offering nothing.

"I know," she says at last.

A pause. "What do you *mean* you know? Have you seen them?"

"Masar, listen—"

"The rest of the Wheel are on this ship. They're *at* the military station, Jun. You can't bring Esek Nightfoot anywhere near them, not after what happened to Nikkelo. They *have* to be protected, no matter what, and you—"

His voice cuts off abruptly, the connections severed. Jun is already reaching to restore it when a new voice fills the car. Jun recognizes it from Kindom bulletins. Six's face shows a different recognition. Jun turns away, casting for a signal location, reaching simultaneously for the controls of the train, as words flood her ears.

"Spokes of the Wheel. This is the First Cleric Aver Paiye, leader of the Righteous Hand, representative of the Kindom, steward of the Godfire and of the Treble entire. We are aware you are hiding amid your Jeveni loyalists under the pretense of Remembrance Day. We know you have instructed all your people, assimilationists and sepa-ratists alike, to converge in this place. Your intentions, whatever they may be, are irrelevant, as your formation of a government clearly vio-lates the Anti-Patriation Act. We must therefore consider all Jeveni in orbit as criminal offenders, subject to Kindom justice. We will show leniency to your people if and when you surrender yourselves to the nearest cloaksaan. If you do not surrender, we will have to consider your actions a statement of rebellion. This will give us no choice but to respond with speed and force, and unavoidable loss of life. I am giving you thirty minutes to surrender in the hopes we can avoid such a tragedy on this day of all days. But that will be entirely up to you."

There is a pause, but it's not an end. Aver Paiye continues, and the formality of his voice relaxes an inch, replaced by something familiar and caustic.

"And to Esek Nightfoot, wherever you are hiding. You have betrayed the Kindom. You have attacked our cloaksaan. You have abandoned all honor and righteousness in service to your own selfish aims, and you will not be forgiven. If those who surround you hesitate to turn you over to us, to give us your body—living or dead—then I remind them that over eighty percent of the Jeveni have yet to dock with *The Risen Wave*. Fail to meet our demands, and we will begin the summary destruction of all ships orbiting Jeve."

A beat of silence, as Paiye lets his message land.

"Peace, under the Kindom. Unity, in the Treble. You have half an hour."

This time, the silence is a statement in itself. Jun looks at Six again, half expecting to see Esek Nightfoot's cruel smirk, or hear some sneering jab (*Do you think they'd mind that she's already dead?*) but there's no such humor on their face. They look grim and shaken and that is what drives home the force of the Kindom's threat.

Jun throws a holographic view into the space between her and Six, a star map with *The Risen Wave* at its center, and hundreds of satellite ships surrounding it. The number of Kindom vessels has doubled since *The Happy Jaunt* docked in Bay 7. It is more than enough to obliterate the Jeveni ships, to say nothing of what the Kindom will do once it has full control of those on the generation ship.

"They wouldn't," says Jun. "We're talking about tens of thousands of people. It…it would be another genocide. They—they wouldn't *do* it."

Saying the words throws her back fourteen years, to the safe house in Riin Kala. *But that's wrong!* she'd cried, and when Six looked at her without emotion—what shame she'd felt at her own naivety.

Six says, "Aver Paiye sent Chono and me on a mission to find a memory coin. He believes the coin implicates the Kindom in the Jeveni Genocide, and he believes the Wheel of the Jeveni has that coin now. What won't the Kindom do, to protect itself from exposure?"

Jun shakes her head in confusion. Her memory coin damns the Night-foots, but it doesn't do anything to implicate the Kindom. She's about to argue as much when Masar's voice sings out through the comm—

"Jun? Are you there?!"

Jun swallows. "Yes, I'm here."

This time he pauses, like someone who knows they might be about to step on a mine. "Are you alone?"

She looks at Six, helpless to think of a response. In the end, Six answers instead, "Masar Hawks. I know you know my voice. And I know you and your leaders must agree with the Kindom that I am on this ship seeking my own interests. You have no reason to trust me, but it is imperative I speak to the Wheel as soon as possible."

Masar makes a sound halfway between disgusted choke and incredulous laugh.

"Yeah, that's not happening. And if you've hurt Jun, I swear to the fucking fertility god you worship I'll—"

"Masar, stop!" Jun cries. "You don't understand, we—"

"Jun, what the *hell* is going on?"

"You have to listen to me," Six barks, eyes flitting toward the unconscious Chono.

"*You* shut up," Masar retorts. "Jun, are you—"

"Quiet, everyone."

The new voice startles them all into silence. Jun, who's got casting lines hooked in about twenty different projects, feels like she's adding another wire to a sketchy bomb as she tracks this latest comm thread to somewhere in the military station. The voice is young, but stern.

"I realize this is a moment of heightened emotion, but there's no time for it. Sa Ironway, if we survive, I look forward to meeting you properly. For now, I am going to ignore you. Esek Nightfoot, I am the Star, the Fifth Spoke of the Wheel. Please confirm you can hear me."

Six glances at Jun. Jun (like she doesn't have enough to fucking handle right now) starts tossing up more holographic views, mapping the positions of the Jeveni ships orbiting *The Risen Wave*. She's not taking any of this shit lying down.

Six says to the air, "Yes, I can hear you, Sa Crost."

A brief silence, full of assessment, before the person continues in a voice that sounds like someone narrowing their eyes, "Yes, my name is Effegen ten Crost. So, the Kindom knows *all* our names. I see. What about Cleric Chono? Where is she?"

Six and Jun both look at Chono, whose med kit shows sluggish progress. Jun hacks a Kindom medical feed and patches its AI to the suture bots, hoping they'll be of some use to each other. Simultaneously, she runs an estimate of how long it would take her to hack all the Kindom ships and crash their weapons systems. First outlook is not good. She's only got one fucking brain, hasn't she?

Six says, "Cleric Chono was shot in Ketch Market. I believe she will survive if your medics—"

"We can address that concern momentarily," interrupts the young voice, and Six's face stiffens. "For now, it's important you answer my questions quickly and honestly. Did you and your kin intend to execute the River when you boarded this ship?"

"I cannot speak for anyone's intentions but my own. I *believe* Cloak Medisogo intended to arrest and interrogate him as a way to reach the Wheel. I do not know if they intend to kill you all. I was not made privy to these plans and was myself a target of the shooting in Bay 7."

Effegen ten Crost asks, "Are your kin in earnest about destroying our ships?"

"Sa, as I say, I was not involved in plans to attack your people, and I—"

"Whether you were or not means nothing to me; there are seventy-six thousand Jeveni out there and I need to know if your kin are going to kill them."

Six hesitates. "I believe they are capable of it, and—"

The Star interrupts, "I am a descendant of the refugees who fled Jeve, Sa Nightfoot, I know perfectly well what the Kindom is capable of. I'm asking you if this was their intention in coming here."

Six falls silent, biting off a curse. Jun looks at them, wanting to help, but she's got her own schemes going right now and no room for extras. Still, she never thought she'd look at *that* face and feel *pity*. They look genuinely lost; they look enraged, unable to say what they clearly want to say. They stare at Chono for two, three seconds, thoughts racing in their eyes.

Then, like a flipped switch, a calm drapes over them. When they speak again, gone is the stranger from the safe house at Riin Kala. It is Esek Nightfoot who chuckles aloud.

"What are their intentions in coming here? What the fuck do you think? They think you're fomenting a damn rebellion. They think you have evidence that implicates them in the Jeveni Genocide, which of course you do. They'd rather wipe you out in one go than let you have power over them."

Effegen ten Crost asks, "It would be better for them to *openly* perpetrate a genocide?"

Six sucks air through their teeth. "The Treble *hates* you, Sa. More than usual. The Kindom made sure of that when it shut down the gates and then gave you permission to jump to Jeve. They've propped you up over the common saan and spread rumors about your union leaders. They've created an environment where all they have to do is say you are rebels, and the systems will dance on your fucking graves. So, yes, you'd be wise to assume they'll act on their threat. The question is what will *you* do? This ship is stacked with artillery. The Kindom probably disarmed it before they turned the ship over, right? But if you're the survivors I know you are, then I'll bet my life you've found a way around that disarmament. So you better get ready to shoot their fucking warbirds out of the Black. Because otherwise they'll kill every last one of you."

Jun's head reels at the never-ending barrage of fucked-up shit she's learned today, but the Star is conspicuously silent. There must be other conversations happening beyond the reach of Jun's bouquet of casting lines, but she hasn't got the time to track them down. She's managed to hack the weapons system of three warhawks, but there's too much going on around her. She can't slip into it, not really, and even if she can program those ships to shoot each other, the Jeveni will still be fucked.

Effegen ten Crost returns.

"Thank you for your honesty, Sa Nightfoot. I can certainly imagine *you* taking such action, given the Kindom has declared your life is forfeit. Unfortunately, we're not willing to put our people in the middle of a firefight. Tell me what will happen if we demonstrate that we are *not* rebels. If we turn ourselves over to them, and bring you with us, what will they do?"

Six pauses. To the Wheel it must read as Esek scrambling for a way to stay alive. But Jun, who's on to plan B (mapping a comm link to every Jeveni ship in orbit), thinks Six's sudden pallor is down to something completely different.

"You can't turn yourselves over," they say woodenly. "You'll all be killed."

"We are willing to die to save our people. Another Wheel will replace us."

"Your people will be put in prison colonies. The ones that aren't executed outright. It'll be the end of the Jeveni."

"The Jeveni have survived massacre before."

"You won't survive this."

"We survived before by fleeing. Tell me what will happen if our ships flee?"

Six makes a strangled sound. "You've got to be—the Kindom will *shoot* them."

"If we create a diversion?"

"There's no diversion that'll get fewer of your people killed than if you shoot the Kindom full of holes. Use your godsdamned guns and *fight*! You can't run!"

Like plugging a cable into its power source, Jun feels the surge of realization go through her. Her whole body stills for an instant. Great Gra's voice whispers in her ear, *When I tell you to run, run.*

And Liis's voice whispers in her other ear, *A con knows when to cut and run.*

And before the thought, the name, the face of that ferocious woman can choke a sob from her, she calls out, "Sa Crost, please listen to me. I have an idea."

Six looks at her narrowly. After a moment of weighty silence, the Star says, "Yes?"

"I think you *should* run."

"They'll be *butchered*," Six snarls.

And Masar cries, "They'll pick us off like target practice!"

"Not if they can't *see* you!"

An immediate, startled silence. Six looks at her doubtfully. Masar makes a disbelieving sound. It's Effegen ten Crost who says, "You're speaking of your Hood program."

"Yes."

"Do you believe you—"

All at once her voice cuts off. First Cleric Aver Paiye returns. "It has now been ten minutes with no response to our ultimatum. We can only assume you have not yet surrendered because you think we are bluffing, or you are executing a plan to fight back. I have ordered the destruction of one of your ships. You have twenty minutes."

He's gone as soon as he came, and a moment later one of Jun's views of the Black explodes like a star. She cries out. Six curses vilely. It only takes Jun seconds to identify the destroyed ship, a transport vessel out of Kator. The manifest lists over five hundred.

"How long will it take you?" Sa Crost's voice slams back into the room.

"We're talking about hundreds of ships, Jun," Masar interrupts. "You can't Hood hundreds of ships at the same time in less than twenty minutes."

"Oh yes I fucking can."

"How?" ten Crost snaps.

Jun throws her hands up, pulls in her lines, starts weaving and building furiously. "I'm already sending something out to your ships.

To them it's going to look like kill ware. Tell them to accept the code and let me in. I'm going to link them together and slingshot this shit from one end of the fleet to the other. Once they're Hooded, they've got to run. Tell them where to run."

Run, whispers Great Gra. *Run!*

And already the dreamscape is pulling her under. She's never been able to resist—as vulnerable as a junkie, as powerful as a god. It rises like water over her head, pulling her in. Distantly she hears ten Crost telling her, "Do it!" and Masar saying, "Where are you? We're coming to get you," and Six, peculiar Six, slipping between Jun's programs long enough to anchor her to their own exquisitely built neural link, a bomb in the head of a pin, a wealth of access and power she doesn't even have time to thank them for. She reaches out; the Jeveni ships are like stars, like lanterns perched upon hillocks. Like birds calling each other's names. She starts to build—*a telephone pole*. Yes! Yes, like in the old stories Great Gra told her. Wire and cable and radio waves. Miracle of early technology, the voice traveling continents in no time at all. Her Hood will travel at the speed of light. All over the hillocks, little birds open their mouths for her, swallow her kill ware, let her into their bellies, and she hooks them, each to each. *Don't worry, little birds, I won't hurt you, I won't hurt you.*

I won't hurt you, Liis swore to her.

But oh, gods, there are so many of them. There are *so many*. The telephone poles stretch for miles and miles but they're not even halfway there. And her Hood! Her little threadbare Hood that she wove to throw over her own shoulders, to shroud her ship—it was never meant to stretch this far. It's unraveling at the edges. It's weaker with every duplication. *Fuck fuck fuck* she *has* to do this. *You have to* stretch, *little Hood, the monsters have come to our station. The monsters are in our shop. They're going to kill us and we have to* run!

The sound of a door banging open cracks the shell of her fugue, brings her out of it long enough to look across the train car. And fuck if this isn't the last thing she needs right now.

Vas Sivas Medisogo is standing in the doorway.

CHAPTER TWENTY-FIVE

1664.

YEAR OF THE CRUX

The Risen Wave
Orbiting Jeve

Chono's body keeps trying to wake up. She can feel herself, like a buoy submerged under mammoth waves, air pressure driving her toward the surface but never quite making it past the next crush of water. She can't move her body, pinned down, helpless. She can't open her eyes, which is even worse. There's a faint sound warbling beyond the waves. Voices. She can hear voices and she recognizes one of them and she wants to go to that voice but...

Gods and fire, she prays sluggishly. *Let me wake. Let me wake.*

She almost does it, the voices starting to clarify, light flickering in her vision, before something drags her down again. *The Six Gods*, she thinks; they are pulling her under—Terotonteris with his many arms and Kata with their many spies and Makala with her greedy loveliness. Chono feels breath on her neck. She feels saliva wet on the side of her face. Hands grip her thighs, and something inside her screams—*no! no! no!*—and bucks and wrenches free.

The hands let go. The waves pull back. Her body is a puppet with cut strings, but her eyes crack open and she sees—

Two figures, squared off. One of them stands between her and the second. The second is a large bear-shaped person in a doorway. All in black. Painted red.

Blood, thinks Chono vaguely, and tastes the same in her own mouth.

The person standing closer to Chono says, "Whatever happens, don't stop working."

With monumental effort, Chono shifts her eyes. There's a third figure in the room, haloed in what must be over a dozen casting views.

"Fuck," Jun Ironway says, and her hands start to move in furious gestures.

"Whatever she's doing is useless," says the bear-shaped person.

Medisogo.

The names click into place as if there were parts of her brain that had switched off and are now turning back on. She tries to focus, noticing next that Medisogo's cloak is gone. There are blast burns on his body armor, and the whole right side of his face is scorched, including his eye. He looks like an undead monster, massive in the doorframe, not a hint of agony on his destroyed face. No. He absorbs everything in the time it takes to blink his left eye: looks at Jun, who works her craft with furious intensity; looks at Chono—though Chono thinks she must still seem unconscious to him; looks, with finality, at the fourth person in the room, the person who flares in Chono's vision like a meteor.

"Not looking so good there, Medisogo," says Esek—

No. No, not Esek, not Esek, not Esek.

The parts of Chono's brain that are trying to switch on judder like they've hit a snag. Her heart rate spikes; she can feel it, a motor rabbiting out of control. She remembers, suddenly, the swarm of suture bots in her chest. *Fucking fuck, what am I awake for?! Fuck!*

She imagines Esek cackling with laughter at this uncharacteristic outburst.

But Esek is dead.

Medisogo lumbers farther into the car (*the train car*—Chono's brain supplies). There are only about seven or eight feet between him and the... person he's looking at.

"And here I thought I blew you up," that person says.

Medisogo looks at them with a single gleaming eye. "Som spared my life so I could feed you to them."

Esek—*not* Esek—responds with bared teeth, a wolf's grin. They draw the bloodletter from its sheath at their waist. Esek's bloodletter. Seeing it makes confusion and anger and hope war in Chono's bleeding chest; one of her pinkie fingers twitches, the nearest she can come to jumping up and throwing herself at the person with the knife.

Medisogo has no bloodletter. No gun, either. He must have lost them both somewhere, along with the cloak, but there's no concern on his face. He glances at the bloodletter as its new owner moves it into a chambered grip. "That toy will not save you."

"This *toy* has killed a lot worse than you," retorts Six.

Six!

But there's no time to be startled. There's no time to be glad or angry. Because all at once Medisogo storms forward.

He's big. He's so big—bigger than Chono. Definitely bigger than Six. In a different space, in a wide-open room, Chono is certain Six and that knife could cut him apart. But they are in a cramped train car, with no room to maneuver. The knife flits out like a snake striking, slicing open the arm that rises to block it, and then Medisogo has them. Grabs them, like they're a child, lifting them up and throwing them across the train car. Six hits the ground with a choking grunt, but is on their feet in an instant. They fly forward. Chono's vision blurs. She can barely process the glint of the knife, the sheer aggression of Six's offense, which drives Medisogo back, and back, weaving and stumbling and trying to bat at Six like they were a fly near his head.

One of those swatting gestures lands, an open palm cracking against the side of Six's head. It sends them sprawling into the nearest bench seat—gives Medisogo the opening he needs. He seizes them by the shoulder, wrenching them up again, grabbing for their throat.

Six drives their knee up into his chest. He drops them with an *oof,* stumbling back.

Chono can move her hand now. She drags it, like an unconscious friend, from where it lies limp on her thigh. The back of her hand touches her sidearm as Six and Medisogo both get their footing, squaring off again, storming forward, and—who does Chono want to win? The one who murdered Nikkelo sen Rieve? The one who is definitely going to murder her? Or the one who murdered Esek? Chono palms the grip of her sidearm, slipping it from the holster, but her hand goes numb, losing hold. The gun slips uselessly onto the ground next to her.

"I need your progress," says a voice—a disembodied voice, unfamiliar—in the air.

Jun Ironway shouts back, "You've got to send help *now!*"

"How close are you?!"

"I—I—I need more time!"

"Do not stop!" Six shouts at her, barely weaving out of the range of a meaty fist. Chono hears the *whoosh* of it cutting through the air, smells the sweat and blood. Then they are a blur of ferocious movement, of parry and dodge and stab. Somehow Medisogo gets behind them, one arm around their waist, one around their throat, locking tight. To Chono it looks like the grotesque approximation of two lovers. Six's feet leave the ground, kicking wildly. Medisogo has their arm immobilized; the bloodletter is useless.

Chono blinks once, very slowly. Her nerveless fingers close around the gun. She barely has enough strength to lift it, braced on her thigh. She hasn't got the control to aim. If she fires, she could strike either of them. Would that be easier? Leaving it to chance? To the Six Gods?

But then her gaze locks with Six. Their eyes have turned glassy, the arm around their throat choking the breath from their lungs. Some-how, they still manage to look *right* at Chono. Chono expects to see a plea in their eyes (*Help me!*) or furious determination (*No! Not like this!*). She doesn't see either of those things. If she lives, maybe one day she'll understand what she sees in their foreign-familiar eyes.

"Almost there!" cries Jun Ironway.

Chono shoots the gun.

Not *at* them (she could never risk that, no, not for anything) but at the wall of the car. It's enough to startle Medisogo. Enough that he flinches, loosens his grip, and Six wrenches free. They hit the ground, half-unconscious and groaning. Medisogo recovers, looks around angrily, and spots Chono, his eyes fathomless with hatred. On the ground, Six tries to get to their knees. Medisogo kicks them in the kidney, dropping them flat as they gag and cry out and turn their head toward Chono. Chono sees their teeth, bared and bloody. She looks up into the ruined face of Cloak Medisogo as he drifts toward her.

"I thought you were dead," Medisogo rumbles.

Chono is silent, defiant. The gun slips from her hand again, and she can't pick it up. She feels sleepy, and weak. She's aware of her threading pulse, and a tremor in her fingers, and she's not *afraid*, exactly, but she is angry. So *fucking* angry.

"I hear you're the only person Esek Nightfoot ever cared about."

Behind him, Six makes a screaming, sobbing sound of effort, trying to get up.

"I'll kill you first," says Medisogo. "To avenge Cleric Paan. And to torment your master as she always tormented mine."

Of course. All those hateful looks from him, all his sneering and glowering over the past few days, like he would tear Chono apart if he could. Ilius did warn her that Khen loyalists sought her death. And now Medisogo has his chance. Chono's mouth is dry, but if it wasn't, she'd spit at him. She doesn't drop her eyes, doesn't flinch, even when he bends over to pick up the gun by her hand. Even when he stands up again, a mountain of a man, and lifts the gun to fire.

And takes a bullet in the back of the head.

He drops like a felled tree, his huge bulk crashing into the ground, nearly on top of Chono. She looks up, expecting to see Six on their feet. But no. It's not Six standing in the doorway of the train car. It's not a cloaksaan, either, nor a Jeveni warrior. The woman in the doorway barely holds herself up, leaning heavily in the frame with an arm wrapped around her own waist, and gripping a pistol. Her other arm is missing. Her face is a rictus of fury and relief, and she's not looking at Chono or Medisogo or even Six. She's staring across the car at Jun Ironway, who has emerged from the fugue of her dozen casting views and chokes out, "Liis!"

The woman in the doorway crumples to one knee. Six, trembling all over, has managed to sit up. Jun shouts the name again and Six shouts back, "Do. Not. Stop!"

But, "It's loose!" Jun cries, voice clogged with elation and panic, lifting her hands as the wall of holograms around her erupt in glittering flashes, a snake of code spreading through hundreds of Jeveni ships that scatter the star map.

"Masar, it's loose!" Jun shouts again. "Tell them to go go go!"

"Hood program engaging," says a disembodied voice.

Six half crawls across the ground toward Chono, coming to kneel before her, doing something to the med kit Chono can't possibly understand.

"What's happening?" Chono mumbles. There's a dirty film over everything now.

Six, who is gray with pain and exhaustion and effort, looks into her eyes. "Pray, Chono," they whisper, their voice a raw and desperate thing. "*Pray.*"

All instinct, she does, mumbling and half-coherent, and Six gasps a sound of relief at her voice.

"*The Risen Wave*, too!" Jun Ironway cries. She leaves her station to stumble toward Liis Konye, who leans panting in the door, covered in blood. "We're Hooded, too, now go!"

"Hooded," mumbles Chono, as Jun drops to her knees before Konye, grabbing the woman into her arms. "Hooded?" Chono asks Six.

"Yes," grits Six, scrambling over the med kit, and Chono gets a glimpse at one of its feeds. *Blood pressure dropping.*

Through the ringing in her own ears, Chono hears a rumble of swelling engines. *The Risen Wave*'s engines. Engines as powerful as jump gates, coming alive. Chono squints at Jun Ironway's star map holograms, watching in dawning comprehension as the hundreds of little Jeveni ships wink out like vanishing stars.

That disembodied voice returns, "Everybody brace."

Six looks at her. Their eyes . . .

"Hold on," they say.

The Risen Wave judders, accelerating in a surge that throws Chono's body sideways; Six grabs her, holds her up, even as they grapple for purchase of their own. The air around them turns close and loud and ear-popping, and Chono wonders what Aver Paiye and Seti Moonback are thinking right now. Just before she falls unconscious, she imagines them watching the Jeveni ships. She imagines them self-assured and unrepentant and determined. All things for the glory of the Godfire. And in that moment of unbreakable confidence, of commitment to the cause, of readiness for the strike, *The Risen Wave* disappears.

CHAPTER TWENTY-SIX

1664

YEAR OF THE CRUX

The Risen Wave
Somewhere

There's no nightmare to fling her awake this time. She rises out of sleep like she's rising from the dead, just a dark void of unconsciousness, blessedly cool and soft. Some hazy instinct tells her to roll over and drag the pillow closer, to seek out Liis's warm body and let the little star lights on the bulkhead wink her back into the void. But when she rolls, she jerks—and nearly falls out of her chair.

She's not on *The Gunner*. She's not in a bed at all. In disorientation she blinks rapidly, looking around and finally locking on the hospital bed in front of her. It's empty. It—

"Liis?" Fear crawls up her throat. She jerks to her feet, shouting, "Liis!"

A voice answers her from across the room. "She's fine."

Jun jerks around. There's another bed, one that wasn't there when she fell asleep. (Was that sleep? It felt like oblivion.) A woman is sitting at a recline, raised enough to meet her eyes across the room. It's—

"Cleric Chono," Jun says, disbelieving.

The cleric was practically dead when she saw her last, and yet now she smiles. It's tight. Exhausted. She looks awful. Pale as ash and with dark bruises under her eyes. Her chest is tightly wrapped and there are tubes coming out of the sides of her, and her hands sit limply on her lap. Yet she watches Jun closely.

"When did you get here?" Jun demands, but doesn't wait for an answer. Liis was in the bed before. Unconscious but alive. "Where did they take her?" She moves toward the hospital door. The handle won't move. Jun casts on instinct for a lock mechanism—and freezes. They've jammed her neural access to the casting net. She's cut off, completely. Fear turns to panic, tunneling down her spine. She jerks the handle harder, half convinced she can rip it out of the door. "Hey!" she shouts, hitting the door with an open palm. "Hey, let me out!"

"She thought you'd be anxious. They promised her they'd bring her right back."

"Why can't I cast? Why is my ocular dead?"

"Mine is as well," says the cleric. "I assume it's a security measure."

"Why the fuck did they take her while I was asleep?"

"She didn't want to wake you."

"That's bullshit," Jun snaps. "They must have drugged me. I—"

"It's been two days since we boarded *The Risen Wave*," Chono informs her. Jun just stares. "I understand you haven't slept in three? The body can only take so much. Believe me. I'm very aware of that, at this moment."

Jun hesitates. Her memories of everything that happened after they jumped are fuzzy. She remembers the train car finally reaching the military station, and Jeveni warriors flooding the compartment. She remembers cradling Liis against her, feeling the slick of blood all over her, and how their eyes met for just a few seconds before Liis's rolled back. She remembers going with Liis to *The Risen Wave*'s hospital, and getting shoved in a room to pace and wonder and receive only intermittent updates. There were surgeries, and complications, and by the time they took Jun to this room, she half expected to find a corpse waiting. But, unnaturally still though she was, Liis lived. Liis is *alive*. Jun hasn't left her side since. Where would they have taken her?

She asks the cleric as much, and Chono opens her mouth to answer, but coughs. Agony crosses her face, makes her look both old and young. Jun thinks of her in the landing bay, trying like hell to get that door open before the cloaksaan could gun her down. And Jun had helped her. Why had she helped her, exactly?

There's a little cup of water on the bedside table. Jun brings it to Chono, tipping it against her lips.

"Here. Here."

Chono drinks, nearly gags, and coughs again. She sips a little more, then drops her head back against the pillows. Her face is sheened with sweat; it glistens on her collarbones and the notch of her throat, giving her a clammy, drowned look, so different from the steely calm Jun first saw on the roof in Siinkai. This close, Jun can see a wealth of injuries. A cut on her throat that has scabbed over. Bruising on her knuckles and arms and forehead. Jun can only imagine what she looks like under the bandages, and yet, like Liis, she's alive. It couldn't have been easy. Why would the Jeveni pour resources into a Hand of the Kindom, after what the Kindom has done?

Voice hoarse, Chono tells her, "Tests. They took your friend for tests."

Jun doesn't really like the vagueness of that, but she also doubts that Chono knows more. And anyway, she's Kindom. Are the Jeveni doctors under some misapprehension that she and Jun are friends or something? Wouldn't Masar have told them the truth?

"She seemed well. Liis Konye. Awake. Alert. She warned me not to wake you."

Jun fights not to show her relief. She's seen Liis injured before, but she has never seen anything like Liis on that train car. Her warm skin leached of color and her lips gone blue, and all of it accented by blood, blood fresh and wet and blood crusty and dark. Blood that smeared and congealed, and blood that pooled under them—

"Truly," says Chono then, and Jun flinches and looks at her, sees a completely baffling gentleness in her expression. "She looked well. I think she'll be fine."

Jun narrows her eyes, wondering at this kindness, this concern for Jun's feelings. In a flare of accusation Jun reminds her, "You shot me. At the Silt Glow Cliffs. You shot me. Or . . . one of your novitiates did."

Chono, half-dead though she looks, seems briefly amused.

"Your Liis Konye nearly blew me up."

"You're lucky. Most of the time she succeeds."

"You're lucky, too. There was a lot of blood on that roof."

Jun rotates her shoulder, mottled with half-healed regenerative tissue and still stiff.

"I suppose we were both perfectly happy to kill each other."

Chono's reaction is muted, but Jun still catches it: the slightest wavering of her stare; the slightest shift in her chin, signaling a dissent. Jun hesitates, and then a memory floods back.

"You called me Six."

Chono just looks at her.

"Up on that roof, you thought I was Six. And you kept telling your novitiates to fall back. You didn't want them to rush me, to kill me. You thought I was Six."

Chono shakes her head a little. "I . . . wondered. I was testing the theory. By then, I more suspected that you were working *with* them, than that you *were* them."

Jun blurts a laugh. Chono blinks, questioning, and Jun laughs again. Actually, she might sound a little frantic. She probably needs more sleep. She wipes a hand down her face.

"It's just ironic, isn't it? You thought I was working with Six. When all that time, I never was. *You* were."

Cleric Chono's already pale face blanches, and she looks away, clearly not finding the humor. For a moment her eyes move restlessly, and Jun has the sense that she wants to get out of the bed. That she wants to run. Her agitation is so stark that Jun feels guilty for the joke, until it occurs to her that Chono's reaction might be grief—grief over the death of Esek Nightfoot. And that is something Jun could never understand, never forgive. She hopes the ground is devouring Esek Nightfoot. She welcomes the day when there is nothing left, not even bones.

Then Chono asks, "Do you know what happened to them?"

Jun hesitates, some vindictive part of her wanting to withhold any information that might be of interest or comfort to Esek Nightfoot's protégé. But in the end she doesn't have the energy, and after all, this is of interest to them both.

"I saw the Jeveni drag them off the train car. I told everyone who they were, but no one seemed to believe me. I've only talked to doctors since then, and the doctors won't say shit, not even if they're alive. But you're alive, so I suppose that's a good sign for them. The Jeveni don't strike me as back-alley executioners, even if they do think...Six...is Esek." Jun flits her eyes up and down the broken body of the cleric. "Then again, maybe they're just waiting to make a show of it. String you both up and make an example of you." Chono offers no reaction. Vindictively Jun adds, "It's what the Kindom would do, isn't it?"

But this has little effect. Chono nods distractedly, her eyes drifting. She's lost in thought for several seconds. Jun starts to think their conversation is over, when—

"I killed a man last year," Cleric Chono says, her voice far away, her gaze distant. Jun wasn't expecting this and looks at her warily. "A cleric," she adds. "He was guilty of horrific crimes, but he was also old. I didn't care. I beat him to death." Jun remembers mention of this from her own research into Chono, but didn't know what was true, and certainly didn't anticipate this description from the mild cleric.

After a moment Chono looks at Jun again, and even in her state of exhaustion she seems focused and sharp. "I was there the night Esek attacked your family. Not there when it happened, but afterward. I was her novitiate. I saw what she did."

Jun's mouth goes dry. A tremble starts in her hands, imagining the scene that she herself never witnessed. Hoarsely she says, "I was in the archivist's academy at Riin Kala. I got a message from my Great Gra, telling me to run, and that was it. I didn't get to say goodbye." Her voice cracks. She clears her throat, hardening. "I didn't get to tell them I loved them. I didn't get to hear them say they loved me, ever again— not one word of love. Just 'Run!' Esek took everything else."

Chono nods, without argument or defense, but then she frowns. "He warned you to run?"

Jun bristles. "What? Yes! Of course he did."

Another nod; a considering look. "That was a word of love, wasn't it?"

Jun just stares at her, unblinking. She can't blink. It's like her face and her lungs and her body are frozen, and that must be why she feels the burn in her eyes, the sudden pressure in the back of her throat. It must be why she cannot look away from the expression on the cleric's face, a gentleness that Jun doesn't want—she doesn't want it! *Fuck her!*

Chono says, "What happened was unforgivable. If you're expecting me to defend myself, or my part in it, you'll be disappointed. I am a murderer and an enabler and a coward. I am as guilty as any Hand in the Treble, even Esek. Som devour me for what I've done."

The words unlock Jun's throat. She breathes in harshly, stepping back. "So why did Six save you? I think they would have given you every drop of blood they had, to save you. *Why?*"

Chono doesn't answer at first, and though Jun is at the height of her impatience, she manages not to press her. Then—

"We've known each other for...a very long time."

It's an unsatisfying answer. Jun wants to say so, to make demands. But maybe it is also the only answer. It's not as if Jun knows how to explain her own strange association with Six. Once again, she finds herself looking up and down Chono's body, studying her face, trying to *see* something, and she's not sure what. The person Jun rescued in the landing bay? The person who murdered a corrupt cleric?

Challengingly she says, "I researched you, you know. After we met at the Cliffs. There's not much, but there are testimonies. Things your parishioners have said about you. Communities you've served across the Treble. They all claim to love you."

Chono looks instantly uncomfortable, her mouth twitching down in a grimace. Jun narrows her eyes.

"If you're as bad as any Hand, why do the people love you so much?"

"Probably because they don't know any better."

"Then you have a low opinion of them." Chono tenses, which must hurt, because she grunts and pushes her head back into the pillow, blinking rapidly. "This cleric you killed on Pippashap. The records are vague, but—was he a rapist?" Chono keeps grimacing, and Jun can't help a humorless chuckle. "Yes, of course. What a monster you are. For killing a rapist."

"I don't regret killing him," Chono says through her teeth.

"So what do you regret? Being a Hand? Working for Esek? *Loving* Esek?"

"Yes."

Jun snorts. "I can't help you with that."

They are at a momentary impasse, the cleric staring at her in stark silence, eyes fierce, as if the intensity of her own feelings is too much for her to think of expressing in words. It's a remarkable picture of anger and regret, and against her better judgment, Jun feels pity. She sucks her teeth. Shrugs a shoulder. "Make amends," she says. It's almost more order than suggestion. "That's your only option, isn't it? Make amends, Burning One."

Chono's look says the thing they both know, which is that nothing could ever be enough. That some things are irreparable. There's no salvation. No absolution. And no excuses for not trying anyway. After several moments the fierceness in the cleric's eyes dissipates, replaced by that quiet weariness again. Her short nod could mean anything—a promise, an acknowledgment, a surrender. But Jun has no opportunity to press the matter further, because the door opens.

The second she sees Liis sitting up in a hoverchair with a nurse behind her, she springs forward. Her heart is in her throat, lungs tight as rocks, her body a torpedo. She brings the chair to a sharp halt (the nurse squawks in surprise), and takes Liis's face in her hands. It's not tender. She holds her face still and looks at her the way she looks at code—scouring for information. There are healing cuts and bruises. There is the feathering of scar tissue along her eyebrow. Her head is shaved, a tragic necessity because one of the cloaks sliced their bloodletter right across her skull, the wound now growing over with regenerative tissue. Jun leans back enough to take in the rest of her, bruised and bandaged, the stump of her arm now fitted with a far less sophisticated prosthetic than the one Liis lost in the battle. Jun grinds her teeth.

"Are you all right?" Her voice is raw.

Liis smiles tiredly. "I am."

Jun glares at the nurse. "Where the fuck did you take her?"

The nurse balks. Liis murmurs, "Jun," and when Jun finally looks at her again, she models a deep inhalation. "Breathe."

Jun's chin wobbles. Liis inhales again and Jun tries to copy her but it's too much. She takes her face in her hands again. She stares directly into her eyes, those eyes like oil slicks, those eyes she loves.

"Don't you ever do that again," she whispers.

Liis's good hand rises to cup her elbow.

"All right."

"Do you hear me? Don't you—don't you fucking *ever*—"

Now Liis's hand is on the nape of her neck, pulling her down, pressing Jun's face into her shoulder. Liis smells faintly antiseptic and a little sweaty, and, underneath, the barest trace of her familiar green smell. Jun remembers the stench of blood all over her, iron and rust and a gagging sweetness. For a second she thinks she's going to be sick, until the hand on her neck clasps tighter. And then all she wants is to crawl into her lap, to crawl inside her, to be subsumed. With a helpless squeaking sound she realizes she's weeping, fat drops spattering on Liis's hospital gown, and Liis is murmuring to her, her own voice thick with tears—*I love you I love you*—

"Now, now," tsks the nurse. "Let me get her into bed—"

A gruff voice answers, "Leave them alone."

Jun pulls back, embarrassed, wiping at her face. But the sight of Masar stops her short again. He's come in behind the nurse and stands with one arm in a sling against his chest, his left eye covered by a bandage. It's a throwback to when they met, after Captain Foxer had blackened his eye. Then she remembers reuniting with him on the train car, his whole face bloody, his eye torn out by cloaksaan shrapnel.

"Fuck, Masar," she whispers.

His lips twitch and then he grins. "Now, don't go weeping for me, too. The doctors are already working on a replacement. Once it rewires, I'll hardly be able to tell the difference."

This isn't strictly true; even with the most advanced technology, a prosthetic eye can never quite re-create the original, but she doesn't say so. Still embarrassed to be caught crying, she gestures impatiently at Liis.

"So why'd you stick a piece of plastic on her?"

Masar's good humor doesn't flag. He chuckles. "They're working on her arm, too. It'll be leagues better than what she had before, I promise you that."

Jun nods tersely, and looks at Liis again, her ire fading as she murmurs, "Are you in pain?"

"A lot less now," Liis replies—which from her is as good as admitting she was in agony before, and Jun's throat closes with the threat of more tears. Liis suggests, "Why don't we let the nurse get me into bed?"

Reluctant, Jun stands back as the hoverchair maneuvers past. Jun watches anxiously as the nurse helps Liis back into her bed. At least none of her injuries seem to have stopped her being able to walk, but nonetheless Jun is ready to step in if needed. Only after the nurse has left and Liis is resting against the pillows (she grabs Jun's hand—a rare sign of vulnerability) does Jun face Masar again. To her surprise, he's looking at Cleric Chono—the two of them watching each other in disquieting silence.

"So…" Jun feels an awkward impulse to break the stalemate. "You here to tell me why my neural link is shut off?"

It works. Blinking his one eye, Masar has the decency to look cowed. "I know that's gotta sting for you. It's not forever. But the Wheel wants to keep some things close right now, and if we give you back your access, you'll hack through every system we have."

That's… fair, though it in no way appeases her. She glances toward the door, probably locked again, and wonders how long "it's not forever" means.

"Will you at least tell me where we are?"

"We're on *The Risen Wave*."

"No shit we're on *The Risen Wave*, but *where* is *The Risen Wave*? Why hasn't the Kindom tracked us down yet? And why have you put a cleric in the same room as us?"

He opens his mouth, looks momentarily stymied, and shuts it again.

"We're outside Treble space," says Cleric Chono suddenly. Everyone looks at her. "Otherwise the Kindom would have found us. We're in the same room because it is convenient to keep all your unknown variables in one place, not to mention I predict the rest of the hospital is full after the battle with the cloaksaan. We're prisoners, but not dangerous prisoners, in your estimation. That's why Six is somewhere else. A real prison, probably. Them you consider dangerous."

At first Masar only looks uncomfortable, but at the end he frowns.

"*Esek Nightfoot* is in our prison."

Chono makes a soft sound, an indrawn breath. "So they're alive?" she whispers.

The sheer intensity of the question takes Masar off guard. His curt nod makes Chono swallow convulsively, her eyes wet with either physical pain or emotion. Jun looks at Liis, and sees Liis watching Chono. It's Liis who tells Masar after a tense pause, "The person in the prison is not Esek Nightfoot."

Masar hesitates, glancing from Chono to Liis. "She's trying to trick us."

Liis shakes her head. "When I found them on the train car, the person who looks like Esek Nightfoot was protecting Jun from Vas Sivas Medisogo. And Cleric Chono, dying as she was, tried to help. Your ships would never have escaped if not for that."

"She was protecting herself. Trying to survive. She—"

"You are wrong," says Liis.

There is so much finality in her voice that Masar closes his mouth. He looks torn, a little grumpy, and then he throws a suspicious glance at Chono.

"Well... If you're both that sure about it, I suppose you won't hesitate to help me."

Jun raises an eyebrow, aware of Liis's fingers gripping hers a little tighter, like she's afraid Masar is going to ask Jun to go on some new caper. Jun rubs her thumb. "Help you how?"

"Help me figure out who she is."

He casts a view into the air. At first all Jun can feel is bitterness that his link works, but then, drawn as ever to shiny casty things, she takes in the wall of text and glyphs that has appeared. It's an obvious encryption code, but unlike the Kindom encryption that strangled the nameday coin, this is wild-built, with a grammatic structure that's gibberish while still being familiar, a hodgepodge of casting logics. Without her neural link she can't dive into it, can't unwind it, and she says so.

"What is it?" she adds.

"It's the encryption preventing us from accessing Esek Nightfoot's neural link." He looks at Chono, like he's gearing himself up for an unpleasant task. "You're Kindom. Can you tell us how to get through a Kindom link encryption?"

Jun scoffs. "That's not a Kindom encryption."

He frowns. "What?"

"That's pure built-in-the-Black chaos cipher. Kindom encryptions are *much* tidier. Six probably built it themself."

He still looks annoyed at hearing her use the name Six, but asks, "Can you break it?"

Jun pauses, glancing at Chono. The cleric looks feverish, eyes red-rimmed and exhausted, her fine black hair lank with sweat. Hacking Six's neural link is a surefire way to prove that Six is not Esek Night-foot, and Jun can see how badly Chono wants her to do this. And Jun, of course, has her own motivation for wanting Six to be safe. Still... Jun's a con artist first.

She looks at Masar again. "What'll your Wheel give me?"

Masar blinks. Liis chuckles.

"Give you?" Masar repeats.

"Yeah. The way I see it I've done a lot of favors for you lately and the most I've gotten out of it is a vague job offer and a few near-death experiences. You're bringing me this encryption because your people can't break it. So if I break it for you, what will you give me?"

He looks at her for a moment, still clearly startled, and then he blurts a laugh.

"You are such an asshole."

"I'm pragmatic."

"Yeah, yeah, whatever. Give me a second."

He turns his back on them, and Jun knows he must be casting a message to someone, maybe the Wheel. It's a silent conversation but he shifts from foot to foot. Jun glances at Liis, who gives her a quick, approving wink, and not long after, Masar faces them again. "All right." He nods his head toward the door. "Someone wants to talk to you. Come with me."

Surprised, Jun hesitates. This is obviously her opportunity to meet another member of the Wheel, but she's not keen to be separated from Liis again. Their knit fingers are like vines that have grown together over centuries, and that's how Jun wants it.

"We won't be long," Masar promises, noticing her expression. "And Liis will be here when you get back. On Sajeven, I swear it."

"It's all right," Liis tells her, with a reassuring nod. "Go with him."

Finally, reluctantly, she lets go of Liis. She follows Masar to the door, pausing to look back on the room. Liis's and Chono's beds are directly across from each other, and they're looking at each other now, faces expressionless. The traitor cloaksaan and the traitor cleric, both as taciturn as ghosts. What interesting conversational partners they will be.

Jun points at Liis. "Try not to lose that arm."

And steps into the hallway.

Jun has only the vaguest memories of the hospital, of being moved from the waiting room to Liis's room, but now she takes note of the equipment against the walls and the personnel walking briskly about their tasks. She knew *The Risen Wave* was a functional city, but it hadn't occurred to her that its hospital would be sufficiently modernized to manage the aftereffects of a battle, or that there would be enough doctors and surgeons among the Jeveni to serve those needs. Masar leads her down the hall, past rooms with open doors and people in beds. She sees the signs of injury and recovery—the Jeveni fighters and civilians who survived the Brutal Hand. Jun wonders for the first time how many didn't survive. She thinks of the ship of five hundred, blown apart in the Black Ocean. She thinks of the crew of *The Happy Jaunt*, who made their last stand as Nikkelo lay dead in the landing bay. Did any of them survive?

She asks Masar and watches the tension gather in his face. He's already walking slowly to accommodate her shorter stride, but the question almost makes him stumble.

"No," he says. "The cloaks got on board. They were all killed."

Queasiness curls, acidic, in Jun's stomach. "I'm sorry."

He nods, a curt gesture, and the silence makes her think that this is no small matter to him, that the grief of it is a monster in his chest. Jun swallows.

"I'm...sorry about Nikkelo, too. I didn't really get to say it before. I liked him."

This time Masar smiles tightly. "Everyone liked him. Some of the Wheel are more likable than others. He was... Well, we loved him."

"Why did he draw on the cloaksaan?"

"To protect the rest of the Wheel." Masar glances at her. "Something you should know about our government—there's no glory in being a Spoke of the Wheel. No self-interest. Spokes resign at the slightest scandal. They've been removed for even minor hints of corruption. It's nothing to a Spoke to let themself be killed, if it protects everyone else. Our Star wasn't bluffing, when she told Esek—or, whoever that is—that the Wheel would surrender to save the rest of the Jeveni. She would have done it. They all would. And a new Wheel would take their place, and the rest of us would find a way to avenge them. We are as ready to die for them as they are to die for us."

Jun considers this, a model of leadership and fealty so unfamiliar to her. She remembers Masar's horror when Nikkelo was shot, realizes with fresh perspective how difficult it was for him not to turn back.

"After what happened, you'll be fugitives. Tens of thousands of you. How can your Wheel possibly protect its people from the Kindom? They'll find you eventually."

Masar smiles again, cunning and self-satisfied. "Don't worry about that."

He pushes open a door and leads them into a new hallway, less populated than the previous. He speaks again, suddenly all business. "We can't leave the hospital. I'm sorry. And I can't tell you all the things you want to know. The man coming to see you—he won't be able to tell you everything, either. But hopefully it'll be enough."

Jun narrows her eyes, wondering which member of the Wheel has been tapped to deal with her recalcitrance. "Okay..." she mutters.

"You know, there's something I've wanted to ask you. All this time you've been saving up to rescue your family—where were you planning to go? You didn't want to hide with us, so I assume hiding itself wasn't in your plans. Were you going to live in the open again? Let your money protect you?"

Jun gives him a cautious, sidelong look. "I had my eye on one of the frontier stations. Out past the boundaries of Kator. It's a three-year trip; the Kindom never bothers them." Masar chuckles, and Jun bristles. "What?"

"Nothing. It's . . . nothing."

"Is that where we're headed? The frontier? My Hood program can't still be shielding the whole fleet; I could barely make it fit long enough to get us through one jump gate."

He shrugs. "We have our own kind of Hood now."

Jun glares. "That's bullshit."

"Well, stop asking me questions I can't answer!"

He tilts his head suddenly; he's getting some kind of comm. He nods. "All right. Good. This way."

They round a corner into an open room, maybe another waiting area for patients' families, though it's empty now. Jun raises an eyebrow at Masar and he gives her a look that means *Wait*—but his expression is warm, not chastising. Sighing, she turns away from him, eyes immediately pulled toward one of the walls. There's a mural drawn on it, ancient and with faded colors. First confused, then amazed, she realizes that it's *The First Portrait of the Six Gods*. But not a re-creation. The *original*. She steps closer, taking in each of the gods in turn. A faded orange-and-yellow sun rises above the six figures, the Godfire burning down on them. Their details, worn and roughened, still manage to convey something majestic. Jun was never much for the gods, never needed worship or Godtexts, never cared about the old riddle—who is the Sixth God? Casting was always her god. Casting, and her family, and Liis. But even she is impressed by the sheer historical significance of what she's looking at.

Her gaze gravitates to Sajeven, always with five eyes in a wheel shape, warm and smiling and secretive. What would it be like to work among the Jeveni, to immerse herself in the culture of this barren god, known for warmth and kindness?

"Was Nikkelo serious?" she calls over her shoulder. "About offering me a job?"

"A lot of people died keeping you alive. He was serious."

That pricks her with guilt, and her eyes drift to Makala, fecund and lovely. Her family's god, though they were never very religious. *Esek's* god—and Esek was far from righteous. Ricari said to Jun once, *The gods are in our actions*, and Nikkelo said, *Our lives are ours to use*—and Jun thinks about weary, regretful Chono, bound by her past mistakes and yet so clearly wanting to be good…

"It's a funny drawing, isn't it?" thinks Jun aloud, stepping back from the wall to observe it more holistically. She hears a door open behind her, and knows that someone from the Wheel must be here. She doesn't rush to turn around. Let them wait.

A voice says, "Jun?"

Something inside her locks tight, a kind of terror. For several moments she doesn't move. She hardly breathes. She tells herself, *I don't know that voice.* Then, at last, she turns around.

There is a man standing in front of her, stocky and not much taller than she is, young and smiling tentatively, his eyes the color of dark wheat…

Jun's heart lurches into her throat, as though it will break through her body, as though it will swell and expand and devour the room. It rises on wings of grief and love, of hope and fear. It puts her into their childhood bedroom, the two of them playing with a busted electrical board that Great Gra gave her to fix. Jun at nine says softly, *Now, careful. That bit'll shock you. But don't worry. I won't let you get hurt.*

The boy, the man, looks at her wonderingly. They look alike, more than they did as children. Her face is in his face. And Ricari's face is in both of them.

"Jun?" he says again, a little hoarse, and he laughs, a little raw. "Don't you know me?"

Jun swallows, trying to hold on to her heart. She says his name like it's a bet she's laying in a game of tiles, like it's her whole life and future and past, gambled on this moment:

"Bene?"

Then with relief he laughs again, and his eyes are blurred with tears—or are those hers?

"Yes," he says, in disbelief, in joy. "Yes!"

And before she can blink, before she can wake up and lose it all again, he rushes her.

And all of these does the Godfire favor. To all of these do its child gods commit their praise. For there is no kingdom but for those who make the kingdom great. So let live the kinship that unites stranger to stranger. Let live the voice of justice in our midst. Let live the spirit of mercy in our hearts. Let live the one who fights corruption, and protects the child in the dark.

The Beatitudes, 1:9. Godtexts, pre-Treble

CHAPTER TWENTY-SEVEN

1664

YEAR OF THE CRUX

The Risen Wave
Somewhere

They don't see anyone or talk to anyone for four days. There was a period of... forced unconsciousness after the Jeveni took them into custody, and when they woke, they were in a cell, which could be on a ship, or on a planet, or on a station. But they know, with a certainty, that they are still aboard *The Risen Wave*.

Meals appear at regular intervals, through a slot under the cell door. The food is generous, rich with the flavor profiles of Jeveni cuisine. The breakfast meal always includes a traditional mint reed, a hand-length, fibrous tube Lucos Alanye often lauded in his journals. The objects and customs of the Jeveni fascinated Alanye, a condescending fascination that sometimes made Six walk away from his recordings, exasperated. Discovering that they are descended of a Jeveni woman has brought Six a vindictive comfort, allowing them to conceive of their lineage as branching from her rather than the insipid Alanye. He was not the genocider that the Treble takes him for, but he was an opportunist and a fool, and Six's disdain for him is tireless.

And yet, like him, they enjoy the mint reed. They sit on their cot with their back braced against the wall. They watch the door and chew the reed. The silence, the solitude, the waiting, are not difficult, after so many months of endless activity. Esek was so... *much*. Always the biggest personality in the room, always the focus of everyone's ire and captivation. It was exhausting to be Esek.

Not that they didn't relish it sometimes—a secret relish, a sensation of victory. Never more acute than when they were with Chono. When they could *see* and *hear* and *talk* with Chono, as Esek had, rather than from an inconspicuous distance.

They have heard nothing about her survival. They refuse any reality where she has died. When Jeveni descended on the train car, everyone pointing guns at Six till they were flat on their stomach with hands behind their back, all they cared about was the group of medics—two squatting down beside Liis Konye, three gathering around Chono. They watched Chono borne onto a stretcher and taken off the train car as they themself were being bound, and for a moment their eyes and Chono's eyes locked, and Chono was alive, and then a dark shaft of unconsciousness cleaved them apart.

There is no reality where Chono has died.

On the fifth day, the door opens. Three armed Jeveni appear, wearing mountain-gray uniforms with the mask of Sajeven appliquéd on their chests. These are what the warriors who descended on Ketch Market were wearing, as well. Apparently, the Jeveni have a standing army. That's good. They'll need their own forces to protect them from the Kindom, going forward.

"Please come with us," says one of the soldiers.

They expect to be shackled, or at least escorted under drawn guns, but the Jeveni do neither. Led by one, followed by the other two, they enter a nondescript hallway, then a kind of garage where a small roof-less warcat waits for them. The soldiers drive them down what seems at first an interminable service tunnel. One of the Jeveni lights a cigarette and offers them one, an unexpected courtesy that reminds them of old stories about prisoners getting one last cigarette before execution. They decline. Esek never smoked.

"I hear you're called Six," says the soldier.

Ah. So. Was it Jun Ironway or Chono who convinced the Wheel who they are?

They nod to the soldier, who drags on his cigarette. "Funny name. D'ya know 'six' means 'spider' in Je?"

The corner of their mouth twitches as they watch the road ahead of them. "Yes."

When the warcat pulls over, the smoking soldier takes a last drag and then grinds out the cigarette in a little metal ashtray in the door. The mundanity of it, after so much, is momentarily fascinating. They absurdly want to ask for a cigarette, just so they can stub it out in the square metal tin. But then the soldiers gesture them out of the vehicle, to a door in the service tunnel. A short flight of stairs later, and they are delivered into some kind of foyer, brightly lit and empty, but for one other person: a very young woman.

"Thank you, friends," she says to the soldiers.

To Six's surprise the soldiers go back the way they came, leaving Six alone with the stranger. Except she isn't a stranger. Six knows exactly who she is.

They look at each other for several moments, before at last Effegen ten Crost asks, "What would you like me to call you?"

Six hesitates. The woman before them is nineteen, *maybe* twenty? She's a foot shorter than Six at least; she's plump and pretty, with greenish-hazel eyes, and it would be very easy to sneer at the idea of answering to such a young person. But Six knows they are not speaking to a girl. They're answering to the Star of the Wheel.

At first they can't answer at all. They examine her instead. Effegen is wearing a bright green robe with elaborate silver threadwork, her hair the color of rich dark soil, intricately braided into a crown. There are rings on her fingers and studs in her ears, black as pitch and red-veined. It can't be real jevite. Real jevite would have paled by now, surely...

"Perhaps...your birth name?" Effegen says. Six's nerves vibrate like the struck strings of a long-hidden instrument. They meet the girl's hawkish eyes, intelligent and watchful. For a split second, she reminds Six of a young Alisiana. But the Star's stare, though assessing, lacks that bite of cruelty. At their silence, she asks, "Or Sa Alanye?"

That name makes them want to growl. They answer, "Every name I have used has been a tool. I have never chosen a name because it mattered to me. You may call me whatever you wish to call me. All my names are the same to me."

A low chuckle, belying her youth. "Cleric Chono said you would be mysterious."

Six's chest tightens, but they keep their stare impassive. "I take it Cleric Chono has survived?"

"She has. Putting those suture bots in her chest saved her life, and our doctors were able to clean up most of the mess. She's still weak, but she'll pull through." A brief silence passes, Six keeping their expression flat, until Effegen ten Crost suddenly smiles, eyes sparkling. "Have you got any idea how strange it is to look at you?" she asks. Her smile brightens. "Esek Nightfoot was a master class of overblown emotionality. And here you are, wearing her face, but looking like you've never had a facial expression in your life. It is totally bizarre. Is this your natural inclination, to be expressionless?"

Six considers. At school, they were never accused of expressionlessness. They were known for a constant scowl, for an air of disdain and distrust that once got them taken aside by the sparring teacher. *I know all the entertainments depict cloaksaan as these constantly grimacing behemoths*, she'd said, *but if you want to be a* real *cloak, you'll have to learn to control that face of yours.*

Later, when Six fled Principes in the cargo deck of a pirate ship, they realized their teacher was correct. They were too conspicuous. If they wanted to survive, they'd need a lot more skills than fighting prowess. They'd need resilience. Control. Brutality but also dispassion. They decided to mimic Chono. Chono had come to school already halfway to perfecting her emotionless facade, a survival instinct from a home she never talked about. Six determined to be like her, and wear composure like a veil.

It had probably saved their life, this decision. This first of many masks.

Realizing the Star is still watching them, Six finally answers, "It took eight facial surgeries to make me look like this. After each surgery, I had to exercise my facial muscles to prevent atrophy. Each time, I had to learn a new face. When I became Esek, no moment passed that I was not exercising my face like a marionette. After all that, there is...some relief to having no expression."

Effegen nods sagely, though she's still looking at them in a disquietingly maternal way.

"You've done a lot to yourself." Six doesn't respond. "After we arrested you, we injected you with a sedative. I apologize. We believed we were dealing with Esek Nightfoot and couldn't risk leaving her conscious. While you were under, my casters extracted several encrypted data packets from your neural link. Or, to put it more honestly, Jun Ironway extracted them." Six isn't sure what happens to their face, but whatever it is, it makes Effegen smile kindly. "Again, forgive our violations. I believe Sa Ironway did it to prove you were not Esek Nightfoot. As you can imagine, we had our doubts. But the contents of those data packets answered a lot of questions we didn't even know to ask."

Still, Six is silent. They have been trying to get into the same room as the Wheel ever since they killed Esek in the Verdant tower. Even for them, a master of infiltration, of subterfuge, of *finding* things and people, the task proved impossible. So good at hiding, the Wheel. How else could they have survived? In the end, Jun Ironway and Masar

Hawks were the best lead they found. They tracked those two space urchins across the Treble, and now, here they are. In the presence of Effegen ten Crost. The thing they've been aiming toward for years. Yet suddenly they are as shy as a kinschool student on day one, voiceless under the force of the history that's brought them here.

The Star is not voiceless. She twirls her fingers, a youthful gesture, and bumps her wrist, tossing an array of images into the air, satellites of revelation orbiting their heads. It's an eclectic collection: shipping manifests, union leader profiles, correspondences, bank accounts, legal records, and, most importantly, a notarized will...

"It's taken us three days to come to any kind of theory of what you've done." Effegen looks up at the holograms like a child watching clouds drift. "We thought at first you had simply consolidated the entire sevite industry under Esek Nightfoot. Under yourself, I should say. Given what Cleric Chono has told us about your long-standing rivalry with Sa Nightfoot, stealing the sevite industry from her makes sense as a kind of revenge. But that's not what you've done, is it? Or... it's not all you've done."

Six says nothing. Six has waited over a decade for this moment, but suddenly they are exhausted. It's as if they haven't slept in years, and all the weight of what they've done instead of sleeping now lands with slow, crushing pressure. When they do speak, they whisper.

"It is my gift."

Effegen cocks her head, quizzical as a bird, waiting for them to explain. Their throat feels dry. They swallow. "It began as revenge but... revenge was not enough." A shiver runs down their spine, which is the memory of Esek's whisper in their ear, a coax and a curse. But Esek was so *small*. She amounted to so little, in the end. "I do not need to tell you the jevite industry was more than anyone could ever avenge. Hundreds of years of theft. Of murder and rape and kidnapping and the destruction of your moon. Of *my*... ancestors' moon. Revenge could never be enough. I wanted more than revenge. I wanted recompense. That is what I have done, Sa Crost. The entire sevite trade is mine now. And I am giving it to you."

The Star looks at them for a long time, and if Six expected any particular reaction, they don't know whether this stare is it or not. Everything feels fuzzy and muted now, a world behind sheets of water, and they are *so sleepy*. Now that it's done, they would give anything for that cot in the cell. They would give anything to crawl into a quiet, dark place, and never emerge.

Effegen says, "That is quite a gift. I see that you distributed the various shares to myself and the other members of the Wheel. My kin and I are fugitives now. Certainly the Kindom will invalidate any transfer of assets? Surely they will invalidate you, the traitor Esek Nightfoot?"

Six sighs and nods. "The Cloaksaan and Clerisy, yes, they will try to. But Kindom law is complex and hypocritical, and easily manipulated if you have the right people in your pocket."

"You mean the Secretaries."

"I mean the Secretaries. Give your scholars more time to review the data packet. You will find I have... thought of everything."

It will be difficult, of course. There will be legal challenges. And all of it hinges on Esek's death—Six's death—which they will have to fake before the transfer officially takes place. But they have used their clever allies to enact a beautiful and vicious revenge, one that will empower the sevite unions and force the First Families to ingratiate themselves to the Wheel. Even the transformation of their own body does not compete with the complexity and genius of what they have done with the sevite trade.

The Star looks at them thoughtfully, nodding. After a moment she says, "We found evidence in your packet—proof of the Kindom's responsibility for the Jeveni Genocide. And Cleric Chono says that while she was Esek's novitiate, you collected records that showed the link between the genocide and the Nightfoots. She says you sent them to her as part of some elaborate game with Esek. Why did you do all of that?"

It surprises Six that they aren't too tired for the sudden warm sensation of amusement. "My purpose was... fourfold, there. First, I collected the evidence to make sure nothing threatened Nightfoot power before I could find a way to steal it. Second, I wished to retain evidence as my own insurance. Third, it kept Esek off the scent of my real purpose. Fourth..." They pause, and they very nearly laugh, but it would probably sound hysterical and they do not want to be hysterical in front of the Star.

Effegen, however, is onto them.

"You did it to fuck with her."

They look at each other. The girl's eyes are sparkling. One could almost think she doesn't carry the weight of her people's government on her back, a weight only increased, now the River is dead. Will they have elected Nikkelo sen Rieve's replacement yet? They will need a strong Wheel, for the work ahead. If the light in this girl's eyes means anything, then she will be equal to the task. And that, Six thinks—that will make it worthwhile, yes? What else can they tell themself, but that it will make everything worthwhile?

"Did you know we searched for you?"

The girl's voice, the gentleness of it, jolts Six out of their thoughts as rudely as if they'd been struck. They stare at her. It's not only her voice that's gentle. Her sparkling eyes have softened. There's a tenderness in her look that wasn't there before. It makes Six flinch inside.

"What?" Their voice is flat.

The Star repeats, "We searched for you. In the past thirty years, we've searched for all the lost children of our ancestors. People like Masar have given up their names and their Jeveni tattoos to do it. Your great-great-grandmother was Drae sen Briit, Alanye's lover. She managed to get off of Jeve in the first hours of the bombings, but succumbed to her injuries later. Her children had been safe on Kator for several months, and one of their descendants, your father, settled on Teros. When we first searched for you, we learned that he had died, and that a secretary took you for a ward. I assume you're the one who killed that secretary twenty years ago? We tracked you as far as the kinschool on Principes, but by then, you had disappeared." Six looks at her stonily, which seems not to disturb the girl at all. Her expression is earnest. "We searched for you. We didn't forget you. But you've been so determined not to be found."

"I was concerned with other matters."

"Yes, we see that now."

There's the faintest hint of recrimination in it. All the years of trying to emulate Chono can't stop Six's jaw from tightening, can't tamp the anger that rises up like a sob.

"And what could you have possibly given, if you had found me?" they demand.

"Purpose, for one. You have gifts, insights—we could have used them. But more than that, we simply wanted you to come home. We could have given you a home."

Six very nearly steps back from her, as if from a threat. Effegen sighs. She twists her wrist, and the satellites of data vanish from the air. "I want to show you something. Will you come? They're waiting for us."

Six doesn't have a chance to ask who "they" are before Effegen has turned away. Six follows her to the set of double doors on the opposite side of the foyer, but no sooner have they stepped through than they come to a startled halt.

The room is vast, and domed. Its whole breadth projects a limitless vista of stars. It's a planetarium, like the one Six visited as a child on Teros. With Da. Before the adopting secretary. Before the kinschool. Before Esek. They stand still and gaze up as if they've never been on a spacecraft before, or a station even. It is so...big, that for a shocking moment they feel small. Small, as if they have forgotten they ever were. Small, like a pinprick. How immutable it is. How spectacular they feel, to be small in the face of something so wondrous, and quiet, and unending.

"This way, Sa Six," says Effegen coaxingly.

But when Six looks the way she is going, their throat closes. The room hosts a large table, ringed with chairs where many occupants sit staring at them, and one voice says—

"Six."

She's twenty feet away, and half-shadowed by the dark of the planetarium. Six would know her anywhere. Six would feel her presence in a pitch-black room. She looks at them solemnly, her near death hanging over her like a shroud, face aged and weary. Six had not planned to tell her who they were. Six had always imagined that Chono would attack them, if she learned the truth. But that was hardly possible with her bleeding to death in that train car.

Chono's eyes snap away, and it's like the severance of a tight and vibrating thread. Released, Six blinks around at the rest of the table and approaches cautiously. There are other members of the Wheel in their green robes: a handsome middle-aged man, the Tree; a silver-haired woman with cool eyes, the Stone; and a person about Six's age, fat and elegant, the Gale. No Nikkelo, no new River. They all watch Six's approach with varying degrees of suspicion, and when Six sits down in a chair across from theirs, it reminds them of exams back at school—a somber jury waiting to see what they'd make of themself.

There are others at the table beside Chono. The pirate Masar Hawks—not really a pirate. The former cloaksaan Liis Konye, now sporting a new arm. When Six discovers Jun Ironway to their right, it actually startles them.

Sunstep.

That scrawny little kid they found in the Riin Kala safe house. Built like a reed and eyes full of fire that was much more than the fever raging through them. Six hadn't expected her to survive. Certainly not to become this caster genius, this con artist turned world breaker. Of all the absurdities.

"I wasn't sure they let you live," Jun says, with feigned brightness.

Six looks at her flatly. "You hacked my neural link."

An indolent shrug, but there's a challenge in it. The caster is obviously curious about them, but also wary.

Chono wears no expression at all, though it is not her usual placid mask. There's a rigidity, a forcedness. She is pretending.

"Were we right?" asks the Stone, her voice as rough as waves on the sand. She's looking at Effegen. Effegen nods and the Stone looks at Six, some of her guardedness fading, though she does not appear welcoming.

The Gale, eyes a deep and watchful brown, says, "Then I suppose we can begin."

Effegen smiles. "Yes. Let's."

Jun's body shifts forward. "Begin what?"

The Star looks amused. "Masar tells me you have not stopped harassing him for information about where you are. We thought it best to make the situation clear to all of you, at the same time. I'm sorry if we have tried your patience."

The caster sniffs. "I threw a Hood over every ship in your fleet and over this generation ship besides and I hacked us transport through a jump gate even though you refused to tell me the coordinates we were going to. I think I've earned a little *impatience*."

Masar groans, "There'll be no living with her."

Jun answers pleasantly, "Fuck off," and demands of Effegen, "Where in the godsdamned Black are we?"

The members of the Wheel look at one another, all eyes finally resolving on Effegen, who sits back in her chair again and manipulates the air with twisting fingers. Her cast grabs the overhead vista and turns it like a dial. Six winces from the disorientation of the stars above blurring, the room itself seeming to flow toward new coordinates. Then all at once something massive and unexpected floods into view.

A planet.

An ice-blue, cloud-strewn, moon-crowned wonder of a planet.

Six is too amazed to take note of anyone else's reaction. They have a distant sense of someone, probably Jun, cursing under her breath, but they don't look at her. They don't even look at Chono, because how could they possibly? How, in this moment, could they do anything but stare in open wonder, and something akin to fear, at the gorgeous curve of a pale planet blotting out the stars? They have visited every planet in the Treble. Every moon. Every space station. They have stood upon the vast green savannas of Ma'kess, trekked the purple mountains of Kator, climbed down into the red clay gulches of Teros, and the jungle ravines of Braemin, and they have floated on their back in the planet-blanketing ocean of Quietus. And in all these places they have looked up into night skies pocked with celestial bodies, but none of those were this bright white orb of a planet now hanging before them.

Effegen says, "We call it Capamame."

Named for a god. *The dear friend*, thinks Six. Little respected by his more powerful siblings but beloved of Sajeven and the Quietans. Chono used to tell his story at school. Six dares a glance in her direction, and she is gazing up at the planet with furrowed brow, lips parted.

Effegen explains, "Before our ancestors colonized the Treble, they considered a number of star systems, and a number of planets. Most were rejected because of either distance or habitability. Capamame failed on both counts. Too far away. Too difficult to colonize." As she continues, an array of planetary data fills the air, which she narrates like a lecturer in a school room. "It's comparable in size to Ma'kess, but has four moons, as you can see. It's composed of four continents, which are altogether equal in land mass to the planet's ocean. There is no terrestrial life beyond insects and microorganisms. There is ocean life, though we're not sure of its extent. Its warmest recorded temperature is only twenty-two degrees, but if you stay within range of its equatorial line and are properly equipped, you can survive year-round. Which is what we intend to do."

Six, whose head has been tilted back like an awestruck child's, now snaps their chin down and looks sharply at Effegen. The young Star is already looking at them, and Six is convinced this whole speech was directed at *them*.

Jun Ironway asks, "Do you mean we're orbiting this planet right now?"

"What, you think we're just showing you pretty pictures?" retorts Masar.

"Um, fuck you, that report says this planet is *forty light-years* away from the Treble. How the hell did we get here?"

"By jump gate," he says.

"You can't just jump to another planet! You need a gate to jump *to*. You need—"

Suddenly the vista shifts again, rotating them around the ice planet until they've circled it entire, and there, balanced on the curving horizon, backlit by a distant, throbbing sun—there it hangs: the mercurial sphere of a jump gate. They sweep toward it, borne closer and closer, as if they are about to enter its shimmering mouth. To Six's amazement, the very fact of the jump gate isn't even the most surprising thing. It's that it looks nothing like any gate they've seen before. None of the trappings of Kindom construction. None of the orbiting security stations. The gate is small; it is…spartan. While Kindom gates are gargantuan cages that both contain and constrain the interdimensional sphere, this gate is slim and elegant and invisible in places, a delicate silver latticework, a miracle of engineering.

After a few moments of stunned silence, Liis Konye asks, "How long did it take you to reach the planet by standard travel?"

Effegen ten Crost replies, "Sixty-three years. We began the journey in 1588, a year before our moon was destroyed. Lucos Alanye"—a glance at Six—"and the Kindom scrutiny he brought with him, forced us to speed up our timetable. The crew arrived in Capamame space in 1651."

Liis nods. Then, bowing her head respectfully, she addresses all four of the Spokes, "Forgive me, Saan, but I studied the Jeveni when I was a student at my kinschool. Even allowing that your people hid a valuable jevite seam for centuries, you were never wealthy after the sevite trade devastated your moon. The resources needed to build a gate—to say nothing of purchasing a ship that could manage a journey that long— how did you do it?"

Effegen's laugh surprises them, as do the responding smiles of the other members of the Wheel. Sharp, self-satisfied smiles. The Tree lays long-fingered hands on the table, tapping them thoughtfully. "How shall we say it…? You and Jun Ironway are not the only con artists in the history of the Black Ocean."

Jun's eyebrows hike upward, excitement in her eyes. "Are you saying you're thieves? Oh, gods, please tell me you're thieves. I *knew* Nikkelo looked like a pickpocket."

The Stone huffs irritably, though there's a quirk of humor at the corner of her mouth. "We are not thieves, Sa Ironway. After the jevite trade failed, and the Kindom abandoned us, we did what so many in the Treble do: We sent our best minds out to make their fortunes. They hid their tattoos, hid their origins, and became collectors. A couple of centuries and strict frugality were enough to amass a fortune. Our generations of poverty were in the service of a higher goal."

Six thinks of Lucos Alanye, exasperated by the Jeveni's spartan lifestyles. How they refused to use the hydroponics and casting equipment he brought them. Now Six realizes they took that equipment and reserved it for their eventual flight. Far-thinking and clever.

"Meanwhile," says the Gale. "We mined our jevite seam for enough raw material to power our ship and a jump gate."

"That was the financial side," continues Effegen. "But it's taken more than money. Over two thousand Jeveni gave up everything in order to spend their lives crossing the Black Ocean. They committed to make new families in transit, to have children, to raise their children and their grandchildren for one purpose: reach Capamame, build a gate, and make a way for the rest of us. They did all of this, knowing their ship might fail en route. Or they might reach Capamame, and find it truly uninhabitable. It's only these past ten years that we've seen true cause for hope. A year since we successfully tested the gate. The Spokes of the Wheel are the only ones who know its coordinates. Which means no one can follow us here. Not even if they know the gate exists. This is why Nikkelo let himself be killed, rather than captured. This is our deliverance from the Kindom. This is something we will build for ourselves."

At that, Jun Ironway leans forward, her brow furrowed. "Are you saying that all the Jeveni—the assimilationists and the collectives—have committed to this together?"

A dry smile from Effegen. "No people could boast a unanimous mission. Only a fraction of our population knew about this plan. We had intended to use Remembrance Day to share Capamame with our entire population so that each Jeveni could choose for themselves. Instead, circumstances have forced us to bring everyone here—and we are still working through the ramifications of that. But we are committed to our secession from the Kindom. There is no other course for us." She pauses, thoughtful. "It is a great irony...The Kindom has long suspected us of plotting treason. They even believed that we allied with Esek Nightfoot to stage a revolt. In a way, they were right. But not the way they thought."

Six feels the following silence like a weight on their chest, before slowly, Effegen looks at them again. Her expression is unspeakably kind, but her words shatter their life.

"I'm afraid we don't want the sevite industry, Sa Six. You see it's... of no use to us. Running the sevite factories gave many of our people a way to live—but a difficult way, an unjust way, as corrupt at times as when we mined Jeve under the Kindom's fist. To take control of such an industry—to wield it and maintain it...that would dishonor our god. I hope you can understand this. I hope you can make peace with it."

Six stares at her. What can they say, after all, that wouldn't be meaningless sounds masquerading as words? It's all beyond language, for them.

Years.

Years and years and years. A whole life passed in dark corners and hidden alleys and empty rooms. A whole life of sweat-soaked, late-night exertions, till there wasn't a weapon in the Treble they hadn't mastered, nor an inch of their skin they hadn't bruised or torn or calloused from overwork. Learning to treat their own wounds in isolation. Learning to speak new languages with no one to speak to. Learning new voices. Training the Six out of their vocal cords, and replacing it with Esek's cruel drawl. Replacing their face and their hands and their *skin* with Esek so someday they could take, and then give away, *everything*. And what would Esek say to all of this, now? Esek would *laugh*. Yes, Six can *see* her, as she was in her final moments: laughing and gurgling, with their ear between her teeth. Her last blow, all mockery and defiance. Her last vow, to haunt them, even into their death.

"What is it you want from us?"

Chono's voice splits the silence, more tired than Six remembers. Six looks at her. She is *barely* recovered. Yet she sits there with her typical proud posture and regards Effegen steadily.

The Star has been looking at Six all this time. Now, she takes in the rest of the room. "A fair question. What we want...is to give all our people a choice. Stay with us, or return to the Treble. You, Six, are a Jeveni, and so you're entitled to that same choice. As for you three"— she looks at Chono, Jun, and Liis—"your choice is more complicated. Though we have made our plans as Jeveni, we are not the supremacists the Treble takes us for. Building a new world is a difficult enterprise. We need all kinds. There are quite a few non-Jeveni among us, including the last of the Ironways."

Six glances quickly at Jun, and sees a new expression on her face, a kind of pure joy that she appears to be trying to control. Like someone embarrassed to be caught skipping. Six themself is baffled.

"How did you find them?" they demand, feeling a prick to their professional ego. "I hid them expertly."

Effegen smiles. "We found them *because* of you. As I told you, we've been looking for you for years, with very few leads. Jun's aunt married a Jeveni engineer on the farm station. She told him about the stranger who rescued her family. The engineer shared the lead with our collectors. It didn't ultimately help us find you, Six, but the family left an impression." She is practically beaming when she looks at Jun. "Your oldest cousin, Bene. He has your ferocity, I think. We could not bear to leave him behind."

Jun beams with pride, tears in her eyes. Liis Konye puts a hand on the back of her neck, intimate and comforting, and Six looks away. They catch Chono's eyes, just for a moment, but Chono breaks contact almost instantly.

Effegen continues, "We would never force you to remain with us on this planet, Jun, and it's not my intention to dangle your family like a carrot. Everyone must make their own choice. What we're asking of you is...a lot. Life on Capamame will be difficult. If it's not the life you want, the jump gate is fully operational. We can send you back to the Treble, with all our gratitude for the service you have already rendered. Sa Konye, of course the same offer extends—"

"I go where Jun goes," Konye interrupts.

Effegen ten Crost nods in respectful understanding, then she looks at Jun again. Jun is wiping her eyes. Six thinks about the day they met, the vehemence of this girl's vow—that she would bring her family together again. Listening to her, they'd felt an unwelcome glimmer of affinity, knowing how much they would give to undo the deaths of their own family. And Jun Ironway's determination, her grit and recklessness, these were things Six carried in their own heart, as well—that gave both of them the power to survive. The young caster clears her throat, striving for composure. "I have to discuss it with my entire family, but if they want to stay... I'm staying."

Even as she says it, Jun's eyes widen a little; she lets out a shuddering breath. Six knows what she is thinking. She is thinking that she has come to the end of a seemingly interminable fight. She is thinking, *Hard life or not... I could finally rest.* And Six thinks with a flutter in their stomach, *So can I.* They can let their life of hunting and scheming go. They can give themself to this other world, this Capamame, beyond the grip of the Hands. Surely Esek Nightfoot's reach won't extend so far? Surely, here, Six could escape the haunting she promised them, and find peace in the icy climes of a new world? All the work they've done, imagined, fought for—Effegen ten Crost wrecked it with a word. But now, she's giving Six something new. And Six's heart blooms with a feeling so foreign it almost frightens them: hope.

"And then there is you, Cleric Chono."

Instantly, the descending cloud of calm shreds apart. Six's dreaming heart leaps up and lodges in their throat as they turn sharp eyes back on Effegen. She and the other members of the Wheel are looking at Chono. Chono gazes back, tired and pale. Six feels pale, too. Because there will be no peace on Capamame if the Jeveni send Chono away.

Effegen says, "I admit there is... debate over what to do with you. Already we have reports from the Treble. Your kin say you are dead. Would it surprise you to know that quite a lot of people are talking about you on the casting net? They paint a picture that, I confess, we weren't expecting. Talk of the good works you've done. Of the gaping hole you leave behind. The people on Pippashap have declared a month of mourning, and they burn lanterns to your memory. It's all enough to make us think you are something different from the ones with whom you've comported, so—"

Chono interrupts, "But that comportment alone is a heavy mark against me."

Tension alights at the table, like electricity sparking from one end to the other. Six, who has learned to scan a room for threats and refuge, scans it now—searches the faces of the Wheel, and Jun Ironway, and Liis Konye, for some hint of compassion. Liis's expression is unreadable; Jun looks conflicted and cautious. Overall, it is not a promising scene.

Effegen nods. "That's true. Whatever your works, you're a Hand. Which is why some people have gone so far as to say we should execute you. There's no need to panic, Sa Six." A quick glance at them, both reassuring and stern, but Six's heart doesn't stop pounding. "We've put that idea aside. The more common opinion is we should simply send Cleric Chono back to the Treble. Let her have a resurrection. Of course, if you do go back, your kin may reframe you as a traitor. I predict they'll torture you for information about our gate coordinates, which you won't be able to give. It's very possible *they* will execute you. Which is why another faction of the Jeveni think we should show you the mercy of our god, and let you remain here, where you'll be safe. The Wheel itself has heard all these arguments. Before we make a decision, we thought we should give you a chance to state your case."

Chono must feel Six looking at her, must feel the imploring intensity of their stare, but she doesn't react to it. She simply straightens her shoulders, looking first at Effegen ten Crost, and then from each of the Spokes to the next. Six thinks of the first time they heard Chono recite prayers. The power and poetry of her voice. The orator in her. If she marshals those skills now, if she shows these people the beauty of her character and the humility of heart, all in that liquid, gods-blessed voice, then they will not send her back to the clutches of the Kindom.

Chono says, "I have no case to make, Sa. With your permission, I intend to return to the Treble right away."

The surprise in the room has a whipcrack intensity, and Six's chest is compressing so tight they can hardly breathe. Their mouth opens, their lips move, preparing to say something. Voice some protest—find *some way* to stop this—

But then, Chono looks at them.

"And you're coming with me."

They remember Esek Nightfoot stumbling back, impaled on the bloodletter Six flung at her. This moment feels like that. Impaled, and carrying the same brutal intimacy. There is no one else sitting at the table, anymore. There is only Chono with her storm cloud eyes. It is the first time since the train that she has really, truly looked at them, and Six holds that stare like a climbing rope—like it is the only thing preventing them from plummeting to their death. For once, Chono does not conceal her emotions. Her eyes search Six's face, a scouring look. A look full of conflict and pain, as she tries to reconcile the face of her mentor with the person of her schoolkin. And Six cannot help her. All Six can do is try to fathom her terrible, incomprehensible words.

Softly, they ask, "Why would we do that?"

Chono has been sitting with her hands on her lap, but now she rests one of them on the table. She holds it there, tensely, as if she's getting ready to strike something. She may seem perfectly steady to the others at the table, but Six has spent a lifetime studying Chono as closely as they studied Esek. Chono is not calm.

"What will happen to the sevite trade?" she asks.

Six hesitates, surprised. Then, irritation sets in. "I expect the Families and the Kindom will kill one another over it."

"That's right," Chono says.

Her stare holds censure now—the righteous cleric, condemning evil. Six begins to understand, and a lance of rage goes through them. "It is not my responsibility."

Chono is unyielding, unmoved. "You wrote to me for years. I've read everything you had locked away in your neural link. I know what you've done, to make sure Esek would inherit the matriarchy. To make sure the trade would belong to her, and all the people indebted to the trade would be indebted to her. You did everything to give Esek that power. And you succeeded. Esek has everything."

"Esek is dead," snaps Six.

"*You* are Esek now."

Six is on their feet in an instant, shouting in fury and terror, "I am *not*!"

Chono never wavers. Her hand is still resting on the tabletop, an uncompleted gesture, and her eyes are huge and full of grief—but also demand. And accusation.

"You *chose* her, Six."

"I did not."

"We both did."

Their breaths come raggedly. Chono holds them pinned, and Esek's ghost flits through the room.

Chono says, "We both chose her. We chose to follow her. To learn from her. We became echoes of her, whether we wanted to or not—whether we were as bad as her or not. Now she's dead, but we aren't. We carry the responsibility for what we chose. We must make amends."

This is unbearable. This is a *sickness*, if Chono believes it. Six grinds out with all the passion of a lifelong hatred, "Esek was a *poison*! The Nightfoots are a poison. What would you have me do? *Redeem* them?"

"What would you have had the Jeveni do, if they accepted the sevite industry?"

Six closes their mouth, stunned. In all the years of bringing their plan to fruition, this was a question they did not entertain. It was not for them to entertain, was it? To give a gift is to let it go, to release one's ownership of it. The Wheel, whom they had known only from a distance, would make something beautiful from their gift, they were certain. Something to shame all the centuries of Kindom tyranny and Nightfoot greed. But Six had never planned to be a part of it.

Chono, they think, can read all of this on their face, and for the first time since they have reunited in this room, her look shifts to something...gentle. The change is more than Six can bear, and Six stands back from the table as if this will give them the leverage they need, when it all comes to violence. But it doesn't come to violence. Quiet Chono looks at them gently. And it is the most terrible, excruciating, exquisite thing...

"It will have to be us now," she tells them. "There is no absolution, otherwise. And I *want* to be absolved." A desperate edge enters her voice; her eyes are wet. "Don't you?"

You'll spend your life having to convince everyone you're me.

I'm going to fucking haunt you, Six, I swear it.

I'll haunt you into the ground.

But what if Chono is there, too, when Esek comes haunting? Could any ghost pass through the bulwark that is Chono? Esek is a phantom. She is ashes in the wreckage of the Verdant tower, and Chono is a cleric who makes the beatitudes seem possible.

"Sa Six."

The new voice cracks their awareness like a gunshot. Startled, blinking, they discover the room is full of people after all, and one of them is Effegen. Six stares at the girl, the Star of her people, who says, "Not all the Jeveni attended Remembrance Day, and not all will choose to stay on Capamame. And more than Jeveni have suffered because of the Kindom and the sevite trade. My people and I do not want the gift you've offered us. But I can't help thinking about the ones we're leaving behind. To stay and fight for them... that would be an extraordinary gift, too."

You must do something extraordinary.

All around them there are eyes, expectant and curious and wary. Somewhere in the room is Esek, too, prowling.

It is not what they wanted. It is not what they planned.

Liis Konye says in her quiet, commanding voice, "The Kindom will seize the trade. There will be no check on their power. You and I know the Kindom, Sa. Can you bear for it to happen like that?"

Six blinks rapidly. They know so little of her. Only that she escaped. And Six wants to escape. They want to escape... but not without Chono.

"Six?" Chono whispers, beseeching.

Six faces her again. For years, they sent Chono letters, not always knowing why. But wanting, needing, to keep the thread between them taut, to send vibrations across it that would ensure Chono never forgot her kinschool friend. For years, they imagined a day when they stood before Chono again, when they looked into her eyes. Eyes that have always reminded them of Esek's cruel game, her life-consuming offer. Now, suddenly, Six knows Chono's eyes will remind them of Capamame, hereafter. Capamame, and promise, and choice.

They look at their old friend, their only friend, under the stars of the planetarium. They open their mouth and choose.

The story continues in...

Book TWO of the Kindom Trilogy

Keep reading for a sneak peek!

ACKNOWLEDGMENTS

One of the most rewarding aspects of publishing a book has been developing a community unlike any I've had before. When I first started to nudge this novel out into the world, I was floored to discover dozens of people who were invested in me as a writer and whose passion, advice, and encouragement have made this journey so rewarding.

I'd like to begin by acknowledging Brenda Drake and all the radical writers, agents, and editors associated with Pitch Wars, in which *These Burning Stars* earned me a spot as a 2020 mentee. Thank you to Rebecca Enzor, who encouraged me in an earlier Pitch Wars submission. She was the first real editor I ever had. She also got me in touch with Michael Mammay, the first person to read any part of *These Burning Stars*. Because of Mike's encouragement, I believed in this book and submitted it to Pitch Wars. That, inevitably, led me to my mentor, Jake Nicholls, a brilliant editor and all-around fantastic human being. Check out Future Worlds Editing to learn more about Jake.

Three big cheers for Ren Hutchings, who tirelessly advocates for and encourages other writers. I've been a very grateful beneficiary of her grace and insight, and her clairvoyance—she imagined my book deal into existence, right down to the editor who would want it, months ahead of time! Thanks also for her community-building efforts—through which I've met many incredible writers in many wonderful Slack groups. Particular shout-outs to Team B (and especially Rebecca Fraimow) and Sci-Fi Squad.

Thank you also to my AO3 readers and friends, who cheered me on from the comment sections!

These communities led me to my agent. Thank you, Bridget Smith, for believing in this book so quickly and so enthusiastically, and for making the process easy for me to navigate while always providing encouragement. From our first phone call, I knew my book would be in good hands!

Thank you to the fantastic team at Orbit US and Orbit UK, including Tiana Coven, Nadia El-Fassi, Emily Byron, and Tim Holman, as well as Alex Lencicki, Ellen Wright, Angela Man, Paola Crespo, Natassja Haught, Bryn A. McDonald, Lauren Panepinto, and Stephanie A. Hess. Thank you to my copyeditor, Kelley Frodel, and my cover artist, Thom Tenery. Finally, thank you to Priyanka Krishnan, my insightful and dedicated editor, who believed in this cast of murderous assholes, and who, most importantly, agrees with me that Liis Konye fucks.

I also want to acknowledge those who had my back long before *These Burning Stars* was a weird throwaway line about pirates. To Anna, for sharing my almost hysterical passion for stories. To Margaret, for believing in me so unequivocally I sometimes wonder where she gets the energy. To all my grad school friends, and my Atlanta friends, and my Buffalo friends.

To my siblings. Julianne, who would I be without your humor, your love, and your relentless confidence in me? Kelly, you've been my audience since we were kids. Everything I write, I write for you. To Mark and Nina, I'll love you forever.

To my parents. A seven-year-old asked you if she could be a writer someday, and you said yes. You may not have realized I was serious, but you changed my life with that answer.

And finally, to Mary, my dearest friend and the one whose faith means more than anything. Let's be silly forever. I love you.

extras

orbit

meet the author

Mary Ganster

BETHANY JACOBS is a former college instructor of writing and science fiction who made the leap to education technology. When she is not writing, she enjoys reading, trying out new recipes, and snuggling in bed with a TV show she's already watched ten times. She lives in Buffalo, New York, with her wife and her dog and her books. *These Burning Stars* is her debut novel.

Find out more about Bethany Jacobs and other Orbit authors by registering for the free monthly newsletter at orbitbooks.net.

if you enjoyed
THESE BURNING STARS
look out for

BOOK TWO OF THE
KINDOM TRILOGY

by

Bethany Jacobs

The story of Six, Chono, and the rest of the Treble continues in the next book of Bethany Jacobs's explosive space opera trilogy.

CHAPTER 1

1648. Year of the Pins

Barcetima
Uosti Sa Continent
The Planet Kator

It was a warm night in the Katish summer, full of dancing and music and laughter, and they used all of this as cover when they slipped into the bar and took a table by the windows. They sat facing the rest of the room, and turned a memory coin in their fingers, and didn't signal for a waiter. They had a perfect view of the road, which wended south and up—toward an estate on the hill that belonged to Ashir Doanye. From their place in the bar, they could see the estate, the grand house, its windows like yellow eyes. They flipped the coin once, but since its tail and head were the same, there was nothing to infer.

They imagined a head and tail onto the coin. If the coin landed on heads, they would give it to her. If it landed on tails, they would kill her.

They flipped it again. Impossible to know.

Someone jostled past them, bumping their chair too hard. Easy as breathing, to turn toward the bump, to slip their hand into the woman's coat and lift the coin purse off her belt. When she was gone, they held the purse under the table, digging through the contents. It was mostly Katish currency, plastic plae, but down at the bottom they found a Ma'kessn ingot. Pleased, they sat for a moment with the memory coin in one hand and the ingot in the other. One side of the ingot showed the face of the goddess Makala, fecund and lovely. On the opposite side of the ingot was an image of the temple Riin Cosas, the most important temple on Ma'kess. Heads and tails.

They flipped the ingot. Makala appeared. *Hmm.*

It was a noisy night. There were too many people around. But they had picked their location wisely. The bar was attached to a very nice hotel, whose best rooms were reserved for a Kindom delegation that, even now, celebrated in the home of Ashir Doanye. The Kindom had signed a lucrative weapons contract, to the benefit of Hands and warmongers alike. They rolled the memory coin between their fingers and watched the road. They would be able to see the delegation come down from the estate. They would see her arrive, and slip from their table, and go to her on the street, and offer her the memory coin. Unless the ingot changed its mind.

Flip. Heads. *Hmm.*

The trick was, she would be expecting it. Because she was always expecting it, always anticipating an assassination attempt. This was one of the things they had learned in the past five years of studying her life—that she never *didn't* expect someone to try to kill her, and that it was this expectation that kept her alive. If they appeared out of nowhere, even just to give her the coin, she would expect a kill. So they had to be fast, so fast, faster than her. She was twenty-seven, practically old, surely not as fast as them.

Of course, they knew that they might be the one who ended up dead. There was no avoiding that. If they tried to kill her and failed, she would definitely kill them. Maybe she wouldn't do it right away. She might torture them first and figure out who they were, but that wouldn't save them. A failed assassin? What good was one of those to her?

Or they might succeed in offering the coin, and still she'd kill them. She had warned them, once, that it could go that way. Just the insult of startling her was worth a death sentence.

They flipped the ingot, and this time the temple shone, a bloody portent. Ah, Riin Cosas. Symbol of the Righteous Hand, of the holy Clerisy. They had never wanted to be a cleric when they studied at the kinschool. Always they wanted to be a cloaksaan, even when Four tried to change their mind. The Cloaksaan, quiet and unnoticed. That was the road for them. And it might all work out, if they gave her the memory coin and she accepted them.

It was all "maybes" now, and they felt somewhat clinical about the possibility of their own death. Not because they were indifferent, but because they had come up against death a dozen times, two dozen times, maybe a hundred. What was their alternative now that this crucial moment had arrived? To walk away? After everything?

Yes, said Four in their thoughts, for Four was a pragmatist and protective. *Walk away.*

Just then a new group came into the bar, taking the table nearest theirs with raucous laughter and congratulatory braying, saying a lot of things, like how well it went, and what a pay day, and who should they fleece next? It wouldn't have even registered, except that one them, a tall man with shoulders as broad as ship's prow, said arrogantly, "Doanye is a sniveling weasel; I never had any doubts."

That name, Doanye, caught their attention. The man with the estate on the hill. Esek's host, even now. The group ordered drinks, and the drinks came. But no one mentioned Doanye again, so Six watched the road through the window. It was already eleven o'clock. Surely the party wouldn't go on much longer. Inside their jacket they felt the weight of two weapons: a pistol strapped under one arm, and a knife in an interior pocket. The knife had a long, curved blade, perfect for gutting fish.

The memory coin was a different kind of weapon. A crystalized moment in time. Or a half hour, to be precise. And what a half hour it was, that this coin immortalized. Revel Moonback, leader of the Moonback family and rival to the Nightfoots, was a cautious man, but he'd been sold out. Six didn't even have to pay much, all things considered, and now they had a recording of him with his mistress—who also happened to be his niece.

It was sordid. And just the sort of secret that Esek Nightfoot would salivate over. If they chose to offer it to her. If they didn't kill her instead. And she didn't kill them.

"When do we get payment, Goan?" asked one of the men at the table next to them.

The tall one laughed richly. "I already got the pay I care about. But the rest of it will be in this weekend. You mark my words, these people need us more than we need them. There's going to be lots more contracts that come out of this."

One of them said, "What do you mean you already got paid?"

A beat of silence, and then the other four at the table were laughing uproariously, mockingly, slapping their ignorant comrade on the back.

"Poor Levye," said Goan. "He doesn't know how these things work!"

Levye looked confused and surly. "How what works?"

"Kinschools," said Goan.

The word was like a gadfly, buzzing at their ear, and though the saan at the table had only had half of Six's attention, now they had it all. But none of them noticed the teenager flipping the ingot.

"I don't get it," sulked Levye. "We got them the invitation to Doanye's party. Now they give us supply contracts. What am I missing?"

At this, Goan leaned conspiratorially closer, clapping a hand onto Levye's shoulder. "Just this," he said. "Kinschools have more than money on offer, and I don't mind taking my finder's fee in pleasure. It's all about connections in this business. You know the right people, you get the best rewards."

Everyone at the table seemed to hold their breath, waiting for the punch line, and Six, too, was waiting for it, wondering—

"A student," Goan crowed.

It took a beat for Levye's eyes to widen in realization. "No!"

Goan nodded. "Sweetest thing, too. Fifteen, sixteen? Big gray eyes—like moons. Not much of a face, but those kinschool students are built like little gods."

Six listened. Six watched.

"But it's illegal," said Levye.

They all laughed again. Goan was a big man, his hands were big. He squeezed his friend's shoulder so hard Six imagined bruises spreading like ink in water. Levye winced.

"It's illegal if the Kindom finds out," said Goan dryly. "And the Kindom doesn't find out because it doesn't want to. The students belong to the schools. They can use them for whatever they want, business, pleasure, you name it. What, you think any Hand starts out a virgin? Or haven't you ever seen the way clerics flirt? Bunch of dogs in heat. And if they're selling, I tell you what—I'm buying. That little student made my week. I could have gone for hours."

The waiter came back with a new round of drinks, and the saan at the table raised their glasses and toasted, and cheered Goan on as if he were a hero. Six supposed he was, to them. Six looked up the road, toward the Doanye estate, and realized that Four was at that party, even now. Four, who they hadn't seen in almost five years, but who they knew had gone out on a recruiting mission with one of the kinschool masters. They thought of Four's gray eyes and strong body, which the man Goan had enjoyed so much. Four, dangerous in its own peculiar way, had never been a sexual performer. Four was quiet, reserved. Four would not have shared Goan's enjoyment.

They gripped the memory coin. They flipped the ingot. Riin Cosas.

It was Four who taught them how to temper their anger, or pretend to. But now those lessons were buckling. Something hot and hard bloomed in their chest. It was a living creature, which thought of the past few years spent trying to emulate Four's calm and could not marshal that calm for anything.

The night was getting later. The people in the bar were getting drunker. The revelry of the summer night was a bad addition to Six's rising emotion, and if they didn't control themself, they would lose their way. Esek Nightfoot was coming down the road soon, a red-plumed bird of prey in her cleric's coat, and she knew nothing of Four, or of Goan, or of Six waiting for her in this bar. Their only advantage was surprise. If the coin landed on heads one more time, they would give it to her. If it landed on tails, they would kill her.

Goan stood, as if answering a signal, bragging, "I need to piss," before he went off toward the restrooms.

Six pocketed the ingot and the coin. They rose like a shadow and followed him.

The restrooms were empty, and as Goan went to the urinal and started to piss, Six stood behind him, watching. It took him longer to notice than it should have, but when he did he threw a startled look over his shoulder. "What are you looking at, you little freak?"

"I heard you like them young," said Six.

Goan barked, a sound half laughter, half scoff. "Fuck off."

He was zipping up his pants. Six said, "I need money."

Goan stopped still. Turned slowly. Looked Six over with slow, perusing eyes. What did he see? Six wondered. A tall teenager, lean and dark-skinned as Kata—not fair like Four. Not built solid, the way Four was built. Small dark eyes instead of gray. Attractive in a conventional and generally unnoticed way. And gendermarked. Unlike Four.

"Really?" said Goan with interest. "You know, prostitution is illegal in Barcetima."

"It is illegal if they find out," Six replied.

A snort. "You're a little spy, aren't you?"

"Fifty plae," Six said.

"Thirty."

"Forty."

Another laugh, Goan clearly impressed with the bargaining. "All right. Lock that door and come here."

"Not here," said Six, stepping back from the aggressive height of the man, who looked displeased. "Somewhere more private. The alley."

They left the bathroom together, walking back toward a rear exit and into an alley that separated the hotel bar from the housing blocks behind it. Six looked left and right, and saw no one, and already Goan was grabbing at them, pawing at their clothes. Six used the confidence of sixteen years learning to survive, and pushed Goan back against the alley wall, distracting him with hands on his belt. They opened it together, and Six reached in. Goan groaned, head leaning back against the wall as he panted in anticipation. Then something hot and wet spilled over Six's hands, and they stepped back.

Goan's head dropped down. He looked at Six with a wide, startled expression. Six held the knife in one hand, the knife with the curved blade. Goan gripped a hand to his belly, his entrails already spilling out of the wide slash Six had cut. He made a gurgling sound, near enough a scream that Six stepped forward and slashed again—this time cutting through his throat. The carotid artery became a geyser, spraying hot blood over Six's face.

It was a gruesome, smelly death, but it went quickly, the two wounds overwhelming all Goan's strength in moments. He slumped against the wall, and then his legs went out. He fell sideways onto the ground, jerking and gagging on his own blood before at last he went still.

Six wiped a hand down their bloody face and grimaced. There was very little light in the alley, but still too much. They found the nearest lamp and determined to crush the bulb and leave Goan in a blanketing darkness.

"What's this, little killer?" said a voice in the shadows. "You're not even going to rob the corpse?"

if you enjoyed
THESE BURNING STARS
look out for

THE BLIGHTED STARS

Book One of
The Devoured Worlds

by

Megan E. O'Keefe

Dead worlds, revolutionary spies, and a deadly secret propel this gorgeous space opera, perfect for fans of Children of Time *and* Ancillary Justice.

She's a revolutionary. *Humanity is running out of options. Habitable planets are being destroyed as quickly as they're found, and Naira Sharp thinks she knows the reason why. The all-powerful Mercator family has been controlling the exploration of the universe for decades, and exploiting any materials they find along the way under the guise of helping humanity's expansion. But Naira knows the truth, and she plans to bring the whole family down from the inside.*

He's the heir to the dynasty. *Tarquin Mercator never wanted to run a galaxy-spanning business empire. He just wanted to study geology and read books. But Tarquin's father has tasked him with monitoring the settlement of a new planet, and he doesn't really have a choice in the matter.*

Disguised as Tarquin's new bodyguard, Naira plans to destroy the settlement ship before they make land. But neither of them expects to end up stranded on a dead planet. To survive and keep her secret, Naira will have to join forces with the man she's sworn to hate. And together they will uncover a plot that's bigger than both of them.

ONE

Tarquin

The Amaranth

Tarquin Mercator stood on the command bridge of the finest spaceship his father had ever built and hoped he wasn't about to make a fool of himself. Serious people crewed the console podiums all around him, wrist-deep in holos that managed systems Tarquin was reasonably certain he could *name*, but there ended the extent of his knowledge. The intricate inner workings of a state-of-the-art spaceship were hardly topics covered during his geology studies.

Despite Tarquin's lack of expertise, being Acaelus Mercator's son placed him as second-in-command. Below Acaelus, and above the remarkably more qualified mission captain, a stern woman named Paison.

That captain was looking at him now—expectant, deferential. Thin, golden pathways resembling circuitry glittered on her skin, printed into her current body to aid her as a pilot. Sweat beaded between Tarquin's shoulder blades.

"My liege," Captain Paison said, all practiced obeisance, and while he desperately wished that she was addressing his father, her light grey eyes didn't move from Tarquin. "We are approximately an hour's flight from the prearranged landing site. Would you like to release the orbital survey drone network?"

Tarquin hoped his relief didn't show. Scouting the planet for deposits of relkatite was the one job for which he felt firmly footed.

"Yes, Captain. Do we have visual on the planet?"

"Not yet, my liege." She expanded a vast holographic display from her console, revealing the cloud-draped world below. "The weather is against us, but the drone network should be able to punch through it in the next few hours."

"Hold off on landing until I can confirm our preliminary survey data. We wouldn't want to put the ship down too far from a viable mining site."

Polite chuckles all around. Tarquin forced a smile at their faux camaraderie and pulled up a holo from his own console, reviewing the data the survey drones had retrieved before the mining ships *Amaranth* and *Einkorn* had taken flight for the tedious eight-month voyage to Sixth Cradle.

Not that he'd been awake for that journey. His mind and the minds of the entire crew had been safely stored away in the ship's databases, automated systems in place to print key personnel when they drew within range of low-planet orbit. When food was so expensive, there was no point in feeding people who weren't needed to work during the trip.

Tarquin's father put a hand on his shoulder and gave him a friendly shake. "Excited to see a cradle world?"

"I can't wait," he said honestly. When he'd been a child, Tarquin's mother had taken him to Second Cradle shortly before its collapse. Those memories of that rare, Earthlike world were vague. Tarquin smiled up into eyes a slightly darker shade of hazel than his own.

At nearly 160 years old, Acaelus chose to strike an imposing figure with his prints—tall, solidly built, a shock of pure white hair that hinted at his advanced age. It was difficult to look into that face and see anything but the father he'd known as a child—stern but kind. A man who'd fought to have Tarquin's mind mapped as early as possible so that he could be printed into a body that better suited him after the one he'd been born into hadn't quite fit.

Hard to see through that, to the man whose iron will and vast fortune leashed thousands to his command.

"My liege," Captain Paison said, a wary edge to her voice, "I apologize, but it appears there was an error in the system. The survey drones have been released already, or perhaps were never loaded into place."

"What?" Tarquin accessed those systems via his own console. Sure enough, the drone bays were empty. "How could that have happened?"

"I—I can't say, my liege," Paison said.

The fear in her voice soured Tarquin's stomach. Before he could assure her that it wasn't her fault, Acaelus took over.

"This is unacceptable," his father said. The crew turned as one to duck their heads to him. Acaelus's scowl cut through them all, and he pointed to an engineer. "You. Go, scour the ship for the drones and load them properly. I expect completion within the hour, and an accounting of whose failure led to this."

"Yes, my liege." The engineer tucked into a deep bow and then turned on their heel, whole body taut with nervous energy. Tarquin suspected that as soon as they were on the other side of the door, they'd break into a sprint.

"It was just a mistake," Tarquin said.

"Mercator employees do not make mistakes of this magnitude," Acaelus said, loud enough for everyone to hear. "Whoever is responsible will lose their cuffs, and if I catch anyone covering for the responsible party, they will lose theirs, too."

"That's unnecessary," Tarquin said, and immediately regretted it as his father turned his icy stare upon him. Acaelus clutched his shoulder, this time without the friendly intent, fingers digging into Tarquin's muscle.

"Leave the running of Mercator to me, my boy," he said, softly enough not to be overheard but with the same firm inflection.

Tarquin nodded, ashamed to be cowed so quickly but unable to help it. His father was a colossus, an institution unto himself, a force of nature. Tarquin was just a scholar. The running of the family wasn't his burden to carry. Acaelus released his shoulder and set to barking further orders with the brisk efficiency of long years of rule.

He gripped the edges of his console podium, staring at the bands printed around his wrists in Mercator green. Relkatite green. The cuffs meant you worked for Mercator's interests, and Mercator's alone. And while the work was grueling, it guaranteed regular meals. Medical care. Housing. Your phoenix fees paid, if your print was destroyed. The other ruling corporate families—who collectively called themselves MERIT—had their own colored cuffs. A rainbow of fealty.

Working for the families of MERIT kept people safe, in all the ways that mattered. While his father could be brusque, and at times even cruel, Acaelus did these things only out of a desire to ensure that safety.

The cuffs around Tarquin's wrists came with more than the promise of safety. Mercator's crest flowed up from those bands to wrap over the backs of his hands and twist between his fingers. The family gloves marked him as a blooded Mercator. Not a mere employee, but in the direct line of succession. Someone to be obeyed. Feared. His knuckles paled.

"Straighten up," Acaelus said.

Tarquin peeled his hands away from the console and regained his composure, slipping the aristocratic mask of indifference back on, then set to work reviewing the data the ship had collected since entering Sixth Cradle's orbit.

Alarms blared on the bridge. Tarquin jerked his head up, startled by the flashing red lights and the sharp squeal of a siren. On the largest display, the one that'd previously shown a dreamy landscape of fluffy clouds under the brush of golden morning light, the words TARGET LOCKED glared in crimson text.

That wasn't possible. There wasn't supposed to be anyone here except the *Amaranth* and its twin, the *Einkorn*. Of the five ruling corporate families, none but Mercator could even build ships capable of beating them here.

"Evade and report," Acaelus ordered.

Captain Paison flung her arms out, tossing holo screens to the copilots flanking her, and the peaceful clouds were replaced with shield reports, weapons systems, and evasion programs. There was no enemy ship that he could see. A firestorm of activity kicked off, and while Tarquin knew, logically, that they'd rolled, the ship suppressed any sensation of motion.

"It's the *Einkorn*, my liege." The captain's voice was strained from her effort.

"Who's awake over there?" Acaelus demanded.

"No one should be, my liege," the *Amaranth*'s medical officer said. Their freckled face was pale.

"Someone over there doesn't like us," the woman to Paison's right said between gritted teeth. "Conservators?"

"It's not their MO," said a broad-chested man in the grey uniform of the Human Collective Army. "But it's possible. Should I check on the security around the warpcore?"

"I iced Ex. Sharp," Acaelus said. "Without her to guide them, the Conservators are nothing but flies to be swatted. Captain, continue evasion and hail the *Einkorn*."

Tarquin cast a sideways glance at Ex. Kearns, Acaelus's current bodyguard and constant shadow. The exemplar had the face of a shovel, as broad and intimidating as the rest of him, and he didn't react to the mention of his ex-partner, Ex. Sharp. It had to sting, having the woman he'd worked side by side with turn against them all and start bombing Mercator's ships and warehouses.

The fact that Naira Sharp had been captured and her neural map locked away didn't erase the specter of the threat she posed. Her conspirators, the Conservators, were still out there, and Tarquin found Acaelus's quick dismissal of the possibility of their involvement odd.

The HCA soldier was right. They really should send someone down to check on the warpcore. Overloading the cores was the Conservators' primary method of destruction. Tarquin rallied himself to say as much, but Paison spoke first.

"My liege," she said, "the *Einkorn*'s assault may be a malfunction. The *Amaranth*'s controls aren't responding properly. I can't—"

Metal shrieked. The floor quaked. Ex. Kearns surged in front of them and shoved Tarquin dead center in the chest. The world tipped and Tarquin's feet flew out from under him. He struck the ground on his side. Something slammed into him from above, stealing his half-voiced shout.

Tarquin blinked, head buzzing, a painful throb radiating from his hips where a piece of the console podium he'd been working at seconds before had landed. Red and yellow lights strobed, warning of the damage done, but no breach alarms sounded.

Groaning, he shook his head to clear it. The impact had pitched people up against the walls. Seats and bits of console podiums scattered the ground. Across the room, Paison and another woman helped each other back to their feet.

"Son!" Acaelus dropped to his knees beside him. Tarquin was astonished to see a cut mar his father's forehead, dripping blood. "Are you all right?"

Tarquin moved experimentally, and though his side throbbed, his health pathways were already healing the damage and supplying him with painkillers. "Just bruised. What happened?"

"A direct hit." Acaelus took Tarquin's face in his hands, examining him, then looked over his shoulder and shouted, "Kearns!"

Kearns removed the piece of podium from Tarquin's side and helped him to his feet. Tarquin brushed dust off his clothes and tried to get ahold of himself while, all around him, chaos brewed. Kearns limped, his left leg dragging, and Tarquin grimaced. Exemplars were loaded with pathways keyed to combat. For one of them to show pain, the wound had to be bad.

Tarquin nudged a broken chunk of the console podium with the toe of his boot. A piece of the ceiling had come down, crushing the podiums, and it would have crushed Acaelus and Tarquin both if Kearns hadn't intervened, taking the brunt of the hit on his own legs.

A knot formed in his throat as he recognized the damage Kearns had taken on their behalf. Tarquin had never been in anything like real danger before, and he desperately missed his primary exemplar, Caldweller, but that man's neural map was still in storage. Acaelus had deemed Kearns enough to cover both of them until they reached the planet.

None of them could have accounted for this.

"My liege," Kearns said in tones that didn't invite argument, "I suggest we move to a more secure location immediately."

"Agreed," Acaelus said. "Captain, what's the damage?"

"Uhhh..." Paison squinted at one of the few consoles that'd survived the impact. "The *Einkorn*'s rail guns tore through the stabilization column. This ship won't hold together much longer."

Brittle silence followed that announcement, the roughed-up crew exchanging looks or otherwise staring at the damaged bridge like they could wind back time. Tarquin studied his father, trying to read anything in the mask Acaelus wore in crisis, and saw nothing but grim resolve wash over him. Acaelus grabbed Tarquin's arm and turned him around.

"Very well. With me, all of you, we're evacuating this ship."

Tarquin stumbled along beside his father, half in a daze. Kearns assumed smooth control of the situation, sliding into his place at the top of security's chain of command. Merc-Sec and the HCA soldiers organized under Kearns's barked orders, forming a defensive column around the rest. Paison threw a brief, longing glance at her command post before falling in with the others. Tarquin found himself in the center of a crush of people, not entirely certain how he'd gotten there.

How had they gone from looking at fluffy clouds to fleeing for their lives in less than ten minutes?

The HCA soldier next to him, the one who'd said this wasn't the Conservators' MO, caught his eye and gave him a quick, reassuring smile. Tarquin mustered up the ability to smile back and read the man's name badge—DAWD, REGAR. That meager kindness reminded him that there was more at stake than his worries. These people had put their lives in the hands of Mercator.

If they died here, they could be reprinted later, but every death increased one's chance of one's neural map cracking the next time it was printed. Neural maps were never perfect; they degraded over time. Traumatic deaths sped the process exponentially, as even the best-shielded backups were never entirely disentangled from the active map.

As if there were fine threads of connection between all backups and the living mind, and sufficient trauma could reverberate out to them all.

Some people came up screaming, and never stopped. Some got caught in time loops, unsure which moment of their lives they were really living through. Neither state was survivable.

Tarquin summoned the scraps of his courage and stood straighter. He had no business in a crisis, but the employees looked to him for assurance. His terror no doubt added to their anxiety, and that was selfish of him.

Something metal groaned in the walls, taunting his ability to hold it together. Tarquin cast an irritated glance at the complaining ship. If only ships would fall in line as easily as people.

Acaelus pulled up a holo from his forearm, but whatever he saw there was blurred by his privacy filters. The information carved a scowl into his face. He slowed and swiped his ID pathway over the door to a lab, unlocking it.

"Everyone, in here," he said.

They hesitated. Paison said, "My liege, the shuttle isn't far from here."

"I'm aware of the layout of my own ship, Captain. Get in, all of you, and wait. I've just received notice that Ex. Lockhart's print order went through. I won't allow my exemplar to awaken to a dying ship. You will go into this lab, and you will wait for my return."

That wasn't right. The secondary printing round wasn't automated; it needed to be initiated. Tarquin frowned, watching the crew shift uncomfortably. Every one of them knew Acaelus was telling a half-truth at best, but none of them were willing to say it.

There was a slim possibility that whatever was causing the other errors had triggered this, but making all these people wait while Acaelus collected one person was a waste of time.

"My liege." Paison stepped forward, squaring off her shoulders. "I can't guarantee this ship will last that long, and we require your command keys to open the hangar airlock."

"I am aware, and you are delaying. Get in the lab."

They shuffled inside without another word, though they were all watching Acaelus warily. The terror of offending their boss was greater than the fear of being left behind to die. You could come back from death. You could never re-cuff for Mercator after being fired. The door shut, leaving Tarquin and his father alone with Kearns. Tarquin's head pounded.

"What are you doing?" he demanded in a soft hiss. "Ex. Lockhart can handle herself. We have to get these people out."

Acaelus shoved him down the hallway. "*We* need to get out. I printed Lockhart to help Kearns handle the crew, but you and I are going to cast our maps back and exit this situation, because I don't know what's happened here, and I'm not risking your map."

Tarquin dug his heels in, drawing his father to a halt. "We can't just leave. I'm not going to allow the Conservators to run us off before I have proof the mining process is safe."

"If this was the Conservators, then we'd already be dead. All the nonfamily printing bays just went active, and I *do not know* who is coming out of those bays. We have to leave. Kearns and Lockhart will handle the rest."

Tarquin rubbed his eyes in frustration. "We can't abandon the mission."

"We can, and we are. Come. This is hardly the place for an argument."

Acaelus jerked on his arm. Tarquin stumbled after him, mind reeling. Sixth Cradle was supposed to be his mission. Supposed to be the moment Tarquin stood up for his family and finally squashed all those squalid rumors Ex. Sharp had started when she'd claimed the relkatite mining process was killing worlds.

While a great deal of what his family had to do to ensure their survival was distasteful, Tarquin was absolutely certain the mining process was safe. He'd refined it himself. Mining Sixth Cradle and leaving it green and thriving was meant to be the final nail in the coffin of those accusations. The one thing he could do for his family that was *useful*.

He wouldn't run. Not this time. Not like he had when his mother had died and he'd fled to university to bury himself in his studies, instead of facing the suffering that weighed on his father's and sister's hearts.

"I'm sorry, Dad, I won't—"

"Kearns, carry him," Acaelus said.

Tarquin was thirty-five years old, second in line to the most powerful position in the universe, and Ex. Kearns scooped him up like he was little more than luggage and tossed him over his shoulder without a flash of hesitation, because Acaelus Mercator had demanded it. Kearns's shoulder dug into Tarquin's ribs, pressing a startled grunt out of him. His cheeks burned with indignity.

"I'm not a child," Tarquin snapped, surprised at the edge in his tone. He never raised his voice to his father.

"You are *my* child, and you will do as I say."

Acaelus didn't bother to look at him. Tarquin closed his eyes, letting out a slow sigh of defeat. There was no arguing with his father when he'd made up his mind. He opened his eyes, and temporarily forgot how to breathe. The door to one of the staff printing bays yawned open, and it wasn't people who emerged from that space. Not exactly.

Their faces were close to human, but something had gone off in the printing. A mouth set too far right. An ear sprouting from the side of a neck. An arm that bent the wrong way around. Half a chest cavity missing.

Misprints. Empties. An error in the printer slapping together a hodgepodge of human parts. The *Amaranth* wouldn't have tried putting a neural map into any of those bodies, but whatever had caused the malfunction had also made the ship release the prints instead of disintegrating them into their constituent parts, as was protocol for a misprint.

What was left of those faces twisted, drew into vicious snarls.

"Kearns," Tarquin hissed in a sharp whisper. His voice was alarmed enough that the exemplar turned.

Kearns pulled his sidearm and fired. The earsplitting roar of the shot in such a small space slammed into Tarquin's ears, but his pathways adjusted, keeping him from going temporarily deaf.

The misprints shrieked with what throats and lungs they had, and rushed them. Kearns rolled Tarquin off his shoulder and shoved him back.

Tarquin stumbled, but his father caught him and then spun, pushing him ahead. "Run!"

Fear stripped away all his reservations and Tarquin ran, pounding down the hallways for the family's private printing bay, praying that he wouldn't find the same thing there.

Kearns's weapon roared again and again, a staccato rhythm drowning out the screams of the misprints. He looked over his shoulder to find Acaelus right behind him, Kearns farther back, his injured leg slowing him down. Tarquin faced forward and sprinted—the door to the printing bay was *just* ahead.

Kearns's gun fell silent. His father screamed.

Tarquin whirled around. Acaelus was chest-down on the ground, misprints swarming over him, their teeth and nails digging into his skin, ripping free bloody chunks. He took a step toward them, not knowing what he could possibly do, and Acaelus looked up, face set with determination as he flung out a hand.

"Go home!" he ordered.

He met his father's eyes. Acaelus pushed his tongue against the inside of his cheek, making it bulge out in warning. New terror struck Tarquin. High-ranking members of the corporate families often wore small, personal explosive devices on the interior side of a molar to use in case someone intending to crack their neural maps attacked them. Acaelus had one.

Tarquin fled. He burst through the printing bay door and slammed it shut behind him, leaning his back against it, breathing harder than he ever had in his life. The explosion was designed to be small. It whumped against the door, tickling his senses.

A gruesome way to die, but it was swift. Gentler suicide pathways had been tried, but they had a nasty habit of malfunctioning. Pathways remained frustratingly unpredictable at times.

He swallowed. The staff back on Mercator Station would reprint Acaelus the second they received notice that his tracker pathway had been destroyed and his visual feed had cut. His father would be fine. Tarquin forced himself away from the door, shaking.

One of the printing cubicles was lit red to indicate it was in use. He crossed to the map backup station and picked up the crown of electronics, running it between his hands.

Tarquin knew he wasn't what his father had wanted. He lacked the clear-eyed ruthlessness of his elder sister, Leka. He couldn't stand to watch people cower beneath the threat of his ire as Acaelus so often had to do to keep their employees in line. His singular concession to being a Mercator was that his love of geology and subsequent studies had aided the family in their hunt for relkatite.

His father never complained about Tarquin's lack of participation in family politics. Acaelus had given Tarquin everything he'd ever asked for and had only ever asked for one thing in return.

When Naira Sharp had been captured and put to trial, Tarquin had taken the stand to prove her accusations false. As a Mercator, as the foremost expert in his field of study, he had disproved all her allegations that Mercator's mining processes destroyed worlds.

It hadn't stopped the rumors. Hadn't stopped the other families of MERIT from looking askance at Mercator and asking themselves if, maybe, they wouldn't be better off without them.

They needed to mine a cradle world and leave it thriving in their wake to put the rumors to bed once and for all.

Tarquin could still give his father that proof, but he couldn't do it alone. Not with misprints infesting the halls and the potential of a saboteur on the loose. He needed an exemplar.

He set the backup crown down and crossed to the printing bay control console, checking the progress on Lockhart's print. Ninety seconds left. Enough time to compose himself. Enough time, he hoped, to get to the planet after she'd finished printing.

Tarquin had never disobeyed a direct order from his father before, and he hoped he wasn't making a colossal mistake.

orbit

Follow us:

�f /orbitbooksUS

🐦 /orbitbooks

▶ /orbitbooks

Join our mailing list
to receive alerts on our
latest releases and deals.

orbitbooks.net

Enter our monthly
giveaway for the chance
to win some epic prizes.

orbitloot.com